Fergus Hu

The Peacock o. Jewels

Fergus Hume

The Peacock of Jewels

1st Edition | ISBN: 978-3-75235-318-1

Place of Publication: Frankfurt am Main, Germany

Year of Publication: 2020

Outlook Verlag GmbH, Germany.

THE PEACOCK OF JEWELS

BY
FERGUS HUME

CHAPTER I

THE ROTHERHITHE CRIME

To find Barkers Inn was much the same to an ordinary person as looking for a needle in the proverbial haystack. Dick Latimer, however, knew its exact whereabouts, because he lived there, and on this foggy November night he was making for it unerringly with the homing instinct of a bee. Leaving Fleet Street behind him, somewhere about eleven-thirty, he turned into Chancery Lane, and then struck off to the right down a by-road which narrowed to an alley, and finally ended in a cul-de-sac. Here the young man hurried through the rusty iron gates of a granite archway, and found himself in an oblong courtyard paved with cobble-stones and surrounded by tumble-down houses with steep roofs of discolored tiles. A few steps took him across this to a crooked little door, which he entered to mount a crooked little staircase, and in one minute he was on the first-floor landing, where a tiny gas-jet pricked the gloom with a bluish spot of light. Hastily using his latchkey, he admitted himself through a door on the left into a stuffy dark passage, technically called the entrance hall. Eventually entering the sitting-room, he hurled himself into a creaking basket-chair, and gave thanks to the gods of home that he had arrived.

The friend with whom Latimer shared these Barkers Inn chambers was seated by the fire clothed comfortably in a suit of shabby old flannels, reading a letter and smoking a briar-root, complacently at ease. He nodded when Dick stormed into the room, and spoke with his pipe between his teeth.

"Beastly night, isn't it?" remarked Mr. Fuller, who had been spending the evening at home very pleasantly.

"You'd say much more than that, Alan, my boy, if you'd been out in the fog," retorted Latimer. "Bur-r-r I'm glad to be indoors and to find you still out of bed at the eleventh hour. I've had adventures: official adventures."

"Connected with your employment as a journalist, I suppose," said Fuller in a lazy manner, and tucking the letter into his breast pocket, "but seriously speaking, Dicky, are adventures to be found in this over-civilized city?"

"Romance stalks the London streets, more or less disguised as the commonplace, my son. I can a tale unfold, but sha'n't do so until I change my kit and have a Scotch hot on the way to my mouth. Is the water boiling?" he demanded, directing his gaze towards the old-fashioned grate where a small black kettle fumed and hissed on the hob.

"It's been boiling for me," said Fuller, indicating an empty tumbler at his elbow, "but I've enough water for your needs."

"I only hope you've left enough whisky, which is far more precious. Poke up the fire and warm my slippers and make a fuss over me. I want to be fussed," said Dick plaintively, as he retreated to his bedroom, "for I'm a poor orphan boy alone in this foggy world."

"Ass!" observed Alan politely, and exposed the soles of his friend's slippers to the fire, "what about supper?"

"I've had that," sang out Latimer, "at someone else's cost."

"You must have ruined him then with your appetite," answered Fuller, laughing; while he tilted back his chair to place his feet against the mantelpiece and his hands behind his head. In this position he smoked quietly and admired the photograph of an extremely pretty girl, which stood beside the clock, while the small black kettle sang the song of home.

The room was both long and broad with a low whitewash ceiling, crossed with black oak beams, a somewhat slanting floor—owing to the great age of the building—and three squat windows which overlooked the dingy courtyard. These were draped with faded curtains of green rep, drawn at this late hour to exclude the cold, and before one stood the writing-table of Latimer, while the escritoire of Fuller bulked largely against the other. Between the two, and blocking the approach to the middle window, stretched a slippery horse-hair sofa, covered with a rugged Eastern shawl to hide its many deficiencies. A shabby Kidderminster carpet concealed the worn floor, but its sad hues were brightened by three or four gayly colored mats, purchased at a cheap price. The round table, the unmatched chairs, the heavy sideboard, the sofa aforesaid, and the chipped bookcase, were all the flotsam and jetsam of auction rooms, belonging, more or less, to the comfortably ugly style of the Albert period. On the plain green-papered walls were various photographs of men and women, with sundry college groups; pictures of football teams, cricketers and boating-crews; odd bits of china and miniature statues on brackets; likewise foils, fencing masks, boxing gloves and such-like paraphernalia of sport. It was a real man's room, suggestive of exuberant virility, and remarkably untidy. All the same there was order in its disorder, as both Latimer and Fuller knew exactly where to lay their hands on any article they wanted. The room was chaotic enough to drive a woman to distraction, but comfortable and home-like for all that.

The journalist returned in a well-worn smoking suit, and proceeded to light his pipe. Fuller brewed him a glass of grog, and handed it across as he sat down in the saddleback chair on the verge of the hearthrug. The two men were fine specimens of humanity in their different ways. Latimer was large and fair and heavily built, with big limbs, and a suggestion of great strength.

He had untidy yellow hair and a yellow mustache which he tugged at hard when perplexed. His blue eyes were keen, but on the whole he did not reveal much brain power in his face, which undoubtedly told the truth, since he was more of an athlete than a scholar. Fuller, on the contrary, was brilliantly clever, and as a solicitor was doing very well for himself in a dingy Chancery Lane office. He was tall and slim, with a wiry frame, and a lean, clean-shaven face, clearly cut and bronzed. Indeed with his steady dark eyes and closely clipped black hair, and remarkably upright figure, he suggested the soldier. This was probably due to heredity, since he came of a fighting line for generations, although his father was a country vicar. Also, in spite of his sedentary occupation, the young man lived as much as possible in the open, and when not running down to his native village for weekends, haunted the parks on every possible occasion, or walked four miles on Hampstead Heath and into the country beyond. It was no wonder that he looked tanned, alert, bright-eyed, and active, more like a squire of the Midlands than a votary of Themis. Since Fuller senior was poor, the boy had to earn his bread and butter somehow, and after he left Cambridge had elected to become a lawyer. Shortly after he blossomed out into a full-blown solicitor, he chanced upon his old school friend, Dick Latimer, who had taken to journalism, and the two had set up house together in the ancient Inn. On the whole they were fairly comfortable, if not blessed with an excess of the world's goods. Finally, being young, both were healthy and happy and hopeful and extremely enterprising.

"Well now, Dicky, what have you been doing?" asked Alan, when his friend, clothed and in his right mind, sipped his grog and puffed smoke-clouds.

"Attending an inquest at Rotherhithe."

"Oh, that murder case!"

Latimer nodded and stared into the fire. "It's a queer affair."

"So far as I have read the newspaper reports, it seems to be a very commonplace one."

"I told you that Romance was often disguised as the Commonplace, Alan."

"As how, in this instance?"

His friend did not reply directly. "What do you know of the matter?" he asked so abruptly that Fuller looked up in surprise.

"Why, what can I know save what I have read in the papers?"

"Nothing, of course. I never suggested that you do know anything. But it's no use my going over old ground, so I wish to hear what you have learned from the reports."

"Very little, if you will be so precise," said Alan after a pause. "In a fourth-

4

class Rotherhithe boarding-house frequented chiefly by seamen, a man called Baldwin Grison was found dead in his bedroom and on his bed, a few days ago. The Dagoes and Lascars and such British seamen as live under the same roof are not accused of committing the crime, and as Grison was desperately poor and degraded, there was no reason why he should be murdered, since he wasn't worth powder and shot. Old Mother Slaig, who keeps the house, declared that Grison retired to his room at ten o'clock, and it was only next morning, when he did not come down, that she learned of his death."

Latimer nodded again. "All true and plainly stated. You certainly think in a methodical manner, Alan. The man was found lying on his bed in the usual shabby suit of clothes he wore. But his breast was bare, and he had been pierced to the heart by some fine instrument which cannot be found. Death must have been instantaneous according to the report of the doctor who was called in. But you are wrong in thinking that the crime was motiveless. I believe that robbery was the motive."

"The papers didn't report any belief of the police that such was the case."

"The police don't know everything—at least the inspector didn't, although he knows a great deal more now," said Latimer, removing his pipe, "but the single room occupied by the deceased was tumbled upside down, so it is evident that the assassin was looking for the fruits of his crime. Whether he found what he wanted is questionable."

"What was it?" asked Fuller, interested in the mystery.

"I'll tell you that later, although I really can't say for certain if I am right. Let us proceed gradually and thresh out the matter thoroughly."

"Fire ahead. I am all attention."

"The police," continued Dick meditatively, "hunted out evidence as to the identity and the status of the dead man, between the time of death and the holding of the inquest. Inspector Moon—he's the Rotherhithe chap in charge of the case—advertised, or made inquiries, or got hold of the sister somehow. At all events she turned up yesterday and appeared at the inquest this very day."

"Who is the sister?"

"An elderly shrimp of a woman with light hair and a shrill voice, and a pair of very hard blue eyes. She heard that her brother was murdered, or Moon hunted her up in some way, and willingly came forward with her story."

"What is her story?"

"I'm just coming to it. What an impatient chap you are, Alan. Miss Grison— Louisa is her Christian name—keeps a shabby boarding-house in

Bloomsbury, and is one of those people who have seen better days. It seems that her brother Baldwin was secretary to a person, whose name I shall tell you later, and was kicked out of his billet twenty years ago, because he couldn't run straight."

"What had he done?"

"I can't say. Miss Grison wouldn't confess, and as the story wasn't pertinent to the murder she wasn't pressed to confess. All she said was that her brother was an opium-smoker and after losing his billet drifted to Rotherhithe, where he could indulge in his vice. She tried to keep him respectable, and allowed him ten shillings a week to live on. But he sank lower and lower, so she saw very little of him. All she knew was that she sent the ten shilling postal order regularly every Friday so that Baldwin might get it on Saturday. He never visited her and he never wrote to her, but lived more or less like a hermit in Mother Slaig's boarding-house, and went out every night to smoke opium in some den kept by a Chinaman called Chin-Chow. Miss Grison sobbed bitterly when she gave her evidence and insisted that her brother owed his degradation to the enmity of people."

"What sort of people?"

"She didn't particularize. He was weak rather than bad, she insisted, and when he lost his situation, he lost heart also. At all events he devoted himself to the black smoke, and lived in the Rotherhithe slum, until he was found dead by the old hag who keeps the house."

"Did Miss Grison's evidence throw any light on the crime?"

"No. She declared that she did not know of anyone who would have killed the poor devil."

"Was there any evidence on the part of the doctor, or Mother Slaig, or those seamen in the house to show who murdered the man?" asked Fuller.

"Not the slightest. The house was open morn, noon and night, and those who lived there came and went at their will without being watched. It's a rowdy locality and a rowdy house, but Mother Slaig keeps fairly good order as she's a formidable old hag resembling Vautrin's aunt in Balzac's story."

"Madame Nourrisau; I remember," said Fuller, nodding. "Then I take it that no one in the house heard any struggle, or cry for help?"

"No. Besides, as I have told you, death must have been instantaneous. No one, so far as Mother Slaig or others in the house knew, visited Grison on that night, or indeed on any other occasion—so they say—since the man was more or less of a hermit. He went to bed at ten and at the same hour next morning he was found dead with his room all upside down."

6

"Was anything missed?"

"There was nothing to miss," said Latimer quickly. "I saw the room, which only contained a small bed, a small table and two chairs. The man had but one, suit of ragged clothes, which he concealed under a fairly good overcoat his sister declared she sent to him last Christmas. He was desperately poor and never seemed to do anything but smoke opium."

"What kind of a man was he to look at?"

"Something like the sister. Small and fair-haired, with blue eyes. Of course, owing to the black smoke, he was a wreck morally and physically and mentally, according to Mother Slaig, and the boys used to throw stones at him in the streets. However, to make a long story short, nothing could be found to show how the poor wretch had come by his death, so an open verdict was brought in—the sole thing which could be done. To-morrow his sister, who seems to have loved him in spite of his degradation, is taking away the corpse for burial."

"Where is it to be buried?"

Latimer looked up slowly. "In the churchyard of Belstone, Sussex," he said.

Alan sat up very straight and his manner expressed his unbounded astonishment. "That's my father's parish," he gasped.

"Yes. And the churchyard is attached to the building your father preaches in, my son," said Latimer dryly, "odd coincidence, isn't it?"

"But—but—what has this murdered man to do with Belstone?" asked Fuller in a bewildered manner.

"That's what I want to find out, Alan. Can't you remember the name?"

"Never heard of it. And yet the name Baldwin Grison is not a common one. I should certainly have remembered it had it been mentioned to me. It is odd certainly, as Belstone isn't exactly the hub of the universe. Grison! Baldwin Grison." Fuller shook his head. "No, I can't recall it. To be sure he may have been in the village twenty years ago, since you say that he has lived since that time in Rotherhithe. I was only seven years of age then, so I can remember nothing. But my father may know. I'll ask him when I go down this week-end."

"There's another thing I wish you to ask him."

"What is that?"

"The romantic thing which lifts this case out of the commonplace. Only Inspector Moon knows what I am about to tell you and he informed me with a recommendation not to make it public."

"Then why do you tell me?" said Fuller quickly. "Is it wise?"

"Quite wise," responded his friend imperturbably, "because I asked Moon's permission to take you into our confidence."

Fuller looked puzzled. "Why?"

Again Dicky replied indirectly. "It seems that Grison, unlucky beggar, had one friend, a street-arab brat called Jotty."

"Jotty what—or is Jotty a surname?"

"It's the only name the boy has. He's a clever little Cockney of fourteen, and wise beyond his years, picking up a living as best he can. Grison used to give him food occasionally, and sometimes money. Jotty ran errands for the man, and was the sole person admitted to his room."

"Well! well! well!" said Alan impatiently. "I'm coming to it, if you don't hurry me," said Latimer coolly. "Jotty on one occasion entered the room, and found Grison nursing between his hands—what do you think?"

"How the deuce should I know?"

"A peacock of jewels!"

Alan stared, and cast a swift glance at the photograph of the pretty girl on the mantelpiece. "A peacock of jewels!" he repeated under his breath.

"Or a jewelled peacock, if you like. Grison put it away when he saw the boy: but that he had such an article is quite certain, as Jotty hasn't the imagination to describe the thing. Now in spite of all search, Inspector Moon can't find that peacock, and you may be sure that after Jotty told his tale the inspector searched very thoroughly.

"Well?" Alan cast a second look at the photograph.

"Well," echoed Dick, rather annoyed, "can't you draw an inference. I think, and Moon thinks, that the assassin murdered Grison in order to gain possession of the peacock, which was of great value. If he wants to make money out of it he will have to sell it, and in this way the inspector hopes to trap the beast. For that reason, and so that the assassin may not be placed on his guard, Moon doesn't want anyone but you and me and himself to know the truth. You can't guess why I have told you this."

"Yes." Alan nodded and rubbed his knees, while a puzzled look came over his dark clean-cut face. "I remember telling you about the fetish of the Inderwicks ages ago."

"Tell me again as soon as you can withdraw your gaze from that photo."

Fuller colored, and laughed consciously. "When a man is in love, much may be forgiven him. And you must admit, Dicky, that she's the beauty of the world. Now isn't she?"

Latimer eyed the photograph in his turn. "She's pretty," he said judicially.

"Pretty," echoed Fuller with great indignation, "she's an angel, and the loveliest girl ever created, besides being the most fascinating of women."

"Oh, spare me your raptures," broke in Dick impatiently. "Your taste in looks isn't mine, and I've met Miss Marie Inderwick, which you seem to forget. She is very nice and very pretty and—"

"Oh, hang your lukewarm phraseology," interrupted the other. "She's the most adorable girl in the universe."

"I admit that, for the sake of getting on with the business in hand. Now what about the peacock of jewels?"

"I told you all I know, which isn't much," said Alan, reluctantly changing the subject. "Marie lives at the big house in Belstone which is called 'The Monastery' because it was given by Henry VIII., to the Inderwick of—"

"Oh, confound Henry VIII. What about the peacock?"

"It's the family fetish, and for one hundred years has been in the possession of the Inderwicks. It was stolen some twenty years ago, and no one ever knew what became of it. Now—"

"Now it turns up in the possession of Baldwin Grison, who has evidently been murdered on its account. And yet you deny latter-day romance."

"Well," observed Alan rubbing his knees again, "I admit that your truth is stranger than your professional journalistic fiction. But how did this man become possessed of the ornament?"

Latimer shrugged his mighty shoulders. "How dense you are! Didn't I tell you how Louisa Grison declared that her brother had been secretary to a certain person, whose name I said I would tell you later on. I shall tell you now, if you aren't clever enough to guess it."

"Rats," said Fuller inelegantly. "How can you expect me to guess it?"

"By using what common-sense Nature has given you. Hang it, man, here is an excessively unique ornament belonging to the Inderwick family which has been missing for over twenty years. Grison's sister says that she intends to bury her brother's body in Belstone churchyard, and declared at the inquest that at one time he was the secretary to a certain person. Now if you put two and two together, you will find that the person is—"

"Mr. Sorley. Randolph Sorley," cried Fuller suddenly enlightened.

"In other words, the uncle and guardian of Miss Marie Inderwick. Well now, you can see that two and two do make four."

"Humph!" Fuller nursed his chin and looked thoughtfully at the fire. "So this murdered man was Mr. Sorley's secretary. According to his sister he lost the situation—perhaps, Dick, because he stole the peacock."

"We can't be positive of that, Alan. Grison, in his secretarial capacity, certainly lived at The Monastery and assisted Mr. Sorley in preparing for the press that dreary book about precious stones which seems to be his life work. He had every chance to steal, but if Mr. Sorley had suspected him he assuredly would have had him arrested."

"Perhaps Grison bolted and could not be traced."

"I think not. He was, so far as I can gather from what Miss Grison says, dismissed in due form. He lived with her for a time at the Bloomsbury boarding-house and later on drifted to Rotherhithe to indulge in his love for the black smoke. No! no! no! my son. Mr. Sorley could never have believed that Grison was in possession of the peacock of jewels."

"Then why did he discharge him?"

"We must find out, and that won't be easy after twenty years. Mr. Sorley is growing old and may not remember clearly. But Grison on the evidence of Jotty undoubtedly had this peacock, and since it cannot be found, he must have been murdered by someone who desired the ornament. The disorder of that sordid room shows that a strict search was made by the assassin, and it could be for nothing save the golden peacock. Now, if the assassin did find it, Alan, and if you and I and Moon and Jotty keep silent, the man will think that he is safe and will sell his plunder."

"Wait a bit, Dick. He may unset the jewels and sell them separately. Then it will be difficult to trace him by the sale of the article."

"True enough of Solomon. However we must take our chance of that. If he is certain that the loss is not suspected he may sell the whole without splitting it into parts. If he does, Moon—who has his eye on all pawnshops and jewellers and on various receivers of stolen goods—can spot the beast and arrest him. But, as a second string to our bow, it is just as well to know all about this family fetish, since its history may throw some light on the mystery of its disappearance. Now what you have to do, my son, is to go down to Belstone and learn all you can about Grison when he was secretary to old Sorley. Ask Miss Inderwick and her uncle about him."

"Marie won't know anything save by hearsay," said Alan, shaking his head. "Remember she's only twenty years of age, and was an infant in arms when the family fetish disappeared. Besides if I make inquiries I shall have to

10

account for my curiosity by revealing what you have told me to keep secret."

"H'm! h'm! h'm!" murmured the other, frowning, "there is that objection certainly. We must put out our sprat to catch the mackerel. However, it wants three days till Saturday, so I shall see Moon and hear what he suggests about the matter. The Inderwicks are poor, aren't they, Alan?"

"There is only one Inderwick left," answered the young solicitor, rising to stretch his limbs, "and that is Marie. Of course she is desperately poor, as I told you ages ago. She has The Monastery, the few acres of the park, and two hundred a year to live on. Sorley is her mother's brother, her uncle and guardian, with another two hundred income. By pooling the cash, the two manage to keep things going."

"H'm! It's a dull life for the girl. Do you like Mr. Sorley?"

"No," replied Fuller serenely. "He's a selfish old animal, who only regards Marie as a necessary piece of furniture. She was at school for many years and only returned home some twelve months ago. Now she acts as her uncle's housekeeper, and leads an infernally dull life. Mr. Sorley never seems to think that Marie is young and requires enjoyment. He's a beast."

"Ho," chuckled Dick shrewdly, "you seem to dislike him excessively. I can easily see that he doesn't favour your suit."

"No, hang him, he doesn't. If Marie married me, the old man would be left with his two hundred a year to get on as best he could, and you may be jolly well sure, Dicky, that he doesn't want to leave the big house."

"Natural enough," yawned Latimer. "Well, my son, you help Moon to hunt down Grison's assassin and recover the fetish of the Inderwicks and perhaps the old man, out of gratitude, may accept you as a nephew-in-law."

"It's worth trying for at all events," said Alan thoughtfully. "Marie's an angel, and I'm bound to marry her sooner or later. I'll go down on Saturday and start operations."

CHAPTER II

AT THE VICARAGE

Alan Fuller thoughtfully tucked the rug round his knees in the third-class compartment of the train which was taking him to Belstone. There was no station at the village, but the Brighton express stopped at Lewes, and thence he could walk or drive to his destination. The young man was in tip-top spirits, as the suggestion of Latimer that he should join in the search for Grison's assassin, and secure the return of the peacock fetish to Marie Inderwick, 'rendered him hopeful that success in this direction would lead to his marriage with the girl. Of course that could not take place for some time since he was not yet making a sufficient income to justify his becoming the husband of the most adorable girl in the universe. Still, if Mr. Sorley would withdraw his absurd opposition—and he probably would do so, were the peacock recovered—Alan concluded that he might become officially engaged to Marie, and so she would not be snapped up by other suitors. Legally speaking he would have a lien on her.

Not that this was really needed, since Marie loved him as much as he loved her, but the position would be more satisfactory to both if matters were arranged on this basis, and in a practical way. After all, Marie was young and impressionable, and if Mr. Sorley found a rich man anxious to become the husband of his lovely niece he might, and probably would, worry her into accepting the suitor. Marie would fight—Alan was quite positive on this point —but she might be worn out by her uncle's persistence, and Fuller knew well enough that the old man was as obstinate as a mule, when once he set his mind on achieving a certain end. On the whole then, Alan was pleased that chance had thrown in his way an opportunity of doing Mr. Sorley a service, as a benefit conferred would undoubtedly soften him. Certainly the peacock belonged to Marie, but—looking upon it, as she would, as a mere ornament— she probably would not mind its remaining in her uncle's possession when it was found. And Sorley was a fanatic about jewels: their glitter and rainbow hues seemed to send him crazy with delight. To recover the radiant splendor of the peacock, he would assuredly concede much and Alan felt quite sure that consent to his marriage with the girl would not be withheld. But everything depended upon the tracing of the miserable Grison's assassin and that was not an easy task.

Before leaving London, Fuller had visited Inspector Moon at his Rotherhithe office, along with Latimer, and the policeman had been greatly interested in the fact that the solicitor knew the original possessors of the article for which Grison had apparently been murdered. He had also been astonished, and with good reason, at the coincidence that Latimer, to whom he had spoken about Jotty's evidence, should have a friend who was—so to speak—mixed up in the matter of the peacock. Since Fate appeared to point out Fuller as an active agent in bringing this unknown murderer to justice, through the instrumentality of the stolen ornament, Moon had readily given the young man permission to speak of the matter to Mr. Sorley and to Marie. Meanwhile the inspector still continued to hunt for the trail, but without success. The assassin had come and gone in the crowd which inhabited Mother Slaig's boarding-house entirely unnoticed, and now that Grison was buried in the

Belstone churchyard as arranged by his sister, it appeared as if the Rotherhithe murder would have to be relegated to the list of undiscovered crimes. Further revelations depended either on the chance that the criminal would pawn or sell what he had risked his neck to obtain, or on some evidence procured from Marie and Sorley, relative to the peacock. Where had it originally come from? who had manufactured it? why did the Inderwick family regard it as a fetish? and finally, why had Grison stolen it? These were the questions which Fuller came down to Belstone to ask.

Meanwhile the inspector still continued to hunt for the trail, but without success. The assassin had come and gone in the crowd which inhabited Mother Slaig's boarding-house entirely unnoticed, and now that Grison was buried in the Belstone churchyard as arranged by his sister, it appeared as if the Rotherhithe murder would have to be relegated to the list of undiscovered crimes. Further revelations depended either on the chance that the criminal would pawn or sell what he had risked his neck to obtain, or on some evidence procured from Marie and Sorley, relative to the peacock. Where had it originally come from? who had manufactured it? why did the Inderwick family regard it as a fetish? and finally, why had Grison stolen it? These were the questions which Fuller came down to Belstone to ask.

It was therefore no wonder that, since Alan's future happiness depended upon his success in solving so deep a mystery, he should be thoughtful on the journey, to Belstone. Dick and he had talked a great deal about the matter but, for want of further evidence could arrive at no conclusion. Until Mr. Sorley explained about the peacock, and stated what he knew concerning Grison, there was nothing more to be done. Alan thought that the uncle would probably know more than the niece, since she had been an infant in arms when the fetish had been stolen. All the same he resolved to question Marie first, on the chance that she might know something, and upon what she stated would depend his future plans. The young man did not like Mr. Sorley, not only because that gentleman thwarted his marriage with Marie, but also for the very simple reason that he mistrusted Sorley's character. His eyes were too shifty; his manners were too suave; and although he always wished to know the private affairs of everyone else, he never by any chance confessed anything that had to do with himself. It was necessary on these grounds, as Fuller considered, to deal with Marie's uncle in a wary manner.

In due course the train stopped at Lewes, and Alan got out with the intention of walking the five miles to Belstone. He had only a gladstone bag containing a few necessary articles for a Saturday-to-Monday's stay in the country, since he invariably kept a supply of clothes at his home. With a nod to the station-master, to whom he was well-known, Fuller left the station, and ignoring the application of several cabmen, struck at an angle to reach the high road. He was soon on the hard metal and walked along swiftly and easily swinging his bag, glad of the exercise to grow warm again, as the day was cold and he was chilled from sitting in the train. As it was now the end of November there was a slight grey fog spreading its veil over the surrounding country, and the sun was conspicuous by its absence. But that Alan thought of Marie's bright face, which he would be certain to see smiling before him on this day or the next, he would have been depressed by the want of sunshine. But what lover who hopes to look into the eyes of the girl he adores within a specified number of hours can feel down-hearted, however gloomy the skies or moist the earth? Not Alan Fuller, who moved on to his much-desired goal with love songs humming in his active brain. And the burden of these was "Marie Marie Marie!" with the delicious name joined to the most eulogistic adjectives in the English tongue.

It was when he was almost within sight of Belstone village that the motor bicycle came along. Alan heard the buzz of the machine round the corner and stood aside to let it pass, indifferent to its coming and going. But when he saw a slim old man with an ascetic, clean-shaven face, smartly dressed in a grey suit with brown gaiters, seated thereon, he both started and called out in his surprise.

"Mr. Sorley. This is unexpected. You on a bicycle?"

The rider shut off the motive power and brought his machine to a standstill a few yards past the young man. "You are astonished," he said, coming back wheeling the bicycle. "Well, Alan, I don't wonder at it. At the age of sixty, it is not many people who would risk their brittle bones in this way."

"No, indeed," replied Fuller, staring at Mr. Sorley's fresh complexion and closely-cropped white hair surmounted by a very juvenile tweed cap. "And I thought you were such an indoor man."

"Pooh! pooh! pooh!" said Sorley good-humoredly. "You know how particular I am about exercise, Alan. I walk every day a certain distance in order to keep myself in health. For years I have slipped out to range the park; but with increasing age should come increasing activity, so, I have bought this," he shook the machine, "and already—in three weeks that is—I have learned to ride it without fear. I can explore the country now, and intend to do so, my dear lad. The park is too small for me, and I must take all the exercise possible if I wish to keep my looks and vitality. Increasing age: increasing activity," said Mr. Sorley again, "there you are."

"Increasing age generally means sitting by the fire and going to bed early, sir," replied Alan dryly, "don't overdo it."

"My boy, there is nothing so objectionable as advice."

"I beg your pardon. I only thought—"

"Then don't think on my behalf at all events," snapped Mr. Sorley, who appeared rather ruffled by Fuller's reflection on his age. "When you come to my years, Alan, I doubt if you will look so healthy as I do."

The young man mentally admitted that it was possible he might not wear so well. Sorley was a marvel of preservation, and although he had turned sixty certainly did not look more than forty-five at the most, save for his white hair. His face was almost without wrinkles; his form, spare and lean, was unbowed, and the up-to-date clothes he always affected gave him quite a youthful air at a distance. In fact he was a very handsome man in an elderly way, and but for his shifty eyes and slack mouth—these marred his appearance considerably— he would have impressed people even more than he already did. But with all his juvenile aspect and ingratiating ways, there was something untrustworthy about the man. At least Alan thought so, and had always thought so, but perhaps he might have been more observant than the usual run of humanity, for Marie's uncle was extremely popular, although his usual life was somewhat after the style of a hermit. But this Mr. Sorley ascribed less to inclination than to the want of money, since he humorously said that he and Marie, unable to make both ends meet, ha ci to make one end vegetables.

"You are wonderful, Mr. Sorley," said Alan, hastening to soothe the old man's easily hurt vanity. "I never saw you look better. How do you manage to knock all these years off your age?"

"Abstention from over-drinking and overeating," said Mr. Sorley briskly, giving his recipe for everlasting youth. "An hour's sleep in the afternoon and plenty of it at night. Cold tubs, dumbbell exercises in the altogether as Trilby says with the window open, judicious walks and an optimistic way of looking at things. There you are," he ended with his favourite catch-phrase as usual.

"Now you must add trips on a motor bicycle," laughed Alan, smiling. "By the way, how is Marie?"

"Blooming as a rose, fresh as a daisy, cheerful as a lark," prattled Mr. Sorley, with a swift and not altogether approving glance at the speaker's face. "She'll be getting married soon. I can't expect to keep such beauty and grace hidden from the world. And she must make a good match, my lad"—this was for Alan's particular benefit as the young man knew very well—"a title and money, good looks and a landed estate, with brains added. That is the suitor I have chosen for Marie."

"You are looking for a bird of paradise," said Fuller, coloring at the hint conveyed, "does such perfection exist in a mere human being?"

"I hope so; I hope so," said Sorley, still cheery and still shifty in his glance, "we must look for the rarity, my lad. But I'm in no hurry to lose Marie. She is a great comfort to her old uncle. I was annoyed the other day, greatly annoyed, and she talked me into quite a good humor."

"What annoyed you, sir?" asked Fuller, not because he cared, but merely from a desire to chat about Miss Inderwick.

"A funeral which took place in the village."

"Oh, Baldwin Grison's funeral?"

Sorley brought his shifty green eyes to the young man's face. "What do you know about Baldwin Grison?" he asked sharply, and, as it seemed to Alan's suspicious nature, rather uneasily.

"All that the newspapers could tell me, Mr. Sorley. He was murdered at Rotherhithe by some unknown person, and his sister brought the body down here for burial in the village churchyard."

"That last wasn't in the newspapers," retorted the other quickly and looking everywhere but at Alan's face.

"No, it wasn't. But my friend Latimer—you may remember meeting him at the vicarage, Mr. Sorley—was at the inquest and afterwards spoke to Miss Grison, who told him of her intention."

"Did she tell him also that her brother was my secretary twenty years ago, Alan?" demanded Sorley, his face growing red and his eyes glittering. "Did she say how he was turned out of the house as a drunken swine?"

"Miss Grison hinted something of those things at the inquest, but did not go into details, and, as they were unnecessary, she was not pressed. But she told Latimer that her brother had been discharged by you for some reason."

"He was a hard drinker, and also smoked opium," said Sorley angrily. "I did what I could for him, but had to discharge him in the long run. That woman had no right to bring the body here and bury it under my nose, as it might be. Decency should have prevented her bringing back the man to a place whence he was kicked out twenty years ago."

"She didn't bring back the man, but his remains, sir."

"It would have been better had she thrown those into a London ditch," replied Sorley tartly. "Grison was a bad servant to me and a bad brother to her and a profligate animal. I don't wonder he was murdered."

"Can you suggest any motive for the commission of the crime?" asked Fuller, looking straightly at the elder man.

"Grison was a drunkard, an opium-smoker, a liar and a loafer. A man like that must have made many enemies, and in the low slum he lived in he certainly risked what has, in the end, happened. The wonder is that he was not murdered before, Alan."

"Well, he had one good point," said Fuller meaningly and to force confidence if possible on the part of Sorley. "He wasn't a thief."

"Can you prove that he was not?"

"Can you prove that he was?" demanded Alan in his turn. "At all events you omitted that particular crime from your category."

"The poor devil's dead and I don't wish to say more about him than I have already stated," said Sorley moodily, and beginning to start his machine, "but I trust that his silly sister will not come and worry me."

"Why should she?" asked Fuller, noticing that the man before him evaded the question of Grison being a thief.

"There's no reason in the world why she should, except that she was infatuated with her brother and believed that I had discharged him unjustly. I shouldn't be surprised if she came to tell me that again, by word of mouth as she has told me dozens of times by letter. She ascribed Grison's downfall to me, and was always asking me to assist him when he was at Rotherhithe during the last twenty years. Of course I didn't, both because I am poor as you know, Alan, and for the simple reason that Grison was not worth helping. I was his best friend, and far from bringing about his downfall I did my best to keep him straight. But all in vain: all in vain. He became quite a scandal in the place and Mrs. Inderwick, my sister, insisted that I should get rid of him. I did so, and he went to the dogs entirely. So there you are, Alan, my boy, and I can't stay here all day talking about a matter which annoys me intensely."

By this time the machine was alive with energy and Mr. Sorley swung himself into the saddle as he ended his voluble speech. With a nod he set the starting gear in motion, and almost instantaneously was a dot on the horizon travelling towards Lewes at the speed of a swallow. Alan looked after him thoughtfully, and tried to arrive at some conclusion regarding his apparently frank speech. By the time he reached the vicarage he came to one resolution at least, and that was to say nothing for the present to Mr. Sorley about the peacock. The young man could scarcely decide himself what made him refrain from speaking, save that the old gentleman's manner and vague speech communicated to him a sort of uneasy feeling, which hinted that reticence was wise for the time being. It might have been some sixth sense which induced the decision, for Fuller certainly could not argue out the matter logically. However, he determined to obey the intuition, and to avoid making a confidant of the uncle, while speaking freely of his errand to the niece. There was no feeling in his mind against discussing with Marie the theft of the peacock as the possible motive for the murder of the man her relative seemed to detest so thoroughly.

As usual the young man received the warmest of welcomes from his parents, who adored their only son and thought him the most wonderful person in the world. The vicar assuredly did not worship the marvellous boy so devotedly as did Mrs. Fuller; nevertheless he took a great pride in Alan's handsome looks and clever brains and general good conduct. He was a bright-eyed, rosy-faced little man, who scarcely came up to his tall son's shoulder, with a kindly nature, which was always being imposed upon. His wife, a sweet-faced old lady, tall, grey-haired, and singularly graceful, was more practical in many ways than her husband. She checked the vicar's too generous way of dealing with those who took advantage of his lavish kindness, and was the true ruling power in the house. Her weak point was Alan, and she often sighed to think that he would never find a woman worthy to be his wife. A dozen of the best women in the world rolled into one perfect creature would never have come up to the standard she had set up in her own mind which the future Mrs. Alan Fuller was to reach.

Alan always enjoyed his home visits, not only because he loved his parents with a tenderness and respect rare in these modern days of revolt against domestic authority, but also on account of the quiet and well-ordered life which made the vicarage so uncommonly pleasant. Mrs. Fuller was a famous housewife, and managed her establishment with such rare tact that she kept her servants for years. Her husband's income was not a large one, but no one would have guessed this, seeing the perfectly appointed dinner-table and the dainty meal prepared. The vicar's wife had brought to her husband by way of dowry a quantity of valuable old furniture, so that every room looked graciously beautiful. And as the house was quaint and old, and kept in perfect repair and order, those not in the secret of the income believed that the Fullers had ample means. But everything grateful to the eye and the touch and the palate was due to the "vicaress," as her husband jocularly called her. The worst-tempered person in the world would have succumbed to the soothing influences which permeated the place.

"Home, home, sweet, sweet home," hummed Alan, when the trio sat in the fragrant old drawing-room after an admirable dinner. "Mother darling, you have no idea how restful this is, after the noise and bustle of London."

Mrs. Fuller smiled from her favorite chair, and went on with her tatting, busy as a bee, for she was rarely idle. In her silver-grey dress with a lace cap of dainty gossamer resting on her white hair, worn cast back after the style of Marie Antoinette, and her old-fashioned set of amethyst ornaments, she looked singularly charming. In the subdued light which came through the pink lampshades she looked like some gentle ghost of early Victorian days, soothingly womanly and motherly. She had grown old gracefully, and as the diamonds flashed from her rings while she tatted diligently Alan thought what a delightful gentlewoman she looked, placid, dignified and gracious.

It was the vicar who answered his son's question, although Alan had scarcely put his remark as such. "Ah, my boy, you'd soon grow weary of this drowsy place, and would long for the crowded hour of glorious life. It is the contrast that makes you appreciate our Eden."

Mrs. Fuller nodded her approval. "White always shows up best against black."

"Well, you have had some London black down here lately, mother." And when she looked at him inquiringly, Alan continued, "I mean the funeral."

The vicar's face grew sad. "Yes! yes! That was indeed an unpleasant reminder of what lies beyond our quiet hills. Poor Grison and poor Louisa tool I do not know which I am most sorry for."

"For Louisa?" said Mrs. Fuller, raising her quiet eyes. "You need not be sorry for her, John. She did her duty and more than her duty by that poor creature who has gone to his account, so she has nothing to reproach herself with. I am glad she is staying for a few days, as I wish to have a talk with her."

"Is Miss Grison staying here then?" asked Alan, wondering if it would be worth while to look her up.

"At Mrs. Millington's, the dressmaker, my dear. She and Louisa were close friends twenty years and more ago."

"That was when Grison was secretary to Mr. Sorley."

"Yes," chimed in the vicar. "But who told you about that, my boy?"

"Miss Grison spoke about it at the inquest and also to Dick and Inspector Moon, father. Then I met Mr. Sorley on my way here and he told me that he had employed the man, but had to get rid of him for drink, and—"

"I don't think that is true," interrupted Mrs. Fuller with some indignation in her usually gentle voice. "Poor Baldwin—we called him so when he was a young man—did not drink to excess, although he certainly took more than was good for him at times."

"Then why was he discharged?"

"I cannot say, Alan, nor can anyone else. Louisa knows, but she would never tell me. But Mr. Sorley was much to blame in throwing Baldwin on the world without a character, since he was too weak to stand by himself. Louisa did what she could, but he fell from bad to worse until—alas! alas! Tell me, Alan, has anything been discovered as to who killed him?"

"Not yet, mother. You have read the papers."

"Oh yes. Louisa sent all the reports down to your father and to me, knowing that we took a deep interest in Baldwin. Don't you remember him, Alan? You were a little boy of six or seven then."

Alan shook his head. "I have a faint recollection only, mother. A little man, wasn't he, with fair hair and blue eyes? But there, I may have got that impression from Dick's description. He saw the corpse."

"Don't talk about such things, Alan," said the vicar hastily. "It worries your mother: she is very impressionable. Let us be thankful that the poor creature has been brought back to lie in our quiet churchyard. As to the person who murdered him, he will suffer for his sin in God's good time."

"I doubt if the truth will ever be discovered," said Alan with a shrug. "By the way, father, do you remember that peacock of jewels which was the fetish or luck of the Inderwicks?"

Not knowing what connection there was between the murder of Grison and the ornament in question, the vicar thought that the apparently irrelevant inquiry was made by his son in obedience to his request that the crime should not be discussed in the presence of Mrs. Fuller. "Everyone in the village, if not in the county, knows about the peacock," he said with an approving smile, "but as to its bringing luck, I do not believe in such superstitions, my boy."

"Perhaps not," said his wife quietly, "but you must confess, John, that since what the Inderwicks call their luck has been missing nothing has gone well with them—that is with Marie, who alone represents the family."

"Nonsense, my dear. Marie is young, healthy, pretty, and happy enough in her own way, as Sorley is kindness itself to her. There's no bad luck haunting the girl so far as I can see."

"No, of course not. But I allude rather to her poverty. The Inderwicks used to be rich, and Mrs. Inderwick was left comparatively well off. Then she lost her money when Marie was born, and afterwards died."

"Inderwick—Marie's father, that is—should not have made Sorley trustee, for he is, and always was a bad business man. He acted honestly enough, I daresay, but even with his sister's consent he should never have speculated as he did. No wonder the money was lost."

"What were the speculations?" asked Alan.

"Land in Australia—in Melbourne chiefly, I believe. There was a big land boom there, over twenty years ago. Then everything failed and bank after bank went smash. Before Sorley could get a letter or even a telegram out, everything was gone. However, Marie has The Monastery and the park and sufficient to keep her in food and dress, so she can't grumble."

"Marie never does grumble," said Mrs. Fuller decidedly, "she is the brightest person I know. But it's a dull life for a young girl at The Monastery. She ought to have a season in London and be presented at Court and have an opportunity," here she stole a shy glance at Alan's expressive face, "of making a good match. With Marie's blood and looks she should secure a title."

"Well, perhaps she will, when the peacock returns to bring back the luck," said Alan, refusing to be drawn into an argument with his mother over Marie.

"It will never be found," said the vicar positively. "How was it lost, father?"

"I can't tell you. But it has been missing twenty years and is not likely to reappear. Marie can do very well without it. Such superstition is ridiculous. And now we must have prayers," ended Mr. Fuller inconsequently. His wife looked up amused, since she knew that he acted thus because he had no patience with her belief in the peacock as a fetish.

And while prayers were being said Alan wondered if the peacock would ever reappear, in spite of his father's doubts, to influence Marie's destiny.

CHAPTER III

A STORY OF THE PAST

The ancient village of Belstone, hidden in a fold of low-lying, undulating hills, is inhabited chiefly by agricultural laborers. One irregular street, four or five narrow lanes, and a few behind-the-time shops, together with many small cottages, constitute this sequestered hamlet. There are a great number of farms and several country seats in the district, but those who own them usually buy the necessaries of life at Lewes, so Belstone cannot depend upon trade for its support. The villagers, however, do not mind this neglect, as they are sleepy-headed and indifferent to all, so long as they earn sufficient for bed and board. The sole houses of any note are the vicarage at one end of the village, and the great mansion of the Inderwicks at the other. Formerly the owners of The Monastery—as the place is called—were Lords of the Manor, but, as their property has dwindled to a few acres, the title has passed to a modern and more prosperous family. The Inderwicks, formerly so rich and powerful, are now of small account amongst the gentry of the county.

The Rev. John Fuller always maintained that the prehistoric name of the village was Baalstone, and that it was so termed after an altar or stone to Baal or Bel, a deity whom the Ph[oe]nicians had introduced into Britain. But it is more than questionable whether these sea-rovers ever traded so far as Sussex, and Mr. Fuller's assumption can be taken for what it is worth, although he held stoutly to his opinion. But be this as it may undoubtedly there was a Druidical temple where the big house now stands, later a shrine to Diana, and afterwards an altar to Woden, until early Christian missionaries built on the same spot a primitive flint and mortar church. Finally came a Benedictine monastery, which lasted until the reign of that arch-iconoclast, Henry VIII. From the expelled monks it had passed into the possession of Nicholas Inderwick, one of Cromwell's favorite gentlemen, and had been owned by his descendants ever since. The spot had therefore always been a holy one, until secularised in the days of the great Tudor monarch, and perhaps for this reason had never brought good fortune to the Inderwicks, who had built up what prosperity they had attained to on the ruin of sacred things and the misfortunes of sacred people. Certainly evil luck had followed them for generations: they had lost land, money, position and authority, and their family tree had been cut down root and branch, until only one feeble twig sprouted from the mouldering trunk. Marie Inderwick was the last descendant of the ancient line, and dwelt in the house of her ancestors on a penurious income which barely sufficed to keep her in food and fire and clothes. And when she married, or died, it was to be expected that the family name would vanish from the land.

All these things Alan knew very well, as all his life they had been talked about in the village and at the vicarage. There was also a prophecy of an expelled monk dating over three hundred years ago, which promised renewed prosperity to the Inderwicks when their fortunes were lowest. The young man could not think how much lower the fortunes could sink, and wondered as he strolled towards the monastery, if now was the appointed time for the fulfilment of the ancient saying:—

"When most is lost and most are dead,
The spoilers then shall raise their head.
Jewels and gold from over-seas,
Will bring them peace and joy and ease."

Of course Alan in his reading of the prophecy modernized the antique diction. There was much more of it, but only Marie knew the whole of Fate's decree, and was accustomed to repeat it hopefully when she felt down-hearted. She always insisted that sooner or later the curse pronounced on the Inderwicks by the monk would be removed.

As there was no money to keep things in order, the place was woefully neglected. The great iron gates which swung from pillars surmounted by the Inderwick escutcheon in the grip of tall dragons had not been opened for many years, and access to the park was gained through a small side entrance set in the mouldering brick wall which encircled the domain. The park itself was so overgrown and wild and tangled and savage that it might have been that very wood which shut in the enchanted palace of the Sleeping Beauty. Alan dreamed that it might be so, and that he might be the fairy prince destined to awaken Marie to a new life. And indeed since she loved him, and he adored her, he had succeeded so far; but how her fortunes were to be mended at the present juncture he could not see. Yet had he been gifted with psychic powers he would have known more or less positively that he was on the eve of entering a new lane down which he would lead the girl towards happiness and prosperity.

A short brisk walk up the neglected avenue brought Fuller into the wide open space wherein was placed the great mansion. Some portions of the original monastery remained, but during hundreds of years it had been so altered that the monks would have had some difficulty in recognizing their former habitation. Parts of the building had been pulled down and other parts built up, that had been altered and this had been permitted to remain in its original state, so that the old house presented an incongruous appearance which could be ascribed to no particular epoch of architecture. With its walls of grey flint, brown stone, red brick, and here and there blocks of white marble somewhat soiled by wind and rain and sunshine, it looked singularly picturesque. And the whole was overgrown with ivy, dank and green and wonderfully luxuriant, since it was never trimmed and never cut. The big building looked as though it were bound to the soil by the tough tendrils and what with the rank coarse grasses and the trees which grew right up to the walls, it might have been part and parcel of the earth itself, so swathed was it in greenery. There was something noble and austere about the dwelling befitting perhaps the Benedictines who had dwelt in it at one time, but it looked altogether too sombre and unwholesome to shelter the fair head of Marie Inderwick, who was all smiles and sunshine. And as Alan advanced towards the huge porch which was supported on twisted pillars, she unexpectedly made her appearance like a gleam of light shooting across a thunderous sky. It was Alan the lover, and not Fuller the lawyer, who made this poetic comparison.

"Darling! darling!" cried Marie, running down the broken steps with outstretched hands. "I knew you would come. But how late you are! I saw you in the church this morning, and have been expecting you all the afternoon. It is now three o'clock and only at this moment do you put in an appearance. No, I won't be kissed. Uncle may be at the window and would make trouble, as he always does. Besides you don't deserve a kiss, when you neglect me so."

"I shall take one for all that," said Alan, suiting the action to the word, "and in spite of possible dragon eyes at the window."

"But your neglect," pouted Marie, playing with his necktie, arranging it and rearranging it after the manner of women whose fingers must always be busy.

"Dearest, I stayed for the midday communion, and when I came out you had gone home with your uncle."

"He hurried me away, Alan. He's always very particular to keep an eye on me when you come down."

"Undoubtedly. He wants you to marry a title."

Marie shrugged her shoulders in a French fashion which she had acquired from a Parisian school friend at the Brighton seminary. "As if anyone would marry a pauper like me.'

"I think any man who has an eye for the beautiful would only be too glad to marry such a lovely pauper."

"That's nice. Say it again and slowly."

"A lovely pauper, an adorable pauper, an angelic—"

"Stop! stop! You flatter too much. You don't mean what you say."

"Not a word," confessed Alan candidly.

Marie grew red and her eyes flashed. "Then how dare you say such things!"

"You expect me to and you shouldn't fish."

"In shallow water? Certainly not! Alan Eric Reginald Fuller," she gave him his complete name and pinched his arm, "you are a bear."

"Bears hug," said the lover, taking her in his arms.

"Oh, my gracious, you will get me into trouble," cried Marie, extricating herself with some difficulty and flying across the lawn, followed hot-footed by Alan. "Come and hide out of sight of those horrid windows. Uncle Ran is sure to see us otherwise, and will order me indoors. Come! come," she sang like a siren and fled after the fashion of Atalanta into the woods.

The trees were bare of leaves, but here and there a fir stood up green and sombre, while the undergrowth of brambles and grass and ferns and various weeds had not yet lost their autumnal tints so that the park did not as yet look entirely wintry. The day was warm too for late November, and pale sunshine irradiated the grey depths of the sky, so that the birds had plucked up heart to sing, perhaps in the hope of averting coming snows. At top-speed Marie flew down a side path which twisted and straightened at intervals for a considerable distance until it ended In a kind of sunken dell in the centre of which was a circle of cemented stones rising slightly above the fading herbage. Over this was a wooden canopy of ancient appearance with a tiled red roof weather-worn and mellow, and beneath, a deep hole which seemed to penetrate into the bowels of the earth. This was St. Peter's Dell and St. Peter's Well since the monastery had been dedicated to the chief of the Apostles. Marie loved the spot, and haunted it in summer for the sake of its coolness. Now she came because she knew that her philanderings with the forbidden lover would not be seen by anyone.

"And Uncle Ran is asleep," she explained as she perched herself on the ragged rim of stones. "He always sleeps for an hour in the afternoon, because he says that it keeps him alive."

"I wish it didn't," growled Alan, placing himself beside the girl, and putting an arm round her, probably to prevent her from falling into the depths. "I don't like your Uncle Ran, dear."

"Since he won't let you make love to me, I can quite understand that," said Marie rather pertly; "but he's all the relative I have so I must make the best of him, Alan. But you haven't told me how I am looking."

"Why, I've used at least a dozen adjectives. But I shall examine you carefully, darling, and give you my honest opinion."

Taking her chin in his hand, he turned her face upward, and looked into the happy blue eyes. Marie was indeed a very pretty girl, although not perhaps so superlatively lovely as Alan imagined. Her face would never have launched a thousand ships, or set fire to Troy Town. But her complexion was transparent and as delicately tinted as a rose, with the dewy look, so to speak, of that flower at dawn. Her hair was golden and waved over her white forehead in rebellious little curls. Then she had sapphire eyes and a straight little Greek nose, and two fresh red lips, which seemed to invite the kiss Alan now bestowed. As her figure was wrapped up in a heavy fur cloak of great antiquity, it could not be seen at the moment, but Alan, who was well acquainted with its suave contours, knew that it was the most perfect figure in the three kingdoms, as her hands and feet were the smallest and most well-shaped. But what really drew his heart to Marie was her sweet expression and candid looks. Some women—few, of course—might have possessed Marie's items of beauty in the shape of form and coloring, but no one, and Alan said this aloud with great decision, ever owned such heavenly smiles or could give such tender glances. Marie sighed and approved of the praise and nestled her head against his rough frieze overcoat.

"You always tell the truth, darling," she said, after he had assured her that she was something higher than an angel.

"Always!" Alan kissed her again for the tenth time. "And now I want you to tell me the truth, Marie."

She looked up somewhat puzzled. "About what?"

"About the peacock of jewels, which—"

The girl drew away from his encircling arm and slipped to the ground. "Why do you want to speak about that?" she asked, standing before him and looking as charming as the Queen of Sheba when she visited Solomon; "it was lost before I was born, and no one ever speaks of it. Except Uncle Ran," she added with an afterthought, "he loves jewels, as you know, and always regrets the loss, although the peacock belongs to me and not to him."

"Marie," said Alan again and gravely, "come and sit down, as I have something important to tell you which you must not repeat to your uncle until I give you leave."

"I shall sit here," said Miss Inderwick, sinking on to the trunk of a fallen tree which was a few feet away, "and I wish you wouldn't look so solemn or talk about such things. You make me nervous."

"There is nothing to be nervous about, my dear."

"Then why am I not to repeat what you say to Uncle Ran?" demanded Marie in an inconsequent manner.

"Because I think if Mr. Sorley got that peacock he would be greedy enough to keep it to himself."

"He couldn't. It's mine."

"He would, because he looks upon your property as his own."

"The peacock was left to me by my father's will, along with the park and the house," insisted Marie folding her hands pensively. "It was particularly mentioned because of the good fortune it will bring—that is when the secret is discovered."

"The secret. What secret?" Alan spoke almost sharply.

"That connected with the golden peacock. You know the story?"

"Only that there is such a fetish, which is supposed to be the luck of the Inderwicks."

"And has been for one hundred years and more. But the secret—"

"I have heard nothing about that."

"Now I come to think of it, I daresay you haven't. I only became acquainted with the real meaning of the peacock of jewels a year ago. I read all about it in a manuscript which I found in the library. When was the battle of Plassey, Alan?"

"In 1757," answered Fuller, who had a good memory for dates.

"It was won by Lord Clive, wasn't it?"

"Yes. But what has that to do with the peacock?"

"A great deal, as you shall hear."

"One moment, Marie. Is this peacock of Indian workmanship?"

"No. It was made by a man called Simon Ferrier, who was the servant of my great great great—I don't know how many greats—grandfather."

"Let us say the grandfather who lived about the time of Plassey. What was his name?"

"George Inderwick. He went to India to—" Here Marie broke off and looked at her lover searchingly. "But why do you ask about the peacock?"

"I'll explain that when I have heard the legend."

"It isn't a legend, but a true story, and you are very mysterious," said the girl somewhat incoherently. "Well then, George Inderwick went out to India long before the battle of Plassey in the hope of restoring the family fortunes. He was only a younger brother and left The Monastery in possession of Julian Inderwick. Things were very bad with the family then and they have been worse since. Now"—Marie sighed—"everything is lost unless the treasure is discovered."

"The treasure?" Alan looked excited. "Is there a treasure?"

"Of course, you stupid thing. That is the secret of the peacock."

Alan became exasperated by the way in which he had to drag things out of her and frowned. "I wish you would tell me the story clearly," he said tartly.

"I shall do so if you won't interrupt so often," retorted Marie. Then looking round the quiet dell, as if for inspiration, and finally finding it in the eager look in her lover's eyes, she began the tale. "George went to India along with his servant, Simon Ferrier, who was his foster-brother—"

"Wait a bit," interrupted Fuller again. "Who wrote this manuscript?"

"Simon Ferrier, and I won't tell you anything if you keep asking questions, Alan. How can I speak when you talk?"

"I am dumb, my dearest virago. Go on."

"I'm not a virago, you horrid boy. Well then, George went to Madras as a clerk of the East India Company, and was lent to some rajah to drill his army. He learned soldiering from Lord Clive, although he wasn't Lord Clive at the time. Simon went with George to some hill fort and palace and the two became quite friendly with the rajah. Then some enemy of the native prince they served stormed the palace or town or whatever it was, and killed the lot of them."

"Even George and Simon?" asked Alan, noting the loose way in which she was telling the tale, and privately deciding to ask for the manuscript, so that he might read it himself.

"No, you silly. They were taken prisoners. But before the place was captured, the Begum—that's the rajah's wife—gave all her jewels to Mr. Inderwick, because he saved her life, and the life of her son. Simon hid them when he and his master were captured by the other king, or rajah, or—"

"Never mind; say captured by the enemy."

"Oh, very well," said Marie obediently, "when they were captured by the enemy. They were a long time in captivity, and George was forced to drill the native troops, while Simon was made to work as a jeweller."

"Why as a jeweller?"

"Oh, it seems that he had been brought up in England as a watchmaker, and having mended some clock belonging to the enemy, he was set to work in a shop to make ornaments for the enemy's wives. He learned how to make Indian ornaments and became very clever—at least he says so himself, but perhaps he was bragging."

"I don't think so, if the stories about the beauty of the peacock he made are to be believed," said Fuller thoughtfully, and recalling certain stories related by old village women who had set eyes on the ornament in question before it had disappeared. "Go on, dear. This is interesting."

"The most interesting part is to come," replied Marie, nodding her small head with a wise air. "Simon managed to get away, and went back to where he had hidden the jewels. He dug them up and came to England—"

"Leaving his master in captivity. How shabby of him."

"He only did what his master told him," said Marie quickly. "He was to take the jewels to England and give them to Julian Inderwick so that the fortunes of the family might be restored. But Simon did not like Julian and found out that he was a spendthrift and a gambler. If he had given him the jewels they would have been wasted, and the Inderwicks would have been none the better for them. Simon therefore said nothing about his mission, but he hid the jewels and then returned to India to rejoin his master, who was now free and was fighting beside Lord Clive."

"Well, and what happened then?"

"When the battle of Plassey was being fought, and before Simon could return to his master, he was taken prisoner by those who had before held him captive. They had come to know about the jewels, and insisted that he should tell where they were. Simon was even tortured to make him tell, but he refused to speak, so they grew tired and set him to work again, as a jeweller. It was then that he made the peacock."

"Why the peacock particularly?"

"Because he wished to let George Inderwick know where the jewels of the Begum were hidden in England, and could only do so by indicating the place through this golden peacock."

"But in what way?"

"I don't know. I can't find out. Simon feared lest the secret should be discovered by the Indians and lest they should send someone to England to get back the gems. He therefore, as I say, made the peacock, and contrived to have it taken to George Inderwick through a native who was friendly to him. He then died, after writing the manuscript, telling his master that the secret was hidden in the peacock. He was murdered, I believe, as he says at the end of his manuscript that he expected to be put to death."

"But what was the use of sending the secret to George when it could not be guessed?"

"It *was* stupid," admitted Marie thoughtfully, "since George never managed to find out from the peacock where the jewels were. In his anxiety to keep the secret from everyone but his master, Simon over-reached himself, and entirely forgot that George would find it as hard to learn the truth as anyone else into whose hands the peacock fell. However, he died, and the ornament with the manuscript came to George. After the battle of Plassey George returned home with some money, and tried hard to learn the whereabouts of the jewels from the peacock. Julian by this time had died, so the younger brother succeeded to the estate—what there was left of it. He—George, I mean—was poor all his life, as he brought back very little from India, and all he could do was to keep what Julian had left."

"Well?" asked Alan, seeing that she said no more.

"That is all. George left a will saying that the jewels were to be found if the secret of the peacock was discovered. But Simon, in his desire to keep them safe, had hidden the truth too securely. Everyone has tried to find the truth, even Uncle Ran, for I asked him, but all have failed."

"How much are the jewels worth?" asked Fuller after a pause.

"Oh," Marie jumped up and spread her hands, "thousands and thousands of pounds, dear! One hundred thousand, two hundred thousand, I don't know how much. There are rubies and emeralds and opals and diamonds and—and—" she stopped for want of breath. "Isn't it wonderful, Alan?"

"Wonderful indeed," admitted the young man.

"So there is one or two hundred thousand pounds attached to the possession of the peacock of jewels if its secret can only be discovered. Hum! It's worth risking one's neck for."

Marie ran up and shook him by the arm. "How can you say such horrid things?"

"I am not talking of my own neck, Marie, but of that belonging to the man who murdered Baldwin Grison."

"Oh." The girl stared. "I know that the poor man was murdered. Mrs. Millington—she's the village dressmaker, and a friend of mine—told me about that crime. Louisa Grison was Mrs. Millington's bridesmaid, and they are very much attached, and—and—but, Alan, what has the peacock to do with this horrid murder?"

"Much. Baldwin Grison was murdered, as I truly believe, so that his assassin might obtain it. Now listen, dear, and be sure you don't repeat what I say to your uncle."

"No, I won't. Though I don't see why you want to keep things secret from him. Go on. What is it?"

Fuller quickly and concisely told her all that he had learned from Dick Latimer and Inspector Moon relative to the Rotherhithe murder, and laid great stress on the fact that Jotty the street-arab had seen the peacock of jewels. Marie listened with open mouth.

"But you can't be sure that the poor man was murdered because of the peacock," she said when he ended. "Besides, how could he have it?"

"Oh, that last is easy. Grison was your uncle's secretary and may have taken the peacock out of revenge, knowing that Mr. Sorley was fond of jewels. On the other hand, Grison may have read the very same manuscript about which you have been telling me and might have tried to learn the secret."

"Then he could not have," cried the girl positively, "else he would not have remained in that horrid slum. Who has the peacock now?"

"The assassin."

"Who is he?"

"No one knows, and no one can find out."

"But are you sure Mr. Grison was murdered because of the peacock?" asked Marie again, and doubtfully.

"I think so, since the room was ransacked, and Grison had no other object of value in his miserable dwelling to tempt anyone to commit a crime."

"Well, it might be so. But why am I not to tell Uncle Ran?"

"Because I wish to find the peacock and deliver the assassin of Grison to justice. If Mr. Sorley goes on the trail also he will get the peacock and will not give it to you, to whom it rightfully belongs."

"I see. Of course I shall say nothing. And Alan"—she laid her arms round her lover's neck—"do find the peacock, and let us look for the treasure."

"And then?" questioned the young man, smiling at the bright face.

"Then! then," said Miss Inderwick, dancing away from him, "why then, you stupid creature, we can marry and defy Uncle Ran."

CHAPTER IV

"Now that we have finished our secret conversation," said Fuller some time later, when the pair were returning towards the avenue, "I shall call and pay my respects to your uncle."

"I don't think he wants to see you," answered Marie very candidly, "he is quite aware that I love you and wishes to keep us apart."

"No doubt, my dear, but I don't intend him to get his own way. He never can, so long as you remain true to me."

Marie squeezed the arm she held. "As if there was any question of that. All the same, Uncle Ran is sure to be nasty if you call."

"He was amiable enough yesterday when we met, and outwardly he has no reason to overstep the bounds of politeness. I intend to call in order to show him that I am quite friendly, and if he objects he can speak out."

"He's asleep yet, I expect," objected Marie anxiously.

"All the better. We shall have a longer time to ourselves, and you can give me a cup of tea."

"Uncle Ran would assuredly object to that," said the girl with emphasis. "He is becoming a perfect miser. Every penny he obtains he turns into jewels, Alan, although owing to want of money he can only buy cheap stones."

"So long as he uses his own money and not yours he can do what he likes, I suppose, Marie. But you have an income and the house, so he has no right to object to your extending afternoon-tea hospitality to me."

"I never get any of my own money except a few shillings a week for my pocket," admitted Marie rather mournfully. "You know Uncle Ran was left my sole guardian, and I do not come of age for another year. Then he says he will account to me for my money, which he declares he is saving."

Remembering Mr. Sorley's shifty eyes and slack mouth, Fuller had his doubts as to the truth of this statement, and merely grunted. But when Marie went on to say that her uncle was selling portions of the furniture he raised his eyebrows. "He has no right to do that without your consent, my dear."

"He says that he has, and that there is too much furniture in the place. I understand from him that he is selling the furniture in order to invest the money for me."

"Hum! It may be so, but I should not be too sure of that. I wish I were your husband now, Marie, and then I could look after your interests."

"You don't trust Uncle Ran?"

"Candidly, I don't, although I have no very strong reason to say so. Do you trust him yourself, Marie?"

"I don't know; I can't say," said the girl slowly; "of course he has been kind to me since I returned a year ago from Brighton, where I was at school, Alan. He doesn't interfere with me, you know."

"He lets you run wild, if that's what you mean, my dear," retorted the solicitor hotly. "Now that it does you any harm of course, as you are a sensible girl. But Mr. Sorley should take you out visiting and let you go to dances occasionally, and you should have a few days in London every now and then. He should not neglect you as he does."

"We are too poor to afford such things, Alan. But some day when we find the treasure, we—you and I of course—shall have a splendid time. Remember the prophecy, my dear," and she repeated two lines of the same:

> "Jewels and gold from over-seas
> Will bring them peace and joy and ease."

Alan was struck by the quotation from a three hundred year old oracle after hearing Marie's story of the secret which possession and examination of the peacock would reveal. "Jewels and gold," he repeated slowly, "yes; it does sound as though that line referred to the Begum's hoard. Odd, very odd indeed."

"It will come true, it will come true," sang Marie, dancing a step or two in her gleeful way, and with the exuberant joy of twenty. "Then we'll pension Uncle Ran off, and have The Monastery and the money to ourselves. Oh, Alan, let us build castles in the air."

"They won't turn into bricks and mortar until we find the peacock," said Mr. Fuller gloomily, "and that will not be easy, seeing it means the capture of poor Grison's assassin. Moon can find out nothing and if he fails how can mere amateur detectives such as Dick and I are succeed. However, we know that he was murdered for the sake of the peacock, and this strange story of yours helps a bit to strengthen the clue. But let me impress upon you again, Marie, not to tell your uncle."

"Certainly not, though I really don't know why you mistrust him."

"I scarcely know myself," said Alan candidly, "but I certainly do."

By this time—walking demurely apart in case Mr. Sorley should be awake and on the watch—they had entered the house, to find themselves in a large

34

and chilly hall, with a black and white pavement and marble busts of the Cæsars set round about it close to the walls. No rosy glow came from the old-fashioned fireplace, since Mr. Sorley deemed it waste of coal to heat such a mausoleum; so, with a shiver, the two crossed into the library, which was at the end of a lordly corridor to the right.

"There's a fire here," said Marie as they entered, "it's Uncle Ran's favorite room, and you can trust him to make himself comfortable, even if he has to pay for it."

"Then he can't be a genuine miser," remarked Fuller, walking towards the fire, which was a tolerably good one; "they starve themselves in every way, my dear, and—oh, I beg your pardon."

This last was addressed to a small elderly woman who suddenly rose from a deep grandfather's chair which looked like a sentry-box. She had sandy hair smoothly plastered down on either side of a sallow, wrinkled face; also thin, firmly compressed lips and hard blue eyes, staring and unwinking. Her figure was lean, her waist was pinched in, and her shoulders were so sloping that the worn black velvet cloak she wore would have slipped off had it not been firmly fastened down the front with large buttons of cut jet. As the cloak was down to her very heels, the dress she had on could not be seen, but her head was adorned with an early Victorian bonnet and her thin hands were covered with drab thread gloves. She had crape on her bonnet, and crape round her neck, but it did not need this evidence of mourning to assure Fuller that he beheld the sister of the dead man, since he remembered Dick's description fairly well.

"Miss Grison," said Marie, coming forward when she heard her lover's speech and offering her hand. "I heard you were down here."

Miss Grison took the hand, gave it a limp shake and dropped it. "Thank you, my dear," she said in a cold, precise voice. "I came down for my brother's funeral. He always wished to rest in Belstone churchyard and have the service read over his remains by Mr. Fuller, so I felt it was only due to his memory to do what he desired."

"This is Mr. Fuller's son," said Marie, introducing Alan.

"How do you do," said the visitor, still coldly. "I remember you years ago as a little boy with bare legs and a pinafore. You have grown since then."

"It is impossible to have bare legs and a pinafore at twenty-seven," said Alan, not knowing if she was laughing at him.

"Twenty and more years ago I saw you," said Miss Grison, who certainly seemed to have no sense of humor. "Ah, how the time passes. You were just born when I left Belstone to live in London," she added, glancing in her hard way at Marie, "a mere infant in arms."

"I have seen you a few times though," murmured Marie politely.

Miss Grison nodded stiffly. "Occasionally I have come down to stay with Selina Millington," she explained, "and we met before you went to school at Brighton. But since your return a year ago we have not met, as I have not been down here. How did you recognise me?"

"You are not changed in any way," said Marie bluntly.

"I should be," remarked the little woman with a sigh, "my poor Baldwin's death has broken my heart."

"It was very terrible," Marie hastened to assure her. "I read about it in the newspapers. Who killed him?"

"That's what I intend to find out," cried Miss Grison with a flash of her blue eyes. "Poor Baldwin never harmed a soul, and had no enemies—except one," she ended with an afterthought, and her lips closed firmly.

"Perhaps the one enemy killed him."

"I don't know. I can't prove anything. And the police seem to be doubtful about tracing the man."

"It was a man then who murdered your brother?" asked Alan suddenly.

Miss Grison gave him a scrutinizing look. "Yes, it was a man, as I truly believe, although there is no evidence to show the sex of the murderer."

"What is the name of the person you think was your brother's enemy?"

"Never mind, Mr. Fuller. I may misjudge him, and until I am sure I shall mention no names. But I shall watch and search and think and work until I avenge poor Baldwin's death!" And the fierce, determined look on her yellow face showed that she thoroughly meant what she said.

"Can I help you in any way?"

"Why should you?" she asked cautiously.

"Because I take an interest in the case," Alan explained equally cautiously. "A friend of mine, Mr. Latimer, who was at the inquest, told me all about the sad circumstances, and the death is so mysterious that both of us wish to learn the truth, if only out of curiosity."

The little woman paused almost imperceptibly and cast a swift look at the young man and the girl by his side before replying. Then she accepted the well-meant offer in her usual unemotional way. "I shall be glad of your assistance, Mr. Fuller," she said, producing a printed card from a bead bag which dangled from her lean wrist; "this is my address in Bloomsbury. I keep a boarding-house."

"So Mr. Latimer told me. You stated as much at the inquest. Tell me," he asked, putting the card into his vest pocket, "have you any clue to—"

"I have no clue you would call reasonable, Mr. Fuller!"

"That hints some ground on your part for—"

"Never mind what it hints," interrupted Miss Grison sharply. "If you call on me in London, and I feel that I can trust you, then I may speak out."

"Anyone could trust Alan," said Marie indignantly.

The visitor gave a thin-lipped smile. "You are quite right to defend him, my dear, and your defence is natural enough since Selina Millington told me that Mr. Fuller admires you. But he's a man and all men are bad—"

"Except Alan, who is engaged to be married to me."

"All men are bad," repeated Miss Grison stolidly. "I only knew one good man, and he was my brother Baldwin.

"H'm!" murmured Alan, remembering what Sorley had said on the previous day.

If Miss Grison heard the ejaculation, and understood its purport, she gave no sign of such knowledge. "What does your Uncle Randolph say to your being engaged to Mr. Fuller?" she asked turning to Marie abruptly.

"He says nothing, because he knows nothing."

"Then don't let him know. He will ruin your happiness in life if he can, as he ruined mine. A hard, cruel man is your Uncle Randolph, my dear."

Marie stared at this wholesale condemnation. "Do you know him well?"

"Do I know him well?" Miss Grison gave a hard laugh, and her eyes glittered viciously. "Yes, I may say that I know him very well."

Alan, looking closely at her, wondered if the enemy of her brother to whom she had referred so positively was Mr. Sorley, and thought that it was extremely likely from the vicious emphasis with which she spoke. But Miss Grison, giving him no time to make any comment on her last speech, continued as though she had not stopped to draw breath.

"I know the house very well also," she said calmly, "and I have been walking all over it, while waiting to see Mr. Sorley."

"Walking all over it," repeated Marie rather indignantly. "A stranger?"

"I am not a stranger either to Mr. Sorley or to The Monastery," replied the small woman with great coolness. "When my brother was his secretary here, years ago, I used to spend days wandering about the rooms and corridors. I know every nook and corner of it, my dear, and could tell you of many a secret hiding-place and hidden passage which were used in ancient times. Your mother made a friend of me in those days, and we used to explore the house together before you were born."

"Still Uncle Ran would not like you walking about the place when I was out and he was asleep. Didn't Jenny or Henny stop you?"

"Do you mean the servants?" inquired Miss Grison smoothly. "Well they did express surprise when I walked into the kitchen. But I told them I had come to see Mr. Sorley, and they showed me in here to wait for him—as if I required showing," ended Miss Grison disdainfully.

Fuller stared at her hard. She seemed to be in her right senses and what she said was reasonable enough, but it struck him that there must be something eccentric about her when she ventured to enter a house and explore it without the owner's permission. Again Miss Grison gave him no time to make a comment, but went on talking in the shrill voice which Latimer had noted and mentioned.

"Henrietta and Jane Trent are twins," she explained to Marie as if the girl knew nothing about her own servants. "I remember them as little toddlers in the village. The mother took in washing. Fine bouncing women they have grown into, my dear: red cheeks and black hair and wooden expressions, just like two Dutch dolls. Are they good servants?"

Marie was so taken aback by the audacity of her visitor that she replied, as she would have done to her schoolmistress: "They are very good and do all the work of this big house."

"There is a lot to do, I admit," said Miss Grison, nodding, "but I notice that many of the rooms are shut up, my dear."

"We—uncle and I, that is—do not require so many."

"I looked into some, and found them bare of furniture," pursued Miss Grison calmly, and with her hard, unwinking stare. "Yet in my time there was a lot of valuable—"

"Pardon me, Miss Grison," interrupted Fuller, seeing the consternation of Marie, "but don't you think you are taking rather a liberty in entering the house and in talking like this?"

"It may appear a liberty to you, Mr. Fuller," she rejoined quietly, "but it will not to Mr. Sorley. We are old friends."

"Friends," said Alan with emphasis.

She turned on him with a flash in her eyes. "Did he ever give you to understand otherwise?" she demanded, drawing quick breaths. "Has he ever mentioned my name to you?"

She waited for a reply but none came, as Alan was deliberating whether it would be wise to inform her of the way in which Mr. Sorley had spoken. Also he wondered if Miss Grison knew that her brother had been murdered for the sake of the peacock, and if she could tell how Baldwin became possessed of the same. But he felt that it would be best not to ask questions, or to make answers, until he knew his ground better. With her hard look, the little woman waited for him to speak, but he was saved the trouble by the unexpected entrance of Mr. Randolph Sorley. He was perfectly dressed as usual in a well-cut suit of blue serge and wore patent leather boots, together with a smart scarf of white silk fastened with a black pearl breast-pin. If he was a miser in some things, as Marie asserted, he assuredly was not so in the matter of clothes, for no one could have been better turned out, or have looked more aristocratic. His carriage was so upright, his hair so short, his face so bronzed and his greenish eyes so alert that he had quite a military appearance. He even looked young in the dusky atmosphere of the big room, and it was only when he came forward more into the light that he betrayed his sixty years. And that was possibly because Alan knew his true age, for the smooth, clean-shaven face looked much younger in spite of the white hair.

"Mr. Fuller! Miss Grison," he said slowly, "this is indeed a surprise. I am delighted to see you both."

And indeed he appeared to be so, for his smile was open, his speech soft and his manner frank. After what he had said about the woman on the previous day Fuller quite expected that he would be rude to her and—since he had other plans in his head—the young man quite expected that he would be rude to him also. But Mr. Sorley was apparently too well-bred to act impolitely in what he regarded as his own house, even if that same house was the property of Marie Inderwick. Miss Grison's blue eyes glittered a trifle more as he shook hands with her cordially but otherwise she remained her impenetrable self. And remembering what she had said about her host, Alan was as amazed at her behavior as he was at Sorley's. As to Marie, she was so relieved that her uncle received Alan courteously that she never gave a thought to the possibility that he might be acting a part for reasons best known to himself.

"Have you had tea?" inquired Mr. Sorley, poking the fire. "Marie, my dear, why did you not offer your guests tea?" And he rang the bell promptly.

"I did not like to without your permission, Uncle Ran," she said timidly.

"My dear child, this is your house, and here you are the mistress. I am only your guardian and live here, as it were, on sufferance. Miss Grison I am truly grieved to hear of your brother's death."

"Oh, indeed," said the small woman sarcastically, "in that case, I wonder you didn't come to the funeral."

"No! no! no! That would have awakened memories of the past."

"There is a proverb," remarked Miss Grison coldly, "which bids us let sleeping dogs lie."

"Very good advice," assented Mr. Sorley, "suppose we adopt it by letting the sad past alone and coming to the sad present. Have the police discovered who murdered your brother?"

"No," snapped Miss Grison impassively.

"Are they likely to?"

"If I can help them, they certainly are."

"Then you know of some clue?"

"I may, or I may not. This is not the time to speak about such things."

"My dear lady," said the host with great dignity, "I am under the impression that you came here to receive my sympathy."

"Then you were never more mistaken in your life," retorted Miss Grison grimly. "I came to say what I shall say, when tea is at an end."

"Nothing unpleasant, I trust?" asked Sorley distinctly uneasily.

"That is for you to judge," she returned, and the entrance of Henny Trent with a tray put an end to this particular conversation.

While Henny, who was large and red-cheeked and black-eyed, and who really resembled the Dutch doll Miss Grison had compared her to, was arranging the tea-table, Alan stole furtive looks at Mr. Sorley. The old gentleman seemed to have suddenly aged, and a haggard look had crept over his deceptive face, while his eyes hinted uneasiness as he watched Miss Grison. It seemed to Fuller that Sorley for some reason feared his visitor, and the fact that she had so audaciously walked over the house appeared to indicate that she was quite sure he would not rebuke her for the liberty. And, remembering the man's bluster, which contrasted so pointedly with his present suave talk, Alan felt confident that there was an understanding between them. He asked himself if such had to do with the murder, but replied mentally in the negative. If Sorley knew anything about the matter, Miss Grison would then and there have denounced him, since she appeared to hate him as much as he dreaded her. But beyond short answers and sinister glances, she gave no sign of her enmity, while Sorley masked his uneasiness under the guise of small talk. In spite of the almost immediate occurrence of the murder, and the fact that Miss Grison had come down for the funeral, Fuller noted that the tragedy was scarcely referred to—at all events during the earlier part of the conversation. Along with Marie, he remained silent, and allowed the other two to converse.

"Are you staying long down here, Miss Grison?" asked the host, handing a cup of tea to her and a plate of thin bread and butter.

"Why don't you call me Louisa as you used to do?" she demanded. "We were great friends, you know, Marie, before you were born." She turned to Miss Inderwick.

"Yes yes," said Sorley, taking his cue. "You called me Randolph; but we are both too old now to use our Christian names." He laughed artificially.

"Are we?" said Miss Grison shortly. "Perhaps we are. How are you getting along with that book on precious stones, may I ask?"

"You may," said Sorley blandly. "I am getting on slowly but surely. It has taken me years to gather material."

"Precious stones, I suppose."

"Certain gems of small value amongst other material, such as legends and superstitions connected with jewels. It will be an interesting book."

"I'm sure it will," said Miss Grison more graciously, "but don't work too hard at it. You are fond of exercise?"

"Yes, I take a great deal."

"Ah, Selina Millington told me that you had bought a motor bicycle."

"Yes," said Sorley stiffly and still laboriously polite. "I ride it round the country."

"And up to London?"

"No," he replied swiftly. "I have not yet travelled on it to town."

"I don't think it takes many hours to get to town on so rapid a machine," said Miss Grison in a musing tone. "But perhaps you are wise; you might get knocked over in the streets."

What answer Sorley made to this speech Alan did not hear. Marie, who had resented his attention to the speech of the elderly couple, now insisted that he should converse with her. He did so rather unwillingly, in spite of his genuine love. But his brain was running on the odd and somewhat spasmodic conversation, and he wondered why Miss Grison so pointedly referred to the motor bicycle. Also it seemed strange that Sorley should be on such familiar terms with a humble woman who kept a Bloomsbury boarding-house. To be sure her brother had been the man's secretary, and Sorley probably had been intimate with the visitor in early days. Perhaps—and here Fuller started—perhaps the two had been in love, and the hatred Miss Grison felt for the well-preserved old gentleman was that of a woman scorned. When he again caught the drift of the conversation she was talking about cryptograms, and this also Alan thought strange.

"My poor brother was always trying to work out secret writings," said she.

"Why?" asked Sorley, again uneasy at this mention of the dead.

"I don't know," answered Miss Grison indifferently. "He wanted to learn some secret that would bring him money."

"In connection with what?"

"I don't know."

"Did he ever decipher the secret writing you refer to?"

"I don't know," said Miss Grison again. "He spent his days and nights in trying to work out the cryptogram.'

"Alan," murmured Marie under her breath on hearing this, "there is some cryptogram connected with the peacock, I fancy."

"Yes! yes, and he had it," said Fuller hastily. Then he raised his voice. "Are you talking about ciphers, Miss Grison? I am fond of solving them myself and indeed I am rather good at it."

"Are you?" It was Mr. Sorley who replied and not the woman. "I think that I could puzzle you."

"No, you couldn't," rejoined Alan deliberately boastful. "Set me any cryptogram and I am sure I can solve it. I go on the system of Poe."

"What is that?"

Before he could answer Miss Grison rose, and shaking the crumbs from her dress walked to the door. There she halted, and turned to fix cold eyes on her astonished host, who had not expected so abrupt a move in the midst of an agreeable conversation.

"I have eaten and drunk in this house," said Miss Grison sternly, "a thing I never believed that I could bring myself to do. Now I shall say what I came to say to you, Mr. Randolph Sorley, and shake the dust from my feet."

"Hadn't you better speak to me privately?" asked Sorley, rising with a wan smile and a white face.

"I think not. What I have to say can be heard by both these young people, who are aware of the opinion I have of you. You are a wicked and cruel and sinful man, worse than the worst of men, although all are bad now that my poor brother is dead."

"Your brother Bald—"

"Don't dare to take his name on your lips," interrupted Miss Grison in a fierce way. "His death is due to you."

"To me? How dare you accuse me of the murder?" Sorley was whiter than ever and seemed much shaken by the abrupt accusation.

"I don't. But I accuse you of having wrongfully dismissed Baldwin from this house, over twenty years ago."

"I dismissed him, if you will have the truth told in the presence of others, because he forged my name to a check."

"He did not. You malign the dead. You turned him out and soiled his name and ruined his life without a shadow of excuse. That he sank to a slum in Rotherhithe is your work; that he was murdered there is your work, for if he had not been in Rotherhithe he would not have died by violence. If you had dared to come to the funeral I should have spat on your wicked face."

"How dare you! how dare you! Marie, go to your room."

"Marie shall stay until she hears what I think of you," cried Miss Grison grimly. "With that meal you hoped to smooth me down. But I shall never forgive you for having laid Baldwin in the dust. You have had your turn: now it is my turn. Wait, wait and see how iniquity can be punished," and, shaking a menacing finger, she stalked out of the room.

"Mad! mad. She is mad," gasped Mr. Sorley and literally tottered out of the library, presumably to follow his denouncer.

"What does it all mean, Alan?" asked Marie with awe. "Why did she turn so suddenly on Uncle Ran?"

"And why did she mention that her brother was trying to solve some secret writing which he hoped would bring him money?" asked Fuller quickly.

"Her brother had the peacock and—"

"Exactly. Now Marie we have a clue to the truth."

CHAPTER V

THE LETTER

What Fuller meant exactly when he suggested to Marie that there was now a clue to the truth may be gathered from one of the frequent conversations he held on the subject with his friend. Fuller had much to say when he returned to town from his week-end visit to Belstone, but for some little time he did not find a favorable moment for an exhaustive talk. He certainly gave Dick a few hints as to what he had learned, and spoke more or less in a desultory manner, but Latimer's time was so fully taken up with journalism that the matter was not discussed thoroughly until the middle of the week. And even then the chance came about in a somewhat unexpected way, as Alan took the opportunity to detain the reporter when he strolled into the Chancery Lane office for a few minutes. Dick had stated that he was off the chain for a time, and simply wished for a smoke and a rest.

"You can fire away with your work, old son," said Latimer, taking possession of the client's chair. "I sha'n't bother you."

"This affair of the peacock bothers me a deal more than you do," retorted the solicitor, "and I am glad to get you to myself for a few minutes to talk it over. Hitherto you have always rushed off when I wanted you."

"Humanity demands my services, Alan," said Dick ironically, "and I have to earn a ridiculously small income by attending to the squalling of brother man. However, I am at your disposal for one entire hour, so you can burble to your heart's content."

"There is much more than burbling in this matter," rejoined the other man gravely. "You don't take so much interest in this matter as I expected you to, Dick, considering our first conversation on the matter."

Latimer, with a lighted match held over the filled bowl of his pipe, looked up quickly. "Oh, but I do, my son. I am very interested indeed, and if you have things to tell me, as I gather from what you have let drop since you came back from the country, I have information also."

44

"What about?"

"First your story and then mine," said Dick imperturbably. "All things in order, old boy. I suppose none of your confounded clients will come in to interrupt."

"I don't think so. Things are slack just now, and I am rather glad that they are, as I shall have time to attend to the Rotherhithe matter."

Dick grunted and shook himself, looking like a huge good-natured bear in the fur overcoat which the bitter cold of the December day demanded. "I don't see the use of your bothering about the business unless you are legally retained to thresh it out. Why waste your time?"

"Far from wasting my time," said Alan quietly, "the solution of this mystery means that Miss Inderwick may acquire a large fortune."

"And you, by marrying Miss Inderwick, will gain possession of the same along with a tolerably pretty young woman," said Latimer dryly.

Fuller's dark eyes flashed. "She's the loveliest girl in the world," he cried vehemently, "and you know it."

"I ought to, since you have told me as much as fifty times. But I say, your hint of a large fortune sounds interesting. How much?"

"One hundred to two hundred thousand pounds."

Dick whistled. "The deuce. We are playing with crowns and kingdoms it seems, old son. Fire away. I'm all attention, in the hope that some of the cash may come into my pockets."

Alan took no notice of this flippant remark, but went into the outer office to tell his clerk that he would be engaged for one hour. As a solicitor with a small but certain practice Fuller only enjoyed the ownership of two dingy rooms very badly lighted and still more badly furnished. His inner sanctum only contained a large writing-table, a green-painted iron safe, a shabby bookcase filled with law volumes bound in calf, and a few cane-bottomed chairs. A window with a slanting silvered glass outside to attract the light and reflect it into the dark room, was opposite the door, and beside it was a small grate in which at the present moment burned an equally small fire. Alan returned and seated himself beside this, taking out his pipe to enjoy the hour during which "he sported his oak," as the phrase goes. Dick grunted and sucked at his briar in an opposite chair, waiting for Fuller to open the conversation.

"I told you that Miss Inderwick had given me a clue," began Alan, but was cut short by his friend.

"Why not 'Marie' to me, my haughty solicitor?"

"By all means," said Fuller readily, "since I keep nothing from you. But I have fallen so much into the habit of speaking stiffly about Marie to outsiders, so as to prevent old Sorley from interfering, that I forget how implicitly I can trust you."

"I sha'n't say a word about your wooing to the man, if that's what you mean," growled Dick, "but if you talk of 'Miss Inderwick' I shall expect you to call me 'Mr. Latimer.'"

"Oh, hang your nonsense. Let us get to business."

"How can we when you talk all round the shop?" protested Dick, raising his eyebrows. "Well, go on. You hinted to me that you spoke to Marie about the peacock."

"I did, but not to Mr. Sorley."

"Why not?"

"Because I don't trust him."

"Why not?" inquired Latimer once more and very stolidly.

"Now you ask me a question which is not easy to answer," said Alan, looking meditatively into the fire. "I can give no reason for my mistrust since, so far as I know, Sorley is straight enough on the whole."

"Well then, if he is straight, why mistrust him?"

"I said on the whole he is straight; but he does certain things of which I do not approve."

"Such as stopping your wooing," chuckled the journalist. "Ho! Ho!"

"I rather refer to his selling certain valuable furniture which belongs to Marie, and which I am pretty sure he has no right to dispose of."

"It sounds crooked. But after all he is her guardian, and you don't know what power the will of her father gives him."

"I mean to find that out by an examination of the will at Somerset House, Dicky. Sorley enjoys Marie's income and his own and has the benefit of living at The Monastery rent free. He is, as you know, crazy about jewels, and from what Marie tells me he uses all the cash to buy them. She only has her clothes and a few shillings a week for pocket money. But he never allows her to go into county society, nor does he take her to town."

Latimer removed his pipe and nodded. "He wants her to remain as a flower unseen until she is of age. Then he will hand over the accumulated money in the form of jewels, and will present her to an astonished world when she come of age in a year and his guardianship ceases."

"Hum!" said Alan dubiously, "so you say. But my impressions are quite different. It is my opinion that this precious guardian will not be able to render an honest account of his stewardship, but, when required to do so, will bolt with the jewels upon which he has squandered Marie's money and with the fortune of the peacock if he can find the same."

"Is there any difficulty in finding it, Alan?"

"Yes. In the first place the fortune is hidden and only by gaining possession of the peacock can the clue be found to its whereabouts. And in the second place, even if that bird—"

"The ooff-bird," suggested Latimer vulgarly.

"If you like. But even if it is found there will be a difficulty in reading its riddle."

"Its riddle? Whatever do you mean?"

"What I say," retorted Fuller impatiently. "The secret of the fortune is connected with some secret writing which has to do with the peacock."

"But how can there be secret writing on a metal ornament?"

"I can't say. I don't know. There's an enigma of some sort, a cryptogram."

"This is very interesting but patchy," said Dick, readjusting his big body in the chairs. "Suppose you tell me all from the beginning. Then I might get a glimmer of what you exactly mean."

"Very good, then don't interrupt." And Alan related the strange story of George Inderwick and his faithful servant, who had preserved the secret so faithfully indeed that not even the master had been able to find the jewels. Latimer listened with great attention, and nodded when the story was concluded with an air of satisfaction.

"It's quite a romance," he declared slowly, when Fuller waited for comment, "and there is no doubt that the assassin stole the peacock by murdering Grison in order to get the Begum's gems. No man would have been such a fool as to risk his neck otherwise for a paltry ornament."

"I am not so sure of that, seeing how valuable the peacock is," rejoined the other doubtfully. "It is—as I learned from my father, who saw this fetish of the Inderwicks—as large as a thrush; of pure gold elaborately worked, and is studded with precious stones of more or less price. The tail is spread out and is also jewelled. Now any of those Lascars or Dagoes in Mother Slaig's boarding-house would not mind killing a man by cutting his throat to gain possession of such an object."

"Ah, but the man was not killed in that way. A seaman of whatever nationality would cut a throat, but would not use a slender instrument which scarcely drew any blood to get rid of Grison. The instrument used—which has not been discovered, by the way—suggests a refined criminal."

"A slender instrument," repeated Fuller musingly, "why not a stiletto which an Italian would use? And there are Italian seamen, you know."

Dick nodded. "There is something in that," he admitted, "but we'll let that point alone for the time being. Evidently the peacock is worth more than its intrinsic value to a man who can solve its mystery. Now the question is, how did Grison get hold of the ornament?"

"I see no trouble in answering that, Dicky," and again Alan told the story: this time that one which dealt with Grison's dismissal from his post by Sorley on a charge of forgery, and with the visit of the sister to the big house. Then he related how Miss Grison had spoken to her host and also how she had talked about cryptograms. "Although," concluded Alan, "since I was talking to Marie at the time, I don't exactly know how she introduced that particular subject."

"That she introduced it at all, shows two things," said Latimer decisively. "One, that she knew her brother stole the peacock; and two, she was aware how he was searching for the solution of the cryptogram connected with the bird in order to secure the gems."

"But how could he have learned about the Begum's treasure?" asked Fuller.

"Undoubtedly in the same way as Marie did. Grison, as Sorley's secretary, must have found the manuscript and—"

"But if he found it, why did he not take it with him?"

"I can't explain that. He would have done better had he secured it so that no one else should learn the true value of the peacock. But it was to get the gems that he stole the ornament, and perhaps told the story in a moment of weakness to the third party who afterwards murdered him for its possession. That's what I think. Have you any reason to believe that Sorley himself knows about the peacock cryptogram?"

Fuller jumped up and, laying down his pipe, began to pace the narrow confines of the office. "Yes, I do, and for these reasons. In the first place, Miss Grison would not have mentioned cryptograms to him without she guessed that he knew something; in the second, when I boasted purposely about my knowledge of secret writings, he would not have told me that he had a cryptogram which would baffle my skill, as he certainly did more or less; and in the third, Dicky, he would not have been afraid of Miss Grison."

"What do you mean by that exactly?"

"Well, Sorley told me that he hated Miss Grison and that she annoyed him by saying that he had dismissed her brother unjustly and had practically ruined his life. She walked into the house and all over the house, and yet Sorley did not dare to object either to her taking such a liberty or to her calling him names when Marie and I were present. Also she asked about his motor cycle which I told you he had bought, and inquired if he had been to London. He denied that he had, and she sarcastically advised him not to go lest he should be knocked over in the streets."

"Then I infer," said Dick, slowly removing his pipe, "that you believe Miss Grison suspects Sorley of knowing both the secret of the peacock and that it was in the possession of her brother. Also that he came up to town by means of his motor cycle and murdered the man for its possession?"

"Yes, I do infer as much," said Fuller bluntly and returning to his chair. "If Sorley has not the peacock, and does not know the story of Ferrier, why should he speak to me about cryptograms?"

"But he only made an idle remark which was natural, seeing that Miss Grison spoke of cryptograms, although I admit that it is strange she should talk about them at all unless—"

"Exactly," interrupted the solicitor, tilting back his chair so as to get at the drawer of his writing-table; "unless she believes that he murdered her brother and now possesses the peacock with an intention of learning the cryptogram by employing me to solve it."

"Sorley would scarcely do that when he knows that if he is guilty, such a revelation of his possession of the peacock would condemn him."

"You forget," said Alan, who had extracted a letter from the drawer, "that the fact of the murder being committed for the sake of the peacock has not yet been made public. As I said, I told Marie, but I did not tell Sorley because I mistrust him, and warned her not to do so either. So if Miss Grison's assumption is true Sorley will have no hesitation in enlisting my services, or in showing me the peacock, always presuming that he is indeed the murderer and has it in his possession."

Latimer nodded three times solemnly. "It *is* strange, and you argue very well, my son. What's that letter you are holding?"

"It's from Sorley and came yesterday morning. I have not had an opportunity of talking about it to you before, as you have been so confoundedly busy. It is a letter," said Fuller, unfolding the missive, "which illustrates the proverb that he who excuses himself accuses himself."

"Ho," said Latimer with a world of meaning, "read it out, my boy."

"There is no need to read it. I can give you the gist in a few words," was Fuller's reply, as he ran his eye rapidly over the lines. "Sorley begs me not to take notice of Miss Grison's wild words, as she is a trifle mad. He had to dismiss her brother for forging his name to a check, but, as the man was also insane—slightly, that is—he did not prosecute him."

"Very kind and Christian-like, Alan, But why does Sorley put up with Miss Grison's vagaries?"

"He declares that he is sorry for her, in this letter."

"And by word of mouth as good as told you that he hated her. Humph! It seems to me that our dear friend is hedging. Well, and what more, Alan?"

"Nothing more on the subject of Miss Grison, save that he declares his contempt for her threats."

"Threats. What threats?" Dick sat up alertly.

"She told him in the presence of Marie, and in my presence also, that he was to wait and see how iniquity would be punished."

"Humph! That looks as though she means to be nasty."

"Exactly. And Sorley's cringing to her implies that he guesses she can make things hot for him. However, he simply ends his letter by saying that when I come to Belstone for Christmas he will have a chat with me on the subject of cryptograms. Did I not say, Dick, that his letter illustrates the proverb I referred to. Why should Sorley think it necessary to explain about Miss Grison and her crazy words—if indeed they are crazy—or why should he wish to talk about cryptograms to me, unless—"

"Quite so," interrupted Dick on the same word and in the same manner as his friend had stopped him previously. "Unless she believes that Sorley made away with her brother. It's a strange case, and grows more complicated as we go into it."

"What is your opinion, Dick?"

"It is rather difficult to give a hard and fast one on what facts we have before us, seeing that we are so much in the dark. By the way, how long has Sorley had the motor bicycle?"

"He told me, or rather hinted at three weeks, but Marie said that he bought it four months ago."

"Humph! So Sorley tells a lie about that, does he? It looks fishy. Certainly on a good machine he could slip up to town and back again in a night without anyone being the wiser."

"Then you think that he committed the murder, by—?" Alan spoke excitedly.

"I can't say that," interrupted Latimer swiftly.

"Oh! You infer then that he is innocent?"

"I can't say that either."

"Then what the deuce do you say?" demanded the lawyer irritably.

"This much. That before we can be sure of Sorley being mixed up with the crime, we must learn for certain if he possesses the peacock of jewels."

"But how can we?"

"*We* can't, but *you* can, Alan. Sorley's request that you should talk cryptograms with him at Christmas can only arise from his desire to solve the riddle of the peacock. Wait and hear what he has to say."

"And then?" asked Fuller, nodding approval.

"Then we shall be able to take another step along this dark path. You mean to travel it, I presume?" asked Dick, looking up searchingly.

"Of course I do," replied the young man emphatically. "If those jewels are in existence they belong to Marie, and I want to find them before Sorley does, lest he should make off with them."

"Well," said Latimer grimly, "I daresay he would bolt, both because he loves jewels and moreover—if guilty—must dread risking his neck."

"Guilty? If he possesses the peacock he must be guilty."

"It would appear so, Alan, since only by means of the peacock can the gems be discovered. If he finds them we can assume very reasonably that he killed Baldwin Grison, but as yet so far as we know the jewels are still hidden." Dick thought for a few moments, then ventured on advice. "You have a week or so before taking your Christmas holiday. Why not visit Miss Grison at her boarding-house? You know where it is."

"Yes. She gave me her card. But she won't speak out, Dicky. Had she been certain of Sorley's criminality she would have denounced him then and there to gratify her hatred."

"She may only have a suspicion of his guilt, or perhaps her wish is father to her thought. But it seems to me that by her allusion to the bicycle, and to cryptograms, she wished to arouse your mistrust of the man."

"Still she cannot be aware that Marie told me about the peacock riddle?"

Latimer ruffled his hair in perplexity. "Oh, hang it, what is the use of speculating!" he cried crossly, and rising to stretch his big limbs. "Before we can arrive at any conclusion we must sound Miss Grison as to what she knows, or what she does not know."

"At all events she detests Sorley and, so far as I can see, will do her best to hang him."

"Perhaps. But it is your task to prevent such a miscarriage. Go and see her, Alan, and then tell me what you learn."

"Very good. I shall write a note and invite myself to dinner."

"Why to dinner?"

"I wish to see what kind of lodgers Miss Grison has, and to hear their opinion of their landlady. Much can be learned in this way. But tell me, Dick, what you have discovered."

"Very little. Moon is still hunting for the assassin and is still at his wit's end how to strike the true trail. The only thing of interest that I have learned is about Jotty."

"The street-arab whom Grison befriended?"

"Yes. He's a clever little animal, and in better surroundings might improve into something useful. Miss Grison intends to give him his chance, and is taking him into her service as a page-boy: She'll have enough to do to teach him civilized habits," concluded Dick cynically.

"Why is she acting so philanthropically?"

"Out of regard for the memory of her brother, as she told Inspector Moon."

"Well," murmured Fuller thoughtfully, "that is reasonable enough since she appears to have had a strong regard for her brother. Perhaps he commended Jotty to her care."

"It's not improbable. The poor wretch may have wished to give the boy a chance, and if so, it shows that there were decent feelings in him. But if you visit this boarding-house I wish you to keep an eye on Jotty."

"Why?" Alan looked up quickly.

"Because I believe the boy knows much more than he has hitherto admitted."

"Oh," said Fuller, after a pause, "so it is probable that Miss Grison's interest in the lad is not wholly philanthropic. You fancy that she may desire to keep him under her own eye lest he should say too much."

Latimer shrugged his shoulders. "I can't say that I quite took that view, Alan, as Miss Grison may really be acting kindly out of regard for her brother's wishes. All the same I believe that Jotty knows things about the murder which he is keeping quiet, and it will be just as well to watch him more or less closely."

"But on what grounds—?"

"On no grounds whatever. It's just an idea I have, and may be all rubbish."

Fuller nodded. "On the other hand it may be useful not to reject your idea, Dick. I shall watch and question Jotty if I get the chance."

"Be careful, Alan. He is a sharp lad."

"I'll see that he does not get the better of me. Dick, isn't it strange how suspicious one gets of everything when on a man-hunt?"

"Yes. But it's natural enough. On a trail one always observes small signs to indicate the direction, and so everything around becomes of value in the way of evidence. However, you know what you have to do?"

"Yes. And you?"

"I shall keep in touch with Rotherhithe and Mother Slaig's boarding-house and Moon. Whatever I learn you shall know. Good luck, Alan, to your hunting."

"Ditto to yours, Dicky, and now clear out and let me get to work."

Latimer tramped to the door and vanished with a friendly growl.

CHAPTER VI

THE BOARDING-HOUSE

The establishment of Miss Louisa Grison was by no means aristocratic as her house was not situated in a fashionable quarter of London and she charged extremely moderate prices for board and lodging. Petty clerks and shop-girls formed the greater portion of those who dwelt under her humble roof, but occasionally people in better circumstances came to the place. Young men learning to become lawyers, students in various metropolitan colleges, actresses in or out of employment, reduced ladies, who had just sufficient income to keep body and soul together, literary aspirants and adventurers down in their luck, were to be found at 2Z Thimble Square, Bloomsbury. It was a fluctuating population which came and went throughout the year. Sometimes the house would be full, at other times it was almost empty but in one way and another Miss Grison always contrived to satisfy her landlord and pay her taxes. She never complained of her lot, or lamented her poverty, but met everything, good, bad and indifferent, in her hard way, without emotion of any kind. Misery seemed to have turned her into stone.

The house was a large corner one, with a vast drawing-room, a vast dining-room, and a sitting-room for Miss Grison on the ground floor, together with a kitchen of no great size and servants' cubicles in the basement. All the rest of the building was given over to bedrooms, so small and so many that they resembled the cells of bees. And the lodgers were exactly like bees, for the greater part of them swarmed out to their various employments in the early morning and swarmed back again late in the evening. Sometimes they had spare money for amusements, but more often they had not, and seemed to be incessantly working like the bees aforesaid to gather honey for other people. Yet as they were generally young and hopeful and healthy, on the whole they contrived to enjoy themselves in a meagre way, their standard of pleasure not being very high. Sometimes the men made love to the women, or the girls flirted with the boys, and so long as these philanderings were innocent Miss Grison did not forbid them. But in her hard way, she was rigorously moral, and any boarder, male or female, who overstepped the line was banished from this penny Eden. However, the inmates of the Establishment—as Miss Grison called it—behaved very well and she rarely had cause for complaint. They were all a trifle afraid of the landlady with her hard blue eyes and stiff manners, and she ruled them after the manner of a schoolmistress, making allowance for youthful spirits yet keeping them in strict order. Some objected to these limitations, but the food was so good and the bedrooms so comfortable and the price of both so moderate that they put up with the lesser evil to enjoy the greater good.

In her reply to Fuller, bidding him come to dinner on a certain day, Miss Grison mentioned that evening dress was unnecessary, an observation which seemed rather superfluous to the young man when he learned the quality of the establishment. He entered the large drawing-room to find the men in their workaday clothes, although the ladies had certainly done their best to smarten themselves for the evening function. Miss Grison, for instance, received him in a worn black silk dress, trimmed sparsely with jet and set off with cheap lace. She still looked as though carved out of wood and still stared with an unwinking gaze which somewhat confused the young man. There is nothing so embarrassing to even a tired man or woman of the world as a steady look, and although Alan was conscious of being a perfectly proper person he yet winced at Miss Grison's hard greeting.

The visitor's good looks and unusually smart clothes—although he simply wore a suit of blue serge—caused quite a sensation. Girls in cheap blouses, cheap skirts and still cheaper jewellery giggled and blushed when he was presented to them, and elderly dames with careworn faces and of antiquated garb, straightened themselves with conscious dignity. There was something pathetic in their assumption of society manners, considering the dire poverty to which they were condemned. The men—they were an ordinary lot as regards looks and brains—were disposed to be hostile as they thought that the female portion of the establishment paid too much attention to the newcomer. But they were civil on the whole and the dull quarter of an hour before the seven o'clock meal was announced by a seedy man-servant—termed grandiloquently the butler—passed off fairly well. Fuller was quiet and observant, and chatted mostly to his hostess, although for politeness' sake he had to address a few observations on safe topics to ladies, old and young and middle-aged.

The dinner was plentiful and nourishing, if not particularly dainty, consisting of Scotch broth, Irish stew, rice pudding with tinned apricots and American cheese. The boarders provided their own liquid refreshments, as Miss Grison merely supplied water in large glass jugs. Consequently there were many private bottles on the table, ranging as to their contents from pale ale to whisky: some of the better-off lodgers even indulging in cheap claret. Miss Grison drank water, and her guest, since she offered him nothing better, followed suit.

"I would banish alcohol of every description from my table," she whispered, with stern apology, "for it was my dear dead brother's curse. But if I kept a temperance hotel I doubt if the business would pay so well."

"Then it does pay," remarked Fuller with a side-glance at her worn dress.

"Oh, yes," she responded indifferently, "I manage to keep my head above water and to save a trifle against rainy days, and old age. Ah, there is our usual late comer, Mr. Bakche. Now his soup will have to be brought back, which puts the servants out. These Orientals have no idea of time, Mr. Fuller."

Alan politely 'agreed and glanced carelessly at the newcomer, only to give a more earnest look later on, for Mr. Bakche was decidedly out of place amongst that shabby assemblage. He was perfectly arrayed in a well-cut evening dress, with pearl studs and patent leather shoes. Tall and slim, he was yet sinewy in his looks and possessed an admirable figure, which the close-fitting clothes set off to great advantage. He had clearly-cut features, a dark complexion, as became an Eastern, and wore a small black mustache, well twisted over very red lips and very white teeth. On the whole he was a handsome fellow and his air was somewhat haughty and reserved. As Alan observed, he ate only plain boiled rice, uncooked fruit, and drank water; just as if he were an anchorite. The looks of the man and the abstinence of the man aroused Fuller's curiosity, and he thought that he would like to talk to Mr. Bakche as well as to Miss Grison. Meanwhile he asked for information.

"He is an Indian prince, so he says," replied Miss Grison in a whisper. "I understand that his full name is Mr. Morad-Bakche, which he told me means, in his own language, 'Desire accomplished.' He is only in England for a few months on some mission connected with the recovery of his family property lost during the Mutiny, and my house was recommended to him by a former boarder who went out to Ceylon."

"He has a striking personality," said Fuller when this information was given, and then asked his hostess about Jotty. "Mr. Latimer told me that you intended to give the boy a chance in life, Miss Grison. It is very good of you to do so."

She shrugged her sloping shoulders. "Oh, I don't know," she answered, sinking her metallic voice. "I want a page-boy to open and shut the door, so as to save the servants' legs. Jotty does as well as another and since my poor Baldwin took an interest in him, of course I feel that it is my duty, to do what I can. I have had him washed and dressed and fed and have given him the more Christian name of Alonzo. The boarders do not know his real name, if indeed it can be called one, and they are not aware that he is the boy who appeared at the inquest."

"They know, I presume, that it was your brother who was murdered?"

"Oh yes, the name appeared in the newspapers, and I had to give evidence at the inquest, so there was no keeping the relationship quiet. But I beg of you, Mr. Fuller, to call Jotty by his new name of Alonzo, as I don't want it generally known that I am helping my poor brother's protégé. As the head of the Establishment," Miss Grison drew up her spare form proudly, "I do not like scandal to be connected with my name."

"But, my dear lady, your behavior calls for nothing but praise."

"Human nature is more prone to blame than praise," answered the hostess bitterly, and gave the signal to the ladies for departure. "We will leave you to smoke with the other gentlemen, Mr. Fuller, and afterwards you can come and talk to me in the drawing-room. Alonzo you will probably see when he opens the door for your departure," and with a stiff bow she left the room at the head of the shabbily-dressed females, who thus followed the customs of the west end.

For a time Alan was left severely alone, and smoked his cigarette in silence, since the men seemed to be too shy to venture on conversation, and had many matters to discuss among themselves. But after a time Mr. Bakche left his seat and moved to a chair at the young man's elbow, offering, as he sat down, his cigarette-case, which was well filled.

"You will find these particularly good," said Mr. Bakche in a deep and mellow voice, which accorded well with his grave dignity. "I received them from a friend of mine in Constantinople."

"Thank you," answered the solicitor readily, and anxious to respond to this politeness, "you are very kind."

"The kindness is on your part, Mr. Fuller."

"You know my name, Mr. Bakche?"

"And you know mine, I observe. We have made mutual inquiries about one another, no doubt. Mr. Potter informed me about you; and Miss Grison, I presume, gave information about me."

"Yes," assented Fuller easily. "She tells me that you are an Indian prince!"

Bakche laughed in a silent manner. "She places me too high, Mr. Fuller, I assure you," he responded quietly. "I come of a princely family, but I am not of princely rank. You can look upon me as a plain Mahometan gentleman of Tartar descent."

"Of Tartar descent," echoed Fuller, who found his companion interesting.

"Yes. Did Miss Grison tell you my full name?"

"Morad-Bakche! Indeed she did and gave me its meaning."

"'Desire-accomplished,'" said the other, with half a sigh, "although I fear that my desire will never be accomplished. However, that is by the way. I wonder, Mr. Fuller, if you have read the 'History of the Moguls.'"

"I regret to say that I have not."

"Well, it is rather an unusual book for anyone to read unless he is a student. But you will find mentioned therein my ancestor, after whom I am called. He was also Morad-Bakche, the youngest son of Shah Jahan, who was descended from Timur the Tartar. My family were rich and famous when the Mogul emperors ruled at Delhi, but everything belonging to us was swept away in the Mutiny, as you English call it."

"I can quite understand that you give it a different name," said Alan sympathetically. "You naturally desired to be free."

"Naturally, but injudiciously, Mr. Fuller. If the British Raj ended, my unhappy country would become the cockpit of contending hosts. We are too divided in India to rule ourselves, and the great powers would interfere, so that we should only exchange King Stork for Queen Log, or the reverse, as I forget the exact details of the fable. But what I mean is that England is a better ruler of our country than Germany or Russia would be."

"Your sentiments are very liberal, Mr. Bakche."

"I have read history," replied the other. "Believe me, Mr. Fuller, that if people only read history more carefully so many mistakes would not be made in this world. The past life of nations is more or less only what the future will be, making reasonable allowance for development."

Bakche talked on this strain for some time, and displayed a great knowledge of history, and betrayed a shrewd observation of men and manners, so that Alan found the conversation very enjoyable. Later on, his companion became particular after general, and gave a few hints about his family.

"At the time of the Mutiny my grandfather was the Rajah of Kam, which was a little-known state which is in the Madras presidency. That is, it was."

"Was," repeated Fuller, surprised, "a state cannot vanish out of existence, Mr. Bakche, since it is land and—"

"Oh, the land is still there and the villages and towns. But the name has been changed and my family have been turned out. I am the sole member left alive, Mr. Fuller. But I have no ambition to get back our former royalty."

"But I understood from Miss Grison that you had come to England on a mission of that sort."

"The good lady is wrong again. I want no forfeited title, but I do want certain property."

"I see. So you are applying to the Government?"

"No," said Mr. Bakche unexpectedly and somewhat grimly, "my property cannot be recovered by the Government. I have to search for it myself. It is—" Here he checked himself. "But I don't see why I should trouble you with all this dry talk."

"It is most interesting, I assure you," Alan assured him quite truthfully.

"Then we must resume it on another occasion," said Bakche, rising. "I have to keep an appointment. Perhaps I shall see you again here."

"Possibly, but if I do not come again here is my card." Fuller passed along his business address. "I shall be glad to see you at any time."

Bakche glanced at the card ponderingly. "You are a solicitor, I see. It is probable that I may want a solicitor."

"I am at your service."

"You may not be when you know what I want," said the Indian dryly, and with a sudden gleam in his dark eyes. "However I am glad that I have met you, and perhaps I may call and see you. Good-night, sir," and with a grave bow Morad-Bakche took his departure from the room which was now almost empty.

Fuller drew a deep breath as he rose to go to the drawing-room. His late companion being of an unusual kind had interested him not a little, but in spite of his suave manners and gentle voice there was something dangerous about him, betrayed for the moment by that sudden gleam of ferocity. Alan felt as though he had been playing with a tiger who had been careful for reasons of its own not to scratch, but would do so when the appointed time came for it to reveal its true nature. He half hoped that Bakche would not come to the Chancery Lane office, and regretted momentarily that he had given his card. But reflection made him laugh at his nervous dread, since he was well able to look after himself and need have no fear of Bakche or of any man. Besides he wanted to get all the business he could so as to make money and marry Miss Inderwick, therefore it would have been foolish to lose sight of a prospective client. Wondering what the precise nature of the man's business could be, Alan sauntered towards the drawing-room, when in the passage he came across a diminutive urchin with a peaked face, arrayed as a page.

"Oh," said Mr. Fuller, stopping, "so you are Alonzo."

"Yessir," gasped the boy in one breath, and looked at the tall gentleman from under light eye-lashes out of light eyes.

"You have another name?"

"Nosir," said the urchin again in a breath and lying glibly, "never was called anything but Alanzer."

Fuller nodded, seeing that the lad was loyal to Miss Grison, and did not try to wean him from his allegiance. All the same he wished to ask him questions about the dead man, but did not think the present moment a judicious one to do so. "Some day you must ask your mistress to let you come and see me at my office," he remarked carelessly, and passed on.

In a moment Jotty was tugging his coat-tail. "What jer want ter arsk?"

"I shall tell you when the time comes. Do you know Mr. Latimer?"

Jotty nodded with bright inquisitive eyes. "Him with the big coat like the bear them Italyains chivy about?"

"Yes. You see that I know something about you, Alonzo. But you are quite right to say what you have said. I don't want you to call and see me unless Miss Grison permits you to."

"Yer a lawr gent?" inquired Jotty, pondering.

"In Chancery Lane." Fuller gave his number. "If you do happen to be passing, Mr. Alonzo, just look in and earn a few shillings."

"I'm game for that anyhow, if it doesn't hurt her." He jerked his head towards the room where Miss Grison was supposed to be.

Fuller turned on him sharply. "Why should anything hurt her?" he inquired.

Jotty did not answer directly. "She's bin good t' me, and he wos good—him es died, sir. I don't want no hurt t' come t' her anyhow," and with a flash of his light eyes the boy sprang down the stairs leading to the kitchen, while Alan entered the drawing-room wondering what the observation meant. It seemed impossible that any harm could come to Miss Grison out of any inquiry into the death of her brother. Again it struck Fuller that the woman's reason for helping Jotty might not be entirely philanthropic.

However he had no time to dwell on this particular point, but looked about for Miss Grison, who was not to be seen. An elderly lady with a simper informed him that the landlady was in her own room, and pointed out the direction, so Fuller knocked at the door softly. The sharp voice of Miss Grison invited him to enter, and he found himself in a small apartment crowded with furniture.

"Oh, here you are, Mr. Fuller," said his hostess, rising from a low chair in which she was seated by the fire. "I thought you would find me here. I cannot stay listening to the twaddle they talk in the drawing-room, having much more serious things with which to occupy my thoughts."

"Very natural, after your great loss," replied Alan, accepting the chair she pushed towards him. "I suppose you wonder why I have come to see you."

"No," said Miss Grison in her sharp, blunt way. "You mentioned at Belstone that you would help me, and I am glad to have your assistance."

"I can give it, if you will be frank with me."

"What do you wish to know?" Miss Grison took a fan from the mantelpiece as she spoke, and used it to screen her sallow cheeks from the fire.

"Have you any idea who murdered your brother?"

"If I had, do you think I should invoke your assistance," she asked, evading his question dexterously.

"Two heads are better than one," countered the solicitor.

"True enough, and yet one head may be able to bring the beast who killed Baldwin to the scaffold."

"Then I must apologise for troubling you," said Alan, rising. "As I told you at Belstone my only desire to unravel this case is one of curiosity, and if you think that I am meddlesome I—"

"No no! no! You are really very good. Sit down and I shall answer what questions you like. After all I should be glad to have the advice of a solicitor for nothing, unless you expect six and eightpence, Mr. Fuller."

"I expect nothing but straight replies to my questions, Miss Grison.

"Go on, then. As to the one you have already asked, I can say nothing at present. I don't know for certain who murdered Baldwin."

"But you have some suspicion?"

"Nothing that has tangible proof."

Apparently she would not put her feeling against Sorley into words, so Alan tried another tack. "Would you mind telling me your history?"

"And that of Baldwin, I suppose. Why should I?"

"Because I may then learn if there is anything in his life or in your life which would cause his death."

"I fear you will be disappointed, Mr. Fuller," she replied coldly, "for my history and that of Baldwin is uneventful on the whole. We are the children of a doctor who practised at Canterbury, and who made money. Mr. Sorley was a patient of my father's and took a fancy to Baldwin when he came home from Oxford, where he was being educated. When Baldwin finished his college career and got his degree—"

"Oh," Alan was plainly surprised, "he got his degree, did he?"

"Baldwin was an extremely clever man," cried Miss Grison impetuously, and her hands trembled with emotion. "I don't see why you should ask me such a question in such a manner. He took his degree with great credit, and came home to go in for the law. But Mr. Sorley, who was writing his book on precious stones, offered to make Baldwin his secretary, and the offer was accepted because my father had died and did not leave us so well off as was expected. My brother went to The Monastery and I stayed with my mother for some years, until she died. Then I paid a visit to Belstone, and Mrs. Inderwick, who was then alive, asked me to remain as her companion. I was with her for years, until she died, and managed to gather enough money out of my salary to start this boarding-house. Shortly after Marie was born her mother died, and she was left to the grandmother of Henny and Jenny to look after."

"Why not to you?"

"Because I had already left the place," said Miss Grison, flushing, and with sparkling eyes. "Sorley quarrelled with my brother as he quarrelled with everyone, and it ended in Baldwin being dismissed."

"But what reason was given for his dismissal?"

Miss Grison hesitated and looked at the fire. "I suppose I may as well talk candidly to you, since so much rests on your knowing the exact truth."

"It will be just as well," said Fuller positively.

"Well then," she drew a deep breath, "although I loved Baldwin and although he was clever and amiable, he had a weak character. He learned to smoke opium and he took more drink than was good for him. In a moment of madness, and because Mr. Sorley paid him so badly, he forged his employer's name to a small check for five pounds. Mr. Sorley found this out and threatened to prosecute him, especially as Baldwin—I don't deny it—made himself objectionable to Mrs. Inderwick. However, Mr. Sorley did not prosecute—"

"Why not? He doesn't seem to me to be a merciful man."

"He's a cruel, hard beast," said Miss Grison fiercely, "and you heard my opinion of him at Belstone. It was no fault of his that Baldwin was not put in jail. I managed to stop that."

"In what way?"

"I sha'n't tell you; there is no need to tell you, Mr. Fuller. It is enough for you to know that I had the power to stop the prosecution and did so. I had just started this boarding-house, and I brought Baldwin here. But what with his drink and his smoking opium, he behaved so badly that, dearly as I loved him, I had to find another home for him, or be ruined. I got him a home with a doctor, who looked after him, but Baldwin ran away and went to Rotherhithe, for there he was near the opium dens. I begged and implored him to lead a better life. He always promised, and he always failed to keep his promise. All I could do was to allow him so much a week, which I did, as I stated in my evidence at the inquest. He lived a degraded life at Mother Slaig's house, which is down a slum, and there he met with his death at the hands of—" She stopped short.

"At the hands of the man whom you suspect," finished Alan bluntly.

"I never said it was a man," retorted Miss Grison abruptly.

"It couldn't possibly be a woman."

"I never said that either."

"Then what do you say?"

"Nothing, because I am certain of nothing. You have heard the story you wish to hear, so make what use you can of it."

"I shall do so if you will answer one other question?"

"What is it?" She screened her face.

"Did your brother steal the peacock of jewels from The Monastery?"

The screen dropped. "Marie has been telling you about that."

"She told me the legend of the jewels and the cryptogram. But of course as she was a child when the peacock was stolen, she could say nothing about the theft. But as Inspector Moon learned from Jotty, your brother had the peacock in his possession.

"That is true."

"And he was murdered on account of the peacock?"

"I believe so." She clasped and unclasped her hands feverishly, not giving him time to ask another question. "Do you know who stole it from Belstone?"

"Your brother, since he had it at Mother Slaig's."

"No. He stole it from me and I stole it from Mr. Sorley."

"You stole it!" Fuller started up in amazement. "Why did you?"

"Oh, I had good reason to, I assure you. I am not ashamed of my theft. That peacock ruined Baldwin, and that peacock shall ruin—"

"Mr. Sorley," broke in Fuller, keeping his eyes on her face.

"No! no." She flung up her hands. "It will ruin me! me! me!"

CHAPTER VII

YULETIDE

Alan could make nothing of Miss Grison's final remark, for after stating—and in a somewhat hysterical fashion—that the peacock would ruin her, she asked him to leave. In vain he asked for a more detailed explanation. Recovering her usual wooden manner, she declined to speak further, and Fuller returned to the rooms at Barkers Inn to report the result of his visit to Dick. It was unsatisfactory, and Alan said as much.

"I don't agree with you," remarked Latimer, after some reflection. "You have seen Jotty ticketed as Alonzo—what a name; and have learned the early history of this unfortunate brother and sister. Finally, you have met with Mr. Morad-Bakche."

"He's got nothing to do with the matter anyhow."

"My dear son, George Inderwick obtained this treasure you are looking for, in India. Simon Ferrier manufactured the peacock in India, and Mr. Morad-Bakche comes from India."

"So do half a hundred other students of the kind," retorted Fuller. "You are too suspicious, Dick, and see a bird in every bush."

"Perhaps I am. But I should like to know why Mr. Bakche was so friendly with you and told you so much about himself. Orientals are generally reserved and don't talk all over the shop. Mr. Bakche told you that he had come to look after some family property. How do we know but what it consists of those gems which the Begum of Kam gave to George Inderwick?"

"Over one hundred years ago, remember. How could Bakche know about them?"

"Orientals have long memories. However, I admit that I may be unduly suspicious, as you observe, Alan. All the same I should like to know what Mr. Bakche is doing in Miss Grison's house and why he was so friendly to you even to the extent of hinting that you might be his solicitor."

"Well then, if he does consult me he will have to state his reason. And if that has to do with the Begum's gems, I shall know where I am. Your imagination is too vivid, Dick."

"It is not imagination but the use of a sixth sense, which gives me impressions contrary to facts," insisted Mr. Latimer, "and if—"

"Oh, I know you believe in all that occult rubbish," interrupted Fuller in a rather rude way, "but I am too matter-of-fact to be superstitious."

"Too obstinate to change your opinion, you mean," replied Dick equably, "Well, well, my son, we will not quarrel over the matter. Time will show if I am right. In the meantime what do you make of Miss Grison's statement that the peacock would ruin her?"

"I can make nothing of it, and ask you for an explanation."

"Humph! The riddle is hard to guess. The only thing I can say is that she dreads lest Sorley should learn of her theft. If so, he would prosecute her and so she would be ruined."

"She is not afraid of Sorley."

"Not now, because he doesn't know—so far as we can see—that she stole the peacock."

"But why did she tell me that? If I told Sorley—"

"Miss Grison knows that you are on her side, so to speak, and will not say anything to Sorley, who is dead against your marriage with Miss Inderwick."

Alan ruffled his hair, as was his custom when perplexed. "I can make nothing of the matter," he cried, greatly exasperated. "What's to be done?"

"See Sorley at Christmas when you go down to Belstone," advised Dick in a calm way, "and hear why he wants to discuss cryptograms with you. In that way you may get on the trail of the lost peacock."

"But if Sorley has it, Miss Grison need not be afraid that he will ruin her, Dicky. If she is a thief, Sorley is a murderer."

"We can't be sure of that."

"If he has the peacock we can be sure."

"First catch your hare," observed Latimer sententiously. "In other words, my son, wait and learn if Sorley has the thing. It's no use theorizing, Alan; we can do nothing until we learn more. Bakche probably will call and see you, so we shall learn what he has to do with the matter."

"He has nothing to do with it, I am sure," said Fuller vehemently.

"My sixth sense tells me otherwise," observed Dick dryly.

"Hang your sixth sense."

"By all means. But to continue: Jotty will come and see you, sooner or later, I feel convinced, and then you can learn." Dick paused.

"Learn what?"

"My sixth sense doesn't tell me. Wait and see."

"Oh, hang it, Dick, what nonsense you talk! It's all moonshine."

"I grant that," returned Latimer serenely. "Until we can gather more facts it is certainly all moonshine. But since seeing you last I have learned a fact which may startle you. Moon told me when I went to look him up yesterday, Baldwin Grison was a murderer."

"What's that you say?" cried Alan, as startled as Dick could wish.

"Ah, I thought I'd raise your hair. Yes, my son. A couple of months ago, in the opium den kept by Chin-Chow—or rather in the lane outside it—a well-dressed man was found dead. He had been knocked on the head with some blunt instrument of the bludgeon kind. From letters and cards found in his pockets it was discovered that he was an independent gentleman who lived in the west end, and who went down to Rotherhithe to indulge in the black smoke. His watch and studs and purse had been taken, so it was supposed that he had been robbed by some scoundrel haunting those very shady parts. Inspector Moon could find nothing, however, to point out the criminal, but has always been on the hunt. The other day he came across the dead man's watch, which had been pawned by Mother Slaig. She said that Grison had given it to her instead of money for his rent and had stated that it was his own watch. Moon thinks that Mother Slaig is quite innocent of guilty knowledge and that Grison, being hard up, must have knocked down and robbed the dead man when they both left Chin-Chow's opium den. Search was made in Grison's room afterwards, and under a loose board the studs of the victim were discovered. So there is no doubt that Grison murdered the man for money and was afterwards murdered by his unknown assassin for the sake of the peacock. It is just as well that Grison is dead, as he certainly would have been arrested and hanged for his crime."

"Destiny gave him a dose of his own gruel," said Alan thoughtfully. "He must have been a bad lot, in spite of his sister's eulogies."

"Well," remarked Dick with a shrug, "Sorley's opinion of the man seems to be more correct than Miss Grison's. Poor soul, I wonder what she will say when she learns that her brother acted in this way?"

"She will be thankful that his violent death prevented his appearance on the scaffold," said Alan dryly. "What is Moon doing about the matter?"

"Nothing. What can he do? Grison is dead, and the relatives of the victim, being of good position and well off, are not anxious to have a fuss made over the matter, since the murder took place in such a locality. You can well understand that, Alan, my son."

"Yes, I can well understand that. Well, Grison had to pay very speedily for his wickedness. You don't think that a relative of the dead man killed him out of revenge."

"Oh, dear me, no! The relatives are most respectable, and never went near Rotherhithe. The first murder has nothing to do with the second, I assure you, Alan. However, there is nothing more to be said about Grison's crime and we must content ourselves in learning who killed him."

"After what you have told me, I don't think he is worth it."

"Worth revenging, do you mean? Well, perhaps not; but the peacock is worth the search for the assassin, since finding him means finding the means to discover the treasure."

"And you suspect Sorley, with Bakche as a factor in the case?"

"I suspect no one at present, and only my sixth sense, which is not invariably to be relied upon, thinks that your Indian friend may be mixed up with the matter. Go down to Belstone, Alan, and see if Sorley still talks about cryptograms. If he does, and submits one for your solution, it will probably have to do with the peacock, if Miss Inderwick's tale of her ancestor and Ferrier is to be believed."

"Of course it is to be believed," said Alan tartly; "however, I shall make quite sure by seeing Ferrier's manuscript for myself."

"It will be just as well," said Latimer, ending the conversation, and so matters were settled for the end of the year. Shortly afterwards Dick went to Paris to keep his Christmas as a kind of heathen festival with an artist friend in the Latin Quarter, while Alan packed his kit to journey to Belstone and enjoy the simpler pleasures of a British Yuletide.

The great season of the Church was on this occasion quite one of the old style, such as would have delighted the heart of Dickens. That is, it had plenty of snow and holly and mistletoe peace-on-earth, good-will-to-men and such like traditional things which had to do with the Holy Birth. The undulating hills around Belstone were clothed in spotless white, and the ancient trees in the park of the Inderwicks stood up gaunt and bare and black amidst the chilly waste. Coals and blankets, food and drink were bestowed on the villagers by the gentry around, who suddenly seemed to recollect that Belstone existed, so that the poor had what Americans call "the time of their lives." Mr. Fuller also behaved philanthropically, although he was by no means rich, and the sole person who did not act in the traditionally charitable manner was Mr. Randolph Sorley. He said bluntly that he had enough to do to look after himself, and gave his blessing instead of more substantial gifts. As to Marie, she never had a single penny, which she could call her own, and lamented that poverty, and Sorley's niggardly ways as her guardian, prevented her from obeying the kind dictates of her heart.

"But when I am of age and have my money," she informed Alan after church on Christmas Day, "I shall make everyone happy."

"You have made me happy anyhow," replied Fuller, enjoying the stolen moment which they had obtained by evading Sorley, "so nothing else matters."

"You greedy boy," laughed Marie, patting his cheek, "you are not the only person in the world I have to consider. My uncle is my uncle."

"And your uncle is your guardian," said Fuller grimly. "I wish he were not, my dearest, for the course of our true love will never run smooth so long as he has a say in the matter. I don't like him."

"You must like him to-night when he comes to dinner at the vicarage," said Marie with alarm. "If you aren't agreeable, Alan, he will be so unpleasant."

"I am always agreeable, in my father's house," said Alan stiffly, and then he kissed away her fears. "There, dear, don't worry; I am a most diplomatic person, I assure you."

Marie agreed, for everything that Alan did was right in her eyes, and afterwards ran away across the snow to join her uncle, who was looking for her. Alan returned to the vicarage to find his mother much exercised in her mind over the Christmas dinner, and had to console her as usual. Every year Mrs. Fuller doubted the success of the meal, and every year it proved to be all that could be desired. Alan reminded her of this.

"My dear mother, you have never had a failure yet. To-night we shall have a very jolly meal."

"I hope so," sighed the vicar's wife, "but I confess that I am not quite at rest in my mind about the pudding."

"And there may be something wrong with the mince pies?"

"It's very likely there will be, since the oven doesn't heat properly."

"And the roast beef will not be up to the mark?"

"Now, Alan, you are making fun of me. You don't know what it is to be a housewife, my dear."

"I don't, mother. Dick and I are very rough and ready in our domestic arrangements. You have asked Sorley to dinner as usual, I hear from Marie."

"Yes, dear," replied Mrs. Fuller complacently, "your father knows he is not well off, and wishes to show him this yearly attention. Besides, since you love Marie, who is a sweet girl, you should be pleased."

"I am pleased," said her son gravely, "although Sorley doesn't approve of my attentions to his niece."

Mrs. Fuller bristled. "What better match does the man want for the girl," she demanded, all her maternal feathers on end; "you have good blood in your veins, Alan, and good prospects, besides being very handsome and—"

"I'm a paragon, mother, there's no doubt of that. All the same, Sorley, as you observed when I was last here, wants a title and wealth for Marie."

"He'll never find either in this back-water of life's river," retorted Mrs. Fuller rather crossly, "and since Marie loves you there is no more to be said, in my opinion."

"There's a good deal more to be said in Sorley's," said Alan dryly.

"He should remember his own love romance, dear, and be more sympathetic with Marie's desire to become your wife."

"I never knew that Sorley had a love romance, mother. I thought he was wrapped up body and soul in his book on precious stones."

"Oh, he has always been writing that, Alan," said Mrs. Fuller, with a shrug to hint that she did not think much of the man's literary abilities, "but he was courting Miss Marchmont over twenty years ago—that was shortly after Squire Inderwick's death, and before Marie was born. You know, dear, her father died almost immediately after the sweet girl's birth, and appointed Mr. Sorley to be her guardian. He settled at The Monastery with his sister. Mr. Inderwick and that miserable man Grison were with them for a time. His sister also stayed as Mrs. Inderwick's companion, but when her brother was dismissed, she went to London and started that boarding-house in Thimble Square, Bloomsbury. Marie was brought up by old Granny Trent, who was the housekeeper. When she grew too old, and Marie went to school at Brighton, her granddaughters, Jane and Henrietta, came to look after the house, and do the active work, although Granny superintends still, I believe. Then Marie returned from school, and—"

"Mother, mother, you are repeating history," interrupted Alan, vexed by this prolix narrative. "I know all this. What about Sorley's love affair?"

"He loved Miss Marchmont, and she died."

"Was she one of the Marchmonts of Augar Place, near Lewes?"

"Yes; the only daughter and heiress. Mr. Sorley would have got a lot of money and property had he married her. But she died, and the Manor, along with the income, passed to distant cousins after the death of old Mr. Marchmont some ten years ago."

"What did Miss Marchmont die of?"

"A chill contracted by getting wet in the hunting-field, dear. Mr. Sorley was very fond of her, and greatly lamented her death."

"Or the loss of her money," said the solicitor doubtfully.

"No, dear. He really and truly loved her. I sometimes think, Alan, that you are not quite fair to Mr. Sorley. He has had his troubles."

"I don't like him personally," said Fuller roundly, "there is an insincere air about him."

"I am not particularly fond of him myself," confessed Mrs. Fuller in an apologetic way, "but he is always agreeable to me. And, although he has lived here for quite five and twenty years, if not more, there has never been a word said against his character save that he is not generous. And his poverty excuses that, Alan. So try and be agreeable to him this evening, dear," finished Mrs. Fuller, making the same request as Marie had done.

"Of course I shall be agreeable. I wish to be very friendly with him."

"That is natural, dear, since you desire to gain his consent to your marriage with Marie. But, dear me, I am quite forgetting the dinner," and Mrs. Fuller hastened to the kitchen with her mind full of the pudding, the mince pies, and the roast beef.

Alan's reason for being friendly with Sorley was not entirely due to the cause mentioned by his mother, although he was anxious enough to gain the man's consent to his wooing. But he felt confident that—unless for a purpose—Sorley would never give that same consent, since he did not think that the vicar's son was a good match for his pretty and long-descended niece. In a year when Marie was of age, the consent of the guardian could be dispensed with; so that particular matter did not trouble the young man overmuch. He really desired to establish friendly relations with Sorley in order to learn if he had the peacock of jewels in his possession, as it was Marie's property and should be given to her. Since the uncle loved jewels, and probably knew that the peacock, besides being covered with precious stones, could indicate the whereabouts of a box filled with similar gems, it was probable that he would seek to keep the ornament to himself. Always provided that he possessed it, of which Alan was not quite sure. But if he did have it, then the supposition would be that he had murdered Baldwin Grison for its possession. It was difficult for Fuller to see what he would say in the way of excuse for owning it.

"But, of course," thought the young man, when he went to dress for dinner, and threshed out the matter in his own mind, "if he has it he won't make any fuss about my seeing it, should he desire me to solve the riddle since at present there has been no public mention that Grison was murdered for its sake.

"But if he does show it to me—" here he paused, greatly perplexed, as he foresaw how difficult it would be to know how to act. Even if the possession of the Peacock proved Sorley to be a criminal, for the sake of Marie, Alan was unwilling to bring him to justice. And yet, on the face of it, the man should pay for his crime. "It's confoundedly difficult to know what to do," was Fuller's natural conclusion.

The Christmas dinner was a great success in spite of the doubts expressed by the hostess, and the five people who sat down to enjoy it, passed a very agreeable hour. Marie had a healthy appetite, and had no reluctance in satisfying it on fare, which was much more dainty than that prepared by Henny Trent, who acted as cook at The Monastery. The girl in a simple white dress and without any ornaments, save a childish necklace of red coral, looked very pretty, and behaved very charmingly. By the end of the quiet evening Alan was more in love with her than ever, and wondered if the earth contained a more delightful little lady. Sorley also made himself most agreeable, being soothed by the excellent dinner, and showed no disposition to frown on the young couple. As to Mrs. Fuller, now that the dinner was off her mind, she beamed on everyone, including her rosy-faced sturdy little husband, who overflowed with Christian charity, which did not need the season of Yuletide to enhance its ready generosity.

Mr. Sorley was perfectly dressed as usual, and looked wonderfully well in his young-old way, which was so deceptive. He was well-informed too, and talked on this subject and that, in a most exhaustive manner, arguing with the vicar and agreeing with Mrs. Fuller, and giving an occasional word to Alan. Afterwards in the quaint old drawing-room the conversation turned on the death of Grison, although Mr. Fuller did his best to taboo the subject, on the plea that it upset his wife.

"Mrs. Fuller always liked the poor man," said the vicar finally.

"He was agreeable and clever, but woefully weak," confessed the old lady. "If he had only stayed here, he would never have met with such a death."

"I would willingly have kept him at The Monastery," explained Sorley in a frank manner, "but he was rude to my sister, and, owing to his drunken habits, kept the house in a constant state of turmoil. I had to dismiss him although I gave him every chance to reform. And you heard, Alan," he added, turning to the young man, who was listening intently, "how his sister blamed me for his death.

"What's that?" asked the vicar sharply.

"Not directly," said the guest calmly. "She could scarcely do that seeing I was fifty miles away at The Monastery when Grison was murdered in Rotherhithe. But his sister said that my dismissal made him take more than ever to opium smoking, and that drove him to the slum where he met with this tragic end."

"Pooh! pooh! Louisa Grison talks rubbish," said Mr. Fuller sturdily. "She was always crazy about Baldwin, although he certainly had his good points, foolish as he was. Don't let us talk any more about the matter. It upsets my wife, and is not a topic for Christmas Day."

"Oh, I don't mind hearing of his death," protested Mrs. Fuller, "I am only too anxious to know who killed him, poor creature."

"I shouldn't be surprised to hear that he killed himself," remarked Sorley in an abrupt way.

"Oh, that's impossible," said Alan quickly; "the medical evidence proved conclusively that he was murdered, stabbed to the heart."

"Well, my boy, a man can stab himself to the heart, can't he?"

"Yes," replied the young man dryly, "but he could scarcely hide the instrument with which he killed himself after his death, and that, as we know, is missing."

"What sort of instrument was it, Alan?" asked Mrs. Fuller.

"A stiletto, it is thought, mother."

"That sounds as though an Italian had a hand in the crime," remarked the vicar; "they generally use the stiletto!"

"I can't say who killed him, or of what nationality the assassin was, father, since nothing can be learned likely to cast light on the subject. But I am sure of one thing from what Latimer has told me, which is that Grison did not stab himself. He had no reason to."

"Mad people never do have any reason," remarked Mr. Sorley pointedly.

"But Grison was not mad."

"Indeed I have every reason to believe that he was," insisted the other; "the father was an eccentric doctor who practised in Canterbury, and the mother of Louisa and Baldwin died in a lunatic asylum."

Mrs. Fuller nodded sadly. "Yes, Louisa told me as much," she said, "and for that reason I excused her oddities and those of her brother. They certainly had queer ways, hadn't they, John?"

"Yes! yes! yes! But no worse than other people," rejoined Fuller senior, in his vigorous fashion, "but Louisa certainly manages her boarding-house in a sane enough manner, as I found when I stayed there."

"Did you stay there, father?" asked Alan.

"Twice or thrice when I went to town years and years ago, although I have not stayed there lately. I wanted to help Louisa, poor soul. But now she is doing so well that there is no need for me to assist her by becoming a few days' boarder. Baldwin may have been a trifle mad," added the vicar, addressing Sorley, "since he sank so low and displayed such weakness; but his sister is sane enough, I am sure of that."

"She did not speak very sanely the other day when attacking me, as Alan heard," said Mr. Sorley significantly. "We were quietly having afternoon tea when Miss Grison rose and suddenly denounced me. She is mad."

"I don't agree with you," retorted the vicar.

"What do you say, Alan?"

The young man shook his head with an embarrassed laugh. "I have not seen sufficient of Miss Grison to pronounce an opinion," he said, and turned to Marie, who was feeling rather neglected. "This is rather dull for you."

"And the subject, as I said before, is not a suitable one for Christmas Day," observed Mr. Fuller. "Marie, my dear, give us some music."

The girl obeyed with alacrity, as she had been yawning during the dreary talk of her elders. In a very musicianly style she played two or three classical pieces, and then with Alan sang some of Mendelssohn's duets, in which their voices blended far more agreeably than Mr. Sorley approved of. The late conversation seemed to have upset his nerves, for he wandered in a restless manner round the room and betrayed a disposition to come between the young people, in strange contrast to his earlier demeanor. When Mrs. Fuller was playing an old-fashioned selection of melodies, called "Irish Diamonds," which her husband loved, Sorley came to sit beside Alan and engage him in quiet conversation, while Marie and the vicar remained near the piano, listening to the variations on Garry Owen.

"You must come over to The Monastery during this week, Alan," said Mr. Sorley in a discreet whisper. "I should like to show you my collection of jewels, which will belong to Marie after I am gone."

"Oh, you will live for a long time yet," said Alan affably.

"I doubt it. I have my enemies like other men, and you need not be surprised if I meet with Grison's fate, poor wretch."

"Whatever do you mean?" demanded the other sharply.

"I mean that in the midst of life we are in death," rejoined Sorley tartly, and in a somewhat enigmatic manner, "What else should I mean?"

"I'm hanged if I know," said Alan frankly, and spoke from his heart. He really could not understand the man's strange reference to a violent end.

"Well! well! well!" remarked his companion with affected cheerfulness, "it may be all imagination on my part. But when one has such a collection of gems as I have in the house, it is not improbable that an attempt may be made to get them on the part of some thief."

"Have you any idea that such an attempt will be made?"

"Oh dear no. I speak generally. For my collection is valuable, Alan, although perhaps not worth so much money as those gems which were given to George Inderwick over one hundred years ago, by the Begum of Kam. Why do you start?" he asked in surprise. "Marie told me that she related the story of the jewels to you."

"Yes—that is—she did say something about the matter," stammered Alan, "only I did not know that Kam was the place where George Inderwick went on behalf of the H.E.I.C. to serve as a native drill sergeant."

"Oh yes. The Rajah of Kam's town and state in the Madras Presidency. You can see the manuscript to-morrow when you come over. Hush, the music is stopping; don't say anything more. Let us keep these matters to ourselves," and having thus forced Fuller, as it were, to be his confidant, Sorley strolled across the room to congratulate Mrs. Fuller on her still brilliant touch.

Alan remained where he was on the sofa, staring at the carpet, and wondering what revelations would be forthcoming when he visited The Monastery the next day, for he was determined to pay the promised visit as soon as he could, lest Sorley should change his mind. But what startled him most was to learn that the jewels had belonged to the Begum of Kam. And that was the very place mentioned by Morad-Bakche as the former territory of his family.

"Dick was right," thought Alan. "Bakche *is* after the gems of the peacock."

CHAPTER VIII

AN EXPLANATION

For the next two or three days Alan enjoyed the rural peace of the country and gave his parents a great deal of his society. Anxious as he was to follow up the hint of Sorley with reference to the story of George Inderwick's treasure, he did not display undue eagerness, since it was better to behave in a casual manner, lest suspicion should be aroused. The young man did not wish Sorley to think that he knew too much about the matter, or had been making any inquiries, for it was not improbable that he might take alarm and decline all assistance. Fuller felt certain that there was a skeleton in Sorley's cupboard, safely locked up, but, "as suspicion ever haunts the guilty mind," it would require a very slight circumstance to render the worthy gentleman uneasy. Therefore Alan pretended to an indifference which he did not feel, and kept away from The Monastery, until his diplomacy was rewarded about the middle of the week, by the appearance of Marie with a request that he should come over.

"This afternoon Uncle Ran wants to see you," said the girl pouting, for she was not pleased that Alan had kept clear of her company. "He has gone this morning to Lewes on his motor bicycle, and will be back at two o'clock to meet you."

"In that case," said Fuller promptly, and glancing at his watch, "since it is just eleven, we can have three hours all to ourselves."

"I don't think you want to pass all that time alone with me."

"Oh Marie, when you know how I love you."

"You don't; you really and truly don't;" said Miss Inderwick, who was looking provokingly pretty in a fur jacket and a fur toque; "if you loved me you wouldn't waste your time as you do."

"Waste my time. Why not, when I am on a holiday?"

"I don't mean that sort of waste, you horrid boy. But you know that you are always in town and I am always here, so when you are down for a few days, you should be with me constantly."

"I should very much like to, my dearest spitfire, but would it be wise when your uncle discourages my attentions to you so pointedly?"

"Oh!" Marie raised her eyebrows and pouted again. "If you are afraid of Uncle Ran there is no more to be said."

"There is a great deal more to be said," retorted Alan, tucking her arm under his own, "and we can say it on our way to The Monastery. When the cat's away at Lewes, we two dear little mice can play at Belstone. Marie, darling, don't make faces; we must be sensible."

"I *am* sensible; you have said dozens of times that I am the most sensible girl in the whole world."

"So you are. All the same we must be diplomatic in case youruncle—"

"Bother my uncle."

"I think you do, my dear," said Alan dryly, "and just now you are bothering me by being cross about nothing. Marie, if you don't smile in your usual angelic way, I shall kiss you here in the open road, Smile, smile!"

"I sha'n't," said Marie, trying to pucker her small face into a black frown, and then had to burst out laughing. "You silly boy!" She hugged his arm. "I spoil you, don't I?"

"You do, you do, like the angel you are."

"There's a want of originality about you, Alan. You are always calling me an angel. What else am I?"

"A goddess, a gazelle, a Queen of the May—"

"In December; how ridiculous!" and Miss Inderwick laughed gayly, her good temper quite restored.

The lovers walked slowly through the village and up to the gates of the neglected park, chatting much in the same strain. Of course they talked great nonsense, as lovers do when together, and the language of Cupid can scarcely be described as instructive. Alan was a sensible and clever young man, and Marie was by no means wanting in mother-wit, and yet their conversation was so characteristic of their several states of mind, which had entirely to do with the wooing of man and maid, that a common-sense person past the turtle-dove stage would have doubted their sanity. But then love is a madness which attacks the young at certain seasons, and custom has so sanctified the lunacy, that those so crazed are not locked up. And mercifully when the glamor of love is on them, they prefer to keep to themselves, so that indifferent people are not compelled to witness their eccentricities. Only when they were walking up the avenue, did the conversation become more reasonable.

"Why does Uncle Ran wish to see you, Alan?" asked Marie curiously.

"He intends to show me his collection of gems," replied Fuller, who did not think it prudent to be too open, until he knew more of Sorley's mind. He did not like the man, and suspected him of having committed a crime; but until he was certain of his guilt, he wished to keep silence. After all, the girl by his side was the daughter of the man's sister, and her guardian, so it was best to say as little as possible.

"Oh, he has got lovely jewels," said Marie, readily accepting the explanation, which certainly was a true one. "I wish he would let me wear some of them. It seems so stupid to lock up a lot of beautiful diamonds and emeralds and sapphires. When they come to me—as Uncle Ran says they will—I sha'n't leave them in their care, but wear them."

"You will look like the Queen of Sheba, my darling."

"Or like a rainbow," replied Miss Inderwick smartly, "all sorts of colors sparkling like—like—like frosts," she finished, taking her illustration from the glittering rime on the bare trees.

It was a perfect December day, and the blue sky arched over a white expanse of snow untrodden save for the track up the avenue along which the young couple had travelled. By this time they had come in sight of the great mansion, and paused to admire its irregular beauty. Its red roofs were hidden under billowy masses of dazzling whiteness, as they caught the sunlight, and the darkly-green garment of ivy which clothed it was flecked everywhere with snow wreaths. Icicles glittered like jewels hanging from eaves, porch, windows, and from the carved stonework, discernible through the greenery, so that the place looked like a fairy palace. Although Marie, its fortunate possessor, saw the house daily, she could not forbear an exclamation of delight.

"Isn't it lovely, dearest?"

"As lovely as you are, my darling," assented Alan readily. "I think you might show me over the house, Marie, as I have never explored it completely."

"I daresay. Uncle Ran won't let anyone go over it, although no end of artists wish to come to it. He wouldn't even let anyone paint a picture of the outside. I don't know why?"

"Nor do I," murmured Fuller, half to himself, "No more than I know why he was not angry with Miss Grison for going over it uninvited."

"That was strange," replied Miss Inderwick thoughtfully, "but I think he is a little afraid of Miss Grison, dear. He thinks she is mad."

"What do you think?"

"I haven't seen enough of her to say. But Mrs. Millington, her greatest friend, told me that she thought Miss Grison's mind was giving way."

"It is certainly not apparent in her management of her boarding-house."

"Well, she may be mad on one point and sane on many," remarked Marie pertinently, "she seems to hate Uncle Ran dreadfully."

"That is because she ascribes her brother's downfall to him. But don't let us talk about such dreary matters, darling, but look over the house, and arrange how we will restore it when we are married."

"And when we find the treasure," cried Marie, skipping lightly up the steps to the open door. "Come in, Alan. We must make the best of our time before Uncle Ran returns."

"He won't be back until two o'clock."

"So he says, but I don't trust him. He's always trying to catch me in mischief, as if I ever had a chance of doing any. I shouldn't be surprised if he pounced down on us unawares."

"In that case I can excuse myself by saying that I have come, at his request to see him," said Alan promptly. "Lead the way, Marie, and let us look over the place from top to bottom."

Marie assented very readily to be her lover's cicerone, and for the next hour they were passing along corridors, peeping into rooms, ascending and descending stairs, and searching for secret chambers and outlets. All the time Marie talked, telling Alan tales about this room and that, which she had heard from Granny Trent, who had lived nearly the whole of her long life in the old building. But what struck Alan most was the absence of furniture. Room after room had been stripped bare, and the vast house gave him the impression of being an empty shell. Yet according to the old woman, whom they looked in to see in her particular den, the place had been crammed with treasures no later than twenty years ago when Mrs. Inderwick had died.

"But he's sold them all," mourned Granny, who did not seem to have much love for her master—"tables and chairs and wardrobes and pictures, and all manner of things, my dears. It's a shame I say, for they belong to you, Miss Marie, and he ain't got no right to get rid of your property."

Granny was a lively, active woman, small and shrivelled in her looks, with twinkling black eyes and an expressive face. Age did not seem to have dulled her faculties, for she spoke clearly and to the point, and what is more, intimated that she could see through a brick wall, meaning in plain English— how easy it was to guess that the young couple were in love.

"And a very good thing too," said granny nodding sagely; "you being handsome and good and kind-hearted, Mr. Alan, or you wouldn't be the son of them dears at the vicarage else. Just you marry my lamb, sir, as soon as you can get your pa to read the service, if it's only to look after him."

"Mr. Sorley?" inquired Fuller pointedly. "You mean him?"

"And who else should I mean, Mr. Alan, if not him? A poor feckless thing I call him, selling up my lamb's goods to waste money on bits of stones. Ah, if the luck of the Inderwicks wasn't missing there'd be plenty of them."

"You mean the peacock?"

"I do. That blessed bird that means good fortune to my lamb here, sir. Them Grisons took it I'll swear when they went away over twenty years ago, and took the luck along with them, for never will it come back—it's the luck of the family I'm talking of, Mr. Alan—until the peacock is under this roof again."

"What sort of luck will it bring, Granny?" asked Marie eagerly.

"Marriage to you and Mr. Alan here, a fortune when the riddle is read as it surely will be, and an outgoing for him, as is your uncle and don't look after you, my lamb, as he should, drat him."

"Oh, he means well, Granny."

"If he means well, why don't he do well," retorted the old woman. "Never mind, the luck will come your way, my lamb, when you least expect it. Now go down to the dining-room, my dears, and I'll tell Jenny to set out something for you to eat. You can't live on love," chuckled Granny, her eyes twinkling.

The two laughed and took her advice, even to the extent of making a very excellent luncheon, plain as the fare was. When the meal ended, Marie carried off Fuller to the library and lighted his cigarette with her own fair hands. When he was comfortably puffing clouds of bluish smoke, Miss Inderwick, perched on the arm of his chair, ruffled his hair and told him that he was the most disagreeable person in the wide world. This led to amiable contradiction, finally to kissing and it was when they were in the middle of these philanderings, that they raised their eyes to see Mr. Sorley standing at the door. He was stiff with indignation, and looked more like a haughty unbending aristocrat than ever.

"So this is the way in which you deceive me, Marie?" he said with an angry look. "How dare you?"

"Why not," said Fuller, as the girl sprang away from his chair in alarm. "I love Marie and she loves me. You must have seen that ages ago, Mr. Sorley."

"I did, sir, but the position does not meet with my approval."

"Who cares," cried his niece defiantly. "I shan't marry anyone but Alan."

"You shall marry the man I select," said Sorley sternly, "unless—"

"Unless what?" demanded Fuller coolly. He was perfectly sure that Marie would remain true to him, and therefore had no fear of her uncle.

"I shall explain that when we are alone."

"Explain now," said Miss Inderwick swiftly, "I have a right to know why you object to Alan becoming my husband."

"He has no money and no position."

"I shall make money and make a position," said Alan calmly, "all in good time, Mr. Sorley, all in good time."

"He will be Lord Chancellor one day," said Marie boldly.

"You will have gray hairs by that time," snapped her uncle, "and until he is Lord Chancellor, you certainly shan't marry him."

"I shall. So there."

"You shall not."

"Unless," observed Alan smoothly, "you said unless, Mr. Sorley."

"Unless you find the Begum's treasure."

"Oh, Uncle Ran," cried Marie in dismay, "when you know that the peacock is lost, and without that no one can solve the riddle, or even know exactly what it is."

"The peacock is—" began Sorley, and stopped short. "Never mind. Go away, my dear, and let me talk to Alan."

He spoke so mildly that Marie began to think better of the position. He did not appear to be so dead against her marriage with Fuller, as his earlier words had intimated. Alan, on his part, guessed from the abrupt stopping of the sentence, that Sorley knew something about the missing peacock which he did not wish to reveal while Marie was in the room. Acting on this hint he took the bull by the horns.

"Look here, sir," he said, rising to address his host more impressively, "I know that the discovery of this treasure is connected with some cryptogram which has to do with the lost peacock. I accept your terms, as, having experience in secret writings, I am sure that I can solve the mystery which has baffled everyone for so long. If I do, and the treasure is found, will you—as you say—consent to Marie becoming my wife."

"Yes," said Sorley tersely and decisively, "but of course part of the treasure must be given to me."

"Oh, I shall buy your consent to my marriage with half of it," said Marie in a rather contemptuous tone.

Fuller secretly did not endorse this too generous offer, and determined that if he did solve the riddle, to hand over the gems to Miss Inderwick. But it was not diplomatic at the moment to insist upon this too much, particularly as Sorley had practically agreed to the marriage. "The first thing to do is to find the jewels," said Alan easily, "and then things can be better arranged, Mr.

Sorley."

"Very well," said the old gentleman, taking it for granted that Alan as well as his niece agreed to the terms, extortionate as they were, "we understand one another. Marie, you can go away."

"But I want to stop and hear everything," she exclaimed rebelliously.

"The time is not ripe for you to hear everything. As yet I know very little, and wish to consult Alan about arriving at the truth. He can tell you all you wish to know later."

"Go, dear," said Fuller in a low voice, and leading the girl to the door, "I can act for us both."

Marie pouted and tossed her pretty head. "You are horrid," she murmured. "I do want to know all about the peacock."

"You shall know if anything is to be discovered about it."

"Very well," she said obediently, "but I think you're horrid all the same."

When she left the library and the door was closed, Sorley, who had removed his overcoat and gloves and cap, sank into a chair with a sigh. He was evidently tired out by his ride to Lewes and back again. Alan waited for him to open the conversation, for having his suspicions of the man, particularly after his hesitation when Marie had mentioned the peacock, it behooved him to be cautious. Sorley thought for a few moments with his eyes on Fuller's face then spoke abruptly.

"You know that Miss Grison hates me, and why?" he demanded shortly.

"Yes. She accuses you of having ruined her brother by having dismissed him wrongfully."

"Quite so, and acts like a mad woman in consequence. As if I could help the man going to the bad. I gave him every chance, and instead of prosecuting him for forging that check I let him go free. I don't see that I could have behaved better. That he sank to the Rotherhithe slum was purely his own fault."

"Miss Grison doesn't think so."

"She can think what she chooses," retorted Sorley, coolly. "I need take no notice of the vagaries of a crazy creature such as she surely is." He paused, and looked oddly at his companion. "Do you know why I dismissed her brother, Alan?"

"You have just explained; because of the forged check."

"That is not the exact cause. I could have overlooked that, since I really was sorry for the poor wretch, even though he was rude to my sister, and a decided nuisance in this house with his drunken habits and use of opium. My real reason for dismissing him was that Miss Grison—Louisa as we used to call her—stole the peacock of jewels."

"Oh," said Fuller with a non-committal air, for he wished to know more about the theft before stating that Miss Grison had confessed to it. And even when he knew all he was not sure if he would be thus frank.

"Yes! she knew how I valued it, both because of its workmanship and the gems set in its golden body, and because it is the clue to a large treasure which was hidden—you know the story—by Simon Ferrier. I told her that if she did not return it I would dismiss her brother on account of the forged check. She refused and I did dismiss him, so she really has only herself to thank for Baldwin's downfall, although, like a woman, she blames me in the silly way she does."

"But if she took the peacock why didn't you have her arrested?"

"I should have done so, but that she declared her intention of destroying the ornament should I act in such a way. She said that she would drop it into the Thames—she was in London when I found out about her theft—or would melt it in fire. As the peacock is the sole clue to the hiding-place of the Begum's gems, you may guess that with such a desperate woman I did not dare to act so drastically as she deserved."

"I suppose she gave the peacock to her brother," suggested Alan artfully, hoping that Sorley would commit himself by confessing the knowledge that Grison held the ornament at the time of his death. But the man did nothing of the sort.

"No, she didn't," he said sharply, "so far as I know she had it in her possession all these twenty years. I went again and again to see her and try for its recovery, but insisting that I had ruined her brother, she refused to surrender it, and lest she should destroy it, I could not use the force of the law. Now I am certain that he had it all the time."

"Why are you certain?" asked Fuller, who was impressed by the frank way in which the man spoke. He certainly did not seem to have anything to conceal, and the solicitor wondered whether he had misjudged him.

Mr. Sorley waved his hand. "One moment," he said slowly, "you may wonder why I am telling you all this, and why I have brought you into the matter? I do so, because you tell me that you are good at solving riddles, and also since you are in love with Marie you are bound to protect her interests. The jewels belong to her, so I am anxious that you should help me to find them, so that Marie may get the benefit of their sale. As she will have this house, her own income, and my collection of gems when I die, I do not think I am asking too much in requesting a share of the treasure, especially when that also will go to my niece after my death."

Alan nodded, since all this was reasonable enough. "I know why you want me to help," he remarked, "but without the peacock we can do nothing."

Mr. Sorley rose and went to an alcove of the room in which was set a tall carved cupboard of black oak. Opening this he took out an object wrapped in chamois leather, and returned to the writing-table to display to his visitor's astonished eyes, the missing peacock of jewels. "On that day when Miss Grison called me names, and by her own confession wandered over the house uninvited," said the man quietly, "she must have brought this back. The day after she departed I found the peacock in yonder cupboard, a place where I frequently go, as Miss Grison knew. Why she should restore it in this stealthy way, or restore it at all, I am not able to say. But I know that she took it from here twenty years ago—from that cupboard in fact, where it was always kept —and her unasked-for visit to this house must have been to replace it."

Alan stared at the glittering bird which was—as Latimer had stated—the size of a thrush, and greatly admired its beauty and perfection of workmanship. Ferrier assuredly had learned a great deal in the East, for the shape and feathers of the bird were truly wonderfully created in delicate lines. The eyes were rubies, and there was a tuft of emeralds on the head but comparatively few stones studded the body, as all were reserved for the glory of the tail. This was outspread like a large fan—and in it were set sapphires, opals, rubies, and many other precious stones which scintillated a glory like a rainbow, especially when Sorley moved the gems to and fro in the thread of sunlight which pierced the dusky atmosphere of the room. But what the young man thought, while he stared at the lovely object, was whether Sorley was guilty or innocent. The presence of the ornament which had been in the possession of the dead man hinted the former, but Sorley's explanation—feasible enough on the basis of Miss Grison's abrupt visit—seemed to declare the latter. As no man is considered guilty in English law until his criminality is proved, and as Alan was a solicitor, he gave Sorley the benefit of the doubt until such time as he had more trustworthy evidence to go upon. Having taken up this attitude he treated the man as innocent, and asked questions about the peacock. It was necessary to do so, if the riddle was to be solved.

"And, so far as I can see," said Fuller, following his train of thought, "there is no secret writing to be seen."

"There is no secret writing," said Sorley unexpectedly.

"But I thought you wished me to solve a cryptogram."

"So I do; but a cryptogram can be other than in letters or figures."

Fuller gazed at the peacock. "I can't understand," he said bewildered.

"Well, Alan," rejoined Fuller with a shrug, "I can't myself, and so have brought you into the business on the assumption that two heads are better than one. I have even opened the peacock to find its secret, but there is nothing inside. In my opinion the secret is hidden in the tail."

Alan was still puzzled. "In the tail?" he echoed.

"In the jewels somehow," explained Mr. Sorley meditatively. "You see there are three semicircles of gems on the tail, and between the second and the third appears a triangle of rubies. Now if we can read the meaning of the three rows of precious stones, they may explain the triangle, which is probably the key to the whole mystery."

"I still can't understand. Why should the mystery be concealed in the jewels of the tail? They may be merely for decorative purposes."

"I don't think so. Of course the gems may imitate the peacock's tail from nature, but you never saw a bird with a triangle marked in this way."

"No," Alan nodded. "You are right so far. Have you any further ideas?"

"Not one. The riddle is to be read on the tail, and by means of the precious stones, but how, I can't say. What's your opinion, Alan?"

"I have none," said the young man hopelessly. "I shall have to turn over the matter in my own mind, and then shall let you know."

Mr. Sorley carefully locked up the peacock in the cupboard and shrugged his shoulders. "I have thought over the problem for years, and I am no nearer the solution than ever I was. But if you solve it, you shall marry my niece."

"With such a prize in view I cannot fail," said Fuller hopefully. All the same the outlook regarding the reading of the riddle was very doubtful.

CHAPTER IX

ANOTHER TRAIL

Alan Fuller left The Monastery in a very perplexed state of mind, as may be guessed, for the revelations, made by Mr. Sorley startled him considerably. On the hints given by Miss Grison he had suspected that the man knew something about the Rotherhithe crime, and now the production of the golden peacock seemed to endorse his suspicions. According to Jotty—who could not have manufactured such a story—the deceased had been in possession of the ornament shortly before his death. Miss Grison also had stated that the same had been given by her to the man, although she admitted having stolen it from the great house. How then did it pass into Mr. Sorley's hands unless that gentleman had committed the crime? Certainly his explanation, or rather his belief, that Miss Grison had restored the peacock to the cupboard when she paid her unexpected visit appeared to be feasible, but before Fuller could entirely believe this, it was necessary that Sorley's suggestion should be supported by the woman's acknowledgment. And it must be mentioned as a point in the man's favor that he did not say positively Miss Grison had brought back the ornament on that occasion, but only gave out the idea to account for his own production of the article.

"And," considered Alan, while plodding homeward, "Sorley is not aware that it is known to Moon, Jotty, Dick, and me that the crime on the face of it was committed for the sake of the peacock. Had he known as much, he might have accounted for its coming into his possession by saying that Miss Grison had brought it back. But since he is ignorant, I don't see the use of his making such an excuse. He could easily have said that the ornament had been mislaid, and that he had found it by chance. Or indeed that Miss Grison had hidden the thing when she stole it in some room, without troubling to remove it from the place. Sorley's explanation certainly seems to point to his complete innocence."

But then again, as the young man considered later, Sorley had, within the last few months, purchased a motor bicycle, and had told an obvious falsehood as to the time of possession. On such a machine he could easily cover the fifty miles between London and Belstone twice over in a night by hard riding, and thus might have been in town about the time when the crime was committed without anyone being the wiser. The ownership of the motor bicycle assuredly hinted that the man had acted in this way, and if so, the chances were that he had murdered Grison to recover the peacock. But in that case, he would hardly venture to show his spoil so openly, knowing at what cost he had obtained it, even though unaware that the police knew how the dead man had been slain on account of the ornament. Certainly he desired Fuller's assistance to unravel the problem connected with the golden bird, but then—as Alan thought—he could have produced a drawing of the article, saying that it had been made by himself or someone else before Miss Grison had stolen the fetish of the Inderwicks. In a correct picture drawn to scale and colored, there would be quite enough to go upon to guess the riddle since the mystery of the peacock was evidently on the surface, and not connected with the interior of the body. Sorley—as he stated, had opened that to find nothing; and, wanting Fuller to help him, he assuredly must have spoken the entire truth.

While Alan was thus turning matters over in his bewildered mind, he heard his name called, and looked round to see Marie flying over the snowy ground. She caught up with him breathless and crimson with the race, to seize his arm with a reproachful expression.

"You *are* mean," she cried, recovering her breath, "I've been waiting for you to come out and tell me what Uncle Ran said to you. But you left without a word. I saw you passing down the avenue, so followed as hard as I was able. Why do you act in this horrid, secret way, you disagreeable thing?"

Fuller halted and looked at her doubtfully. Since he had imparted to the girl that knowledge regarding Grison's possession of the peacock, which he had obtained from Inspector Moon, through Latimer, he certainly did not intend to reveal that Sorley had displayed the ornament in the library. Should he do so, Marie would at once, on what she knew, jump to the conclusion—and very naturally—that her uncle was guilty. Being of an emotional nature she would probably refuse to remain in the house with the man, in which case the truth would have to be told. If it were, and Sorley learned that he was suspected, he would probably place obstacles in the way of what really happened coming to light. That is, assuming he really was the criminal, a fact of which Alan, after thinking over things was by no means certain. And if the man was innocent, he might make an outcry to clear himself, which would be equally prejudicial to the solution of the problem. The more secretly all operations were conducted until positive knowledge was forthcoming, the better it would be for the cause of justice. And in this case, justice consisted in bringing the assassin of Baldwin Grison to the gallows.

"Oh," said Alan lightly, and smiling at her inquiring look, "your uncle only asked me to assist him to learn the riddle of the peacock."

"But how can that be done when the peacock is missing?"

"Your uncle had drawings of the bird," replied the young man evasively.

"I have never seen them," declared Marie rather crossly, "and as the peacock belongs to me, I should see them."

"I will show them to you in a few days," answered Alan quickly, and made a mental resolve to prepare the drawings himself. And indeed it was necessary that he should have them, since he could not take the actual bird to town, and required something tangible upon which to work. "Don't you bother your uncle about the matter, Marie, or he may withdraw his permission."

"What permission?"

"That I should become engaged to you."

"Oh Alan! oh Alan! oh Alan!" Marie could only gasp and blush.

"That is," said Fuller correcting himself, "he does not directly sanction an official engagement. But he says that if I solve the problem and find the jewels that he will agree to our marriage. Meanwhile we can be together as often as we like."

"That is as good as an engagement," cried Marie, clapping her hands with delight, "how good of Uncle Ran. I love him for this."

"Don't tell him so," interposed Fuller hastily; "he's an odd fish, and if he knows that I have told you of his yielding so far, he may change his mind, my dear."

Marie nodded very wisely and solemnly. "I see; I quite understand. I shall say nothing to Uncle Ran."

"And ask no questions?"

"Not one. But you will tell me everything, won't you?" she said, pressing up to his side in a coaxing manner.

"Of course," Alan assured her, "whatever discoveries I make regarding the riddle you shall know," and the girl was satisfied with this, not guessing that her lover was withholding information connected with the more serious matter of the Rotherhithe murder.

Having—as she now presumed—full permission from Sorley to display her preference for Alan, Marie boldly took his arm and walked through the village with him in a most open manner. There was no chance now that her Uncle Ran would appear to make trouble, and the girl declared as she clung to her lover that all their troubles were over. "For of course, such a very clever boy such as you are, dear, will easily solve the riddle."

"I hope," replied Fuller doubtfully, "but it is a hard riddle, Marie, and has baffled everyone for over one hundred years."

"Well," said Miss Inderwick, arguing from a feminine standpoint, "if anyone had guessed the riddle the jewels would have been sold by this time, and probably the money would have been spent. So it is just as well that the truth has not become known. You will guess the riddle, dear, clever boy that you are, and then we shall become very, very rich, even though the half of what you find goes to Uncle Ran."

"Nothing shall go to Uncle Ran," said Alan grimly, "because Uncle Ran has no right to ask for a share—unless, of course, he solves the riddle. The peacock and the treasure it can point out, Marie, both belong to you, so don't go making hasty promises to Mr. Sorley; and above all, dear—mark what I say, little featherhead—don't sign any paper if he asks you to."

Marie nodded meditatively. "I understand what you mean, Alan. Of course Uncle Ran is fond of jewels, and—well then I shall sign nothing without consulting you, dear."

"And don't tell him that I advised this."

"Of course not; he would take a dislike to you if I did. Don't worry, Alan darling, for I know exactly how to behave."

"Behave just as you have done, Marie, and do not let Mr. Sorley believe that anything new is afoot, or that there is any understanding between us."

Miss Inderwick nodded vigorously to imply that she knew what she was about, and the two walked on for some distance in silence, over the cobblestone pavement of Belstone main street. Occasional smiles and looks of approval were cast at the young couple by stray villagers, for Alan was a great favorite in his father's parish, and Marie was much more popular than her uncle. The inhabitants of Belstone believed that if Marie became Mrs. Alan Fuller, that the old day of plenty would return to The Monastery in which all would share, for they credited the young man with brains which would enable him to make a great deal of money. And if he did, seeing that he had a generous nature, it was just as well that he should marry the last descendant of the ancient family who had ruled the neighborhood. All public sympathy was on the side of the lovers.

But to this Marie and Alan paid no attention, since they were wrapped up in one another. The girl felt quite happy in Fuller's company and occasionally glanced at his meditative face. Alan appeared to be thinking deeply, and apparently of something not connected with herself. With the natural jealousy of a woman in love, Marie could not permit this.

"What are you thinking about, dear?" she asked suspiciously.

"About Morad-Bakche!"

Miss Inderwick opened her eyes on hearing this strange name. "Who is he?"

"He is an Indian gentleman, dear, whom I met at Miss Grison's."

"Why should you think about him just now when I am here, Alan?"

Fuller answered the first part of the question, and passed over the latter. "I am wondering if he has anything to do with the peacock?"

This remark put an end to Marie's egotism for the time being. "Why should he have anything to do with it?" she demanded, astonished.

"Well," exclaimed the young man quietly, "he has come to England, so he told me to search for some mislaid family property. He is descended from that Rajah of Kam to whom George Inderwick was sent by the H.E.I.C., my dear."

Marie, having read and re-read the story of Ferrier grasped the connection at once. "Then he knows about the peacock?" she cried in dismay.

"That is what I wish to learn. The Begum of Kam certainly gave the jewels we are looking for to George Inderwick, from whom they descend to you, so as Morad-Bakche represents the Kam family it is just possible that he has come to get back the gems if he can."

"He sha'n't have them," cried Marie, becoming flushed, "don't let him take them, Alan."

Fuller laughed. "We have to find them first," he remarked coolly. "When we have them in our possession, then we can talk over Morad-Bakche's claim."

"He sha'n't have them," murmured Marie, much disturbed; "they are mine. And after all, Alan, he may not have come for the Begum's treasure."

"He may, or he may not. I am unprepared to give an opinion. Only it is so strange that he should live at Miss Grison's boarding-house, considering that she knows about the peacock, which is to reveal the whereabouts of what the man probably desires. He didn't get to that boarding-house by chance, I am certain. And Dick fancies also—by his sixth sense, as he declares—that Morad-Bakche may have designs on the treasure."

"It is very strange," said Miss Inderwick, pondering over this speech; "but how could he find out that Miss Grison knew about the peacock?"

"We must learn. Have you ever seen an Indian gentleman in the village, my dear, or haunting The Monastery?"

"No. If I had I should have told you, or would have written about it. We see so few people about here, Alan—strangers that is—that anyone new is quickly noticed."

"Well, you may not have seen the man, but others may have. Who is the greatest gossip in the village?"

"Oh, Alan, as if you didn't know, when your mother is always talking about her. It's Mrs. Verwin, of course."

"Ah yes! and she keeps The Red Fox, our one and only inn. Marie, she is the very person to know, for besides being a gossip, she is the landlady of an inn to which a stranger would go even if he only came for the day. Come and let us interview Mrs. Verwin."

Marie assented eagerly, for the search was like a game, and interested her greatly. The pair simply retraced their steps and entered the green space in the centre of Belstone, whence streets and lanes diverged, to behold the shabby old inn facing them directly. It was an ancient Georgian building, ugly without, and comfortable within, and had been more notable in the day of stage-coaches than it was now. Its walls sadly needed a coat of paint, its roof required patching, while both doors and windows would have been the better for a little attention. In fact, there was a half-hearted look about The Red Fox, which showed that the good lady who owned it had given up any idea of making her fortune, and was content to exist for the day without troubling about the morrow. Sometimes tourists stayed in the old place, more frequently artists, attracted by the romantic beauties of The Monastery, for the shabby rooms were fairly comfortable, and the cooking, within limits, was tolerably good. Mrs. Verwin's money mostly came from the pockets of laborers and yokels, who drank the very inferior beer she supplied while they talked over the news of the countryside in the smoky taproom with the sawdust floor, and cumbersome settles. In the evening when the day's work was ended, that taproom was the meeting-place of gossips both male and female.

And Mrs. Verwin was the greatest and most famous gossip of the lot. How she gathered all the news she did was a mystery to everyone, since she never left her abode, and worked from morning until night in order to keep things going. But somehow she managed to hear all that was going on both near and far, and used her long tongue freely in discussing what she heard. But that the villagers were so somnolent Mrs. Verwin would many and many a time have been in danger of a libel action, but reigning as a kind of rural queen, no one was bold enough to bring her to book. If anyone had dared to venture on such a course, he or she would have been excluded for ever from the taproom, and such excommunication was not to be thought of by anyone who desired to see life. And life was nowhere to be seen in Belstone save under the noisy roof of The Red Fox.

Mrs. Verwin herself welcomed the young couple the moment they set foot on the threshold, as she had already espied them from the window. Being a very stout woman, she could scarcely curtsey, but did her best, and invited her visitors into the best parlor. It was a great honor that the vicar's son and the leading lady of the neighborhood—for that Marie was by virtue of descent if not of money—and Mrs. Verwin was quite overwhelmed. As the inn was quite respectable and well-conducted, Alan had no hesitation in taking Marie into the place, although Mrs. Fuller would scarcely have been pleased, because she disliked the landlady's too ready tongue. But as that lively, black-eyed dame was a good churchwoman and really kind-hearted, the vicar had a better opinion of her.

"Lor' sir and miss," cried Mrs. Verwin, energetically dusting a chair for Marie to sit down on. "Who'd ha' thought of you an' Mr. Alan coming to see me, friendly like. And very well you're looking miss, though Mr. Alan there could do with a little red in them pale cheeks of his. London smoke," added Mrs. Verwin in disgust, "and London food, and the milk that blue with watering as the sky is gray to it. Now do have a cup of tea, sir, and—"

"No, thank you, Mrs. Verwin," interrupted Alan quickly, for there was no chance of getting a word in edgeways save by cutting short the good lady's voluble speech; "we have only come for five minutes. I want to ask you a question, if you don't mind."

"Mind, Mr. Alan, and why should I mind, me being all straight and above the sky-line, respectable as my parents were before me, as anyone who can read is able to see on their tombstones in the right-hand corner of the churchyard looking from the porch. Ask me what you like, sir, whether it means weddings or funerals, or all that goes between in—"

"I simply wish to know if during the last year you have seen an Indian gentleman in the village," interrupted Fuller again, and with a look at Marie to show that he desired to conduct the conversation himself.

"Well, I never, and to think as you didn't hear of him, stopping here as he was in July last for one night, and saying as the rice he ate was boiled in a way he admired."

"Oh, so there was an Indian here?"

Mrs. Verwin nodded and placed her stout arms akimbo, with curiosity in her snapping black eyes.

"Quite the gentleman he was, though I hope there's nothing wrong with him, meaning courts and docks and lawyers, as is all the sons of Old Nick, asking your pardon, Mr. Alan, for saying so, and yours, miss, for talking about him, as shouldn't be spoke of, nohow. Now if—"

"There's nothing wrong about him," said Alan, again stopping the flow of the landlady's conversation, or rather monologue; "but I happened to meet him at Miss Grison's boarding-house in London and—"

"Lor' sir," said Mrs. Verwin again, and taking her turn to interrupt, "may I never speak another word, if she don't owe me a good turn for having told him to go there, where he'd be comfortable, though I never could see as Miss Grison, and Louisa's her name, was much of a housekeeper."

"You told Mr. Bakche to go," said Alan, remembering how the Indian had mentioned to Miss Grison that someone in Ceylon had sent him to Thimble Square, "and why?"

"Batch. Yes sir, Batch was the name, and he was a very dark gentleman with eyes like gimblets for boring a person through and through, haughty like and grand in his manners, speaking English like a native in spite of his having been reared in a country where they chatter French and German, the last a language I never could abide, since a waiter of that sort went away when the house was full, and I needed all the hands I'd got besides a few more. Oh, Mr. Batch was a gent sure enough, though a son of Ham as we are told in the Bible, your pa, Mr. Alan, having read about them children of Noah only three Sundays back, and then he—"

"Why did you send Mr. Bakche to Miss Grison's?" asked Alan impatiently.

"Well, I didn't in a way, sir, because it was the peacock as sent him to—"

"The peacock," repeated Marie, and looked at Alan anxiously.

"And well do you know all about it, miss," cried the voluble Mrs. Verwin, turning to face the speaker, "it being the luck of your family as will never have no fortune till it's brought back again. And that Grison person as was your uncle's clerk took it over twenty years back, as I'm a living woman, which we all said when we heard as he was gone and it was missing. I said and others said as Mr. Sorley should have persecuted—"

"Did you tell all this to Mr. Bakche?" questioned Fuller quickly.

"And why shouldn't I tell him, Mr. Alan?" inquired Mrs. Verwin, wiping her heated face with a corner of her apron and bridling. "He asked if there wasn't people called Inderwick hereabouts, and I up and told him all about the family. Mr. Batch says, as his father knew some of 'em in his own land, and said as how him he met—not mentioning names, though it was an Inderwick as spoke, and perhaps, miss, a cousin of your very own—well, him as he met mentioned a peacock. So I tells Mr. Batch all about the story of the peacock being the luck of the family, as all the countryside knows, and says as how we believed that Grison person had took it. He said he'd like to ask him or her about the peacock—meaning them Grisons—since he liked to hear them sort of stories, so I recommended her house to him as being comfortable, and heaven forgive me for the lie, seeing Miss Grison—and Louisa's her name—

ain't got no more idea of cooking than a cat."

"Oh, Mr. Bakche is very comfortable there," said Alan easily, and very glad that he had learned so much; "did Mr. Bakche say nothing about any treasure connected with the peacock?"

"No," cried Mrs. Verwin, her face alive with curiosity, "never a word did he mention of a treasure, and where—"

Fuller saw that he had made a mistake in hinting a thing which was known only to the Inderwicks to this gossip, and hastened to repair his error. "I am talking of the peacock itself, which is a treasure," he said quickly, "for it is made of gold with precious stones—"

"I know, Mr. Alan, of course I know, sir, for didn't I see it on my wedding-day forty years ago, when your dear ma, miss, was alive and well along with your late pa. My husband—poor Verwin as is dead and gone—said as he give me a wedding treat, and he takes me to see The Monastery and asked Squire Inderwick to show that blessed peacock. Oh," Mrs. Verwin raised her fat hands and closed her eyes in ecstasy, "well may you call it a treasure, Mr. Alan, for such glitter I never did see. It was like the New Jerusalem for shine and—"

"Well that is the treasure I meant, Mrs. Verwin."

"And you never spoke a truer word, Mr. Alan. But I hope sir, and you, miss, as I didn't do wrong in telling Mr. Batch—and a pleasant gentleman, though dark, he was too—about the peacock, for it's a story as we all know for years and years and years. The luck of the Inderwicks! Why I heard my dear, dear pa as is dead these fifty years tell all about the blessed idol, so I thought t'was no harm to let Mr. Batch know as we'd something in Belstone he hadn't got in his own country, wherever that may be, though they do say as it's across channel somehow, and, if he—"

"You didn't do wrong, Mrs. Verwin," said Alan, striking in hastily, as he was anxious to get away with Marie, "and I merely asked about Mr. Bakche because he seemed to know something of Belstone."

"He know. Now I ask you, sir, what can he know, staying but for one day, and only giving an eyewink at The Monastery where he—"

"Oh, he went there, did he?" asked Fuller, turning back at the door.

"Yes sir, he did, saying he'd like to see such a lovely place about which I'd told him such a queer story, for queer he said was the name for the luck of the peacock. I think Mr. Batch was one of them gents who write and who ask others for things as they can't think of themselves, to—"

"Yes! Yes. Very probably, Mrs. Verwin. Thanks for answering my questions. I just did so because I chanced to meet this gentleman at Miss Grison's."

Alan, and Marie, who had taken scarcely any part in the conversation, managed to get outside the door, but were followed into the open by Mrs. Verwin, talking all the time, and curtseying at intervals with difficulty as she said good-bye. "For I do hope miss, and Mr. Alan, sir, as you'll come in again, you not forgetting, miss, as I was kitchen-maid at The Monastery before Verwin came along to make me a happy bride; and so have the interest of the family at heart. Sitting on a throne is where you should be, miss, with all under your pretty feet as you will be when the peacock comes again to its own. And if that Grison person is dead, murdered they say with much blood, and serve him right, I hope as he's sent back the peacock by post, if his sister —Louisa's her name—ain't got it, which is just as likely as not, taking into— Well good-day, sir—good-day, miss—and bless you both for a nice-looking couple," and Mrs. Verwin's voice arose to a perfect scream, as the distance between her and the visitors increased. Not until they were on the verge of the green entering the lane which led to the vicarage, did the sound of her adieux die away.

"Marie," said Alan seriously, "if you ever talk so much, I shall divorce you at once. Poor Verwin. He must have been glad to leave the world."

"She always makes my head ache," said Marie laughing.

"And other people's hearts ache, owing to her gossip. However, she can't make any mischief about what we have been talking, since I explained exactly what I meant. So Bakche came down here to ask after the peacock. That shows, as I thought long ago, that he is after the Begum's gems."

"What will you do, Alan?" asked Marie anxiously.

"Consult Dick, and tell him what I have found out. Meanwhile Marie, you need not tell your uncle what we have discovered."

"Mrs. Verwin will probably do that," said Marie darkly.

Alan frowned. "We can't stop her tongue, worse luck," he said with a sigh.

CHAPTER X

MR. SORLEY'S JEWELS

There was no doubt that the evidence of the village gossip would be valuable in connection with the Rotherhithe crime, since it showed that another person besides Mr. Sorley desired to obtain possession of the peacock of jewels. From oral tradition or perhaps from some family paper, it was apparent that Morad-Bakche had learned how his great great grandmother, or whatever the relationship might be, had presented the gems to George Inderwick. Also the mere fact that he had sought to learn the history of the fetish from Mrs. Verwin indicated that he knew in some way, not yet to be explained, how the golden bird could reveal the hiding-place of the treasure. That he had met with a cousin of Marie's in India, as he had told the landlady to account for his knowledge of the peacock, was merely an excuse, as no relative of the Inderwick family was in India at the present time. But of course only Bakche himself could explain how he had managed to trace the fetish which had to do with the family treasure of his ancestors, and he might do so when he called on Fuller, which the young man quite expected him to do.

"Mrs. Verwin," thought Alan, as he retired to bed, "undoubtedly must have told him that I was paying attentions to Marie, so that was why Bakche behaved so amiably to me at the boarding-house. Dick was right after all, for the man is seeking for the gems, and his politeness to me had something to do with his hope of getting them. He is certain to look me up again, and if I pretend to know nothing, he will have to speak out himself if he desires my assistance. But then there's Sorley—"

It was at this point that the young man's senses became confused, and he fell asleep. But next morning he determined to see Marie's uncle, and ask if he had seen Bakche in the village or haunting the grounds of The Monastery. Of course the Indian was working secretly to regain what his people had lost; all the same he might have gone boldly to Sorley, and sought to learn if that gentleman knew details of the gems and their whereabouts. Alan remembered vaguely that Sorley had talked of the possibility of his being murdered, and although the man insisted that the chance had to do with his own private collection of jewels, yet it was not improbable that Bakche had threatened him. The Indian was not the man to stick at murder if he wished to gain his ends, and Alan wondered if he had killed Baldwin Grison in order to get the peacock. But this supposition he dismissed as ridiculous, since had Bakche secured the plunder he assuredly would not have sent it to Mr. Sorley. However the sole chance of learning more or less of the truth lay in questioning both men. Alan began with Sorley.

Also he wished to make a drawing of the peacock, so as to have before his eyes an exact representation of the bird. Alan had a fair idea of art, and had at one time amused himself with sketching, but not being particularly successful had abandoned his hobby. However, he possessed sufficient technical skill to draw the bird and color the drawing, so looked out his japanned tin paint-box and took it in his pocket to The Monastery. This was a couple of days before he returned to town, and at the beginning of the New Year. Luckily on this occasion Marie had gone to see a schoolgirl friend at Brighton, so Fuller was glad that she would not be at home to interrupt his interview with Mr. Sorley. She asked too many questions, and having regard to her uncle's very peculiar position, Alan found a difficulty in answering them. Finally although he intended to show her the sketch of the peacock, he did not desire her to see him preparing it, since that would have given the lie to his assertion that Sorley already possessed such a drawing, and moreover might reveal that the peacock itself had returned to its old home. Therefore Fuller entered the big house feeling thankful that Marie was out of the way for a few hours. Being very much in love with her he had never expected to have such a feeling, and felt rather ashamed of himself in consequence. But as he knew that he was acting straightforwardly under particularly difficult circumstances he cheered up and saluted his host with a smile. Henny Trent with a grin on her Dutch doll face had introduced him into the library, and here Mr. Sorley was writing letters.

"How are you, Alan," he said, rising to greet his visitor, and looking as spick and span as though he had just stepped out of a bandbox. "I thought you had returned to your duties in Chancery Lane?"

"I go back the day after to-morrow," replied the solicitor, shaking hands, and wondering if he was doing so with a man who ought to be in the New Bailey dock; "I came to say good-bye and to ask you to allow me to make a drawing of the peacock."

"For what reason?" questioned Sorley suspiciously and uneasily.

"My reason is very apparent, sir. The riddle is to be read on the exterior of the peacock, you say?"

"I think so, since I have opened the bird and found nothing inside it."

"Then I must have a representation of the article before my eyes in order that I may ponder over the signs."

"What signs?"

"There you have me," answered Fuller frankly; "so far as I can see there are no signs of hieroglyphics or writing on the bird, so I don't see that it can in any way indicate the hiding-place of the Begum's gems. But if I have a picture and examine everything about it carefully, I may hit on the solution."

"You don't appear to be very certain of success," said Mr. Sorley dryly, "yet you told me that you were an adept at solving cryptograms."

"If they consist of signs," Alan explained cautiously, "and I can see no signs on the peacock. Well sir, will you let me draw it?"

"Certainly, since I wish you to work with me in the endeavor to learn where Ferrier concealed the treasure. But I don't want you to show the drawing all over the place, lest someone else should guess the secret."

"Oh, I shall be careful," said Fuller cheerfully, but making a mental reservation that Dick Latimer should see the sketch.

Satisfied with his promise, Sorley took the golden peacock from the cupboard of black oak, and unwrapped the chamois leather covering to display it on the table. But before doing so he locked the library door without apologizing, an action which seemed highly suspicious to his visitor. But if cautious with others who were in the house, Sorley was certainly very frank in his dealings with Alan, and although the young man could not bring himself to entirely trust his host, he admitted privately that the man did not act in a way which suggested terror of the law, And if he had murdered Grison to gain possession of the fetish, he assuredly would be more cautious in showing it to a lawyer. But Fuller never could make up his mind as to Sorley's innocence or guilt, and wavered between belief and disbelief in a way which annoyed himself. But there was nothing else to be done until more evidence was forthcoming.

The young man looked searchingly at the beautiful specimen of goldsmith's work which glittered on the table. Ferrier knew his trade thoroughly, and probably had acquired some skill when in India. The feathers, the form, and the head of the bird were perfectly done, and in a minute, delicate manner, which showed how painstaking its creator had been. The tiny emeralds on the head-tuft trembled on golden wires like the filaments of flowers, and the ruby eyes were set admirably in their sockets. The breast shone with few gems, but the body of the bird was of feathered gold, and the artist seemed to have reserved the full blaze of beauty for the outspread tail. Yet there were fewer jewels in this than might have been expected, for in the three curved rows which followed the semicircular outline of the tail, Alan counted only fifteen precious stones, namely: eight gems in the first row, four in the second, and three in the third. Then between the second and third was the triangle which contained fifteen minute rubies on each one of its three sides.

"Fifteen gems in the lines," murmured Fuller thoughtfully, "and fifteen of them in each line of the triangle. I wonder, Mr. Sorley, if the number fifteen is the key to the secret."

"I can't say, I don't know; I certainly cannot see how it can be," replied the host doubtfully. "I have tried in every way to solve the riddle, but I cannot even see how to make a beginning, The secret may be contained in the position of the stones, the shapes of the stones, or the color of the stones." Alan faced round. "What do you mean by the color answering the riddle?"

"It is just an idea I got from a man who is a theosophist. In what they—the theosophists I mean—call the aura of a human being, which can be seen by those gifted with astral sight, the colors all mean something."

"I don't quite follow you, Mr. Sorley, although I have heard something of this sort from Dick. He believes in these occult things. Do you?"

"I can't say that I have looked into them," rejoined Sorley in a careless manner. "I only attended to the matter so far as the meaning of colors was concerned—a kind of color alphabet as it were. Pink means affection, blue means religion, green sympathy, and so on. I applied the principle, but it wouldn't work."

Fuller quite believed this, as he did not see how the principle in question could be applied. However, he was too engrossed in drawing the bird to go into the subject at the present moment, but promised himself to ask for a more thorough explanation of the color alphabet—as Mr. Sorley aptly called it— from Dick Latimer. Meantime he drew the outline of the peacock, filled in the details, being particularly careful as to the position of the stones in the tail, and then slowly colored every part in accordance with the original object. When finished he laid down his brush with a tired sigh and held out the sketch at arm's length. Mr. Sorley restored the peacock to its chamois leather wrapping and to the cupboard, after which he returned to examine Alan's artistic effort.

"Very good, very good," he said nodding, "you have done it very exactly, although the drawing is very stiff."

"Rather architectural isn't it, sir? But the original is stiff also, and I am not drawing from an artistic point of view, but with the idea of getting an exact representation of the thing," said Alan, and slipping the sketch into an envelope, he put it along with the paint-box into his pocket.

Before leaving, Fuller determined to speak to Sorley of what he had heard from Mrs. Verwin regarding the visit of Morad-Bakche to Belstone. He had immediately after the interview warned Marie not to mention what had been said to her uncle, but on reflection he thought that it would be just as well to learn what he could. Moreover Mrs. Verwin being loose-tongued would probably talk about the matter, and if it reached Sorley's ears he might get it into his suspicious mind that Alan was working against him, rather than with him, an attitude which was not to be permitted, since in this case union was strength. Whether Sorley was guilty or innocent the young man—as had been said before—could only decide on what evidence he possessed; but in any event, seeing that the gentleman in question was Marie's uncle, Fuller wished to arrive at the truth without too much publicity. For publicity on the face of it, meant the intervention of the police.

"Do you know that I went to dinner at Miss Grison's boarding-house?" asked Alan in a would-be careless manner.

"No," retorted Sorley, again looking uneasy, "and it does not interest me if you did," his manner gave the lie to this statement. "That woman hates me and is trying to injure me!"

"In what way?"

Sorley looked hard at the speaker. "By bringing back the peacock."

"I don't quite understand." And Fuller did not, as the remark puzzled him a great deal, lacking, as it did, a feasible explanation.

"The woman stole the peacock," said Sorley gloomily, "because she knew that I valued it and knew also that there was a riddle connected with it which would probably result in a treasure being found. For over twenty years she resisted all my supplications and threats to give it back, and I did not dare to move in the matter—as I told you before, Alan—lest she should destroy it. Yet here she comes down secretly and puts back the peacock in its old place without a word of explanation."

"Have you asked her why she behaved in this manner?"

"No; I am only too content to have the golden bird back again without asking questions. She would probably tell a falsehood since she hates me."

"But if she hates you, Mr. Sorley, why did she give you back what you so very greatly desired?"

"That is what I wish to know," cried the elder man excitedly. "It is for no good object I am certain. She means to cause trouble in some way, but how, I fail to see. Remember her threats in this very room when she was here."

Alan nodded. "It is very strange," he murmured, and wondered if Sorley really meant what he said, or whether he was preparing an excuse for himself should he be told—say by the police—that Grison at the time of his death had possessed the golden peacock. "It is very strange," said Alan again, and pondered deeply, while Sorley watched him gloomily and in a shifty stealthy manner. He seemed more uneasy and anxious than ever.

"Why did you visit Mrs. Grison's boarding-house?" he asked abruptly.

Fuller roused himself. "To hear all I could about the Rotherhithe crime, Mr. Sorley. Dick was at the inquest—"

"Dick. Who is Dick?"

"Dick Latimer, a reporter, the man who shares my rooms. We were at college together. You have met him down here, Mr. Sorley."

"Yes, yes, I remember now. His name slipped my memory. So he was at the inquest, was he?"

"Yes, and like myself he is very interested in this crime."

"There is nothing interesting about it," said Sorley abruptly once more; "some scoundrel of a sailor murdered the poor devil."

"But the motive?" asked Fuller, wondering if his host hinted at the dead man's possession of the peacock.

Sorley shrugged his shoulders. "Have those sort of people ever any motive, Alan," he asked skeptically.

"Certainly. A man doesn't put his head in a noose for nothing."

"A noose." Mr. Sorley shivered and put his hand to his throat with an uncomfortable look, "no I suppose a man would keep clear of the gallows if he could. But—but—well never mind, Alan, let us change this disagreeable subject. I promised to show you my own private collection of gems."

"Yes, I shall be pleased to look at them," answered the young man, who saw that his last remark had greatly affected his host, a fact which again aroused his suspicions, and made him shrink from the dapper gentleman.

Mr. Sorley made no reply, but went to a panel marked with a cross cut in its wood, which formed a portion of the inside wall of the library. He fumbled at some spring for a moment and then the panel slid into a groove to display a cupboard with many shelves upon which were ranged trays of jewels. One by one the man brought them to the central table, and his eyes glittered with fanatic joy as he pointed out their various beauties. And certainly throughout many years he had succeeded in gathering together a number of precious stones.

"Little by little I have collected for over thirty years," explained Mr. Sorley, mounting his hobby-horse, "buying here and there whenever I had the chance, and sometimes selling at a bargain what I had bought, so as to get some particular gem. There are quite six thousand pounds worth of jewels here, Alan, and only my poverty has prevented my buying more."

Fuller did not hint, as he might have done, that the collector had used his ward's income as well as his own to indulge his expensive taste, and had also sold furniture to which he had no claim for the same reason. Under the circumstances it was foolish to quarrel with Sorley on this point. Until the mystery of the murder and the peacock was solved Alan wished to keep on good terms with the man, who evidently had to do with both. He therefore examined the gems and listened patiently to Sorley's explanations. And the jewels were certainly well worth looking at. There were diamonds cut and uncut, rubies colored like port wine, and some of the true pigeon blood hue; emeralds displayed their verdant tints, and there were sapphires the color of a summer sky. Pearls were conspicuous by their absence, as if kept in a collection and not worn, Sorley explained this—they became discolored; but beryl stones, amethysts, carbuncles, and opals, many-hued as a rainbow were displayed on the black velvet of the shallow trays. The collection was not of extraordinary value, but Sorley gloated over his darlings, streaming the stones between his fingers, holding them up to the light, and pointing out to Fuller the particular excellence of each.

"It's an expensive hobby," said Alan, after an hour had been passed in this way, for Sorley talked on with the merciless zeal of a collector.

"In a manner it is, my boy; but then gems are always worth money, and I can always sell these if necessary." He shuddered, "I hope it will not be necessary. It would be like parting with my life to give up these. I know every single one and each represents days and weeks of bargaining. I could tell you the history of each gem."

"I fear that would be too long," said Fuller hastily, for he was growing weary of this enthusiasm; "but are you not afraid of these being stolen?"

"No," snapped Sorley, putting back the trays and adjusting the panel, so that it looked exactly like a portion of the wall, "no one would ever guess that the jewels were behind that cross. You know, but I don't think you will rob me, Alan. Ha! ha! ha!"

"I am not fond enough of gems to do so," said the young man indifferently; "but you said at the vicarage that you feared lest you should be murdered for the sake of your collection."

"Did I? Did I? I forget."

"You certainly did," insisted Fuller, looking at him searchingly; "and you seemed to be very much afraid."

"Well of course there is six thousand pounds worth of gems there. Some one might—"

"Have you any particular person in your mind?"

Sorley turned gray and gasped. "Why do you say that?" he asked sharply.

Fuller looked at him harder than ever. "I told you that I dined at Miss Grison's boarding-house," he explained; "while there I met with a man, who called himself Morad-Bakche!"

Mr. Sorley gasped again. "The Indian," he muttered nervously.

"Ah!" Alan gasped. "So you have seen him."

"Seen him, seen him. What do you mean?"

"I mean that this Morad-Bakche came down to Belstone to ask after the peacock, and gained some information from Mrs. Verwin at the inn. She told him how it was suspected that the Grisons had stolen the ornament, and gave him the Bloomsbury address."

"So Morad-Bakche is at Miss Grison's," muttered Sorley, sitting down; "that makes it more certain that she is up to no good in connection with me."

"I thought it strange myself," said Alan dryly.

Sorley did not reply, but looked hard at the carpet, "What do you think of this Indian?" he asked abruptly.

"I think he is a man who will stick at nothing to get the peacock."

"Then he is after that?"

"You should know," said Alan meaningly.

"How should I know." There was a note of defiance in the man's voice.

"Because Mrs. Verwin declared that Bakche went to look at The Monastery. If he did, I think—from what you hinted just now—that you saw him."

"Yes, I saw him, and what is more I spoke to him. Confound that woman! She chatters too much."

"Why should she not?" questioned the solicitor. "The story of the peacock is well known—that is the history of its being a fetish of the Inderwicks. That it can reveal a treasure is not known, I fancy."

"No. Quite so. After all Mrs. Verwin only said what everyone else can say, Alan. But I wish she hadn't told Bakche about the Grisons."

Fuller shrugged his shoulders. "What does it matter now. You have the peacock in your own possession."

"Yes, I have the peacock, and if Bakche learns that, he may try and murder me. He is just the man—as you say—to stick at nothing."

"Oh, then, that was what you meant when you hinted your fears to me on Christmas Day at the vicarage?"

"Yes." Sorley wiped his face again, looking still gray and anxious, "and of course Miss Grison had brought back the peacock by that time. If I hadn't got it I should not be so afraid. Ah," he rose and began to walk up and down in a startled way. "I see her game now Alan. She will tell Bakche how I have the peacock and he will—and he will—oh Alan!"

The man gripped Fuller's arm and appeared to be thoroughly frightened at the idea of a raid being made by the Indian. The solicitor gently forced Sorley to sit down again and asked for an explanation. "You must be frank with me if I am to help you," said the solicitor.

"Oh I shall be frank," panted Sorley, as though he had been running for a long distance. "I can trust you, and you want to marry my niece. It is to your benefit to be on my side, and then—"

Alan cut short this vague chatter. "Tell me about Bakche?"

"Well then, he did come to The Monastery about July last. He called here openly, and told me what Mrs. Verwin had stated. He gave me to understand that he was the representative of the Kam royal people, and knew all about the peacock."

"How did he learn?"

"From some family papers which stated that the Begum had given the gems to George Inderwick because he saved her life and the life of her son."

"Hum!" murmured Alan to himself. "So the excuse of having been told by an Inderwick in India it was lost."

"Bakche wanted the peacock, and I told him that it was lost?"

"Did you say who had stolen it?"

"No, I didn't. I thought if I did, that Miss Grison out of spite might give it to him, and so I should lose the treasure."

"Did Bakche know that the peacock would reveal the whereabouts of—"

Sorley interrupted eagerly. "Of course he did. The papers in question told him that Ferrier had manufactured the peacock as a guide. Bakche declared that the Begum had no right to give family jewels to Inderwick, and insisted that I should surrender the peacock so that he could trace and recover them. I said that the bird was lost, and he went away greatly dissatisfied, saying that he would look for it."

"Of course," said Alan nodding; "and as Mrs. Verwin had told him that the

104

Grisons had stolen it, and had given him the boarding-house address, he went there to get it from her."

"I wonder why she didn't give it to him to spite me," groaned Sorley.

Fuller was on the point of saying that she could not because her brother possessed the desired article, but checked himself. He did not wish to let Sorley know that he knew how Baldwin Grison had been murdered for the sake of that very peacock. And apparently from what had just been said, Sorley believed that the sister had always possessed it. "She preferred to give it to you," said Alan.

"Yes," cried the man, "and why? Because she knew that Bakche wanted it. Now she will tell him and he will come and murder me to get it."

"He may not be so bloodthirsty," said Fuller encouragingly, "and after all if you fear that, why not give him the peacock."

"No," said Sorley energetically, "I shan't give up the chance of getting the treasure. It belongs to Marie. I can't as her guardian give up that."

"No." Alan thought that Sorley was rather thinking of himself, than of his niece, "but what's to be done?"

"Nothing, I tell you, nothing," said the other man almost fiercely, "I shall hide the peacock along with my own jewels behind that panel. No one will ever guess that it is there, and I shall ask the village policeman to keep an eye on The Monastery in case Bakche tries to rob me ... And what will you do, Alan?"

"My course is obvious, Mr. Sorley. I shall try and solve the riddle."

"Yes, yes. And we can then get the treasure, and Bakche will be outwitted. Even if he steals the peacock, we have the drawing to unravel the problem. Go! go! Alan go! and hold your tongue, for Miss Grison may not have told the man that I have the bird."

"Perhaps," said Fuller dubiously, "time alone will show!" and he took his leave feeling that Miss Grison had probably informed Bakche about the peacock, on the chance that he would trouble the man she hated.

CHAPTER XI

In due course Mr. Fuller returned to his office and to the chambers in Barkers Inn, only to find that Dick had not yet put in an appearance. Alan regretted his absence greatly, since Latimer was the one person to whom he could talk freely. Needless to say, the young man was bubbling over with the information he had acquired, and found it very difficult to think of anything else, which was scarcely a good state of mind in which to attend to his clients' affairs. Had the solicitor been able, he would have set everything else aside until he had solved the mystery of the Rotherhithe murder, and had learned the secret of the peacock; but as he had to earn his bread and butter, such indulgence in gratifying his curiosity was not to be thought of. Alan felt very unsettled for quite a week after his arrival in Chancery Lane.

Nor were his anxieties allayed when he heard from his clerk, that during his absence, an urchin who called himself Alonzo had haunted the office, demanding on every occasion to see Mr. Fuller. And the odd thing about the matter was, that when Alan really did return, Jotty—to give him his slum name—failed to put in an appearance. The solicitor did not dare to write to the lad saying that he would be glad to accord him an interview on a settled date, since Miss Grison might read the letter and prevent the boy's attendance. For the same reason Fuller did not call at the Thimble Square house, lest its landlady, being extremely sharp, might—and probably would—guess that he was tampering with Jotty's loyalty. As a matter of fact Alan was not, as he did not seek to question the page about the lady, but simply wished to learn what he had to say concerning his association with Baldwin Grison. And as the dead man's sister desired that the assassin of her brother should be captured and punished, Fuller deemed that he was right in using every means to forward her aims. Jotty—Alan felt sure of this—was a valuable witness, and, if dexterously questioned, might be able to throw some light on the darkness which environed the crime. It certainly seemed that the next step to be taken was the examination of the street-arab, but as the lad did not put in an appearance, and Fuller—on the before-mentioned grounds—did not dare to awaken Miss Grison's suspicions by sending for him, he had to wait patiently. And this, coupled with the continued absence of Latimer, did not tend to sweeten the young man's now irritable temper.

In fact the wear and tear of thought so displayed itself outwardly that when Dick did arrive he commented openly on his friend's sorry looks. The reporter came back to London by the night mail, and finding when he got to Barkers Inn that Alan had already gone to his office he followed him there as soon as a bath and a change of clothes had made him respectable. Breakfast he had already dispatched in a restaurant on his way from the railway station. Dick, having enjoyed his holiday, was in a happy frame of mind, but his smiles left him when he saw his chum's anxious face.

"What the deuce is the matter?" asked Mr. Latimer, when the first greetings were over, and he was smoking comfortably in a chair, "you look sick."

"I am sick—with worry," said Fuller emphatically, "it's that infernal case."

"Oh," said Dick leisurely; "which part of it in particular?"

"The whole. I have much to tell you, as I want your opinion. The more I look into the matter the more confused does it grow."

"Have you been looking into the matter?" asked Dick provokingly calm.

"Yes, I have, and in consequence I have scarcely enjoyed my Christmas at home," cried Alan.

"Not even with the most charming girl in the world?"

"No. Because she asks questions, and I have to keep a great deal from her."

"On account of her uncle?"

"Precisely!"

"Hum! Is he guilty?"

"I don't know. Anyway he has the peacock."

Latimer pushed back his chair and let his pipe fall. "What?"

"He has the peacock. I've seen it, and what is more he allowed me to make a drawing of it," and Alan fumbled among his papers for the sketch. "Here it is, Dicky!"

"The devil!" ejaculated the journalist staring at the painted bird; "then the man murdered Grison after all."

"I'm not sure. I have my doubts."

"But hang it, man, you know that Grison was murdered for the sake of the original of this." He laid his finger on the sketch, "and if Sorley has it, he must have taken it out of the murdered man's room."

"Well you won't be so sure of that when you have heard my story," said Alan in a tart way, for his nerves were all jangling.

"Tell it, old son," remarked Latimer, recovering his pipe, and not another word did he utter until he was in full possession of Alan's information.

The solicitor told him everything from the time he had arrived at Belstone until the moment of departure, and carried up the narrative as far as London by relating how Jotty had been haunting the office.

"And now that I am back, the little fool won't turn up," finished Fuller, greatly exasperated, "and I dare not send for him."

"No," nodded Dick grimly, "that is very obvious. The quieter you keep this business the better it will be until we get at its truth. Hum! It's a most extraordinary complication, Alan." He stared at the sketch which was now lying on the table. "Have you solved this riddle?"

"No. So far as I can see there isn't any riddle to solve."

"It looks like it," murmured Dick, looking hard at Fuller's artistic effort; "so my sixth sense was right when it told me that Morad-Bakche was mixed up in the matter."

Alan nodded crossly. "But I wish that your sixth sense would tell you who murdered Grison."

"We shan't learn that until we question the sister. If she admits that she took the peacock to The Monastery at Belstone, Sorley will be exonerated. If she declares that she did not, Sorley will have to account for its being in his possession."

"But confound it man, can't you see that if—as Sorley says—she wishes to get him into trouble, she will certainly decline to tell the truth."

"What is the truth anyhow?" asked Dick, after the fashion of Pontius Pilate.

"Lord knows!" replied Fuller disconsolately. "Of course Jotty never said that Grison had the peacock on the precise night of his murder. The boy only saw it on previous occasions. It is quite possible that the dead man may have given it to his sister to send to Sorley and make trouble. They both hated the man, and evidently with good reason."

"Yes; but if that were the case, it would argue that Grison knew he would be murdered, which is ridiculous. Besides Sorley told a lie about his motor bicycle, which shows that he does not wish it known he was able to slip up to town and back again without making use of the publicity of the railway. I am inclined to suspect Sorley as the guilty person."

"Do you think Bakche may have killed Grison?"

"No; for if he had he would scarcely have given the peacock to the sister for Sorley's benefit."

Alan nodded. "I thought that myself," he said slowly. "Well what is to be done now, Dicky?"

"Inspector Moon ought to know," said Latimer significantly.

Fuller jumped up quickly, "Not just now, Dick; don't say anything to him. He would certainly arrest Sorley straight away, and I wish to spare Marie the disgrace."

"But the truth is bound to come out sooner or later, Alan," remarked Dick, perplexed how to act.

"The truth! Quite so. Still, when known, the truth may not implicate Mr. Sorley. For all we know he may be perfectly innocent."

"He may be," retorted Latimer dryly, and with a shrug, "but to my mind he seems to be deeply involved in the matter. The evidence is strong—"

"The circumstantial evidence," corrected Alan quickly.

"I don't see that your interpolated word matters a cent, sonny. The peacock being in the man's possession points to his guilt."

"Unless Miss Grison left it secretly at The Monastery."

"There is that chance certainly," admitted Dick with another shrug. "However as Sorley is not aware that he is suspected he won't try to bolt, so under the circumstances I shall hold my tongue until things straighten out a trifle. But if he does try to leave the country, I must speak, Alan, and so must you, else we may be accused of compounding a felony. As a lawyer you ought to know that much."

"I do know it," said Fuller impatiently, "and if Sorley is guilty he assuredly must be arrested and punished when the case is proved. All the same we must give him the benefit of the doubt until his criminality is placed beyond all question."

"Why do you defend the man so?" asked Latimer suspiciously; "you don't approve of him, as you have told me dozens of times."

"I am not thinking of the man so much as of Marie. The shame of having her uncle tried and hanged for a sordid murder would certainly break her heart, Dick."

"Well there's something in that. How love does complicate honest behavior. But that you love Miss Inderwick you would have no hesitation in telling Moon the truth."

"I admit that. But things being as they are, I must ask you not to speak to the police until I give you leave."

"Very good, old son. I see we'll both end in jail, for tampering with the course of justice. All the same I shall hold my tongue. And now that being settled so far may I ask what you intend to do?"

"I can hardly say. What in your opinion is the step I should take?"

"Question Miss Grison and learn if she took back the peacock," said Dick without a moment's hesitation.

"But hang it all man, she will only tell lies."

"Why should she?"

"Your common-sense, let alone what we talked about a few moments ago, should tell you," said Fuller impatiently. "If she did take all that trouble to implicate Sorley, she won't give herself away by acknowledging it. The admission that she concealed the peacock in its old cupboard would exonerate Sorley. You can see that?"

"Yes! Of course since she hates the man, she–– Hullo, what's up?" Latimer asked this question because Alan suddenly started to his feet and listened intently to a noise in the outer office.

"I hear a boy's voice," said the solicitor hastily throwing open the door just in time to permit Jotty to be pushed into the room by the indignant clerk with whom he had been arguing. "Oh it's you, young man. I thought so. That's all right, Seymour, I'll attend to him," and Fuller, closing the door, pointed out a chair to the page. "Sit down, Jotty."

"Alonzer, please sir," said the lad quickly, "I don't want t' hey anythin' t' do wiff m' ole bad self. I've turned over a new leaf, Miss Grison ses."

"We'll take a look at the old leaf before you do that finally," said Alan, seating himself at his desk. "Just now and for the next half hour, you are the disreputable Jotty, and not the Sunday-school Alonzo."

The boy grinned cunningly and nodded, glancing round the office and at Latimer in a furtive and stealthy manner. He did not wear his page's suit of

110

many buttons, but a civilian kit of badly-cut tweed clothes. But as his sleek hair was well oiled, and he had a penny sprig of holly in his button-hole it must be presumed that Jotty was out for the day, and was very pleased with his general appearance. Being small and wizen, his legs scarcely touched the ground, when seated, and he looked not unlike a monkey. But his very shrewd and restless eyes, which were taking in everything to be stored in his active brain, showed that he was a clever and decidedly dangerous lad.

"Who's him, sir?" asked Jotty, pointing at Dick in negro fashion with his sharp chin, "d'y wan' me t' tork wen he's here?"

"Yes, and you know this gentleman, so don't pretend ignorance."

"Ho yes," murmured Jotty with pretended surprise, "y'wos at th' inquitch wosn't y'sir."

"I was, Jotty. You and I and Inspector Moon had a talk."

"'Ad we, sir?" asked the lad with a vacant look. Fuller leaned over and gave him a shake. "No nonsense, boy," he said sharply, "you have to answer a few questions. I'm glad you have come to see me at last, you young rip."

"At larst, sir," protested the page meekly, "why I've bin an' bin an' bin ever so oftin and couldn't spot yer nohow, sir. An' t'aint easy t' git out of th' house wen she's got her eyes abaout nohow. But it's m'day orf an' I come along t' see if I cud make a quid or two."

"Your price is a high one," said Alan dryly, "how do I know what you have to tell me is worth a pound, or a quid as you call it."

"Oh I ain't got nothink t' tell," said Jotty readily, "but I thought es y'd help a pore cove es wants t' be respectable."

"I shall help you at a price," said Fuller, who did all the talking while Dick smoked in silence and kept his ears and eyes open. Latimer had not a very good opinion of the witness, as he thought him cunning, and likely to tell lies unless he was driven into a corner, and perhaps for that very reason. "Do you know this?" asked Alan, pushing the sketch under Jotty's shrewd blue eyes. Dick frowned at the action, as he deemed it wise that Alan should have kept the fact of the peacock being in Sorley's possession to himself, in the meantime at all events.

"Yessir," said Jotty quickly, "it's a picter of him es was kind t' me's goldbird es he showed me times an' agin."

"Well then," said Alan, and Dick's frown relaxed as he spoke, "this picture, as you call it was taken long ago, before Mr. Grison got the peacock. Was the bird like that sketch, or is there any change."

"Nosir. It wos just like that here. Wiff a big tail and shiny things on it. Them spots is th' shiny things ain't they, sir?"

Alan nodded, while Dick grinned at this compliment to his friend's artistic abilities. "When did you see the peacock last?"

"On the very night es he es wos kind t' me wos murdered."

"Can you swear to that?" asked Alan with secret dismay, for this reply seemed to prove that Sorley was guilty.

"Yessir. I kin swear hard I kin," said Jotty with a frank smile.

"Are you sure that Mr. Grison didn't give the peacock to someone, say a day or so before he met with his death?"

"Him give it away," cried Jotty with supreme contempt, "why sir, he es wos good t' me, ses t' me es he'd rather die nor give up thet shiny thing. An' die he did, when it wos took."

"Who took it, boy?" demanded Dick suddenly.

"Him es slipped the knife int' th' pore cove."

"Are you sure that Grison had the peacock on the night he died?" asked Alan, fighting against hope for Marie's sake.

"I'd swear t' it anywhere, sir," said Jotty confidently. "I liked t' hev a look et that there shiny thing, and him es wos good t' me, he shows it t' me most every night, saying wot lots of swell things it cud buy. Every night he showed it t' me," repeated Jotty with emphasis, "and afore he went t'bed that night he let me 'ave a squint."

"On the night he was murdered."

"On the night he was done for," said Jotty in his own simple way.

"That seems conclusive, Alan," put in Latimer.

"Yes," said the lawyer with a sigh, then added under his breath. "Poor Marie, what a shock for her. Jotty, you liked Mr. Grison, didn't you?"

"Yessir, no end. He wos good t' me, and guv' me things t' eat an' drink. Oh my," Jotty rubbed his lean stomach vulgarly, "the baked taters an' corfee and saveloys I hed when he stood sam."

"Then you would like the man who stabbed him to be punished?" pursued Fuller artfully.

"Yessir; and bring him t' th' gallers I shell somehow."

"But you have no idea who murdered Mr. Grison?" remarked Latimer quickly.

"Oh hevn't I? Perhaps not, and praps I ain't sich a fool es you'd think me t' be, mister. I knows whot I knows anyhow."

"What is that, Jotty."

The lad looked indescribably cunning. "I ain't agoin' t' tell till I'm a dead cert es I'm right."

"But if you tell me, Jotty, I can help you."

"I don' want no help," said the boy sullenly.

"If I speak to Inspector Moon you'll have to tell," said Dick sharply.

"Sha'n't, so there," growled Jotty, his shrill voice becoming gruff as if the change to manhood had suddenly taken place.

"You shall."

Jotty made no reply, but looked at both gentlemen with a mulish expression evidently determined not to speak. "It's wuth a quid or two," he muttered after a long pause.

"What is worth a quid or two?" demanded Alan, eyeing him with a strong dislike, for he objected to the brat's obstinacy.

"What I knows."

"What do you know?"

"That's tellin's."

"If I give you a quid, as you call it, will you tell."

"Yessir," said Jotty promptly, and held out a curved claw in which Alan, as promptly, placed a sovereign. The boy bit it to prove its quality and then spat on it for luck. "I knows someone es wos with him es wos good t' me, on that night," said Jotty, agreeably supplying the information.

"Who was the person?" asked Latimer, while Alan winced, quite expecting to hear the name of Sorley.

"Sha'n't tell."

"Do you know the name?"

"Yessir. Leastways I spelled it out fro' th' letter. Oh I've 'ad schoolin', I 'ave, gents both, and knows m' letters somehow."

"What is this letter?" asked Alan in a peremptory tone.

"A letter es the cove es came wrote sayin' he'd come. I never sawr him es

113

wrote the letter," explained Jotty, "cos, after I seed the peacock on th' night; him es wos good t' me turned me out to dos elsewheres. But I fun' the letter I did in them ole clothes."

"Whose old clothes?"

"Him es wos good t' me."

"Mr. Grison?"

"Yessir. He fell an' got covered with mud like. An' he ses t' me he'd like me t' taike the mud orf, and I did. In th' coat I fun' th' letter, an' wrapped up marbles in it. I furgot t' put it back," added Jotty in an apologetic manner, "an' es he es wos good t' me didn't ask fur no letter, I never said anything, I didn't, nohow."

"When was this?" questioned Alan anxiously. "On the day afore he es wos good t' me wos made a dead un."

"Have you the letter?"

"Yes sir!" and Jotty clutched the breast of his ill-fitting jacket, "but I want another quid or two for it."

"You know how to make a bargain, young man," said Latimer humorously; "just hand over that letter at once."

"I sha'n't. So there," said Jotty, turning obstinate again. "It's wuth another quid anyhow. An' I sawr him es wrote it when he called t' see him es wos good t' me afore."

"Oh this person called to see Mr. Grison before, did he."

"Onct or twice he did. Allays at night, and then they torks."

"What about?"

"I dunno, sir. I never heard. Him es was good t' me, he allays turned me out wen the gent came."

"Oh," said Dick meditatively, "so this visitor was a gent?"

"Yes sir. A real gent, wiff slap-up clothes and—"

The description sounded like that of Sorley, and Alan stretched out his hand. "I want that letter, you imp?" he said impressively.

"Give me a quid an' it's yours."

Fuller shrugged his shoulders and glanced at Latimer, who nodded. It was unpleasant being dictated to by a boy, but the issues were so great that Dick's nod intimated it was best to agree, and get the epistle in question with the least possible trouble. Money was scarce with Fuller, but so anxious was he to arrive at the truth that he reluctantly brought forth another sovereign. Jotty clawed it and went through the same ceremony. He then produced a letter written on very excellent paper, which was dirty with having been in his pocket for some length of time, probably to wrap up the marbles he had mentioned. In his anxiety Dick rose and looked over his friend's shoulder to read the letter. It did not take long, as it only consisted of a date, a line and the writer's initials as follows, on a plain sheet of gray note-paper without any address:—

"11 *November*.

"Will see you seven o'clock, 13: 11: 08.

"R. V. S."

"Is it his writing?" asked Latimer, referring to Sorley, but not mentioning the name because of Jotty's presence.

"I think so. I can compare it with the letter he wrote me. The initials are certainly his, and the appointment is for the night of the murder."

"But he wos up afore," put in Jotty, who grinned in a very satisfied manner, as he well might do, considering he had just made two pounds.

"Who was up before?" asked Latimer sharply. "Him es wrote thet letter."

"Can you describe the man?"

"Ain't I done so," said Jotty in an injured tone, "he wos a real gent wiff slap-up clothes. Hadn't got no hair on his face he hadn't and torked es if every cove wos dirt. Stiff-like, too, an' an ole 'un, tryin' to look like a young toff."

Alan winced again as both the letter and Jotty's very excellent description seemed to prove that Sorley was the guilty person. "How do you know that this gentleman you describe wrote the letter?"

"Cos I seed him coming up an hour or so afore him es wos good t' me kicked th' bucket. I wos turned out, long afore he come in. So I goes away an' dosses wiff a friend o' mine, and never hears no more till nex' morning when Mother Slaig, she ups and ses es murder had bin done cruel."

"Is that all you know?"

"Every blessed bit, sir," said Jotty cheerfully. "Why didn't you tell this to Inspector Moon at the inquest?" demanded Latimer sharply.

"Cos there wasn't no quids in it then," retorted the boy impudently, "an' I do nothin' fur nothin', I do anyhow. An' now I've got wot I arsked fur," he placed his cap on his head, "I'm on t' give m'self a treat."

The youth had edged near the door by this time, and held it slightly open, evidently expecting to be stopped. Indeed Fuller put out an arm to detain him and ask further questions, only to cause Jotty to vanish in a remarkably swift space of time. Dick prevented Alan, who was about to follow.

"Let him go," said Latimer quickly, "we can always get hold of him when we want. Compare the letters?"

Without a word Alan did so, and placed both the one he had received from Sorley and that which Jotty had sold, under Dick's eye. The latter drew a long breath. "There's no doubt about it, Alan," he said sadly, "they are written by one and the same man. Sorley had an appointment with Grison at Mother Slaig's on the night of the crime, as this letter proves. Also Jotty declares that he saw him, for the description is very accurate. Hum! I wish you had not shown the boy that drawing of the peacock."

"The moment I did show it, I guessed that I had made a mistake," said Fuller quickly; "and so I was forced against my will to tell a necessary lie in order to lull the lad's suspicions. But it seems evident, Dick, that Sorley got the peacock from Grison, and that the yarn about the sister leaving it, is wholly untrue. What's to be done now?"

"Sorley must be arrested for murder," said Dick decisively.

"No, no. He may be innocent after all!"

"Innocent when you have seen that note and heard Jotty's description?"

"Well," said Alan anxiously, "wait for three days before doing anything."

Dick wavered then made up his mind abruptly. "All right, I'll wait," he said gruffly.

CHAPTER XII

AN INDIAN CLIENT

Dick Latimer had promised to hold his peace for three days before imparting to the inspector who was in charge of the Rotherhithe case what had been discovered with reference to Sorley. All the same he was troubled in his mind, as he could not be sure if he was acting rightly. Much as he sympathized with Fuller because the man likely to be arrested was the uncle of the girl to whom his friend was engaged, it did not seem right that a criminal should remain at large. The journalist indeed thought that Alan's objections were rather sentimental, and that justice should be done in spite of Marie's feelings, which assuredly would be outraged. Nevertheless he admitted that Fuller was placed in a difficult position, and it was natural that he should wish to gain time in the hope of proving Mr. Sorley's innocence, and so avert the scandal.

But, so far as Dick could see, there was no chance of clearing the man's character. He had been with Grison, whom he openly detested, on the very night when the murder was committed, and shortly before it took place, as was conclusively proved not only by the letter, but by the evidence of the street-arab, who certainly could never have invented such an accurate description of the guilty person. Then again, Jotty had sworn that on the night of the crime he had been given his usual treat of a display of the peacock, and since that was now in Sorley's possession, it could only have passed into it directly from the dead man. And as the presumed criminal's full name, Randolph Vernon Sorley, was intimated by the initials R. V. S., and the note to Grison was certainly in his handwriting there appeared to be no doubt that he had murdered the miserable creature to obtain wrongful possession of the Inderwick fetish. Finally, since that had been stolen, all Sorley's energies had been bent upon getting it again, and in desperation he probably had struck the fatal blow. Of course the story of Miss Grison having taken the peacock back to The Monastery was one—so Dick thought—deliberately invented to implicate the woman and account for the reappearance of the desired article.

Upon this evidence it could scarcely be doubted that Sorley was guilty, and when the fact that he had purchased a motor bicycle was taken into account, Latimer could see no flaw in the indictment. More than ever he considered it necessary to have Sorley brought to justice, which would be done as soon as Inspector Moon was informed of these discoveries. But having made a promise, Dick faithfully kept it, in spite of the many qualms of conscience he daily felt. Then on the third day he took up a newspaper to find a new and extraordinary development of the case. After mastering the article, which appeared in *The Latest News*, a daily paper much given to gossip, he jumped into a hansom and drove direct to Fuller's office. It chanced that Alan was not engaged, so Dick entered at once into his friend's private room, flourishing the paper.

"Have you seen this?" he asked, placing it before Alan.

"Seen what?" asked the other, glancing at the heading indicated, and then he took in the meaning at once. "Good Lord!"

He might well utter the ejaculation, for the article contained an account of the Inderwick fetish given—as was intimated—by no less a person than Miss Louisa Grison. The story of Ferrier was narrated, much in the same fashion as it appeared in the manuscript at The Monastery, and it was very plainly stated that a treasure was to be found when the riddle attached to the peacock was solved. Finally, Miss Grison ended the interview with the man, who had written the article, by saying that her dead brother had possessed the golden bird at the time of his death, and that in her mind there was no doubt that he had been murdered for its sake. "Find the peacock," said Miss Grison, "and you find the assassin of my dear brother." Then the article terminated with comments by the writer on the extraordinary and romantic story which had been set forth, and with the original remark culled from Hamlet, "That there were more things in heaven and earth, etc., etc."

"I wonder he didn't add that truth is stranger than fiction," remarked Dick, while Alan hastily skimmed the account. "It is just as original. Well, my son, and what do you think now?"

"I think," replied Fuller, very decisively, "that Jotty has repeated to his mistress what he told us, and she has taken steps to trap Sorley."

"But she doesn't know that he has the peacock—for certain that is?"

Alan shrugged his shoulders. "My mistake in showing the drawing to the boy has proved that Sorley has the bird. Miss Grison, I daresay, knew that no sketch had been made of it before it was taken away; and in any event what Jotty told us is sufficient evidence to secure Sorley's arrest."

"I think so indeed. There is no longer any need for me to keep silence."

"Well," said Fuller hesitatingly, "I suppose there isn't. Moon is certain to see this account, and will come to ask Miss Grison why she has made the matter public after promising to be silent. She can only excuse herself by repeating Jotty's story, and Moon will certainly go down to Belstone to arrest Sorley. Poor Marie!"

"I'm not so sure you can call her that," put in Dick hastily. "After all if the man is a criminal, it is better that she should not be in his company."

"But the disgrace to the name—"

"To Sorley's name, not to Miss Inderwick's. Besides when she marries you she will change her name. It is no use being sentimental any longer, my boy," said Latimer resolutely. "The man must be punished. I'm off to see the inspector, and tell him what I know."

"But Dick won't it be best to question Miss Grison first, and learn if she really has heard Jotty's story."

"I am quite sure she has," said the reporter emphatically, "else she would not have broken her promise to Moon. The matter of the peacock was kept silent so that the assassin, feeling safe, might betray himself—as he has done, by the way to you. Miss Grison, learning from the boy that Sorley is guilty, has taken the opportunity of making the story as public as possible so that the man can't escape."

"He may see the papers and take warning," suggested Alan. "I expect this tale will be in every paper in the kingdom to-morrow."

"All the more reason that I should see Moon at once. I am not going to dilly-dally any more, Alan, but do my duty, as I expect you to do yours."

"I can't blame you. Go and see Moon."

Latimer hesitated at the door. "You won't wire to Sorley, or send that paper to him, I suppose."

"No. If the man is guilty and it certainly looks as though he were, he must be punished. I shall not interfere, unpleasant as the scandal will be for Marie. Go and do your duty, Dick, by telling Moon, and I shall do mine by keeping perfectly quiet."

Latimer argued no longer but took his departure, leaving Alan much disturbed in his own mind. And no wonder. Marie did not love her uncle, who had always treated her with indifference, and had made use of her money for his own purposes. Still, it would be a terrible shock for her to hear that he had murdered the brother of Miss Grison, and of course the shame of having a relative hanged would be great. And Fuller did not see how Mr. Sorley could escape the gallows, since the evidence on the whole was so very decisive. At the best he could only defend himself by putting forward the story about Miss Grison, and that was but a weak line to take up.

"Hum!" said Alan, opening the drawer of his desk to look at the sketch he had made, "I wish I had not showed this to Jotty. He must have mentioned it to Miss Grison, and from that fact she probably guessed that Sorley had the peacock. The man will certainly be arrested, for he will have no time to escape."

As Alan murmured this he glanced idly at the paper which Dick had brought, and saw that it was dated the previous day, and of course had been issued yesterday morning. It occurred to the young man that chance might possibly bring the paper to Sorley's notice, since four and twenty hours—if not more— had elapsed since its publication. And if the man was warned in time he assuredly would escape, before Inspector Moon could lay hands on him.

Fuller hoped that this would be the case, if only to spare Marie the shame and pain of the scandal. But after all it was doubtful if the account would fall into Sorley's hands immediately, as few newspapers arrived at Belstone, and the doings of the world were always hours and days and, at times, weeks late. The solicitor shook his head dubiously, and wrapping up his sketch in the journal, he placed both in the drawer of his desk. There seemed nothing for it but to wait for Sorley's arrest, and to hear what defense he would make to the charge brought against him.

Shortly a card was presented to the lawyer by his clerk, and on seeing the name Fuller ordered the owner to be shown in at once. In a few moments he was face to face with Mr. Morad-Bakche, who looked calm and aristocratic and—as Alan judged—indifferent. Yet if he had seen the article in *The Latest News*, and really had come to England to search for the treasure, Bakche surely would not feign a nonchalance he could not possibly feel.

"How are you, Mr. Bakche?" asked, Alan, polite and watchful, while placing a chair for the Indian, "so you have come to see me as you said you would."

"Yes, sir, and about a very important subject," replied Bakche, sitting down stiffly, and taking a newspaper out of his pocket.

"Yes?" said Alan inquiringly, though of course the moment he saw the paper produced he knew why the man had come to see him.

Bakche doubled back the journal and pointed out the article with a slender brown finger. "Have you seen this?" he asked quietly.

It was not to Fuller's interest to admit anything, as it was necessary to conduct this interview with great caution. The young man quietly read again the account of the interview with Miss Grison. All the time, Bakche was looking at him hard, trying to guess by the expression of Alan's face what he truly thought.

But the solicitor was prepared for the scrutiny, and kept an unmoved countenance. "Very interesting," remarked Fuller coolly, when he had finished.

"But not new to you, sir, I presume."

"Well no, Mr. Bakche. The story told by Miss Grison is well known in Belstone, the parish of which my father is the vicar. I have heard it before."

"Have you heard before that this man Grison was murdered for the sake of the peacock?" demanded the Indian rather impatiently, and thereby showed that his indifference was mainly pretence.

"It was commonly reported in Belstone that the Grisons, brother and sister, had stolen the peacock from the Inderwick family when they left The Monastery some twenty years ago. But, pardon me, Mr. Bakche, why do you come here and ask me these questions?"

"Can't you guess, sir?"

"How can I guess?" retorted Fuller cautiously.

"By putting two and two together, as is your English way," said Bakche in a calmer manner. "I told you when you dined at Miss Grison's that I had come to England in order to recover certain family property."

"You did. Well?"

"The property I referred to is the peacock of jewels,"

"How did you expect me to know that, Mr. Bakche?"

"I can answer that if you will reply to a question?"

"What is the question?"

"Do you know the story set forth in this article?" asked the Indian quickly.

"Yes. As I told you the whole countryside knows it."

"Then you must be aware that the Begum of Kam gave the jewels to Simon Ferrier. I told you that I am a descendant of the Rajah of Kam, so you must have guessed that I desired to obtain possession of the peacock."

"Quite so," said Fuller coolly, "but there was no need for me to say so."

Bakche was honest enough to admit this. "You are very cautious, you English gentlemen," he said with a faint sneer, "and no doubt you did not wish me to get the peacock."

"I fail to see how my telling you what you have now told me would aid you to get what belongs rightfully to another person."

"It does not belong to another person, but to me," cried Bakche wrathfully.

Alan raised his eyebrows. "How do you make that out?" he demanded in an exasperating manner. "George Inderwick's servant, Ferrier, manufactured the peacock for his master and—"

"And so manufactured it that in some strange way it reveals where the jewels of the Begum are concealed," finished the Indian sharply. "Understand Mr. Fuller, that I do not exactly claim the peacock—"

"You did just now," interrupted Alan in his turn, and shrugging.

"Only because I wish to learn where the jewels are hidden."

"Indeed. You will find that difficult, since for over one hundred years, the riddle of the peacock has been unsolved."

"Never mind," said Bakche doggedly. "If I see the bird I shall probably be able to learn the truth."

"And then?—" Alan raised his eyebrows again.

"Then," said the other confidently, "I shall take the jewels."

"You may not be allowed."

"Why not. The jewels belong to me as the descendant of the Rajah of Kam."

"You forget," said Fuller smoothly, "that the rajah's wife gave the same to George Inderwick because he saved her life and the life of her son."

"She had no right to do so," cried Bakche loudly, "the jewels were not her private property to dispose of, Mr. Fuller. They belonged to the family—to the state as it were. Royal treasure cannot be parted with in this way."

"I am not prepared to argue the matter, Mr. Bakche," remarked Fuller in a dry manner, "since—beyond the known story, which has become a Sussex legend —I am not acquainted with the exact facts. But I would point out that the rajah may have given his wife permission to reward her preserver in this way. Inderwick assuredly deserved a return for what he did."

Bakche bowed stiffly. "I admit that the gentleman acted bravely, and as I am descended from the young prince he saved I am indebted to him for the fact that I exist at all. Nevertheless, Mr. Fuller, the reward need not have taken the form of almost the whole of the royal treasure of Kam."

Alan shrugged his shoulders again. "The Begum was apparently a very grateful woman, Mr. Bakche. And if she had retained the treasure, it would have been confiscated by the British Government when the royalty of Kam was abolished."

"It is probable," said Bakche dryly; "but I think that the priests would have taken care to preserve the jewels and give them, when times became quieter, to the rightful owner."

"In which case you would now be in possession of them, I presume?"

"Certainly. I am a direct descendant of the prince saved by Mr. Inderwick, sir. As it is I shall certainly claim them."

"You have to find them first," retorted Alan coolly.

"Show me the peacock and I shall try to solve the riddle and find them."

Fuller laughed and shrugged. "Does that mean I am the criminal?"

"Oh no," Bakche hastened to explain smoothly; "but you may know where the peacock is to be found."

"Really, I don't quite follow your line of argument, Mr. Bakche.

"Let me put the matter in this way," said the Indian deliberately: "The peacock is not only valuable in itself, but also indicated the whereabouts of a great treasure. Miss Grison declares that her brother was murdered for the sake of the bird, so it is plain that the assassin must have known the meaning of the riddle."

"Still I cannot follow your line of argument," persisted Fuller; "so far as I know the riddle has never been solved, unless Baldwin Grison, who had the bird for over twenty years—according to his sister that is—guessed what has baffled everyone."

"Well," said Bakche sullenly, "whether he solved the riddle or not, some one who wanted the treasure murdered him to obtain the clue."

"On the other hand some rough sailor may have killed the man merely for the sake of getting the bird. It is valuable enough, as you say yourself, to account for the assassin risking his neck. But why come to me, Mr. Bakche, since on the face of it I can possibly know nothing."

"You know who wants the bird!"

"Oh yes. Miss Inderwick, from whose house it was stolen, and to whom I am engaged, wants the bird very much, since it belongs rightfully to her. But I hope you don't accuse a girl of twenty of the crime."

"No! no! no!" said Bakche earnestly; "but other people know of the value of the peacock."

"I agree. The whole countryside knows the story. If you suspect anyone in Belstone you had better go down and look for the individual."

"I suspect Mr. Sorley!"

"Why?" demanded Alan, who had quite anticipated the question.

"Because he wanted the peacock."

"So did Miss Inderwick, so did many other people. Everyone who knows the story would like to find the jewels." Alan paused for a reply but as none came he continued coolly: "How did you trace the possession of the peacock to Baldwin Grison?"

"I didn't—that is, I did in a way," stammered the Indian nervously.

"In what way?" asked Fuller relentlessly, and trying to make Bakche tell what was already known to him, "for instance how did you come to live at Miss Grison's boarding-house?"

"I explained when I met you there, sir."

Fuller laughed ironically. "You did, and I beg leave to doubt the truth of the explanation, Mr. Bakche."

"How dare you, sir; by what right do you doubt me?" demanded the man furiously, and his dark eyes shot fire.

"By the doubt of common-sense. You were in search of the peacock in order to gain a clue to the hiding-place of these jewels you claim. Come now, Mr. Bakche, it was not mere chance that guided you to Miss Grison, who of all the people in London, knew about the matter."

Morad-Bakche looked sullenly at the carpet, and evidently saw that Alan was one too many for him. After a long pause, which Fuller took care not to terminate too soon, he looked up with a would-be frank smile. "As I wish you to help me in the matter," he declared, "I may as well make a clean breast of what I know."

Alan nodded, and neither refused or agreed to accept the man as his client, but intimated that he was ready to give his attention to the confession. Morad-Bakche at once took exception to the word.

"It is not a confession I wish to make, sir, but merely a statement to show how I came to learn about the matter we are discussing."

"Oh, I beg your pardon," said Fuller ceremoniously, "go on please!"

Bakche frowned at the irony of his tone, but made no further objection to relating what he knew.

"My explanation as to how I came to Thimble Square was not wholly true, Mr. Fuller," he said abruptly.

"So I thought at the time?"

"Why did you think so?" asked Bakche quickly.

"Because I got it into my head that you were after the Inderwick fetish, although when you spoke I did not know that it was the Begum of Kam who had given away the jewels. That fact I learned later. However, it struck me that if you had come on some such errand, you went for that reason to Miss Grison's boarding-house, and not because your Ceylon friend recommended it."

Bakche nodded. "Very creditable to your intelligence," he said in a patronising manner. "To be plain, sir, I learned the story which is set forth in the newspaper, from some family documents."

"As I thought," murmured Fuller softly.

"Seeing that the Begum had given away jewels which should rightfully belong to the family I determined to find them. I came to England and went to Belstone, where the documents I mentioned informed me the Inderwicks lived. At the inn there I learned from a very voluble woman all that was to be known about the loss of the peacock... Afterwards I visited Mr. Sorley, who is, I understand, the guardian of Miss Inderwick, to whom the peacock is supposed to belong. He told me that the ornament was lost, but he did not say who had taken it from The Monastery."

"Quite so," said Alan, remembering that Sorley had withheld such information lest Miss Grison should give the peacock to the man; "but of course Mrs. Verwin at the inn hinted that the Grisons had the bird."

"She did, sir and what is more she gave me the address of the boarding-house in Thimble Square. I returned to London in July last and took up my abode there, determined to learn all that I could."

"Well?" asked Fuller, when the Indian paused.

"Well," echoed the other, "I learned nothing particular."

"Hum!" remarked Alan doubtfully, and looking hard at the speaker, "did you tell Miss Grison the story of your search?"

"Yes I did, at a later period when I had become more or less friendly with her. I even stated that it was reported how she and her brother had stolen the peacock."

"What answer did she make?"

"She said nothing to the purpose, only stating that she believed there was such an ornament, but that she did not know where it was. Of course in the light of this interview," added Bakche, placing his hand on the newspaper, "you can see that for her own ends she spoke falsely. Evidently Baldwin, her brother, was the thief, and possessed it the whole time. The wonder is, Mr. Fuller, that being desperately hard up as he was, he did not sell or pawn the peacock."

"I rather think that the man hoped to learn the secret and get possession of the jewels. Did you ever see Grison?"

"No," said Bakche so quickly that Alan felt sure he was not speaking the exact truth, and became more sure of the fact when he elaborated his denial. "Miss Grison refused to give me her brother's address, which I knew was in some slum. And of course, not guessing that Grison had the peacock, I did not push my enquiries. Had I known that he had the bird I should have placed the matter in the hands of a private detective, and in some way I should have learned his whereabouts."

"And then?"

"Then," said Bakche, drawing a deep breath and clenching his small hands, "I should have forced him to surrender it to me."

"You would have used violence?" asked Alan in A peculiar tone.

"Yes! That is—" Bakche broke off with a laugh of contempt. "Why do you look at me so suspiciously, Mr. Fuller? Do you think that I did see the man and did use violence even to the extent of stabbing him? You are entirely wrong, sir. Had I murdered him and obtained the peacock I should by this time have been far away on the Continent out of danger, and until things grew quieter, I should have remained absent trying to solve the riddle. I am not the criminal, and I am not the possessor of the peacock."

"I grant that," said Fuller quietly, who knew well that the man spoke the truth, since Sorley owned the bird at that moment. "Well, and what do you expect me to do, Mr. Bakche?"

"I wish you to find out who murdered Grison, so that the peacock may be recovered and handed over to me."

"On behalf of Miss Inderwick I am doing that," said Alan dryly, "so I cannot possibly act on your behalf."

"The peacock is mine," cried the Indian, rising to his feet with a snarl which again reminded Fuller of his tigerish nature.

"The peacock is Miss Inderwick's, and should I find it, I shall hand it over to her so that she may discover the treasure."

"You are—" began Bakche violently, then suddenly and dangerously restrained his anger and smiled meaningly. "Well, since you are engaged to the lady, it is natural that you should want her to gain the jewels—"

"Mr. Bakche, stop that if you please." Alan rose in his turn with indignant looks.

The Indian shrugged his shoulders and walked to the door. "It is a duel between us," he said smoothly, "you want what I want, so we shall see who wins. And I can tell you what is your best step to take."

"Very kind of you, Mr. Bakche. And that is—"

"To find the boy Alonzo, formerly called Jotty. He knows the truth."

"Then why not question him, since he is at Miss Grison's house?"

"Indeed he is not; Jotty has been missing since last night!" and refusing to explain further, the Indian departed, leaving Fuller greatly astonished and greatly annoyed also, that the boy should have disappeared.

CHAPTER XIII

AN UNEXPECTED VISITOR

Dick's remark when he brought news of the Rotherhithe crime, that there were more romantic than commonplace events to be found in present-day life, seemed to be verified by what had taken place. A hidden treasure, a riddle in gems and gold, a mysterious murder, a melodramatic Indian, and the necessary pair of lovers to spice the whole—these were certainly details out of which to weave a tale worthy of more highly-colored days. And Destiny who was relating the story to an interested world was doing her best to involve her characters in a whirl of unhappy things. For even if Sorley were arrested and confessed his guilt and suffered punishment, the story—as Alan considered—would by no means be ended, since the jewels had to be discovered and detained from the clutch of Morad-Bakche. Marie had to be comforted and married, and Miss Grison—the Atê of the tale—had to be appeased. There was a great deal yet to be done before things could be settled, and Fuller, as the hero of Fate's fiction, felt that he ought to do something towards bringing about a necessary climax. But as yet he could not see his way to do anything.

And to make matters worse, Latimer next day arrived with the news that Sorley had disappeared. On the previous day Inspector Moon had been duly told the story, and the evidence of Sorley's complicity had been placed under his official eye. With the joyful feeling that here was a case which would reflect credit on him if dexterously managed, Moon procured a warrant, and took the night train to Lewes. About midnight he arrived at The Monastery, only to learn that Sorley had gone away early in the day, and neither Marie, nor the three Trents, were able to tell the inspector whither he had departed. Hastily packing a small bag, and wearing an unpretentious tweed suit, the suspected man had vanished from The Monastery and Belstone on his motor bicycle. Moon, having acted immediately on Latimer's information, was furious at the escape, and could not understand how the man had been warned. Henny Trent however threw some light on the darkness of this point by stating that Mr. Sorley had been visited by a small boy with light hair and blue eyes. The urchin had not been seen since the departure of Marie's uncle, so it was presumed that he had left earlier. In disgust at his bad luck, Moon installed an officer in the house to watch for the possible return of Sorley, and had come back in the morning to London, where he informed Dick that the bird had flown. Now Latimer had come in the afternoon to the Chancery Lane office to explain to his friend.

Alan was much surprised to hear that Sorley had been warned, and from a suspicious look in Dick's eyes fancied that Latimer suspected him. "I did not break my promise," he protested sharply and stiffly and unasked.

"No one suggested that you did," growled the reporter, who was annoyed that the criminal—as he truly considered Sorley—had escaped.

"Your eyes suggest quite enough," retorted Fuller, hurt by the suspicion, "and you should know me better, Dick, than to think that I broke faith."

Latimer flushed. "I'm sorry, Alan, but I really did have some such thought, although I see now that it was unwarranted. But you had every temptation to save the man, seeing that he is Miss Inderwick's uncle."

"You should have known me better," persisted Fuller stubbornly. "I gave my promise, and I kept it."

"I am sure you did." Latimer extended his hand. "Forgive me Alan."

The other gripped it. "Of course. A vague suspicion such as you have entertained won't spoil our friendship. And yet, Dick," he added, when they had both cooled down, "I am not exactly surprised, now I think over Bakche's last words."

"Bakche, the Indian? Has he been to see you?"

"Yesterday. He came as a client, and confessed much of what we already know."

"Then my sixth sense?—"

"Oh, hang your sixth sense. We agreed that it was right when I related Mrs. Verwin's story. Bakche's yarn is merely corroborative. He did find the history of the peacock in some family papers, and did come to look up Belstone village to see if he could get the peacock and find the treasure, and yesterday he came to me to ask if I would engineer the job."

"Hum! You refused, I expect."

"I should jolly well think so, Dicky. Bakche claims the treasure, as he says that the Begum of Kam had no right to give it away. He wants to find the assassin of Grison, and recover the bird and read the riddle."

"Does he know that Sorley is the culprit?"

"He didn't yesterday, whatever he knows now. I declined to receive him as a client saying that I was working for Marie, and intended to give her the treasure when it was discovered."

"Will it ever be discovered?" questioned Latimer skeptically.

Alan sighed. "Lord knows! I have been trying my hardest to read some meaning into the sketch I made, but so far I have failed."

"We'll have a look at it together," said Dick encouragingly, "my sixth sense may help you where others have not been able to arrive at any conclusion. I owe you that much for having suspected you had broken faith with me, even for a moment," and Dick looked very repentant.

"Oh, that's all right, old man," said Alan heartily "seeing that I love Marie so much it was natural you should credit me with trying to spare her pain by getting her uncle saved. But I thought it was best to let the law take its course, as in any case if he was saved now, he would only be discovered and arrested later on."

"I suppose you and Bakche are enemies now?"

"He gave me to understand that he would do his best to get the better of me," remarked Fuller a trifle dryly, "and then like a fool, he gave me a hint as to who knew the truth."

"I don't think I should take that hint coming from such a quarter," said Dick reflectively, "who knows the truth according to Bakche?"

"Jotty!"

"H'm. He may be right after all, although it is odd he should give you a chance to outrun him in this way. I always did think that Jotty knew more than was good for him. Of course he gave Sorley warning."

"Of course," assented Fuller quickly; "only Jotty could have been the blue-eyed, fair-haired lad, who called to see the man. He disappeared from Thimble Square, as Bakche told me, the day before yesterday, so I expect he saw the news about the peacock in that paper, and bolted to warn Sorley."

"But why should he do that?" asked Latimer with a puzzled air; "he evidently told Miss Grison—guessing the fact from the drawing you showed him—that Sorley had the bird. And on account of that, Miss Grison related what she did to the interviewer. But I can't understand why Jotty having brought about the trouble, should try to save Sorley from it."

Alan shook his head. "It is impossible to say, unless we can get hold of the boy again and make him speak out. He may return to Miss Grison—"

"No," said Dick decisively, "he won't. She has done her best to get Sorley into trouble, and won't thank Jotty for giving him warning. I wonder where he has gone?"

"Jotty?"

"And Sorley; both of them. Moon has left a detective at The Monastery on the off-chance that Miss Inderwick's uncle may return. But I don't think he will. Probably he has taken those jewels of his own, you spoke of, and has left the country."

"It looks as though he were guilty," observed Alan with a groan.

"It does," assented Latimer quickly; "but it is just as well that he has got away, and so avoided arrest and trial, and probably hanging. I don't expect you'll set eyes on him again or on Jotty either, as maybe he has taken the lad with him."

"Why should he do that?"

"Jotty—as I always suspected—knows too much, and Sorley wants to get him out of the way."

"It is too late," replied Fuller doubtfully. "Jotty has given us the letter, and has told us enough to hang Sorley unless the man has a very good defence. Probably he hasn't any, else he would have stood his ground. Oh, my poor Marie, how dreadful it is for you to have a criminal for an uncle."

Dick patted Alan's shoulder. "See here, old son," he remarked with rough sympathy, "I was annoyed when I heard that the man had bolted. Now I am very glad for your sake. As I said you won't hear of Sorley again. So go to work and solve the riddle of the peacock; marry Marie and tell Bakche he can go back to India with his tail between his legs."

"But Sorley has probably taken the bird with him."

"What does that matter? You have the drawing, and can solve the riddle from that, as you have always expected to do. The mystery of Grison's death is an open secret now, Alan, my boy, so let the past bury itself, and look forward to your marriage with the girl, and possession of the treasure."

Fuller nodded in an absent-minded way, but did not reply. Before he could make up his mind what to say, there came a knock at the door, and Seymour, who was the solicitor's one and only clerk, appeared with the intelligence that a lady wished to see his employer. Thinking that this was a client, Latimer moved into the outer office, only to come face to face with Marie. The girl looked ill, and all the bright color of her face had faded to a dull white, while there were dark circles under her eyes.

"Miss Inderwick," cried Dick in amazement, and, on hearing the name, Alan appeared at the door with a look of equal astonishment. The last thing in the world expected by either man was the visit to London of Marie.

"My dear girl, what are you doing here?" questioned Alan in tones of alarm when he saw her pale face and anxious eyes. "Come in, Dick, close the door," and shortly the three were in the private office, and Seymour had received orders to admit no one.

"I had to come up, Alan," said Marie, clinging to his sleeve. "Oh, my dear, it is dreadful. Last night a policeman came with others, and they say that Uncle Ran murdered Mr. Grison. But it's not true, I am sure it is not true," and Marie burst into tears.

"I can't say if it is or not, dear," replied Alan uneasily, and kneeling by the side of the chair she dropped into. "But—but Mr. Sorley has not been arrested has he?"

"No," wailed Marie, "and that is what makes me so afraid. Some boy came in the afternoon, and Uncle Ran went away on the motor bicycle, after giving me twenty pounds and saying that he would not return for a few days. The boy left the house also; I suppose so, although neither I nor Henny nor Granny nor Jenny saw him go. If Uncle Ran were innocent he wouldn't run away, I'm sure. Oh, Alan, what is to be done? I can't stay in the house, and as I had the money I came up to ask your advice."

"Dear," said Fuller, placing his arm around her waist tenderly, "the best thing for you to do is to return to The Monastery and wait."

"But I'm all by myself Alan, and that horrid detective person is staying in the house. I can't stop on there alone."

"The girls and their grandmother are there, darling."

"Oh, but what use are they. I want you," she leaned her head on his shoulder, weeping profusely.

"But I can't come and stop in The Monastery while your uncle is away, my dearest girl," cried Alan much distressed; "people would talk. Suppose you go and stay with my mother for a time."

"But if I did I should have to tell her the truth," wept Marie; "and how can I say that Uncle Ran did what he didn't do."

"It has to come out sooner or later, Miss Inderwick," remarked Dick in a voice full of regret, for the girl's tears made him feel ashamed of having brought about the catastrophe.

"What has to come out?"

"The fact that Mr. Sorley murdered—"

Marie sprang to her feet and the color flew to her wan cheeks. "I don't believe it; I don't, I don't, I don't," she said almost fiercely. "Uncle Ran has his faults, and never did care much for me, besides using my income and being nasty to Alan because he loved me. But he would never kill anyone, I am sure, Mr. Latimer. What Miss Grison says in that paper is a lie."

"Oh," cried Fuller quickly, "you saw that paper?"

"Yes; *The Latest News!* That boy brought it to Uncle Ran, for I saw him give it through the window of the library while I was walking on the terrace. Uncle Ran left it behind in his hurry, and—"

"He left in a hurry?" asked Dick suddenly.

"Yes. He told me that he had received bad news and would be away for a time and that I was to use the money—the twenty pounds I mean—to keep things going."

"Did he say anything about returning?"

"No. He was in such a hurry that he had no time to say much. And then very late at night there was a ring at the door, and Henny went down to find a man with another man who said they had come to arrest Uncle Ran for murder. I had to get up and answer questions, and then one man went away while the other stayed. He's at The Monastery now," cried Marie with a fresh burst of tears, "and I haven't been in bed all night. Henny made me lie down for a time this morning, and then I came up by the midday train to see you, Alan. Oh, what does it all mean?"

Alan glanced at his friend, for the situation was very painful. He opened his mouth to speak, but could not, while Marie looked at him so appealingly. Dick, more hardened to the world, and not being in love, solved the question, as to frank speech or silence.

"Miss Inderwick," he said bluntly, "believe me I am very sorry for you in every way, but it is just as well that you should know the truth. What Miss Grison says in that interview is true. The holder of the peacock is the person who murdered Grison for its possession."

"But not Uncle Ran, not Uncle Ran!" she pleaded anxiously.

"I fear so," said Latimer turning away his head; "he has the peacock."

"It's not true, it's not true, Alan—"

"I fear it is, Marie," said the young man sadly. "I saw the peacock myself in your uncle's hands when I was down at Belstone for Christmas."

"Oh! and you never told me."

"I did not wish you to learn the truth, and tried to keep it from you. But since the matter has been made public, you have become acquainted with what has happened, and the flight of Mr. Sorley seems to suggest a guilty conscience. I hope he is innocent, but—"

"He *is* innocent," interrupted Marie with the tears streaming down her face; "nothing will ever make me believe that Uncle Ran murdered anyone. How did he account for possession of the peacock?"

"He declared that Miss Grison must have left it in the cupboard where it had been stored twenty years ago."

"On that occasion when she came and walked all over the house; when we found her sitting in the library?"

"Yes."

"Well then," said Marie triumphantly, "Uncle Ran is innocent, and Miss Grison is a wicked woman to say that whosoever holds the peacock murdered her brother, since she had herself—"

"But, Miss Inderwick," broke in Dick, "we cannot be sure if Mr. Sorley's explanation is a true one."

"It is; I am sure it is. But what does Miss Grison say?"

"We have not questioned her yet."

"Then I shall question her," cried Marie, starting to her feet with a very determined air, "she shall confess to me that she brought the peacock to The Monastery so as to get Uncle Ran into trouble. She always hated him, and you heard yourself, Alan, what she said on that day. She is mad, she is mad. Uncle Ran said as much, and now I quite believe him."

"Dear Marie," said Fuller, taking her hand, "let us hope for the best. You may be certain that for your sake I shall do my best to prove your uncle's innocence. But there is no doubt that the evidence against him is very strong, and his flight seems to prove that the charge is true."

"I don't believe it," said Miss Inderwick obstinately, and sitting down again to tap a vexed foot on the ground. "Uncle Ran will come back again with an explanation. I'm sure he will."

"Let us hope so," murmured Latimer skeptically; "but I doubt it."

"As to the evidence against him—what is it, Alan?"

He told her, relating Jotty's discovery of the letter, and showed her a copy of the same, which he had taken before Dick passed on the original to Inspector Moon. "So you see, Marie," he ended, when she was in full possession of the painful facts, "that it seems almost certain—"

"I don't care what it seems," interrupted Marie in her wilful feminine way, "Uncle Ran never murdered that wretched Grison."

"Then why didn't he remain and say so?" asked Dick sharply.

"He will explain that when he returns," she retorted in a lofty tone. "In the meantime we must learn the truth."

"We know the truth," Latimer replied.

Marie stamped. "How horrid of you to take it for granted that Uncle Ran killed this man. I say he didn't, and nothing you say, or Alan says, will convince me that he did."

"I say nothing," put in Fuller quickly; "things look black against Mr. Sorley, but I wish to give him the benefit of the doubt."

Marie flew at him and threw her arms round his neck. "Bless you, Alan, for the words you have spoken. I am not very fond of Uncle Ran as you know, but I am sure he is innocent and you must try and prove his innocence."

"I shall do my best, darling, if you will leave the matter in my hands and return to Belstone."

"No, Alan don't ask me to. I want to go down to Rotherhithe."

"What for?" asked Dick surprised.

Marie looked at him disdainfully, for she gathered very plainly that he was not on her side. "To ask questions of that woman who keeps the house where Mr. Grison was murdered."

"Mother Slaig? Oh, my dear Miss Inderwick you can't go and see her. She is a virago, and her house is most disreputable. Besides she cannot help you, as she gave her evidence at the inquest—"

"And didn't accuse Uncle Ran at all," interrupted Marie. "I shall get at the truth if I see her."

"Marie," said Alan quickly, "you can't go down to Rotherhithe."

"I can and I shall," cried Miss Inderwick with another stamp, and looked like a small goddess of war. "Uncle Ran shan't be hanged for what he never did, if I can help it."

"So long as he keeps away he cannot be caught to be hanged," said Alan in a pacific manner, for it was necessary to deal in a wary manner with the infuriated girl. "Meanwhile I shall look into the matter and do my best to clear his character. If you go to see Mother Slaig, you may prevent Mr. Sorley's innocence from being proved."

"But I want to help," cried Marie, weeping again; "he is my uncle."

"You shall help," said Alan, taking her in his arms, "when I know in what way you can aid us. Marie, doesn't everyone in the village know about the accusation of your uncle, and that a detective is in the house?"

"Yes. It's horrid. Everyone is talking about it."

"Then you can have no hesitation in going to my mother and father and in laying the true facts of the case before them. My mother will surely ask you to stay at the vicarage, so remain there while I look into the matter, dearest. Believe me it is the best course to take."

"Then I shall do what you want me to do. But tell me, Alan, when it is necessary for me to come into the matter. I must have a hand in proving the innocence of Uncle Ran."

"I promise you, that as soon as I require your aid I shall ask for it."

Satisfied with this promise, Marie dried her tears, and then asked Alan to get her something to eat, as she was very hungry, and it was now close on five o'clock. Her lover put on his hat and coat and took her out to a restaurant near at hand, where she made a fairly good meal. Dick came with them, as he did not wish Marie to go away with the impression that he was hostile to the accused man.

"Believe me, Miss Inderwick," he said when they were at the table, "no one will be more pleased to hear of your uncle's innocence than I shall be."

"You believe that he is guilty?"

"Well, the facts are against him, but I shall adopt Alan's line and give him the benefit of the doubt. When we face Miss Grison she may exonerate him. It is not likely, since she hates him for some reason, but—"

"She won't, she won't; and I don't care if she doesn't, Mr. Latimer. In some other way we must save Uncle Ran. Will you see her?"

"This very evening," promised Dick earnestly. "And so shall I," said Alan suddenly. "Hope for the best, darling."

"Yes," sobbed Marie, who felt better after her meal, but still was unable to restrain her tears, for the poor girl was greatly shaken, "but is it not terrible, Alan?"

"Very, my dear. But you must be a heroine and keep up, for your uncle's sake. Now we must take a taxi to Victoria, and you can catch the something after six train to Lewes. There is one about this time, I know. Have you enough money to take a fly to Belstone, dear. No, don't take a fly. On second thoughts I shall wire to my father to send his trap to meet you; that will be best."

"But the trouble, Alan," faltered the girl as he handed her into the taxi.

"It's no trouble. Dick, will you come, or—"

"I am coming of course," said Dick, bestowing his burly form in the taxi. "I don't want Miss Inderwick to go away with the idea that I'm a beast."

"I'm sure I never said so," sighed Marie, "and if I was rude, Mr. Latimer, you must put it down to my being so upset."

"My dear young lady, you are right to stand up for your uncle, and I have nothing but praise for your conduct. With all my heart I trust that he will return again to face the accusation and prove his innocence."

"Thank you," replied Marie softly, and gave him her hand. Then she sat close to her lover, and the three spoke very little until the station was reached. Here Alan sent a telegram to his father, and placed the girl in the train. He bought her a first-class ticket, and asked the guard to look after her comfort, as he did not like the idea of such an unsophisticated damsel travelling all alone. Her freak of coming to London so unexpectedly, though natural enough under the circumstances, caused him great anxiety, and he heaved a sigh of relief when the train steamed out of the station. Marie would be looked after by the guard as far as Lewes, and then the Rev. John Fuller would meet her and take the stray lamb to the vicarage, where his wife would console her. Dick laughed when he heard his worried friend sigh so thankfully.

"All's well that ends well, my son," he said, clapping the young man on the back, "and Miss Inderwick has behaved like a heroine."

"I daresay; but I hope she won't come to London again, as she is not used to being by herself, and may get into trouble."

"She certainly will," said Dick grimly, "if she goes to see Mother Slaig in that Rotherhithe slum."

"Oh, I shall see to it that she does not go. Well, I am tired, Dick. Are you coming home, or have you business to attend to?"

"I'm coming with you," responded the big man, affectionately, taking out his pipe, as the presence of Marie had hitherto prevented his indulging in a smoke, and he felt the need of the soothing weed. "I have nothing to do this evening—nothing particular that is—so I may as well have a few quiet hours at home, and talk this case over with you."

"There's nothing to talk about."

"Well, I don't know. It seems to me that the Indian is mixed up in the business somehow. From what you describe I believe that he guessed Baldwin Grison had the peacock."

"I thought so myself, but then if he had killed the man and got the peacock he wouldn't have sent it to Sorley."

On the way to Fleet Street and Barker's Inn they went over the same old ground, but without coming to any definite conclusion. Besides the strain of the last few days was telling on both men, and they felt very weary. It was with a sigh of relief that they arrived at the dark cobblestone court and mounted the crooked staircase. Alan used his latchkey and admitted both himself and Dick into their chambers. When they entered the sitting-room they received a surprise and a shock. In a chair by the fire sat a figure, and in a moment he was recognized in spite of his shabby looks.

"Mr. Sorley!" cried Alan and Dick in a breath.

CHAPTER XIV

FACE TO FACE

It was indeed Mr. Randolph Vernon Sorley who spread out his hands to the fire in a crouching attitude, but woefully changed from the debonair and juvenile gentleman of former days. His aggressively shabby overcoat and worn boots showed that he had some idea of disguising himself, since he had both money and clothes at his command to dress better. He was unshaven, his cheeks and chin being covered with a silvery stubble, and in his sunken eyes there lurked a hunted look. The man looked both broken up and broken down, and had aged at least twenty years since Alan had last set eyes on him. The terror he displayed when the young man entered the room showed how apprehensive he was of being arrested by the police.

"Oh, it's you, Alan," he gasped with a sigh of relief, when the newcomers, in sheer surprise, called out his name. "I'm glad it's only you and your friend."

"I am Fuller's friend," remarked Latimer with emphasis, "but not yours."

"Ah!" Sorley shivered and cringed fearfully, "you're against me too. Am I to find an enemy in you also, Alan?"

"No," said the young man briefly; "I never kick a man when he is down."

"I'm glad to hear that, Alan, for I am very down indeed. A few days ago and I could hold up my head with the best; now I am hunted for a crime.

"If you are guilty—"

"I swear I am not," interrupted Sorley, his voice rising to a scream, "on my soul I swear to both of you that I am not."

"Then why did you run away?" asked Dick.

"Because, after reading the newspaper interview with that vile woman, I saw that appearances were against me. I fled to gain time."

"Time for what, Mr. Sorley?"

"To prepare a defence."

"Oh," said Latimer doubtfully and staring at the limp figure of the fugitive, "then you have a defence."

"Yes—that is, I can—I can—oh, Alan," wailed Sorley piteously, "in heaven's name give me some wine or brandy. I have scarcely touched food since I left Belstone, and I am that weak I can scarcely speak. Give me drink and food, then we can talk."

Fuller nodded silently, and went to a cupboard, whence he brought out a loaf of bread, some butter, and a jar of *pâté de foie gras*, which had been given to Dick by a friend, together with a bottle of good port wine. The hunted man, who had sought the sanctuary of their hearthstone, staggered to the table and began to eat and drink with avidity. Both men pitied the unfortunate creature, whose arrogance had been thus laid low. Whether he was innocent or guilty they could not say on what evidence they possessed; but it seemed terrible that a gentleman should be brought to such a sordid pass. While Sorley methodically filled himself with food, there was silence for quite a long time. Alan finally broke it.

"Why did you come here?" he asked abruptly.

"I want you to help me," mumbled Sorley hastily.

"How can I help you, man? You know that there is a warrant out for your arrest, so if either Latimer or I assist you to escape we shall be compounding a felony."

"I never asked for your assistance to escape," retorted Sorley tartly, and in a stronger tone, for the food and drink had put life into him.

"Then why did you come here?" asked Alan again, and stiffening, as the old arrogance was perceptible in the man's tone.

"I have told you; I want help."

"What sort of help?"

"To prove my innocence."

"How can I, or how can Latimer? We know nothing."

"I think you know a great deal," returned the other acidly, and shuffled to the fire again, as the night was chilly and he required warmth; "from what Jotty told me, you brought about my arrest."

"Pardon me, Mr. Sorley," struck in Dick before his friend could speak, "but I am the one who did that. Since you have seen Jotty you must know that he found the letter which you wrote making an appointment with Grison on the very night and about the very time when the poor devil was killed. He showed that letter to us, and Alan was all in favor of leaving the matter alone, since he has some sympathy for you as the uncle of Miss Inderwick. But I declined to compound a felony, and I went to Inspector Moon to explain that you were the criminal."

"I am not the criminal," cried Sorley furiously. "I did not murder the man. As to Jotty showing you my letter—"

"Then you admit the letter?" demanded Dick swiftly.

"Certainly I do. Why should I not? But the boy never told me that he had acted in such a Judas way. He came down to see me with a copy of *The Latest News* in his pocket, and when I read the interview I went away on the impulse of the moment, recognizing how dangerous was my position."

"Why did the boy go to warn you?"

"Because he wanted money. Didn't he get money for giving up that letter?"

"Yes," answered Alan readily; "two pounds."

"He received five from me for bringing down the newspaper," said Sorley in a hasty tone, "he sold me to you, and later he sold you to me. You expected to have me arrested, but the boy's warning enabled me to escape. It is all a question of money. Jotty, as I knew and Grison knew, would sell his soul for gold."

"Where is the boy now?" asked Dick suddenly, and watching Sorley through half-closed eyes.

"I don't know. He got his price and left The Monastery, shortly before I went away on my motor bicycle. He may have gone back to Miss Grison for all I know."

"I don't think that is likely," said Alan dryly, "since she hates you, and will not be pleased if she finds out—as she must have done by this time—that Jotty has thwarted her revenge."

"There you are, there you are," cried Sorley, greatly excited and gesticulating vehemently, "that beastly woman hates me. It is she who has got me into this trouble. What did I tell you, Alan, what did I tell you? That she had some reason for bringing back the peacock and leaving it in its old place. Now you see the reason; she wished to implicate me in the death of her infernal brother."

"Did she really bring back the peacock?" was Dick's question.

"Yes, she did; I swear that she must have brought it back on the day she came unexpectedly to The Monastery and walked—as I learned later—all over the house. It's a trap—a trap I tell you. I am innocent; oh yes, I am innocent as a child unborn, but she is doing her best to put a rope round my neck. What are her words in the interview. 'Find the peacock and you find the assassin of my brother!' Those are her words, because she knew that I had the bird, and that the mere possession could hang me. Oh, the devil, the cruel vampire that she is!" and he trembled with rage and terror.

"But there is not only the peacock to be considered, Mr. Sorley," put in Latimer, struck by the vehemence of this defence, and wondering if the man was really innocent after all. "The letter—"

"I wrote the letter," admitted Sorley swiftly, "and—but one moment Mr. Latimer, you had better present me with a full statement of the evidence upon which you and the police base your charges against me. Then I shall be able to defend myself."

"I hope so, sincerely," murmured Alan, who sat back in his chair with folded arms, and allowed Dick to conduct the conversation.

The journalist wasted no time in preliminary explanations, but bluntly set forth the whole story from the time he had entered that very room in November to report the murder, down to the moment when Marie departed from the Victoria station for Belstone *via* Lewes. Sorley still crouching and still haggard in looks, though stronger in voice, listened intently, but did not interrupt. Alan noticed, however, that at certain portions of the recital he trembled, probably from overstrained nerves. When Dick ended, and relighted his pipe, the old man nodded gravely.

"I am indeed in a dangerous position," he said, striving to steady a voice that would quiver with ill-concealed alarm, "all the same I am entirely innocent. I swear to it."

"A judge and jury will not believe in such swearing without proof," said Fuller, shaking his head.

"Proof! Proof! What proof can I give? Only Louisa Grison can prove that the peacock was brought to The Monastery without my knowledge, and she hates me too greatly to confess as much. Do you think," cried Sorley bitterly, "that she will spoil the trap she has set? Not she. I know her venomous nature too well."

"There's the letter, you know," Dick reminded him.

"Yes! The letter. I don't deny the letter, which that Judas of a boy showed to you. He betrayed me—"

"And he saved you," interpolated Alan quickly.

"For money in both cases," sneered the other, "if the truth is to be found that lad knows it. If so, he is aware that I am guiltless, and thus he may have come to warn me because his conscience smote him."

"I scarcely think that Jotty is sufficiently evolved to possess a conscience," said Latimer dryly; "he helped you for the five pounds, as he betrayed you for the two pounds. It is all a question of money. But since you insist so strongly upon your innocence, Mr. Sorley, I should like to hear on what grounds you do so."

"On the grounds that Miss Grison brought the bird to—"

"Yes, yes; but the letter; your presence at Rotherhithe on the night and about the time the crime was committed?" put in Alan hastily, for he felt that they were losing time.

The old man was silent for a few moments, and his fingers played in a senile manner on his unshaven chin. Then he appeared to gain a sudden strength from the steady looks of his companions, and spoke with some dignity and considerable strength. "I make an admission to you both," he said in a surprisingly clear tone. "I knew that Grison had the peacock."

"Oh!" said the listeners simultaneously, and looked at one another, wondering if Sorley was about to confess his guilt. The man saw this and smiled in a sardonic manner.

"If I were what you suppose me to be," he said coldly, "I should scarcely admit as much; but being innocent, I can do so. For many years I believed that Louisa Grison had stolen the peacock out of revenge, because I dismissed her brother." Alan nodded at this point, as he had heard the woman acknowledge as much, but did not interrupt. "It was twelve months ago when I became aware that Grison possessed it. He wrote me a letter saying that he could not live long, and was ready to give up the peacock on condition that I came to hear on what terms he was prepared to surrender it. I went up to town and to Rotherhithe to that dreadful woman's house."

"Mother Slaig's, I suppose. Did you ride your motor bicycle?"

"No, I did not have it twelve months ago," said Sorley quickly. "I went up and found Grison better than I expected. He had rallied since writing to me, and refused when we met, to give up the peacock. I departed, and later—in a few weeks, went up again, when I saw that he was very sick indeed with his profligate ways. He said that if I would promise to give his sister half of the treasure when it was discovered, he would hand me back the peacock. I refused, as I had no right to dispose of Marie's property in that way."

Alan smiled grimly when he remembered how this scrupulous man had disposed of furniture which belonged to the niece whose goods he was supposed to safeguard. However he did not make any remark on this point, but asked a pertinent question: "Had Grison discovered the secret?"

"No; he had tried to, but had failed, as everyone else has done up to the present," said Sorley, continuing his narrative with an effort, for he appeared to be very weary. "When I refused to give up half the treasure he declined to restore the golden bird. Up till November last I continued to call on him and urge him to return what his sister had stolen, and it was because of my frequent visits that I purchased the motor bicycle."

"Ah," said Dick, who was nursing his chin, "you didn't want your visits to be known to the railway authorities."

"You are quite wrong, Mr. Latimer. If I chose to go up to town every now and then that was no business of anyone. Had I contemplated murder I might indeed have shirked giving color to my doings by travelling so often by train. But I bought the bicycle to save expense in one way, and because I found it easier to slip out of the house and up to town in this style."

"Hum!" murmured Latimer, to whom the explanation sounded weak, "we'll admit so much for the time being. Well, sir?"

"Well," said Sorley taking no notice of the implied doubt. "I went up and down constantly. Sometimes Grison when sick would agree to give up the peacock without terms; then, when well, he would refuse to surrender it on any condition. Also sometimes he wanted half the treasure for his sister, since —as he put it—she had stuck by him in his fall. Finally, so as to get the bird and try to unravel the secret I compromised by offering to give a third of the jewels to Louisa."

"You had no right to promise that without submitting the proposition to Marie," said Alan.

"I didn't want Marie to know anything about the business until it was entirely settled and the jewels were in our possession," said Sorley doggedly, "she never dreamed that I went so frequently to London, for I was often by myself for days, and had my meals alone. When I got the motor bicycle she and the other women more than ever were unable to learn about my movements. Things went on in this way until November last, and I could do nothing with Grison, who was as obstinate as a mule. He then wrote me saying that he wanted to see me on the evening of the thirteenth November, and this time would really make terms. I replied that I would be there at eight o'clock."

"Seven o'clock," corrected Alan quickly.

"Thank you; it was seven, but my memory is not so good as it was, my boy. I went up on my bicycle and saw Grison at the appointed time at Mother Slaig's. He was as difficult to manage as ever, and I came away about eight, quite angry at my constant failures to get what I desired. I rode back during the night and gained The Monastery as usual. Next day, or rather the day after, I heard through the medium of the newspapers about the murder. Having regard to the time and place and my presence on the spot I saw in what danger I stood, so I held my peace. In one way I fancied that I could not be taxed with the commission of the crime, since I had not the peacock. Then I found it in its old place after the unexpected visit of Miss Grison, and guessed that she had brought it. I guessed also—since I knew that her brother had possessed it —she was setting a trap of some sort. Had I been wise," he looked frankly at the young men, "I should have told the police at once about the matter; but I saw then, as I see now—and as you, Mr. Latimer, have so plainly set before me that everything was in favor of my guilt."

Dick nodded and pulled his mustache meditatively. "You didn't improve matter by bolting when Jotty warned you," he remarked pointedly.

"I lost my nerve," gasped the other man, his pale face becoming still more pale, "and on the impulse of the moment I fled."

"Why did you fly here?" asked Alan, irritated by the problem presented to him as to letting the man go, or handing him over to Inspector Moon.

"I have told you twice, my boy; I wish you to help me. Long ago I told you that I believed Louisa Grison was laying a trap for me with that peacock. Now you can see that I was right, and your evidence that I spoke as I did, will help me at the trial."

"At the trial." Dick looked swiftly at the fugitive. "Then you—"

"Yes; I intend to give myself up." Sorley rose and stood up lean and haggard, yet with something of his old self-assertion, "but before doing so I wish you both to come with me to Thimble Square and see Miss Grison."

"Why?" demanded Fuller, jumping up with an inquiring look.

"I desire to face her in your presence, and accuse her of having brought the peacock down to The Monastery to get me into trouble."

"But how could she get it from her brother, when Jotty said that he saw it on the night of the murder in Grison's possession?"

"I can't explain," said Sorley with a vexed air, "and I am sure that Louisa hates me too much to do so. She may have induced him to give it back, lest he should return it to me; she knew of my visits."

"Did she know of your visits?"

"She must have. Baldwin doubtless told her, for he never could keep his own counsel, being as weak as water. And if he did hold his peace, I am very sure that Jotty did not. The boy saw me frequently."

"Yes," said Alan reflectively, "he told us that he did, and described you."

Sorley smiled bitterly and revengefully. "The boy seems to have given me away thoroughly. Had he come to me I could have paid him more than two pounds, and would have done so to close his mouth and regain that letter."

"It is just as well that Jotty did speak out, and has placed you in your present position," said Latimer coldly, "for if Miss Grison did lay the trap you speak of, the exposure would only have come about in another way.'

"I daresay you are right," sighed the old man, putting on a shabby cap which also formed a portion of his disguise, "and after all, Jotty, by coming down to warn me, gave me a chance of escape."

"Hum!" said Alan after a pause, "your flight only lent color to the suspicions against you, on the evidence we gave to Moon. It is just probable since Jotty is in league with Miss Grison—for I believe the brat is—that the warning was arranged so that you should incriminate yourself."

"I shall do so no longer," said Sorley opening the door, "come both of you with me. You need not fear that I shall try to escape as I quite intend to give myself up, knowing my complete innocence. If you doubt me take each of you an arm."

"Oh, we'll trust you," said Latimer with a shrug, much to Alan's relief. All the same Dick intended to keep a sharp eye on the man, since the talk might be mainly for effect, and there was no knowing if an escape might not be attempted.

And when the trio got outside, it proved to be a night very propitious to a fugitive, since an unexpected fog had rolled down on the city. London was enveloped in a dense gray smoking cloud chilly and clammy, and intensely disagreeable. Alan and his friend had, after all, to take Sorley's arms to guide him out of the court and through the rusty iron gates, and he went along so passively between them that Latimer became ashamed of his suspicions, since the old man appeared to be acting very straightforwardly. It was not easy even for those who knew the neighborhood, to get out of the labyrinth surrounding Barkers Inn, for the dense fog made the place as unfamiliar as the desert of Sahara. But in some way they managed to reach Chancery Lane, and turned up towards Oxford Street on their way to Thimble Square in Bloomsbury. So thick was the fog that all traffic had ceased, although it was still early in the evening, so the three men, by keeping close to the houses, had to literally feel their way like the blind to their destination. It was a long time before they managed to strike the Square, and longer still before they found the house. But in the end they crossed the threshold, and told the Swiss waiter, who opened the door that they wished to see Miss Grison. As the man was going upstairs, Latimer called him back to press a shilling into his palm.

"Where is Alonzo?" he asked under his breath.

The waiter threw up his hands and explained that the boy had gone away and had not returned, and madame was greatly vexed by his absence. "Hum!" said Dick to himself when the waiter finally departed to announce their arrival, "Jotty seems to have engineered Sorley's escape on his own account, and fears lest his mistress should turn crusty."

Shortly the Swiss came back and conducted them up the stairs and into the private room of Miss Grison. Looking more acid than ever she stood by the fireplace to receive them, but smiled in a wintry fashion when the two young men—who had sent up their names—entered. But they had—for obvious reasons—omitted to inform her that they brought a companion with them, and Miss Grison's face grew hard and malignant, when she saw Sorley steal in behind them. Her shallow blue eyes flashed like sapphires, and if looks could have killed her enemy, Sorley would have fallen dead that very instant. Hate was written all over that wasted face.

"How dare you bring that beast here?" she demanded shrilly, yet—as Dick observed mechanically—lowered her voice lest those in the near drawing-room should overhear, "he ruined my brother and murdered him."

"It's a lie," said Sorley savagely, and glared fiercely at her.

"Beast! beast! it's the truth, it's the—" she stopped, and her hand went to her heart suddenly, "My drops, my drops," she staggered to the door, avoiding her enemy even at the moment of pain. "Wait, wait," she breathed hurriedly to Latimer, "weak heart—drops—a moment a—" she almost reeled out of the room, seeking medicine to recover her from the shock which Sorley's presence had inflicted upon her.

"Is her heart weak?" asked Alan, turning to the man.

"Not that I ever heard of," he retorted sharply, and wiping his face, "she was all right when at Belstone twenty years ago. Perhaps it is weak now. I wish it would break and she would fall dead."

"You mustn't say such things, Mr. Sorley," said Dick frowning.

"But I shall. What would you say of a woman who ruined you?"

"She's not ruined you yet," remarked Alan, soothingly; "if you are innocent you will be set free."

"Oh, I shall be set free all right, even if I have to drink poison to rid myself of my bonds," said the old man, recklessly. "Oh, that woman, that woman, you don't know of what she is capable. Wait till she returns and hear the lies she will tell. All is against me, and only she can prove that I did not take the peacock from her brother. But I am innocent; I swear before heaven that I am innocent."

"Hush! Don't make a row," said Dick, who did not wish the house to be disturbed, and for the next ten minutes both he and Alan were trying to reduce the excited man to a quieter frame of mind. Miss Grison was absent quite that time, if not a few moments longer, and when she returned her looks were much stronger and more composed.

"Why did you bring that man here?" she demanded again, and took up a defiant position on the hearthrug.

"I wish to ask you a question," said Sorley feebly, for his wrath had almost worn him out, and he felt that he was at the mercy of his enemy.

"*You* ask me a question," she echoed contemptuously, "the police wish to ask you one or two, you—you criminal."

"I—I—I am not a criminal," panted the other, sitting down suddenly.

"You are. Inspector Moon has been to see me. He related how Mr. Latimer—and I thank Mr. Latimer for doing so—gave him the letter you wrote to Baldwin which proves that you were with him on that night. I know also what the police know, that you have the peacock which you took from his body, you beast!"

"It's a lie! a lie, Louisa, and you know it. It was you who brought the peacock to The Monastery when you came down for the funeral."

"Ha! is that so?" she said tauntingly; "and how are you going to prove I did such a thing?"

"You don't deny it, Miss Grison?" asked Alan, with some sharpness.

"Yes, I do. I deny it at once and with all truth. I stole the peacock to punish that brute who ruined us, and I gave it to Baldwin. He had it in his possession when he was murdered, and since he has it," she pointed an accusing finger at Sorley, who winced and wilted, "he is guilty."

"You brought it to The Monastery to trap me," said the man resolutely.

"I did not," she retorted equally resolutely, and the two argued the question on and on and on until Alan and Dick both felt their heads reeling. For almost an hour the conversation continued, Latimer sometimes putting in a question, and sometimes Alan suggesting an explanation. But every time, the result was that Miss Grison refused to acknowledge that she had taken the peacock to Belstone. Then, while they were in the full tide of talk, she rose unexpectedly, and pointed towards the door.

"Come in, come in," she almost shouted, "this is the beast."

Inspector Moon appeared, and behind him were two policemen in plain clothes.

CHAPTER XV

THE BLACK BAG

Sorley shivered and shrank back when he saw the uniform of Inspector Moon and the two men behind him. Miss Grison, with an exulting look on her hard face, pointed to her prey, glorying in the way she had trapped him. And that it was a trap, Fuller now truly believed, since the police had appeared at so opportune a moment for the capture.

"There he is," cried the woman excitedly; "take him away, the beast!"

Moon moved forward and laid a heavy hand on the shoulder of the wretched man, who moaned and trembled at the fatal touch. "I arrest you, Randolph Sorley, in the name of the King, for the murder of Baldwin Grison," he said in unemotional tones, and reciting the regulation formula; "anything you say now will be used in evidence against you."

"I am innocent, I am innocent," was all that Sorley could say.

"And upon my soul I believe he is," murmured Alan softly to Dick.

"If so it is just as well to have the whole matter threshed out in a proper manner," rejoined the reporter. "How did you come here, Mr. Inspector?"

Miss Grison replied before the officer could open his mouth. "I telephoned for him," she said sharply. "You thought that I left the room to take medicine, but it was to send for the police."

"Then you were not ill?" said Latimer taken aback.

"No," she answered coolly; "it was all acting; didn't I act well?"

"I told you she was a wicked woman," moaned Sorley, who stood passively between the two plain-clothes men.

"Wicked!" repeated Miss Grison with scorn; "if I am wicked, what are you?"

Inspector Moon made a sign that she should be silent, and explained his speedy presence quietly. "Miss Grison telephoned to me at Rotherhithe," he said; "and as I happened to have business in the Bow Street police office my clerk repeated the telephonic message to that place. I was thus enabled to drive here in a cab with my men, in spite of the fog, although I must say that we drove very slowly. However," he looked at Sorley, "we are in excellent time. May I ask what you two gentlemen are doing here?"

"We brought Mr. Sorley to see Miss Grison at his request," said Latimer.

"You should have sent for me as this lady did," rebuked Moon sharply.

"There was no need," put in Alan. "Mr. Sorley intended to give himself up."

Moon smiled derisively. "I doubt that, seeing how he ran away from his own house at Belstone."

"I did so on the impulse of the moment," cried Sorley, drawing himself up with some dignity; "but later I saw that my flight gave color to the charge against me. As I am quite innocent, I intended to give myself up so that the matter could be inquired into, and I do so now."

"Because you can't help yourself," said Moon with a shrug; "come away, sir, at once. I have a cab at the door."

"Oh, I sha'n't try to escape, for I am innocent," persisted the old man; "because I have the peacock it is supposed that I murdered Grison."

"It is very good evidence, you know," Moon assured him.

"It was that woman, who brought the peacock down to The Monastery."

Miss Grison laughed scornfully. "I told you he would say that," she said, addressing Moon, "and I solemnly swear that I did no such thing."

"You stole it from me over twenty years ago," cried Sorley insistently.

"I took it, certainly," admitted the woman coolly, "because you owed my brother money, and it was necessary to hold something valuable belonging to you so that he might be paid. You never paid, and preferred to get back your property, or rather that of your niece, by crime."

"It is wholly false."

"Tell that to the judge and jury," she sneered, "I warned you that you would be punished for your iniquity, and now the time has come."

"The time has not come," said Sorley furiously; "you have involved me in difficulties somehow, and I am trapped. But I believe that the Indian who lives here has been used by you to bring about my disgrace. He also knew about the peacock—

"Come! come," interrupted Moon in a peremptory manner, "remember what you say will be used in evidence against you. Better hold your tongue and come away at once. I regret to say—" He stepped forward clinking handcuffs.

"No," almost screamed Sorley, backing against the wall with a gesture of refusal, "there is no need for that shame. I won't run away; I intended to give myself up, indeed I did, I did."

"Put them on, put them on," cried Miss Grison, clapping her hands with delight, "he murdered Baldwin and deserves punishment."

"I won't run away, I won't run away," whimpered Sorley piteously.

Alan, sorry for the man, interfered. "Indeed I don't think that there is any need to take such a precaution, Mr. Inspector. He really came to me and Mr. Latimer this evening to surrender himself to the law."

Dick nodded. "I agree with Fuller," he remarked, and Sorley cast a grateful look in his direction, as Moon after a moment's hesitation placed the handcuffs in his pocket.

"I won't put them on in the house," he said graciously, "so when we go, no one will see that you have been arrested on so serious a charge. But in the cab—"

"I don't mind that," said Sorley eagerly; "only spare me the shame of being seen with them on by my fellow-creatures. Oh, dear me, and I am quite innocent," he maundered on in a senile way, "quite innocent. When—"

"Come," said the inspector imperiously; "I don't wish to use force."

"I should drum him out of the house with the Rogue's March," said Miss Grison laughing fiercely, "beast that you are!"

Sorley did not reply, for he was already tottering towards the door between the two officers, and followed by the inspector. As he passed out of the room, he turned and looked significantly at Alan, "The black bag, don't forget the black bag," he said, and, as Moon touched him on the shoulder he went stumbling out of sight. Strange to say no one attached much meaning to his last words, and Alan himself was bewildered.

"What the dickens does he mean?"

"Something bad, you may be sure," retorted Miss Grison malignantly.

"I think Sorley is a better man than you admit him to be," remarked the young man indignantly. "Dick, where are you going?"

"I intend to follow Sorley and Moon," answered Latimer, "come with me."

"No," said Fuller with a glance at the landlady, "I wish to ask Miss Grison a few questions."

"They won't be answered," cried Miss Grison exultingly, "my enemy has been trapped, and there is nothing left for me to wish for."

Latimer was so annoyed at the malignity of the woman, that he turned at the door as her victim had done. "Let me remind you of an excellent proverb, Miss Grison," he said quietly: "there's many a slip t'wixt the cup and the lip!" and then he went out quietly.

"There will be no slip except that of Sorley when he is hanged," said the woman savagely. "Now, you can go, Mr. Fuller, I have no quarrel with you."

"There is one on my part, however," said Alan, taking a seat; "you have disgraced Marie by this arrest of her uncle."

"Oh, indeed. And you say that because you love her. Is the course of justice to be stayed for the tears of a chit?"

"Marie is not a chit," retorted the lover angrily.

"Yes she is; yes she is," taunted Miss Grison in quite a schoolgirl manner. "I hate her, I hated her mother, who made me a slave to her whims. I hate Sorley, and have paid him out."

"Not yet."

"What do you mean with your 'not yet,'" asked Miss Grison contemptuously.

"I mean that he may prove his innocence at the trial."

"He can't; everything is against him."

"So far I admit that. But some new evidence may turn up."

"I don't care what turns up," said Miss Grison vehemently; "the man is a guilty beast and must be punished. I hate him, oh, how I hate him!"

Fuller was about to ask why, when the door opened slightly and the brown haughty face of Morad-Bakche peered in. "Pardon my intrusion," he said in his best English, "but the whole house is in commotion about a reported arrest. How are you, Mr. Fuller." He stepped into the room as he spoke.

"Wait here," said Miss Grison to Alan imperiously. "I must explain to these people, as there is no need to make bad worse. Sorley has ruined me before, and my brother with me. He will ruin me now by coming here to be arrested, since many of my boarders will leave the house."

"Let me remind you, Miss Grison, that you are responsible for his arrest."

"Because you and Mr. Latimer would have allowed him to escape," she said in angry tones. "Better that I should lose every boarder I have than let that beast go free," as the murmur in the near drawing-room increased. She opened the door which Bakche had closed. "Wait here," she said again to Alan, and vanished to pacify the inmates of the establishment.

Left alone with Morad-Bakche, the young man made no remark, as he did not feel inclined to talk to the man. But he was not permitted to be at peace, for the Indian advanced eagerly, his eyes sparkling. "Has Mr. Sorley been arrested?" he asked swiftly and anxiously.

"Yes," answered Fuller shortly.

"On a charge of murder?"

"Yes!"

"How did he come here?"

"I think you had better ask these questions of Miss Grison."

"I shall do so," rejoined Bakche calmly, "when you are gone. But there is one she may not be able to answer."

"Probably!" Alan shrugged his shoulders with feigned indifference, guessing what the question was, and not choosing to reply to it immediately.

But Bakche was not to be put off by a contemptuous manner. "Has Mr. Sorley given up the peacock to the police?" he demanded.

"I cannot say. If he has, the police will give it back to me."

"Why should it be given back to you?"

"Because it is the property of Miss Inderwick; and until her uncle is free I intend to look after her interests."

The other man sneered. "I can understand that."

"If you do, there is no necessity for you to ask questions," rejoined Alan coolly. "You are no client of mine, Mr. Bakche."

"It would be better for you if I were."

"I fail to see that. You want the peacock, and I don't intend that you should have it, or the treasure either."

"Both belong to me," cried the Indian angrily.

"I think not. And as our interests are opposed, you can scarcely expect me to reply to your questions further."

"But if we join forces, we shall be stronger to learn the truth."

"Possibly, but if the discovery of the truth—I suppose you mean in connection with the whereabouts of the treasure—means your having half the jewels, I prefer to work alone." Fuller thought for a moment, then added slowly, "of course Miss Inderwick may be willing to make terms with you regarding the sharing of the gems on one condition?"

"What is that?" demanded Bakche eagerly, and with flashing eyes.

"She believes her uncle to be innocent, and I am half inclined to agree with her, notwithstanding the weight of evidence against him. Now if you can prove his innocence, and thus do a service to Miss Inderwick, why then—"

"But how can I prove his innocence?" asked Bakche in a puzzled manner. "I know nothing about the murder."

"I never supposed you did. However, the proving of Sorley's innocence is your affair, if you want to get a share in the jewels."

Bakche took a turn up and down the room. "I may know more of this affair than you think," he said abruptly.

"Probably you do since you say so. Well?"

"Well, if I get Mr. Sorley released can I take your word for—"

"Certainly you can take my word," replied Fuller stiffly; "and my offer is such a sporting one, that it is not worth while committing it to paper."

Bakche nodded. "I have always found that an English gentleman keeps his word, sir," he said cordially, "so on those terms I shall hunt for the assassin of Grison."

"Don't you then believe that Sorley is guilty?" asked Alan suddenly.

"On those terms I shall hunt for the assassin of Grison," said Bakche once more. "I decline to speak further, and—" he stopped short as Miss Grison re-entered the room and moved towards the door. "We can talk further, Mr. Fuller, when you are more at leisure," was his final remark as he stole out and closed the door swiftly behind him.

"What is that?" asked Miss Grison with a searching look at Alan.

"Bakche wants the peacock and the jewels, as he says that they rightfully belong to him. He wishes me to help him."

"Will you do so?"

"No. They belong to Miss Inderwick."

"And you intend to marry Miss Inderwick," said the woman with a hard laugh; "well you are wise. But Mr. Bakche is the rightful owner."

"On what grounds?"

"The Begum's jewels, which she gave George Inderwick were temple treasures and should not have been parted with."

"Hum!" said Alan meditatively. "I remember Bakche saying something about priests. Is he one himself?"

"No," answered the woman quietly, "but he is the rightful heir to the jewels, as you can see from the snakes on his right arm."

"I don't see how that proves his ownership!"

"Many of the ornaments are in the form of snakes set with gems."

"Still I don't see," persisted Fuller doubtfully.

Miss Grison sat down impatiently, as apparently the late excitement had affected her nerves. "I'm sure I can't explain further. Mr. Bakche declared that the jewels are sacred and that he wants to get them back. The snake sign I mention is tattooed on his right forearm twisting in spirals up from the wrist to the elbow. Ask him to show it to you."

"I don't think it interests me," said Fuller dryly. "Mr. Bakche assuredly shall not get Marie's property if I can prevent it."

"I think the peacock prevents it," said Miss Grison spitefully. "Until you guess the riddle you can't find the gems, and I hope you never will.'

"Why?"

"Because I hate Sorley, and I hate the girl, and the whole horrible lot," she cried furiously.

"So you said before. This conversation is getting monotonous."

"End it then; I don't want you. But if you will take my advice you will give the peacock to Mr. Morad-Bakche. He has sworn to have it."

"And I have sworn that he shall not have it. Do you think that I am afraid of a black man, Miss Grison? Moreover I have not got the bird."

"Oh!" She shrugged her shoulders, "I daresay Sorley has concealed it somewhere, and will tell you where to find it before he is hanged."

"He never will be hanged."

"Yes he will. He can't escape."

"Unless it can be proved that you took the peacock to Belstone."

"I never did," said Miss Orison coldly; "Sorley made up that story to account for its possession and to implicate me."

"Well," said Alan rising, "I shall ask Jotty, for I verily believe he is aware of much more than he chooses to say."

"He has never told me anything," snapped the woman; "and moreover is the most ungrateful little reptile I ever met. I gave him a good home and a new name and food and clothes and every chance of being respectable; yet he ran away, and heaven only knows where he is."

"I can't tell you his whereabouts now, Miss Grison, but I can tell you in what direction he went on leaving the house a few days ago."

For the first time the landlady showed some curiosity. "Where did he go?"

"To Belstone with a copy of your interview in his pocket to warn Sorley that—"

He got no further, for Miss Grison jumped up with her hard blue eyes flashing with rage. "The traitor," she said in an ominously calm voice. "After all I did for him, he tried to save Sorley, did he?"

"For money?"

"Of course. The boy is a born miser. Well, if he returns here, I shall know how to punish him. Never mind how; don't ask; I may box his ears, or I may have him put in jail for theft."

"But since you have given him a chance of being respectable why ruin him?"

"Because he has sided with my enemy."

"Why do you hate Sorley so?" questioned Fuller, bluntly.

"You wish to know. Then you shall. I hate him because he ruined my brother Baldwin, because he murdered my brother Baldwin, and because he deserted me twenty years ago."

"What do you mean?"

"I mean what I say, Mr. Fuller. Do you know who I am? You don't. Well, I am Mrs. Sorley." Alan stared. "His wife?"

"His deserted wife," corrected the woman bitterly. "Yes; Randolph married me because I was a pretty girl. But he grew tired of me, and then he wanted to make a rich lady his wife."

"Yes; I have heard that," said Alan recalling the story of his mother, about Miss Marchmont.

"It was a secret marriage," said Miss Grison; "he asked me to keep it secret, as he feared lest his sister, Mrs. Inderwick, should ask him to leave The Monastery if she learned what he had done. The lady he wished to make his wife died, or I should have spoken out. But Baldwin forged that check, and the sole way in which I could prevent Randolph from putting him in the dock was by promising to hold my tongue for ever. He gave me money, and I came here to set up this boarding-house. And I took the peacock to punish him, afterwards giving it to Baldwin. Randolph fought me, but I said that I would destroy it if he used force. And then—well," she broke off abruptly, "can you blame me for hating this man? He ruined my brother and he ruined me and I —hush! What's that? Mr. Latimer!"

It was indeed Dick, who came hastily into the room.

"Alan! Alan, come with me to the police office."

"What is the matter?"

"Sorley has escaped."

"Escaped," Miss Grison screamed, and then suppressed her emotion lest more trouble should be caused in the house. "How—how did he escape?" she asked, clenching her hands so tightly that the nails were driven into the flesh.

Dick was recovering his breath by degrees. "When the cab stopped at Bow Street police office, and we alighted—that is, when Moon and his officer and Sorley alighted, for I followed him in another cab—Sorley suddenly darted away and was lost in the fog."

There was a look of mingled dismay and anger on Miss Grison's face at this unexpected intelligence. She tried to speak and could not, so Fuller asked the necessary question.

"Didn't the detective hold him when he alighted?"

"Yes, and there came in Sorley's cleverness. On the way out of this house he managed to slip his arms out of the sleeves of that overcoat he wore and simply left it buttoned on his shoulders. When one of the men held him by the arm, he suddenly slipped the coat and ran away. Of course Moon and his underlings followed, but the fog was so thick that they could not catch him. I arrived a moment later, and then came back here to tell you."

"He is guilty, he is guilty," said Miss Grison persistently. "What do you say now, Mr. Fuller?"

Alan was puzzled. "He certainly gave himself up," he remarked.

"And intended to give the detectives and Moon the slip whenever he had the chance," retorted the landlady. "Bah! Don't tell me; the man is the murderer of my brother, and came here to try and force me to prove his innocence by admitting that I took the peacock down to Belstone, which I certainly did not. What is your opinion, Mr. Latimer?"

"I can't say," replied Dick with a perplexed air. "To-night, since the man was giving himself up so frankly, I half believed that he was innocent. I have my doubts now. But it is a very puzzling case," ended Dick with a sigh.

Fuller, preparing to take his leave buttoned up his coat and picked up his hat. "There is one thing to be said in Sorley's favor," he remarked, addressing Miss Grison, "if he did murder your brother, he did you a service."

She threw back her head scornfully. "Oh indeed! I should like to know in what way, Mr. Fuller?"

"I heard—and Latimer there is my informant—that your brother murdered a man just outside the opium den he frequented in order to rob him of watch and money and general jewelry. Since this is the case, Sorley saved your brother from being hanged, and your name from being further disgraced."

Miss Grison's head drooped. "Inspector Moon told me about the matter," she admitted, "and how the watch had been traced. But I don't believe Baldwin killed anyone. He was much too kind and thoughtful."

"My dear lady," said Latimer impatiently, "let me point out that no one but yourself entertains this good opinion of your late brother. According to everyone else he was a bad lot. I regret having to say this, but you must be just. If Sorley has acted wickedly—and of that we cannot be sure—your brother is not free from blame. That he murdered this man is certain, so his own violent death is simple justice."

"I don't believe what you say, Mr. Latimer; you are prejudiced in favor of that beast."

"On the contrary, as Mr. Fuller will tell you, I have been hot against the man, Miss Grison. Now I have my doubts of his guilt."

"In spite of his escape?"

"Yes It is a perplexing case, and until I can gain more evidence, I am not prepared to give an opinion. Why do you hate him so?"

The woman gave the same answer to Latimer as she had given already to Alan, detailing the circumstances which led her to become her enemy's wife, and emphasizing his desertion. "And I kept silent for Baldwin's sake," she ended in a grating voice; "but he is dead, so there is no longer any reason for me to deny that I am Mrs. Sorley. Not that I shall ever take my real name, seeing how my husband has disgraced it. Now I don't want you to make any remarks, thank you, Mr. Latimer. You can go, and you can be sure that I shall do my best to get Randolph arrested again."

"You won't find it easy to discover him in this fog," said Dick dryly, and with Alan took his immediate leave, for there seemed no necessity to remain and listen to Miss Grison's wrath which was that of an unreasonable woman obsessed by one bitter idea.

The fog was still thick, and Fuller remarked that he wondered how Moon had managed to get a cab. "We couldn't do it, Dick."

"The fog gets lighter at times and then thick again," said Latimer absently. "I suppose when Moon took his cab, traffic was resumed for the moment."

"It seems to have stopped now," answered Alan, trying to peer into the darkness blurred by the street lamps. "Let us go home. Why do you want to go to the Bow Street office again?"

"I only wished to learn the latest details with an eye to copy," said Dick, "but I think I shall leave things until to-morrow, as I am quite tired out."

Having arrived at this conclusion, the two groped their way back to Chancery Lane and to Barkers Inn. The true reason why Latimer had so readily yielded to Fuller's suggestion was that he greatly desired to learn if Sorley had again sought shelter with them. But on entering their chambers they found that no one had come during their absence, and Dick heaved a sigh of relief, which was echoed by Alan.

"I'm glad he didn't come back," remarked Alan, "we should have had to give him up."

"I think he knew as much, and so did not return. However, the fog will afford him an excellent chance of escape, and I doubt if he will be caught a second time. What's the matter?"

"The black bag," gasped Fuller, pointing to an article of that description which was on a chair in the corner of the room, "he mentioned that when he went away with Moon." Alan picked up the bag. "What is in it?"

158

"The peacock for a hundred pounds," cried Dick swiftly.

He was right, for when the bag was opened, Fuller found wrapped in the chamois skin the golden bird, which was the cause of all the trouble.

"Ha!" said Latimer staring at it, "now we can try and solve the riddle."

CHAPTER XVI

MISS INDERWICK'S EXCURSION

While these events were taking place in London, Marie, isolated in The Monastery, anxiously waited to hear news from her lover. As arranged, Mr. Fuller met her at the Lewes station and drove her to Belstone in his trap. As Alan had guessed, the vicar was in full possession of all that had taken place, and invited the girl to stay with himself and his wife until matters were more settled. While in London Marie had complained of her loneliness at the big house, and had looked forward to some such invitation. But on the way down in the train she had changed her mind, since she felt that she could think things out better when alone. However, she did not object to dining at the vicarage, and explained the whole matter to her hostess. They were naturally horrified, as no such event had ever before disturbed the village.

"I can't believe that Mr. Sorley would commit a crime," said Mrs. Fuller, greatly distressed, "gentlemen don't do these things."

The vicar drew down his long upper lip. "I fear that gentlemen do what suits them, when the temptation is strong, my dear."

"Does that mean that you believe Uncle Ran is guilty?" flashed out Marie in a resentful tone.

"Not necessarily. I am not yet acquainted with the whole story, save what scraps you told me as we drove here."

Marie looked round the room, and seeing that the servants had taken their departure, leaving those at the table to walnuts and wine, she concluded that the moment had come to make a clean breast of things. In a low voice, and entirely without emotion, she related all that she had heard from Alan and Dick. The story sounded black enough, and the faces of Mr. and Mrs. Fuller grew longer as she proceeded. When she ended there ensued a silence which rasped Marie's nerves.

"Well?" she asked sharply, and looking from one to the other, "what do you think of it?"

"The weight of evidence is decidedly in favor of Sorley's guilt," said Mr. Fuller sadly.

"I daresay. All the same he is innocent."

"How can you prove that, my dear girl?"

"I can't prove it," responded Miss Inderwick in a truly feminine way, "but Uncle Ran never did it for all that."

"It is all very dreadful," moaned Mrs. Fuller, shaken out of her usual state of placid happiness. "I wonder you can speak so quietly, Marie."

"I cried awfully in London," acknowledged the girl frankly; "but I can't cry any more. Tears won't help Uncle Ran, and common-sense will. He is not going to be hanged if I can help it."

"Oh, my dear." Mrs. Fuller shuddered at the mention of the sinister word.

"You intend to prove your uncle's innocence—or what you presume to be his innocence?" asked the vicar, looking at her doubtfully.

"Yes, only I don't presume anything. I know that Uncle Ran never killed that poor thing. I don't know who did, but he didn't."

"How are you going to set about the matter?"

"I can't say," said Marie curtly, although this statement was not quite true, for she had an idea of making a start, which she did not intend to place before these two ordinary people.

"Of course, if your uncle had the peacock, my dear—"

"Mrs. Fuller, I am quite sure that Miss Grison brought down the peacock on that day when she paid a visit unasked to The Monastery. She hates Uncle Ran because she thinks he ruined her brother, and is only too glad to get him into trouble."

"But how could she get the peacock?"

"From her brother. He had it all the time. Alan said so, and he knows a very great deal about matters."

"Alan has a good head," said the vicar approvingly. "I think Marie you had better allow him to look into the matter, and stay with us meanwhile. We can send over to The Monastery for your clothes, my dear."

"No thank you. I wished at one time to stay here until Uncle Ran was proved innocent, but I think it is best for me to return to the house in case he should come back again."

"Oh, I hope not," cried Mrs. Fuller in alarm, "he would assuredly be arrested as soon as the news got about."

"It wouldn't get about," said Marie resolutely, "for I should hide Uncle Ran somewhere until we learned the truth. There are plenty of secret places in the house where he could be concealed."

Mr. Fuller passed over this latter statement to remark upon the first. "The question is, what is the truth? If Sorley is innocent, and I sincerely trust that he is, who murdered this unfortunate Baldwin?"

"Morad-Bakche," said Marie promptly.

"Who is he? You never mentioned him before," said Mrs. Fuller, startled.

"Did I not?" observed Miss Inderwick with a lightness she was far from feeling. "Oh, he is an Indian who wants to get the jewels because he says that they belong to the royal family of Kam. He came down here and stopped a night at The Red Fox."

Mr. Fuller nodded. "I fancy I heard something about a foreigner staying there," he said quietly, "in July last was it not?"

Marie nodded. "He learned all about the peacock from Mrs. Verwin—the common talk of the village, that is."

"Oh that woman is a terrible gossip," exclaimed Mrs. Fuller distressed. "I dread her tongue. What did she say exactly, my dear?"

Marie reported the interview between herself and Mrs. Verwin and Alan, and shortly, the vicar and his wife were acquainted with the way in which Morad-Bakche had traced the peacock to Belstone and afterwards to London. "And I believe that he learned Mr. Grison had it," finished Marie, "and must have tried to get it from him. A man like that is much more likely to murder a person than poor dear Uncle Ran, though he has his faults, and has always been horrid over my engagement to Alan."

"But are you really engaged to Alan?" asked the vicar sharply.

"Yes, I am. Uncle Ran said that if Alan found the jewels that we could be married, so I look upon myself as being engaged to him."

"But Alan has never found the jewels," objected Mrs. Fuller tremulously. "He may never find them, my dear."

"It doesn't matter," replied Marie, getting on her feet; "we shall marry all the same. But the first thing to be done is to save Uncle Ran, and I am doing what I can—that is, I intend to do what I can. Alan will work also, and Mr. Latimer, though he doesn't seem to think Uncle Ran is innocent.'

"On the face of it it looks as though he were not," said the vicar doubtfully, and rising in his turn, "however we can talk over the matter in the drawing-room."

"No," said Marie standing very erect, and looking at the elderly pair with very bright eyes. "I am now going home to think out things."

"Oh, Marie, won't you stay here?"

"I think it is best to go home," repeated the girl gently, but kissing the soft and withered old cheek. "I am all right with granny and Henny and Jenny to look after me. If Mr. Bakche comes I shan't be afraid."

"My dear girl, you may suspect him wrongly," said Mr. Fuller.

"Well, other people are suspecting Uncle Ran wrongly," retorted Miss Inderwick, "so that balances things. Now I must go away. Good-night Mr. Fuller; good-night, Mrs. Fuller. If I learn anything I shall come and tell you."

"I shall write at once to Alan and ask him to explain things precisely," said the vicar, as he saw his guest at the door; "and keep up your heart my dear child. This trouble, like all troubles, is a blessing in disguise."

"It is a very good disguise, then" said Marie sadly, "no, don't come with me," she added when Mr. Fuller assumed his soft hat and took his stick. "I can get home by myself."

"No," said the clergyman grimly, and took her arm, "after you have hinted about that Indian, I think it is just as well to see you safely into the hands of your servants."

"But you don't think—"

"I think that one should always be on the safe side, my dear. If this man wants the peacock, he may try and enter the house. If he does I am sorry for him, as Henny and Jenny are as strong as men. By the way where is that wretched bird, which has caused so much trouble?"

"I don't know," sighed Marie, as they walked through the village, "uncle took it away with him I think, although he has left his gems."

"I should think if Sorley clears his name he will have had enough of gems for the rest of his life," remarked Mr. Fuller rebukingly, but as Marie did not answer, and he did not wish to cause her pain, he said no more. They passed through Belstone, and into the park, and Marie said good-bye to the vicar when Henny with a noisy joy received her at the door. Mr. Fuller was now at ease in his mind, as he knew how devoted the Dutch dolls were, and returned home wondering how these crooked things would straighten out.

Granny and the two servants were overcome with delight when their young mistress was within doors, for they had troubled considerably over her visit to London. Marie laughed them out of their fears and assured them that she was quite able to look after herself. They asked after Mr. Sorley, who was no great favorite with the three, but of course Marie, ignorant of what had taken place at Miss Grison's, could give them no information. In her opinion Uncle Ran had gone abroad, and would wait there until his innocence could be proved.

"Well, my dear Miss Marie," said granny polishing her spectacles. "God forbid as I should say what I shouldn't say, but there's no doubt as Mr. Sorley ain't the proper person to be your guardian, my dear. He's took your money and kept you short and mewed you up here like a nun, to say nothing of having behaved very badly to that poor Miss Grison, not that I'm fond of her myself."

"Did Uncle Ran ever care for her?" asked Miss Inderwick anxiously.

"Well he did and he didn't. She was pretty, in a light-haired skimpy way, I don't deny, and I thought as he loved her; and then—but it's too long a story, Miss Marie. I'll tell it you to-morrow when you are rested. Let us hope that Mr. Sorley won't be hanged, which would be a sore disgrace to the family, and that you'll marry Master Alan, who is just the kind-hearted gentleman to look after your interests properly."

"Look after them and me also, you mean, granny," said Marie, who was really too weary to listen to an account of her uncle's early delinquencies. "I shall go to bed now," and she did, feeling quite worn out. But before falling asleep she arranged in her own mind to go to London the next day.

The fact is, Marie being anxious and wilful, was not at all pleased to remain passive while things were so unpleasant for her uncle, and incidentally for herself, since she was his niece. Alan had insisted that she should not see Mother Slaig, whereupon Marie, although promising to obey him, mentally vowed that she would do so. Mother Slaig, if anyone, would know the truth and might be persuaded to reveal it to a dexterous questioner. Of course this was Marie's own opinion, and she intended to prove to Alan that she was right. Sorley had given her twenty pounds, so there was no lack of money, and the girl decided firmly to do a little detective business on her own account. For no visible reason she believed that Bakche had something to do with the death of Grison, if not indeed the actual doer of the deed. Should her surmise prove to be correct Mother Slaig might be able to say if the Indian had haunted the slum, or had come into touch with the deceased. And Marie wished her uncle would return home if only to tell her that he had seen Bakche at Rotherhithe, which was not impossible, considering that Mr. Sorley had been too often to interview Grison. But Sorley, as she sadly reflected, did not dare to come back, for the detective left behind by Moon was still in the house, and would arrest him at once.

Of course granny made an outcry the next morning, when Marie announced her intention of going again to London. All her arguments were in vain, however, and Miss Inderwick left the house early so as to catch a morning train. She promised to be back again by six o'clock, but did not tell granny where she was going—that is she admitted that the metropolis was her goal, but did not specify whither she would precisely go. Granny, believing that the wilful girl was to meet her lover, felt fairly comfortable in her mind. Had she known that Miss Inderwick purposed exploring a slum, she would have sent a telegram to Fuller to stop the excursion. Marie guessed this, so held her peace.

The girl knew exactly how to get to Rotherhithe, as she had peeped into an ABC. before leaving Belstone. On arrival at Victoria it was necessary to take the underground route, which would conduct her directly to her destination. When on the spot Marie hoped by enquiries to learn the precise whereabouts of Mother Slaig, and moreover had a faint idea that the slum the harridan lived in was called Gibson's Rents. To explore this low neighborhood she had put on an old serge frock and a shabby black jacket, so that she was as well disguised as her uncle had been when he sought Barkers Inn. Not that Marie was ever so well dressed as Mr. Sorley, for he never gave her sufficient money to be extravagant.

The venturesome damsel duly reached Victoria Station, and had no difficulty in dropping downward to the nether railway line. Being yet a schoolgirl and feeling hungry, she bought some pastry of the jam-puff order and devoured it in the first-class compartment, which she shared with other ladies. Marie travelled in this most expensive fashion, because she thought she would be safer from being accosted by strangers. Destiny protected her in this especial way, and she gained Rotherhithe without having a single remark addressed to her. When she emerged into the open air once more, she looked helplessly around, not knowing which way to go. But she felt sure that Gibson's Rents was the name of the slum, and asked a tall and burly policeman where it was to be found.

The officer looked at her keenly, and saw that she was a lady in spite of her shabby clothes. "Why do you wish to go there, miss?" he asked, and touched his helmet, "it's a rough place."

"I wish to see a woman called Mrs. Slaig."

"Mother Slaig. Why, miss, she's one of the worst creatures in the slum. I don't think it is wise of you to go, miss, I don't indeed. You're a district visitor, I take it, miss," went on the man, who could conceive of no other object but philanthropy which would take the young lady into such a hole, "and Mother Slaig don't want tracts."

Marie did not deny the identity the policeman attributed to her, as she was quick enough to see that such a character would expedite her journey, and would conceal her real intentions. She did not wish to be asked questions lest she should get into trouble, by interesting herself in a police-court case, such as the murder of Grison truly was. "I shall be all right, officer," she answered lightly; "no one will hurt me."

"Well, miss, I don't think they will, for they think a heap of district visitors at Gibson's Rents, as these ladies give them money. But I can take you to the end of my beat and pass you on to another officer, who will show you the way. Come along, miss."

Marie conceived a high estimate of the guardians of the law, for her friend passed her along to another, who transferred her to a third, and all three men were courteous and considerate in every way. Perhaps Marie's good looks, and engaging manners had something to do with this suavity, but she was certainly charmed with her guides. It was a fourth policeman, tall, slim and military-looking who conducted her down the crooked alley, near the riverside, where Mother Slaig had her boarding-house. There were numbers of disreputable people about, both male and female, and when the oaths of these unfortunate creatures struck her ear, and her eyes rested on their animal faces, the girl felt glad that she had a constable at her elbow. In her ignorance, she had never thought that the neighborhood was so vile as this, and half regretted coming. However, she had the high spirit of the Inderwicks, and declined to turn back, for having put her hand to the plough, the did not intend to leave it until she had driven her furrow.

The fourth policeman saw her shudder of disgust, when they stopped before a disreputable house, dingy, tumble-down, and dilapidated. "I shall stay here while you give Mother Slaig your tracts, miss," he said politely, also taking her for a district visitor, "and if anything goes wrong, you just call for me."

Perhaps for this reason Mother Slaig received Marie graciously, when she ventured into the evil-smelling place. It was like a rabbit-warren with innumerable doors, passages, stairs, and rooms, all equally foul. Men and women in ragged garbs swarmed in and out, while children tumbled here there and everywhere, shrilly crying and swearing and quarrelling. The police introduced Marie to the landlady of this thieves' kitchen, as it truly was, and then took up his station at the door with his thumbs in his belt, to look benignly on the ebbing and flowing of the populace in and out of the lane, and in and out of the dens which bordered it. Mother Slaig, not approving of district visitors—for Marie had been presented as one—led the young lady into a small dark room on the ground floor, and sat down with a sniff, prepared to battle for her rights as an Englishwoman, who declined to be converted. She was a shapeless stout old creature swathed in various rags which had long since lost their color. Her face was so swarthy as to suggest gipsy blood, and her snappy black eyes and the quantity of cheap jewellery she wore emphasised the fact that she probably belonged to the gentle Romany.

"I don't want no Bible talk, young lady," she said in a harsh voice, "nor no tracts, nor no arsking if I'm saved. Whether I am or I ain't's my look out, so just say your say and git, though I don't deny," added Mother Slaig in a whining tone, "as a shilling or two, let alone gold, would help me to bear me sorrers better, bless you, my dearie."

"I shall give you a pound if you will let me have a talk with you," said Marie, smiling, for in spite of the woman's disreputable looks there was something oddly attractive about her.

"A pound, and what's a pound, miss?" grumbled Mother Slaig.

"Not much, but it is all I can afford. You are a kind-hearted woman, Mrs. Slaig, I am quite sure."

"Me!" Mother Slaig stared. "Why I'm the tork of the place for me languidge and slappings."

"Ah," said Marie diplomatically, "no one has taken you in the right way."

"P'raps they 'ave an' p'raps they 'avn't," growled the woman restlessly, for Marie's charm of manner softened her, "an what's all this oil and butter for, miss. You want something, you do. Oh trust you fur that."

"Yes, Mrs. Slaig, I do want something, and I am going to throw myself on your mercy, because I trust you."

The old hag stopped scratching her elbow, and stared harder than ever. "I never was spoke delicate-like to afore," she muttered. "You ain't the sort of lady with tracts as I' 'ad 'ere, bullying me no end."

"I hope I'm not," said Marie with a girlish laugh, which brought a perplexed smile in answer on the old woman's dirty wrinkled face. It was rare that such pure innocent laughter was heard in Gibson's Rents. "I know you will help me, Mrs. Slaig."

"Well, I don't say as I won't, for there's no denying you've got a way with you, as ain't bad. What is it?"

"It's about the murder of Mr. Grison?" said Marie slowly.

Mother Slaig aroused with a subdued screech, "Blimme if you ain't one o' them wimin 'tecs. Now ain't y', ain't y'?"

"No; I am the niece of Mr. Randolph Sorley who is accused of the crime."

Mother Slaig dropped again into her chair a shapeless bundle of clothes, and with a bewildered look in her eyes. "Ho! you're her, are y'?" she growled, but not in a hostile manner. "Moon—he's the head peeler hereabouts, dearie's been nosin' round about that murder. Only this mornin' he comes an' ses as they caught that Sorley cove larst night, and he got away in th' bloomin' fog. Yuss," said Mother Slaig, anticipating Marie's question. "I knows the Sorley cove. Many a time he's come t' see that Grison chap, as was a rotten bad egg, and guv me shillin's and tanners endless. A swell, a toff, he was tryin' to look what wasn't his age, but a good 'un wiff his cash. I 'adn't got no row with him, nohow," and she nodded vigorously.

"You don't think he murdered Mr. Grison?" asked Marie apprehensively.

"Blimme if I knows," said Mother Slaig reflectively, and scratching her elbow again, "and what odd's 'f he did anyhow, miss. Grison was better undergroun' than above it in my opinion. Never paid his rent rigler he did, cuss him," swore Mother Slaig furiously, "an' if I'd knowed about that gold hen as they're makin' sich a fuss round, I'd ha' had it out of him for a whelp as he allays was, an' that same, you kin taike fro' me, miss."

"Well I don't believe that my uncle murdered Mr. Grison," said Marie in a resolute voice, and looking hard at the harridan.

"That's right, dearie, allys stick up fur them as is relatives, though I don't think much o' mine leavin' me 'ere to slave cruel, and never givin' no cash whiff their stingyness. He was 'ere that night y' know anyhow."

"He came away at eight o'clock and Mr. Grison wasn't killed till after," declared the girl.

"So he ses," murmured Mother Slaig, "p'raps some frien' of him es Grison stuck paid him out in th' saime waif."

"What do you mean?" asked Marie who had not heard of the man's act.

"Didn't y' know," cried Mother Slaig with relish "why, bless y' miss—an' bless y' I kin, fur I've kind o' taiken a fancy t' y'—Grison killed a cove es he smoked wiff in, that Chinky's den. We fun' the watch of th' cove an' his juwulery in Grison's room. A frien' of him es wos done fur may 'ave stuck Grison out of revenge, and no blame t' him, dearie."

"Do you know if any relatives of this dead man came down here?"

"No, I never did. I don't know anything, miss, and what's more I don't want to i' case I shud come bunkin' against them beastly perlice, as is allays interferin' with an honest woman who's tryin' to git 'er livin'."

"Well then," asked Marie coming to the point "can you tell me if an Indian called Morad-Bakche ever came to see Mr. Grison?"

"Don' no th' naime," said Mother Slaig, after a moment's thought, "an there's lots of them dagoes abaout 'ere, lascars an' mulletters and all that sort o' scum. Grison torked t' one an' all. What like's the cove's y've got in yer mind, miss?"

As Marie had heard Bakche described both by Alan and Mrs. Verwin she was able to convey to Mother Slaig's shrewd intelligence a fair picture of the man. The old hag reflected again, then slapped her fat knees with both fat hands. "Know 'im, dearie; 'course I knows him, 'Aughty-like, fur a nigger, an' looked on me, es is a free born British woman jus' like mud. I guv him bits of m' mind when he sneaked round 'ere."

"Then he *did* come to see Mr. Grison?" asked Marie, delighted that she had succeeded in establishing the fact of Bakche's acquaintance with the dead man. "Did he come often?"

"Carn't keep count, miss, me not 'aving a 'ead fur figures, tho' me sister was grand at them, dearie. But he comes times an' again. Oh, yuss," she went on as the memory returned to her, "he was stan'orf fur a nigger. 'Thort he was a lascar at fust, but he wasn't, tho' he did live on rice and water like them sweeps. Dress'd like one of them stokers tho'—if y' know what a seedee boy is, miss, which of course y' wudn't, bein' a lady. I sawr as he was a cut above them, I did. He wore a snake?"

"Wore a snake," repeated Marie bewildered.

"On his right arm, below th' elber," explained Mother Slaig, "'tattooted it was, as them sailors 'ave a fancy fur; twistin' round' an' roun' till it made me giddy t' look at it."

Marie was glad she had heard this mark of identification was to be found on the haughty dark gentleman who had visited Grison. She was certain that the man in question was Bakche in search of the peacock, but it was just as well that Mother Slaig could identify him by means of the tattooed snake. "Was he here on the night of the murder?" asked Marie anxiously.

"Ah, now you 'as me," said Mother Slaig in an expansive fashion, "me, on th' night as he was done fur, bein' 'appy."

"Happy?" Marie did not know what was meant.

"Gin," explained Mother Slaig rocking to and fro. "White satin as some call it, tho' blue ruin is my naime fur it. I got half a quid fro' that Sorley chap, es he come in or wen' out—I dunno which. 'Laid it all out in gin wiff frien's o' mine, and we did 'ave a time t' dream of. Never thort I cud ha' swallered such oachings o' gin; but I did, an' the thust as was on me nex' mornin', dearie, you'd never believe."

"But isn't it bad to drink so much," asked Marie, rising timidly.

"Fur sich es you es is a flower it is," agreed Mother Slaig, rolling out of the chair and getting on her feet with an effort, since she was so stout, "but not fur me, es 'as a 'ard time, dearie. You've fun' me sober thro' me not 'aving—where's that there quid y' promised?" she demanded suddenly.

"There," said Marie, taking the money from her pocket, "but don't drink it away, Mrs. Slaig. It's a pity such a nice woman as you should drink gin."

"Well, I don't git no shampin down 'ere, dearie," said Mrs. Slaig crossly, and, like Jotty, biting the gold to make sure it was genuine. "We taikes what we can. Wan't t' know anythin' else, lovey dovey?"

"No," answered Marie, walking into the passage, for the smell and closeness of the place was making her feel faint. "But you needn't tell anyone what I asked you about."

"Sha'n't nohow," said Mother Slaig firmly. "Y've browt back daiys when I was a pretty girl and 'ad all the men arter me, furious-like. You're a breath o' fresh air an' a smell of country roses, an' a sight o' green fields, t' yours truly, dearie. An, never a word shell I say, save as you're a visitor with tracts—tho' you ain't guv me one, but summit better." Mother Slaig felt for her sovereign as she spoke. "But if there's police, dearie, an' I 'as t' saive m' bacon, I mus' speak."

"There will be no trouble with the police," Marie assured her in a low and hurried voice, for her friendly constable was just at the end of the passage. "Good-bye, Mrs. Slaig."

"Go'bye, dearie," she attempted a curtsey, but failed for want of breath. "'An bless y' fur an angil o' delight wiff stars roun' yer 'ead."

Marie laughed and hurried away in the shadow of the policeman, who refused to accept a tip. Again she was passed from one constable to another, until she regained the station, and every one of her temporary guides declined money.

"The most chivalrous men in the world," said Marie afterwards, "are London policemen!" and she never changed her opinion on this point.

CHAPTER XVII

THE SECRET

Considering that Marie was inexperienced in worldly matters, she acted with extraordinary foresight and determination. Few girls would have risked that journey to the Rotherhithe slum, or would have conducted the interview with Mother Slaig so discreetly. Certainly her lucky star was in the ascendant when she plunged into those malodorous depths, as she had been guarded from all peril by the various policemen; but her own diplomatic behavior had accomplished the impossible with the old harridan. Marie returned home with the full belief that Morad-Bakche was the guilty person, since he desired to obtain possession of the peacock, and he had been haunting the house wherein Baldwin Grison resided. That Sorley had held the bird—a fact vouched for by Alan—she believed was due to the machinations of Miss Grison, who evidently was working in concert with the Indian to ruin the man. And Bakche's reward would be possession of the jewels, since Marie fancied the dead man's sister had possibly guessed the riddle of the ornament. If this was so, there was no need for either of the conspirators to retain possession of the peacock, since it had yielded up its secret.

With this idea Marie came back to Lewes, and there she sent a telegram to Alan asking him to come down the next day. She was anxious to impart her discovery to her lover, and to show him that she also was able to kelp in the matter of tracing Grison's assassin, and obtaining the treasure. On the evidence she had discovered concerning Bakche's presence at Rotherhithe, a new departure might be taken relative to the conduct of the case. But Marie felt that she could venture no further along the dark path unassisted, and therefore wished for Alan's co-operation. She knew that the telegram would bring him to her at once, and retired to bed with the conviction that he would lose no time in coming to Belstone. Of course on her return, she had to answer numerous inquiries from granny and the maids as to what she had been doing, but managed to answer without stating too plainly what her errand had been. She was very weary when she placed her head on the pillow, and fell asleep almost immediately.

Fuller duly arrived by an early morning train, and it was ten o'clock when Marie—who was watching for him like a veritable Sister Anne—saw him walk up the avenue. She rushed out of the house and led him into it, hanging fondly on his arm, while asking innumerable questions.

"Oh, darling, I am so glad to see you. And how are you? and when did you arrive? and how long are you going to stay? and will we go into the library? and what have you in that black bag?"

The young man laughed at her eagerness, and was surprised to see how gay and happy she looked, which was indeed remarkable, seeing that Sorley was in such straits. He replied to her questions in sequence. "I am quite well, dearest; I arrived an hour ago, and walked direct from Lewes to you, not even troubling to go to the vicarage; I shall stay for the whole day, as I want to be with you, and have much to tell you; we may as well go into the library for a purpose which I shall explain soon; and in this bag I have the peacock of jewels."

"Oh," cried Miss Inderwick greatly astonished, "how did you get it?"

"Mr. Sorley left it in my chambers last night."

"Then you have seen Uncle Ran?"

"Yes; and so has Latimer."

Marie looked nervous. "Mr. Latimer doesn't like Uncle Ran," she said thoughtfully, "but I hope he has not given him up to the police."

"Your Uncle Ran gave himself up of his own accord," said Alan grimly, "but repented at the eleventh hour and made his escape."

"I'm glad of that," remarked the girl thankfully, "as I believe Uncle Ran is quite innocent. But why did he give himself up at all?"

"I don't know, no more than I can say why he changed his mind and bolted, my dear. However, I can tell you the whole story if you will listen." And when Miss Inderwick signified by a gesture that she was all ears, Fuller detailed all that had taken place on the previous night. By this time they were in the library with the door closed, and Alan related his story seated in a deep armchair with Marie balancing herself on the table.

"Poor dear Uncle Ran," she said when Fuller ended; "he wished to give that horrid Miss Grison a chance of confessing her guilt."

"Confessing her guilt! What do you mean, Marie?"

"I mean that she knows more about the murder than she admits, and that she is in league with that nasty Indian to ruin Uncle Ran."

Alan shook his head gravely. "You can't be sure of that, Marie."

"But I am," she insisted positively. "Mr. Bakche knew that Mr. Grison was at Mother Slaig's and went there heaps of times. She saw him."

"How do you know?" asked Alan, surprised by her decided tone.

"Because she told me herself. Of course she didn't know his name, but her description is exactly the same as yours—haughty, dark and—"

"Marie! Marie! How do you know this?"

"Because I visited Mother Slaig yesterday."

Fuller looked startled. "Darling you never went by yourself to see that dreadful old hag?"

"Yes, I did, and I don't think she's so very dreadful. She was very nice to me in every way, and what she told me only cost a sovereign."

"Marie, you shouldn't have gone to Rotherhithe without telling me."

"If I had you would have stopped me," pouted Miss Inderwick; "and I did so want to do something to help Uncle Ran."

"But has your visit helped him? Mother Slaig may be wrong about Bakche, and may have mistaken a lascar for him."

"There was no question of mistaking anyone," retorted Marie quickly, "for Mother Slaig did not know the name. I described Mr. Bakche as you did, and she said that she had seen a man of that description—the snake man she called him."

"The snake man," repeated Alan swiftly. "Why?"

"On his right arm from the wrist to the elbow he had a snake tattooed in spirals."

Fuller slapped his knee, and spoke excitedly. "Mother Slaig is right, dear, and so are you. Miss Grison told me that Bakche had such a mark."

"Then he must have been at Rotherhithe and known Mr. Grison," said Miss Inderwick.

"Certainly; since Mother Slaig would otherwise have known nothing about the tattooed snake. Tell me exactly what she said, Marie."

Miss Inderwick did so, omitting nothing, and shortly Fuller was in possession of all that had taken place at Rotherhithe. The recital so excited him that he rose to his feet and began to pace the room. "And Bakche denied that he visited Rotherhithe, or knew Grison," he cried. "Marie you have undoubtedly found valuable evidence which may help to clear your uncle's character, I admit that."

"I am quite sure that Uncle Ran is innocent, and that Miss Grison is conspiring with Mr. Bakche to ruin him," said Marie firmly.

Alan shook his head. "No, dear, I don't think that there is any conspiracy between them. If Bakche gained the peacock by murder, he certainly would not have sent it to your uncle. And if Miss Grison knew that he had the bird, she must have guessed that he stabbed her dearly-beloved brother. In that case she would have denounced him. Of course, she denies having brought the peacock down here; but if she did, Baldwin gave it to her before his death."

"And if she did not, Mr. Bakche must have sent it."

"Why should he do that?"

"To get Uncle Ran into trouble."

"My dear, Bakche did not wish to get Mr. Sorley into trouble. All he desired, and still desires, is to obtain the peacock."

"Then why did he haunt Rotherhithe?"

"To get the peacock," repeated Alan; "and if he did get it, he certainly would not have given it to your uncle. No, Marie." Fuller shrugged his shoulders. "What you have discovered implicates Bakche plainly enough, but it does not solve the mystery of the death. That is as great a riddle as ever."

"What is to be done now, then?" asked the girl, fuming at the judicious way in which her lover talked.

"We must tell Inspector Moon about Bakche's visits to Rotherhithe, and then the Indian can be questioned. I shall do that to-morrow. Meanwhile—" Alan opened the black bag—"look at this."

Marie greatly admired the peacock, as it was the first time she had set eyes on the beautiful object. The glitter of the gold, the radiance of the many gems appealed to her feminine love of color, and she clapped her hands with delight when the gorgeous ornament glowed like a rainbow-hued star in the sunlight. The lovers sat down and admired the luck of the Inderwicks, which held a secret hard to solve, a secret which would, if guessed, bring a fortune to the last member of the family and restore the faded splendors of the line. The girl with her eyes fixed on the treasure, murmured words from the ancient prophecy:—

> "Jewels and gold from over-seas
> Will bring them peace and joy and ease."

Alan nodded. "If that is applied to this bird," he said slowly, "it is perfectly true, since the riddle, when guessed, means a gigantic fortune. You will be a wealthy woman, Marie, and then I shall have some hesitation in keeping you to your engagement."

"Oh, Alan, darling, why?" asked the girl jumping up in dismay.

"People might call me a fortune-hunter."

"I don't see how they could, seeing that you love me now when I have next to nothing. And if the fortune is found it will be through you, dearest, so you will have a right to share it. And after all," ended Marie earnestly and inconsequently, "what does it matter what people say seeing that we love one another?"

Alan kissed her. "That being the case, Marie, I promise you that no wealth shall part us. But had we not better put the peacock away?"

"Won't we try and solve the riddle?"

"It's impossible. I've tried in every way to do so, and am still quite in the dark as to how that jewelled bird can indicate the hiding-place."

Marie took up the luck of her family and turned it round upside down, and looked at it from every side. "It does seem impossible," she confessed with a reluctant sigh. "I suppose we must give up trying to guess its riddle for the present. Where shall we put it, Alan?"

"In the cupboard, I suppose," said the lawyer carelessly, and pointing to the dark oak press, out of which Sorley had produced the peacock when it first appeared on the scene; "it has always been there."

"If so," said Marie shrewdly, "someone—Miss Grison for one—may know where to find it, and she is quite capable of telling Mr. Bakche who is in league with her, I am sure. No, Alan, I shall put it along with Uncle Ran's private collection of gems," and she moved towards the panel marked with a cross, which Fuller remembered very well.

"Can you open it, Marie?" he asked, walking beside her to the place.

"Yes! See!" She touched the hidden spring, and the panel slid aside into its groove. "Uncle Ran showed me how to work this before he left, in case—as he said—he should never come back."

"Hum!" muttered Alan, staring into the dark recess with its many shelves, "he seems to have his doubts as to whether his innocence will ever be clearly proved. Put the peacock back on the table, Marie, and let us look at the gems. If your uncle does not return they belong to you."

"Yes, he said that," replied Miss Inderwick, putting down the peacock near the black bag. "Many of the gems are bought with my money. I always thought that you were hard on Uncle Ran, dear; he saved money for me."

"Marie, I have every wish to think well of your uncle," confessed Alan, "but it seems to me that he does not act quite straightly. For one thing he undoubtedly treated Miss Grison very badly, and—" Fuller checked himself, as it did not seem necessary at the moment to reveal the strange truth regarding the woman's claim to be Mrs. Sorley.

"And what, dear?" asked the girl innocently.

"Nothing. I shall tell you later. Let us think the best we can of your uncle, and examine his gems. I have seen them before, but I should like to admire them again. Bring the trays to the table, Marie."

The girl did so, and tray after tray of jewels was placed in the flood of sunshine which streamed through the windows of the room, until the whole table glittered with rainbow fires. When the shelves were empty, Marie put her hand in and groped round to see if she had missed any gem. Suddenly she uttered an exclamation, and brought out a long steel instrument, with a silver handle set with rough turquoise stones. "Oh, Alan, look at this, dear," she said, bringing it to her lover.

Fuller started and frowned, remembering how Grison had been stabbed with a slender instrument, a stiletto for choice. And here was a stiletto in the secret hiding-place of Sorley's jewels. There was blood on the handle, and the young man looked at it with a shudder. Was Sorley guilty after all, and were these stains the life blood of Baldwin Grison? It would seem so, he thought, and his thoughts showed themselves in his face, for Marie uttered an exclamation and grew pale. "Oh Alan, dear, you don't think that, do you?" she asked piteously.

"Think what, dear," he asked in his turn, and evasively.

"That Uncle Ran murdered Mr. Grison with that stiletto."

She had made use of the very word mentioned at the inquest. "It looks like it, dear," said Fuller sadly. "The evidence showed that Grison was murdered with a weapon of this sort, and now that we find it in a secret place known only to your uncle—"

"Miss Grison knows it also," cried Marie, determined to believe nothing against her relative.

"We can't be sure of that, dear. And if she did, she would not have placed the weapon there. You surely don't think she killed her brother?"

"Oh no; oh no. Still, if only to revenge herself on Uncle Ran because he—as she says—ruined Mr. Grison, she may have—"

"Marie, it is no use building up theories," interrupted Alan firmly; "the presence of this stiletto looks bad, I don't deny. Still Mr. Sorley may have some explanation to make of its presence."

"I am sure he is innocent, and will return to explain everything," said Marie obstinately. "Nothing will ever make me believe that Uncle Ran killed the poor thing. We won't think anything more about the matter until he comes back," she ended, and returned the stiletto to the hiding-place.

"If he ever does come back," murmured Alan under his breath, for he looked on the presence of the weapon—and stained with blood as it was—as a very good proof of the man's guilt. However, so as not to vex Marie, and because he could not, in legal words, prove his case, he made no remark. For the next quarter of an hour they examined the gems, and, becoming absorbed in this one and that, (so beautiful were the objects), both quite forgot the discovery of the stiletto which seemed to incriminate the collector.

Marie tried the effect of several jewels against her fair skin and admired herself in the mirror over the fireplace. Amongst the loose ornaments—for some of the gems were set in gold—she found a curious ring of silver entirely circled by precious stones. "Isn't that odd, Alan," she asked, slipping it on her finger, "and how uncomfortable to wear, dear. The stones go right round and hurt one so between the fingers. Oh!" she pulled it off, "I could never wear that with pleasure. Perhaps it is a nose ring—one of the Begum's treasures."

Fuller examined the object, which was a broad band of silver set with gems at various intervals, entirely round its circle. "It's not of Indian workmanship, Marie," he said, after a pause; "there's an English look about it. I wonder why the stones are set all round it, though?"

Marie peering over his shoulder pointed out a point that had escaped Alan's attention. "See, there is a letter," she observed, "it's a 'K.' Look, Alan, between that bit of coral and that pearl."

"So there is. I wonder what 'K' means," Alan mused, then threw back his head trying to remember something. "I have heard of a ring set round with stones before," he said thoughtfully, "and it was explained to me why the gems were all over it. Who has that ring? Oh!"—a memory suddenly came into his mind—"it was my grandmother who showed it to me when I was a tiny boy. It was a golden ring with six stones, and each meant a letter."

"How do you mean meant a letter, dear?" asked Marie, greatly puzzled, "and what word did it make?"

"Regard," answered Alan carelessly, "the first word of each stone-name gave the meaning: Ruby, emerald, garnet, amethyst, ruby again, and diamond."

"Regard," repeated Marie, clapping her hands. "Oh, how clever. You must give me a ring like that some day, Alan. Only we'll have love on it. Lapis lazuli, opal, and—and—what precious stone begins with 'V,' Alan?"

"There is none," he said smiling at her earnestness, and glancing at the silver ring he still toyed with, "no more than there is a gem beginning with 'K.' I expect the maker of this ring chose a word which contained that letter, and as he could not suggest a stone, engraved the word on the silver in this fashion. Strange that he had not more foresight."

"Let us see what the word is, Alan," cried Marie much excited, "begin with the letter 'K.' That's a start. Next is a piece of coral—that's 'C.'"

"Then an opal standing for 'O,' another piece of coral—"

"C," said Marie anxiously, "an amethyst for 'A,' an emerald for 'E'—"

"And a pearl for 'P.' The word therefore reads K. C. O. C. A. E. P. And that, my dear, makes nonsense," finished Fuller with disgust.

"Spell it backwards," suggested the girl, "we may as well try all ways."

Almost before she ended, Alan, following her advice, had arrived at the truth swiftly. "Peacock!" he shouted, "Marie, this ring was made by Simon Ferrier."

"But it isn't of Indian workmanship," she protested.

"No; but Ferrier, although he learned from Indian jewellers, was an English workman first of all. Peacock"—he twirled the ring—"Darling, I really and truly believe that we have discovered the secret."

"Oh Alan! oh Alan!" the girl shrieked in her excitement and ran to the table quickly, "I see your meaning. We take these stones in the tail and—"

"And read them as we have done those of the ring, making the first letter of each stone stand to spell the word.

"Yes! yes! yes!" Marie clapped her hands. "But there is more than one word in that tail, Alan. Oh—perhaps it indicates the hiding-place?"

"I'm sure it does," cried Fuller, taking out a pencil. "Marie, read out the stones in order, beginning at the top, and I'll set them down."

Almost too excited to speak, the girl did so with sparkling eyes, and the result when finished was as follows, with the three lines and the triangle of rubies, indicated plainly:

Δ

Sapphire, Turquoise, Pearl, Emerald, Turquoise, Emerald, Ruby,
Sapphire, Pearl, Opal, Onyx, Lapis lazuli.

Ruby, Emerald, Diamond.

Alan rapidly set down in order the first letter of each stone, and Marie, looking over his shoulder saw that they read thus:—

"ST PETER'S POOL Δ RED"

"Oh," she cried with a grasp.

"St. Peter's Pool, the triangle, red," murmured Alan, still perplexed, till the feminine intuition of the girl came to his aid.

"It's the well," she cried, "St. Peter's Well in St. Peter's Dell, can't you see. The jewels are hidden in some place marked with a red triangle. Oh I am sure of it, because the word is 'red,' and the stones of the triangle are rubies."

"By heaven, Marie! I believe you are right."

"Of course I am. Simon Ferrier came back to England to hide the jewels."

"No Marie, he returned to give them to Julian Inderwick. But since that man was a profligate and would have squandered them, Ferrier evidently hid them somewhere about St. Peter's Well, or pool, as he calls it on the tail of the bird, and marked the hiding-place with a red triangle. And of course, if George Inderwick had been able to read the riddle he would easily have found the gems. My word!" Alan stared at the golden bird, now reft of the secret it had held for so long, "and to think that the solution is so easy after all. Why those rings such as I have described my grandmother having, are by no means rare."

"I believe Simon Ferrier did make this silver one," said Marie, fingering the article thoughtfully, "since it is a kind of key to the riddle."

Alan shrugged his shoulders. "I believe that George Inderwick found it as hard to guess as the mystery of the peacock. At all events he never arrived at the solution of the thing. And so easy, so easy after all."

"Perhaps the very ease made it difficult to guess," suggested Marie.

"Like Columbus and the egg," laughed Fuller, taking back a tray of gems to the hiding-place. "Let us put these away, Marie, and then go down to the well. We must close the panel in case that man Moon left behind should come in and learn too much." He was thinking of the stiletto as he spoke.

"Oh, that is all right," said Miss Inderwick, assisting to replace the jewels; "he went away this morning. Inspector Moon sent him a wire saying he was to go back to town."

"Oh!" said Alan thoughtfully, as he closed the panel, and it resumed its innocent look. "I expect Moon has given up all hope of Sorley returning to this place. Well, I expect he is right. It would be foolish of your uncle, dear, to thrust his head into the lion's jaws."

"I am sure he will return and prove his innocence," cried Marie resolutely; "and won't he be pleased when he learns that we have found the Begum's jewels, Alan?"

"We haven't found them yet," answered Fuller, determined in his own mind that whether innocent or guilty the man should not meddle with the girl's property. "Let us go and look, Marie. Ask Henny or Jenny for a crowbar."

"What for?"

"We must pry up the stone under which the treasure is hidden. I expect, as you suggest, that it is marked with a red triangle."

"I don't expect we have a crowbar," said Miss Inderwick dubiously, but went into the back part of the house on her errand, nevertheless, while Alan took his way to St. Peter's dell. He surveyed what Ferrier had called "The Pool" in his cryptogram, and expected that he had done so, since there was no gem's name beginning with "W" which he could have placed in the peacock's tail. The man had engraved the letter "K" on the ring as a hint to his master, as was evident, but had not taken the same liberty with the peacock, since it might solve the riddle too easily.

"And hang it, how easy it was after all," said Alan, who could not get over this point. Then, while awaiting the coming of Marie, he surveyed the well.

There it was, standing amongst the still leafless trees, and amidst the rank slushy grasses, a circle of stone, surmounted by the wooden canopy with its mellow red roof. The windlass was rotten with age, and the rope, formerly used to wind up the bucket, was conspicuous by its absence, as was the bucket itself. Fuller peered into the depths and saw the water far down twinkling like a star in the uncertain light, which filtered to the depths. The sides of the well were of massive masonry, green with moss and slime, while the circle above ground was overgrown with herbage. In the hope of finding the marked stone, he began to tear away the grasses and briars and ivy, scratching his hands considerably as he did so. To save these he put on his stout deerskin gloves, which he fortunately had slipped into his pocket. Marie found him thus occupied.

"We have a crowbar after all," she cried, bending under the article she mentioned, along with a spade and a coil of rope. "One of the workmen who was building a new wall at the back of the house, left it a year ago."

"Why have you brought the rope, Marie?"

"I thought you might have to go down the well," she said quickly, "we can fasten it to the windlass."

Alan eyed the same dubiously. "I fear it's too rotten to support us, or rather to support me," he remarked; "and we may not have to explore the depths of the well."

"The pool, the pool," cried Marie, throwing down her load; "why do you drag away those grasses, Alan?"

He explained, and she saw the necessity of helping, although to save her tender hands he transferred his gloves to her. The two, buoyed up with the hope of treasure went to work with a will and soon the cemented circle of gray stones round the well was quite bare. Alan searched, as did Marie, but on no stone, could they find the desired red triangle.

"It must be down the well," said Fuller with a shrug; "but I'm not going to trust that rotten windlass.

"Tie the rope to this tree," said Marie pointing to a young beech which was growing close to the opening, and, as Alan thought this was an excellent idea —he gave her a kiss for the suggestion—he fastened the rope to its trunk and then made a slipknot, which he bound under his arms. "Now dear take a turn on the rope round the tree and lower me gently, that will prevent the strain being too great."

"I hope so," said Miss Inderwick, doing as she was told. "I don't want you to be drowned."

Alan slipped over the edge of the well, and the rope grew taunt from himself to the beech, where the several twists round the trunk stopped the drag being too great on Marie. Nevertheless she felt anxious when she saw her lover disappear into the dark depths.

"Oh do take care, darling," she cried holding on to the rope at the part beyond the twists round the beech-tree trunk, "do take care."

A laugh came up which sounded very clearly, for Alan was only a few feet below the surface. He looked round and round, twisting himself with his hands, and thrusting his toes into the crevices of the stones to gain foothold, and not to strain either the beech-tree's strength or that of the girl. But the moss and the lichens grew so thickly that he could not see the surface of the stonework, and therefore could espy no triangle. And small wonder, since it was over one hundred years since the treasure had been stowed away by Inderwick's faithful servant. "I wish I had a knife," muttered Alan, and Marie heard him.

"Get out of the well, and I'll fetch one," she said fastening the rope to the tree trunk firmly; "I sha'n't be a minute," and she flew up the path.

"Bring a carving-knife," Alan shouted after her, getting his head above the surface circle of stones, and Marie waved her hand to show that she heard him. But he did not get out of the well, as she advised, but braced his feet and shoulders against the masonry and continued his examination. But when she returned with the knife he was still at fault.

"Clever darling," he said, taking the carving-knife and dropping down again. Then he went to work, while Marie called out every now and then from the beech-tree to know if he was safe. Everywhere he scraped the moss off the stones and laid bare one row after the other, but for at least one hour he failed to find what he sought. He was just thinking that it would be as well to get out and have a rest, particularly as Marie was imploring him to do so, when suddenly she heard him shout.

"Dear, have you found it?" she cried, not daring to leave the rope or the tree, lest the first might slip from the last.

"Yes! yes. Here is the red triangle marked on the fourth row of stones—on one big one, that is. Tie up the rope, Marie and give me the crowbar. I won't need to descend further."

The girl did as she was told, and leaning over the edge of the well, handed her lover the crowbar. Already Alan had worked away at the interstices of the marked stone with the knife point. He deepened these sufficiently to slip in the point of the crowbar, which was rather blunt, and then began to strain in his effort to loosen the block. Marie anxiously looking down, heard him breathing hard with the effort, and implored him to take a rest. But Fuller was too anxious to find the treasure to do so, and with aching arms and legs—for he was resting his weight on them with his toes in a crevice—worked away desperately. Little by little, the mortar in the interstices of the block crumbled, as he drove in the crowbar, and finally the stone became so loose that he could ease it with his fingers. Again he shouted, and this time with relief, as the big stone splashed down into the dark waters below.

"Have you got it, Alan?" cried Marie, quite sick with excitement.

"Yes, I think so." He was feeling in the dark hole which the displaced stone had revealed; "but it doesn't seem to be very much. Only a small box. Oh Marie, there can't be many jewels in this." He handed up as he spoke a tin box of no great size, which Marie received with manifest disappointment, and went on groping. However he found nothing else, so emerged from the well, with his clothes considerably damaged, and with a red perspiring face, for the task had made him quite hot.

"How can we open the thing?" asked Marie, when they sat on the edge of the well to examine the box, "It's locked."

"Pooh! it's only tin," said Alan, and looked rather annoyed. "What a sell if this little thing contains the whole treasure."

"Perhaps it's a big diamond," said Marie, watching her lover pry open the locked lid with the edge of the spade.

"Perhaps," assented Alan dubiously, and worked away hard. It was not an easy job, in spite of the box being merely tin, but in the end he managed to get the lid off. "Huh! it's only papers."

And that was all. Papers wrapped up in linen to preserve them from damp, though the box was dry enough, since it had been hermetically sealed by the stone block. One paper, on examination, proved to be a statement signed by the Begum and Rajah of Kam and their vizier, saying that the jewels, which were enumerated, had been given to George Inderwick because he had saved the life of the royal woman and her son. Then there was a letter to Inderwick written by Ferrier, which stated that he had placed the jewels in Yarbury's Bank, Monks Lane, Cheapside, London. "To be given up to you when you produce to Mr. Yarbury the peacock of jewels," ended the instructions.

CHAPTER XVIII

THE TREASURE HUNT

"Have you the papers, Alan?"

"Yes dear."

"And the key which came out of that box?"

"Yes, dear."

"Then I have the golden peacock in this bag of Uncle Ran's," ended Marie, quite satisfied that all was well.

With Fuller she occupied a first-class carriage of the London express from Lewes, and the two had it all to themselves, since Alan had bribed the guard to keep out other passengers. As the lovers were so excited over their solution of the riddle and their discovery—if not of the treasure—at least of certain evidence that the same existed, it was little to be wondered at that they could talk of nothing else. Hence the necessity for a compartment all to themselves, for they did not wish anyone else to know of their newly-acquired fortune, until it was in their own possession. Then Alan intended to advertise the affair far and wide through the medium of the daily newspapers, so that Mr. Sorley —wherever he might be—should become cognizant of the fact, as well as Mr. Morad-Bakche. It was just as well to let both these gentlemen know that Miss Inderwick had the jewels, and intended to keep them. Fuller was quite certain that he could safeguard her interests in every way, should the Indian try to gain what he had come so far to seek. As to Mr. Sorley, that gentleman being in his present straits, scarcely counted. But Marie wished him to know the truth, as she believed he would then return. Alan was of a different opinion.

On the previous evening there had been great excitement at the vicarage when the lovers returned from their investigations and told the story of how they had guessed the riddle together, besides narrating, with much wealth of detail, the search down the well. Both Mr. and Mrs. Fuller had expressed the greatest surprise, as well they might, and both congratulated Marie on her good fortune. If indeed the jewels—as was hinted in Ferrier's story—were worth from one to two hundred thousand pounds, she would indeed be able to restore the family prestige and repair The Monastery. And then, as Marie intimated firmly, she intended to become Alan's wife, a declaration which Mrs. Fuller received with unfeigned joy, as she loved Marie as fondly as though she were her own flesh and blood. The vicar also was gratified, as of course if his son became the Squire of Belstone, that fact would help him greatly in controlling the parish.

On the whole they had a very happy evening, and when Marie returned to The Monastery, she could not close an eye. Also next morning when Alan met her to catch the express, she informed him that she had heard strange noises during the night, and had been rather terrified. But of these things the two did not talk much until they were travelling towards London, and until Marie had assured herself that both she and Alan possessed the necessary articles to secure possession of the jewels. There was the letter of Simon Ferrier, and the signed agreement that the gems belonged to George Inderwick, besides a curiously shaped brass key which was supposed to open the box of gems now at Yarbury's Bank, Monks Lane, Cheapside, London. Finally Marie held tightly on to the bag which contained the golden peacock without the production of which she would not be able to take the jewels away, as she intended to do.

"And I only hope," said Alan, when they were both satisfied that all was in order, "that Yarbury's Bank is still in existence."

"Oh, Alan! I hope so. Why shouldn't it be?"

"Well the jewels were deposited there one hundred and fifty years ago more or less my dear, and it is possible that the bank may have smashed. There have been plenty of panics during the century."

"What would have become of the gems had the bank smashed?" asked Marie in a timid and rather tearful voice, for it was a terrible thought to think that her dreams might dissolve into thin air.

Alan shrugged his shoulders. "Really, my dear, I can't say. They might be passed on to another bank, or might remain with the reconstructed old one.

On the other hand they may have been stolen and dispersed. I never heard tell of Yarbury's Bank myself; but then I am not closely acquainted with what goes on in the city."

"I daren't think of it not being there," shuddered Miss Inderwick. "Oh it would be a shame if we lost everything at the eleventh hour."

"Well," said Fuller with a philosophy he was very far from feeling, "let us hope for the best, and talk of other things until we arrive at Monks Lane. These noises, Marie? weren't you dreaming?"

"No, dear, no. Certainly not. I was wide awake. I fancied I heard a scream; it sounded like the cry of a woman in distress. Then there were footsteps—muffled footsteps far below. Of course The Monastery is haunted, so I thought it was the ghosts."

"Are there more than one?" asked Alan, suppressing a skeptical smile.

"Oh yes. There are two monks, and one cavalier, and a lady who has no head at all," said Marie solemnly. "Granny knows all the stories, and some of them are just horrid. This morning when I told her about the noises, she said that Henny and Jenny and she had heard them several times during the last week, but she believed they were only the ghosts. Granny is quite proud that we should have them, as we are such an old family."

Alan shuddered. "Well, dear, I sincerely hope that when we live at The Monastery, these uneasy spirits will take their departure. I don't believe in ghosts; all the same, I don't like odd noises. Marie," he sat up suddenly as a thought struck him.

"I know what you're going to say, Alan," she cried quickly.

"What?" He looked at her sharply.

"That the noises might have been made by Uncle Ran."

"Yes I did, my dear. It is just possible that he may have come back secretly to The Monastery, knowing that Moon would not search there. And a very good idea it would be if he did; safe as houses."

Marie shook her head solemnly. "No. If Uncle Ran had returned he would have let me know, since he could be certain that I would not betray him. And he would require food and drink, which would be another reason for him to let me know he was hiding. No, Alan. I tell you the cry I heard was that of a woman, and I believe that Miss Grison is in the house."

Fuller stared. "What on earth put that into your head?"

"Well, she knows all the secret passages and chambers of The Monastery better than I do, since she lived there for so long before I was born. As Uncle Ran had the peacock, she may have thought that he left it behind, and may have come down to steal it. She uttered that cry I am sure."

"I don't think so," said Fuller scouting the idea, "She wouldn't be such a fool, Marie. However, when we have been to Yarbury's Bank—if the blessed place still exists, that is—we can drive to Thimble Square, and see if she is in or out of London."

"She's out of it, and in The Monastery," cried Miss Inderwick very decisively, "It's no use talking, Alan, I am sure it was she I heard screaming. And if she is there—which I am sure of—she will probably let that horrid Indian into the house, so that he can take the peacock. I sha'n't sleep there to-night, Alan, but at the vicarage, I don't want to be murdered by that Mr. Bakche as he murdered poor—"

"Marie, that is all theoretical."

"I don't care, it is true," insisted Marie, and although Fuller argued the point until they arrived at Victoria Station, she still held to her opinion, rather to the young man's annoyance. He had not thought Miss Inderwick was so obstinate, and told her as much in a most provoking manner, whereat the girl pouted. Of course Alan had to kiss her into a more amiable mood and admit that he was entirely wrong, and make sundry apologies for being the most disagreeable man in the world. The two were driving along Piccadilly in a taxi, before this comedy was finished, as such comedies always do, with the subjugation of the stronger by the weaker. "And you're quite horrid, aren't you?" finished Marie, pinching his arm.

"Quite," admitted Alan gravely.

"And I'm an angel."

"Rather; an archangel if you like!"

"Then I forgive you, dear. No, don't kiss me. You'll spoil the set of my hat, and make the driver turn round. And—and—oh Alan," she suddenly dropped her bantering tone and became anxious. "I do hope Yarbury's Bank is in existence. Where did you tell the man to drive to?"

"Monks Lane, Cheapside, dear. As he is doing so, thank heaven *that* is yet in existence. So much we have to be thankful for."

In Cheapside, and at the entrance of a narrow side street which the driver assured them was the lane in question, they alighted, and walked down it after the taxi had been dismissed. Both Marie and Alan crooked their necks staring upward to see the much-desired name; but not finding it, the lawyer asked an office-boy who came out of a near building if he could direct him to Yarbury's Bank. To the relief of the couple, an answer came terse and sharp, that it was number twenty, just round the corner, which meant that the place was situated where the lane suddenly, so to speak, crooked an elbow.

"Oh thank goodness!" murmured Marie, when they came face to face with a very dingy building, black with age and grime, and wedged in between two tall houses which overtopped it considerably. "It's Yarbury's!"

"Sure enough," replied Fuller, staring hard at the wire blinds—half blinds they were—which displayed the magic name in dull gold letters. "Cheer up, Marie; since the bank is here, we are certain to find the treasure."

"I hope so," answered the girl doubtfully, "but I shall believe nothing until I see the gems with my very own eyes."

Alan laughed, and led the way into a broad and low room of vast proportions filled with mahogany counters, protected by shining brass railings, and a number of desks, high and low, with shaded electric lamps over each; for the place was darkish even at noon. A number of clerks were busy with the usual business of the bank, and two or three customers were paying in, and drawing out money. On inquiring if the manager could be seen, a message was sent and an answer received that the great man would accord an interview to the strangers. Alan sent in his card and that of Miss Inderwick, and after another short delay the two were conducted into a fair-sized room at the very back of the building, to be welcomed by an elderly gentleman with white hair and a brisk expression. He was small and neat and very well dressed, and his manners were scrupulously polite. Yet as he placed a couple of chairs for his visitors, Alan noticed that he cast a curious glance at Marie.

"What can I do for you?" he asked, addressing himself to Fuller.

"You are the manager of Yarbury's Bank?" inquired Alan rather unnecessarily, but anxious to be quite sure of his ground.

"Certainly. Berwick is my name, and I have been in charge for some years."

"It is a very old bank, isn't it?" asked Marie timidly.

"Very, my dear young lady!"

"One hundred and fifty years more or less," put in Fuller suddenly.

"More rather than less," said Mr. Berwick with a genial smile, "but how do you know, Mr.—er," he glanced at the card lying on his table, "Mr. Fuller?"

"If you know the name of Inderwick, Mr. Berwick, you may have some idea of how I come to know."

Again Berwick cast a look in Marie's direction. "Inderwick! Yes, I do know that name. It was mentioned in the newspapers some little time ago, and had to do with a murder case connected with Rotherhithe."

"And with a peacock," said Marie quickly.

"Yes." Berwick scratched his chin meditatively. "It was supposed—I am quoting from the newspapers—that the man at Rotherhithe was murdered for the sake of the peacock, not a living bird, of course, but a certain ornament."

Marie nodded. "Which is the luck of our family," she finished.

"Oh, then you are one of the Inderwicks of Belstone?"

"Yes," said Alan slowly, "she is the last representative of the family, and the heiress of George Inderwick. Do you know that name?"

"I do," assented Berwick alertly. "On reading the newspapers it led to my recalling certain transactions, which—but pardon me." Mr. Berwick interrupted himself, "how can I be sure that this is Miss Inderwick?"

Marie was about to indignantly assert that she alone had the right to the name, when Alan prevented her. "That is a very natural question, sir," he remarked, opening the black bag, "perhaps this will assure you of the identity of this young lady."

Berwick stared when the peacock in all its glittering glory was placed under the electric light, and his ruddy face grew a trifle pale as he pushed back his chair uneasily. "It's the peacock," he muttered.

"You know about the peacock then?" questioned Alan sharply.

"Yes! When taking charge of the affairs of Yarbury's Bank I looked into all business old and new; also searching amongst old documents and examining deeds and papers dealing with various transactions which are in our strong-rooms below. I came across the account of the peacock, and the meaning of the peacock, belonging to George Inderwick, although a certain box which had to do with that bird was placed here by Simon Ferrier."

"Inderwick's servant," said Alan dryly, "hum! it seems to me that we are on the right track, Marie."

She nodded again, but Mr. Berwick, who still seemed much perturbed, moistened his lips and spoke unsteadily. "I can certainly supply you with information, which I can guess you require; but before doing so, I should like to send for Inspector Moon."

"But why—" began Marie hotly, only to be interrupted by her lover.

"I quite understand what you mean, Mr. Berwick," he said calmly, "and, of course, under the circumstances, it is necessary that you should take every precaution to safeguard the interests of the bank."

"Precaution, Mr. Fuller?" stammered the manager uneasily.

"I also," continued the lawyer imperturbably, "have read the account in the newspapers of the interview with Miss Louisa Grison. She declared therein that if the peacock were discovered, the assassin of her brother could be brought to justice. Is that not so?"

"Yes," admitted Berwick readily, "it is so."

"Since we have brought the peacock, which it is necessary to do, in order for Miss Inderwick to obtain possession of the box deposited here over one hundred years ago by Simon Ferrier, you naturally wish to know how we come to possess it."

"But surely Mr. Berwick doesn't think that we murdered Mr. Grison to obtain this," said Marie indignantly, touching the glowing splendor of the bird.

"No! no! no!" the manager assured her hastily, "nothing was further from my thoughts, my dear young lady. But, as Mr. Fuller sensibly observes, it is necessary for me to safeguard the interests of the bank."

"All the same you did think that I or Mr. Fuller had killed Mr. Grison," persisted Marie, her obstinacy again coming uppermost.

"No! really, really—"

"Never mind," remarked Alan impatiently, and cutting short the man's protestations, "it is natural that Mr. Berwick should suspect us, in the face of Miss Grison's statement. Better send for Inspector Moon, who has charge of the Rotherhithe case; and also I must ask you to send to the office of *The Latest News* for Richard Latimer."

"Why?" asked the man rising and staring. "Because he can prove how I became possessed of the peacock."

"I shall do what you ask, and you will excuse me, Mr. Fuller, if I am rather punctilious in dealing with the matter."

"I quite understand, Mr. Berwick. The affair is an odd one, and when we tell you what we know, you will find it even odder than you suspect. In the meantime, please telephone for Mr. Latimer and Inspector Moon, mentioning my name to both of them, and Miss Inderwick's also, if you like."

With a look of wonder written all over his ruddy face Berwick departed and personally telephoned for the two necessary persons in question. Marie rather fumed while he was absent, as woman-like she expected to be taken as genuine on her bare word. "He thinks we are swindlers," she said crossly.

"And small blame to him," rejoined Alan good-humoredly, for it was evident that the gems were all right, as he judged from Berwick's hints. "You can't expect the man, my dear, to hand over thousands of pounds worth of jewels without making inquiries.'

"The peacock is enough," said Marie stubbornly.

"The peacock is the cause of the trouble," retorted her lover; "but here is Mr. Berwick. Well, sir?"

"I have received a reply from both," said the manager, resuming his seat, and looking apologetically at Marie, "they will be here as soon as possible. Pardon me taking these precautions, and perhaps while you are waiting for Inspector Moon and Mr. Latimer, you will explain how you came to find out that the box of Ferrier was in our bank?"

"We guessed the riddle," said Marie suddenly.

"Oh!" Berwick looked at the peacock in a puzzled way. "I knew from what the newspapers said that there was a riddle to be solved, although I can't see what this golden ornament has to do with it. Did you not know that the box was at Yarbury's Bank?" he addressed Miss Inderwick.

"No; nor did anyone else, Mr. Berwick. Only when Mr. Fuller and I guessed the riddle did we learn the whereabouts of the box. It is here then?"

"Certainly," Mr. Berwick assured her promptly, "and has been here for over one hundred years. When I looked into matters on taking charge of the bank, I, like all former managers, became acquainted with the fact that a box of jewels had been deposited with us by Simon Ferrier on behalf of his master, George Inderwick, shortly after the Battle of Plassey. We have the letter of instructions concerning it."

"What are the instructions?" asked Alan.

"The box of jewels is to be held by the bank authorities, whom I at present represent, until someone brings a certain golden peacock studded with gems, certain papers explaining the peacock, and others dealing with the transfer of the jewels from the Rajah and Begum of Kam to George Inderwick, and finally a key which will fit the box."

Marie looked at Alan, who brought out the objects named. "There you are, Mr. Berwick," and he placed them under the manager's very nose.

"Oh, ah, excuse me," said Berwick, deeply interested at the sight of the old documents, and forthwith devoted himself to reading them. As the English was odd, to say the least of it, and the handwriting was crabbed—apparently that of a somewhat uneducated person—he was some time deciphering what was before him. Both Marie and Alan waited his pleasure quietly. "I am quite satisfied," he said when he finished his reading, "that these are the necessary papers, and the key can speak for itself if it fits the lock of the steel box. Meanwhile, and until our two friends arrive, Mr. Fuller, perhaps you and Miss Inderwick will explain how you came to guess the riddle which is referred to in the letter from Simon Ferrier to his master."

"And you can tell him also how we come to have the peacock," said Marie, who still felt annoyed by the suspicious attitude of Berwick, although that was considerably modified by the production of the papers and the key.

"No," said Alan decisively, "I shall tell that when Moon and Latimer arrive; there is no need to repeat the story twice. But it will serve to while away the time if we tell Mr. Berwick about the riddle."

"Certainly it will," said the manager in a lively tone; "and don't be angry with me, Miss Inderwick, I must protect the interests of the bank, you know."

Marie smiled and began to be somewhat ashamed of her irritation. "You must excuse me, Mr. Berwick," she said cleverly, "but the discovery of my fortune has somewhat excited my nerves."

"Very natural, very natural indeed. Well, Mr. Fuller, what about the riddle?"

Fuller lost no time, but related the various stages by which he and Marie had been led to guess the mystery of the peacock's tail. He produced the silver ring by way of illustration, and finally convinced Mr. Berwick of the manner in which the secret had been discovered. "And the annoying part of the whole business," concluded Alan, "is that the riddle is so easy."

"When guessed, Mr. Fuller, when guessed," said Berwick staring at the peacock, "but I assure you that I don't wonder it has been hard to solve, and had not the accident of the silver ring, or rather that of the letter 'K' on the silver ring led you to the truth, I doubt if you would ever have solved it." Berwick still eyed the bird steadily. "Most extraordinary! Ferrier was too clever, however, if I may say so; he concealed the treasure so well that the man he intended to benefit never did. Fate—" he bowed gallantly to Marie— "reserved the gems of the Begum for fairer hands."

"Then you will give me the box," said Marie, timidly.

"Of course; it rightfully belongs to you, since you have fulfilled the conditions of Ferrier's letter of instructions to the then manager of Yarbury's Bank. Here is the key, the peacock, the letter of Ferrier to his master, and the assignment of the jewels to the same person by the rulers of Kam. Oh yes, Miss Inderwick, the fortune is yours, and I congratulate you."

"What is the value of the jewels?" asked Alan abruptly, and drawing a breath of relief when he heard this speech.

"Really I can't tell you, Mr. Fuller. There is no mention of their value in the letter of instructions, and of course the box has never been open, since only the key you have brought can do that. Then—"

Berwick was interrupted by a clerk entering with a card inscribed with the name of Latimer, and Dick entered all alive with curiosity to hear why he had been summoned to such an unexpected place. After greeting Miss Inderwick and his friend he began to ask eager questions, which Alan proceeded to answer, until Inspector Moon arrived a few moments later. The officer opened his eyes wide when he saw the golden peacock on the table.

"How did it come here?" he asked suspiciously, and looked at the company.

Berwick explained the circumstances of Alan and Miss Inderwick's visit, and gave both Moon and Latimer an account of the trust held by Yarbury's Bank. Then Fuller explained more directly about the peacock.

"Sorley called at my chambers on that night he escaped," said Alan, addressing the astonished inspector. "Mr. Latimer and I took him to Miss Grison as he wished her to acknowledge certain things. He intended to give himself up, but—as I learned—he ran away at the eleventh hour. Have you arrested him yet, Mr. Inspector?"

"No. We have searched far and wide, but he is still at large. Still, Mr. Fuller, this explanation doesn't show how you became possessed of the peacock."

"Mr. Sorley left it behind in this black bag," said Alan readily, "you may remember, Mr. Inspector, that when you were taking him away, he called out to me to remember the black bag. I did not know what he meant, but when Mr. Latimer and I returned to our chambers, we found the bag there, and in it the golden peacock."

This seemed satisfactory to Moon, especially as Latimer vouched for the truth of the story. "Sorley is undoubtedly guilty," he remarked, and Alan had to press Marie's arm to prevent her bursting out with an indignant denial, "but you should have brought the peacock to me."

"Not at all, Mr. Inspector," said Fuller coolly and resolutely, "that is the property of Miss Inderwick here, and was stolen by Miss Grison over twenty years ago, because she thought that Mr. Sorley had treated her brother in a cruel way. It is only just that it should return to its owner, and I don't think that you can take possession of it."

"No," said Moon reluctantly, "I suppose not, since Miss Inderwick certainly possesses it legally, and came by it—according to your story, vouched for by Mr. Latimer—in a perfectly honest way. I understand from hints given, Mr. Fuller, that you have solved the riddle alluded to by Miss Grison in her published statement."

"Have you, Fuller?" asked Latimer in excited tones.

"Yes. Marie and I found it out, more by accident than in any logical way, Dick. See here!" and to Moon and the other man Fuller explained the method pursued, and showed the meaning of the precious stones in the tail of the bird. Berwick chuckled and rubbed his hands at the astonishment displayed by the newcomers, then quietly left the room. While Moon and Latimer were still expressing their surprise, and examining the bird, Berwick returned with one of the clerks carrying a good-sized box.

"Here are the jewels," he said expansively, when the clerk had been dismissed, and the box was placed on the table. "Use the key, Miss Inderwick."

They all crowded round to admire the box, which in itself was really curious and artistic. It was of polished steel, greatly tarnished by damp and age and sundry batterings which might be ascribed to its career in India before Ferrier had used it to store the jewels. The steel was enclosed in a network of delicate brass, scrolled and twisted and plaited and woven in a most elaborate manner. It was deep and rather large, which augured well for the quantity of gems it contained. Marie with a fluttering heart inserted the key, while the others looked on eagerly. She had some difficulty in turning it, since the lock had not been used for so long; but Alan aided her with his strong wrist, and with a click the key did its work. Then appeared the sandalwood lining of the box and a rich piece of Indian silk covering the contents. Miss Inderwick twitched this away, and a cry of amazement and admiration rose from everyone. In the glare of the light a perfect glory of color and radiance flashed out.

"Why, there must be a million pounds' worth," muttered Moon, astonished.

He might well say so, for the sight was enough to bewilder a miser. No pearls were visible, as they would have lost their color in the long darkness to which the gems had been submitted. But there were emeralds, rubies, sapphires and opals of many hues. Some of the precious stones were loose and polished, while others, also loose, were uncut. Still many jewels were set in various golden and silver ornaments, such as nose-rings, bangles, anklets, brooches, belts, and adornments for the head. Four trays piled with these treasures were lifted from the box, and at the very bottom, lying on a pad of rose-colored silk, were many loose diamonds glittering with multi-hued fires like the suns of innumerable solar systems. It was a royal heritage that Marie had entered into possession of, and worthy of a princess.

"And all for you and me, Alan," she whispered, joyously slipping her hand into that of her lover. "No more trouble now, dear."

"Well," said Moon, reflectively. "I don't wonder that Sorley risked his neck for an Arabian Nights' heap of jewels of this sort."

"He did not," cried Miss Inderwick, who could not be restrained this time; "my uncle is perfectly innocent."

"For your sake I sincerely trust that he is, Miss Inderwick," said Moon in grave tones; "and I hope he will prove your trust in him by giving himself up to the law. But this is not the time or place to talk of these things, and I do not wish to spoil your pleasure in inheriting a fortune of gems sufficiently beautiful to make a queen envious."

"I shall devote the fortune to proving my uncle's innocence," said Marie haughtily and stubbornly. "In the meanwhile, Mr. Berwick, put the box back in your strong-room along with tile peacock."

"Don't you wish to take it away with you?" asked Alan quickly.

"No. I don't like those noises in The Monastery, and I am sure that Miss Grison and that horrid Indian have something to do with them. If I took the gems down she and he would steal them."

"Noises," repeated Inspector Moon reflectively, "and in Mr. Sorley's house?"

"It is my house," said Marie quickly, "and if Miss Grison is down there, I shall order her out."

"You will be quite right in doing so, Miss Inderwick," said Inspector Moon with a bow, "and now I shall take my leave with renewed congratulations."

He went out repeating under his breath the word "Noises!" and Alan overhearing guessed that Marie's statement had aroused his suspicions as to the whereabouts of the much-wanted Sorley. He hoped that, after all, these same noises were due to Miss Grison, and felt anxious to call at Thimble Square after the box of gems and the peacock had been carried back to the strong-room of Yarbury's Bank.

"Let us visit Miss Grison now, Marie," he said when they were in Monks Lane again, with Dick beside them.

"You won't find her at home," said Latimer. "I called, but she has gone away."

Marie turned triumphantly to Alan. "There!" she cried, "what did I tell you, my dear? That horrid woman is hiding in The Monastery after all."

CHAPTER XIX

AT DAWN

It had been Alan's intention to send Marie back to Belstone by herself, and ask his father to meet her at Lewes, so that she could sleep at the vicarage. He had spent a great deal of time over the business connected with the murder of Grison and the finding of the jewels, therefore his clients were being neglected, much to their annoyance. His days of searching could scarcely have said to have been wasted, since they had ended in the acquisition of a fortune. Certainly it did not belong to him, but as he was to marry the girl who possessed it, in the end he would undoubtedly benefit. All the same he decided that he would have to attend to his own affairs, and it was only the fact that Miss Grison was not at Thimble Square, which caused him to change his mind. He therefore returned to the village with Marie, and what is more, insisted that Dick should return with him.

"We must get to the bottom of these matters," said Alan late that afternoon; "and if Marie will not sleep at The Monastery, Dick, you and I must do so."

"Oh, Alan," cried Miss Inderwick nervously, "why need you and Mr. Latimer do that when there is no need?"

"I think there is every need," rejoined her lover dryly. "Your remark as to inexplicable noises has aroused Moon's suspicions, and I should not be surprised if he either sent back that detective to keep watch, or came himself to-night or to-morrow."

"But how can our sleeping there alter Moon's intentions?" asked Latimer.

"I want to learn the meaning of these noises, so you and I, Dicky, can keep watch, while Marie is safe at the vicarage."

"If the noises are caused by Sorley," said Dick leisurely, and rather uncomfortably, "and we find that he has gone to earth there, you can't expect me to hold my tongue."

"Uncle Ran is innocent," protested Marie furiously.

"If he is—and I sincerely hope for your sake, that such is the case—it will be much better for him to come forward and face the worst. Otherwise, he will remain a hunted fugitive. Believe me, Miss Inderwick, by refusing to compound a felony—for that is what silence in this matter amounts to, as Alan will tell you—I am doing Mr. Sorley a greater service than you think."

"I agree with Dick," said Fuller quickly, and before Marie could make another protest; "it is best to bring matters to a head. If Mr. Sorley is indeed hiding at The Monastery, he is bound to be discovered some time, especially after the unconscious hint you gave Inspector Moon, my dear."

"I don't believe Uncle Ran is there," declared Marie pouting. "If he were he would look to me to give him food and drink, and he knows—as I said before, Alan—that he can trust me. It is that horrid woman."

"If Miss Grison is there, all the more reason Dick and I should sleep in the house, and learn what she is driving at."

Latimer nodded. "I'll come with you, Alan," he said quickly. "Since Miss Grison is not in her house, it's just possible she may be at Belstone."

"When did you call to see her?"

"Yesterday afternoon," explained Dick quietly. "I wished to learn how she knew that her precious brother had murdered a man outside Chin Chow's opium den."

"Moon told her that, and she swore that Baldwin was incapable of such a wicked deed," replied Alan with a shrug; "she seems to have a most touching belief in the creature, even though he is dead."

"Well, I learned that Miss Grison had gone away at noon for a few days."

"Where has she gone to?" asked Marie sharply.

"Her servants could not tell me, since she has left no address. All she said was that she would be absent for a few days, and she left her establishment in charge of the head waiter."

"That secrecy shows that she is at Belstone," cried Miss Inderwick triumphantly; "it is just the kind of underhand thing she would do."

"Well," said Alan, settling the question, "she may suspect that Sorley is hiding in The Monastery and may wish to catch him. If she gets into the house, Dick and I can compel her to state her reason. But indeed, Marie, I don't see how she could enter The Monastery without Henny or Jenny or Granny Trent seeing her."

"You don't know what a curious house it is, Alan. There are ways of getting out and in and hiding and spying, which no one would believe. I know of some myself, but Miss Grison is better acquainted with the place than I, as Granny always said that she explored the house thoroughly when she was my mother's companion. I'm sure you'll catch her; and if you do, tell her that we have found the jewels. That will settle her."

"Nothing will settle her until Sorley is proved innocent or guilty," said Fuller gravely. "The woman is obsessed by one idea, and that is revenge. I only wish we could find Jotty, for he knows a lot, I am sure, which could put things straight."

"Jotty can't be found," said Latimer lazily, "although Moon and his underlings are keeping their eyes open. He hasn't gone back to Miss Grison's or to Mother Slaig, either. He has vanished as completely as Mr. Sorley has. However, we shall see what can be done by our sleeping a night in your old family mansion, Miss Inderwick. I'll come down."

This being settled, the trio went to the station, and in due time arrived at Lewes. They talked during the journey about the jewels, and Dick had again to listen to the account of the solution of the riddle, in which, after all, he was so deeply interested that he did not object to the twice-told tale. Then Marie chattered about her good fortune, quoted the prophecy which certainly now seemed to be fulfilled, speculated on the amount of money which the sale of the gems would bring her, and talked of the improvements she would make in her family mansion. All this may seem rather heartless, when her uncle was under a cloud of suspicion; but the girl was so thoroughly convinced that the man was innocent and that her newly-acquired fortune would enable her to prove his innocence, by employing the best detective talent to hunt down the true criminal, that she did not worry over the matter so much as might have been expected. Moreover, her uncle had always behaved selfishly to her, so she did not think that trouble would harm him for the time being. Indeed she hoped that it might improve him into something less egotistical.

On arriving at Lewes, they found Mr. Fuller in person waiting for them in his pony-chaise, bubbling over with unexpected news.

"I am glad you have returned, Marie," he said, as he assisted the girl to get in; "a man has been asking for you."

"Who is he?"

"An Indian gentleman called—"

"Morad-Bakche," interrupted Alan breathlessly, and with a glance at Dick. "What does he want with Marie?"

"Perhaps he has learned that I went to Rotherhithe," murmured Marie, but too low for the vicar to hear.

"I don't know what he wants," said Mr. Fuller rather irritably, "he is stopping at The Red Fox, I hear, having come down this morning. He called at The Monastery to see Marie, and not finding her there, he came to the vicarage. He declined to believe that Marie was in town, although Henny told him so. However I convinced him."

"You didn't say why Marie had gone up, father," said Alan, in alarm.

"No no. Why should I? I simply said that Marie would return, and Mr. Bakche is on the watch."

"Don't see him, Marie," said Alan quickly. "Dick and I can interview him privately and learn what he has come about. And father, Marie will sleep to-night at our house, since she is afraid to remain at The Monastery. I and Latimer stay there.

"Why?" asked the vicar sharply.

"Marie will tell you while you drive back to Belstone, father. We can't all get into this small trap, so Dick and I will walk."

"Very good," said Mr. Fuller gathering up the reins, "but tell me, both of you, about the jewels."

"We have found Yarbury's Bank and the jewels also," said Marie gaily, "I can relate our day's experience while you drive, dear Mr. Fuller. And, Alan, do come to the vicarage before you go to sleep at The Monastery."

"Yes; Dick and I can spend the evening with you and mother and father. Afterwards we can walk over to your house to sleep there. I shall call and tell granny—with your permission—to get a couple of beds ready for us. Only don't you speak to Morad-Bakche, my darling; refer him to me."

Marie nodded and waved her hand as the vicar—who was rather bewildered by all this mystery—drove the pony-chaise out of the station yard. The two young men braced their muscles and started on the five miles' tramp to Belstone in very good spirits. Alan fancied, and communicated his fancy to his friend, that the presence of Bakche augured good, since the man undoubtedly knew something, and would be willing to impart it if he shared the fortune.

"But why should he?" objected Dick, lighting his pipe; "the assignment of the gems to George Inderwick puts him out of court."

"Marie wants to use some of the money to clear her uncle's name," explained Alan gravely, "and although I don't like Sorley, I am willing that she should do so. It will be worth the money."

"That depends if Bakche can say anything useful," growled Dick doubtfully.

"I am certain that he can, since he hinted something of the sort to me. He knew Grison at Rotherhithe also, and knew that he had the peacock."

"No!" said Latimer, greatly surprised.

"Yes, indeed," and Alan related Marie's daring visit to Mother Slaig, and what she had discovered regarding the movements of the Indian.

"She's a plucky girl," said Dick, referring to Marie; "fancy her tackling that horrible old woman. Hum! So Bakche was in the swim also, was he? I wonder if he murdered the man himself?"

"I don't think so; but we can ask him, for here he is."

Fuller's sharp eyes had seen the tall figure of the Indian almost running along the high road, and as the atmosphere was very clear he saw at some distance the brown tint of his face. Bakche met them quite breathless, and explained his haste. "I came down to see Miss Inderwick," he said, rather short of wind. "I met her—in the carriage—with—the—the clergyman. She refers me to you —Mr.—Mr. Fuller."

"I am conducting all business on Miss Inderwick's account," said Alan in a quiet tone; "but why are you in such a hurry, Mr. Bakche?"

"I thought that I might lose you. I stay at the village inn to-night, as I stayed last July; but I wish to see Miss Inderwick this evening, or you as her representative," he looked hesitatingly at Latimer.

"My friend knows all about the matter of the Rotherhithe crime," said Alan quickly, "you can speak frankly before him."

"How do you know that I came down to speak of the crime?" asked Bakche in a haughty tone.

"Because you know more about it than you have hitherto chosen to confess."

Bakche replied, still haughty, "I object to the word 'confess,' Mr. Fuller; I have no feeling of guilt in the matter."

"I don't say that you murdered the man yourself, but you know who did."

"Perhaps I do," answered the man significantly; "but you can't expect me to give you that information without payment."

"Oh, if you want money—"

Bakche flushed through the clear brown of his skin. "I do not want money, Mr. Fuller; a gentleman of my rank does not take money. I only desire a share of the jewels which rightfully belong to me—the whole of them."

"I think not," said Alan, while Latimer kept step beside him in silence, leaving his friend to adjust matters. "There was a proper assignment of the jewels made by the Rajah of Kam, the Begum and their vizier. All is in order, Mr. Bakche, and you have not a leg to stand on."

The man was silent for a few moments in sheer surprise at this very authoritative statement. "How do you know this, Mr. Fuller?"

"I read the statement myself, and saw the jewels of—"

"You saw the jewels," almost shrieked Bakche, clenching and unclenching his hands; "then you have—you have—" he could speak no further.

"Yes," growled Dick, breaking his self-imposed silence, "Fuller and Miss Inderwick have solved the riddle of the peacock, and have found the jewels."

"Where are they? where are they?"

"In a certain bank in London," said Alan quickly; "they are there now in Miss Inderwick's name along with the peacock."

"So if you intended to burgle The Monastery," growled Dick grimly, "you only waste your time."

Bakche drew himself up proudly. "You speak to an Indian gentleman, sir."

"I speak to a man who wants certain jewels, and who will stick at nothing to get them," retorted Latimer bluntly; "how do we know but what you may have murdered Grison?"

"I did not; and," added the man superciliously, "you will have some difficulty in proving that I did."

"I am not so sure of that, Mr. Bakche," put in Fuller; "after all, Mother Slaig can prove that you frequently saw Grison at her house."

Bakche looked startled and turned gray. "How can she prove that?"

"By means of that tattooed snake you have on your right arm."

"Ah-r-r-r! So you have been making inquiries? No," Bakche threw up his hand with a haughty gesture. "I don't want to hear what you have to say, for I admit that I often visited the house you mention. I knew that Grison had the peacock through his sister. She told me. I tried to get it from him, but he refused to surrender it. But I did not murder him."

"But you know who did?"

"Perhaps," said the Indian ambiguously, "only I shall not tell unless Miss Inderwick—as you suggested yourself, Mr. Fuller—gives me a portion of the jewels. If they did not belong to me rightfully I should not ask for even a part. I am," he drew himself up again, "an Indian gentleman."

"Well," said Fuller, who wished to be fair, "I don't deny but what your family jewels being given away is hard on you. Miss Inderwick wishes to clear the character of her uncle, and will be willing to give you some of your own back —I expect you put it in that way to yourself—if you can denounce the true murderer."

"I think I can."

"Are you not sure."

"I shall be sure if you can bring me face to face with that boy."

"Jotty?" cried Latimer, taking his pipe from his mouth. "I always said that the brat knew a lot."

"Yes. He knows a lot, and so do I," answered Bakche smiling dryly. "However you must give me a night to think over matters. To-morrow I shall call at The Monastery early in the day, and if we can come to an arrangement you shall have your minds set at rest. Always," ended the Indian taking off his cap, "always presuming that the boy is confronted with me."

"Do you hint that Jotty is guilty?" asked Fuller suddenly.

Bakche, who was turning away, looked back with an enigmatic smile. "A weak arm can drive a stiletto into a sleeping man, as easily as can a strong one, sir," and, still smiling, he walked off rapidly in the direction of Lewes, evidently objecting to further questions.

"By heaven!" muttered Alan aghast, "he knows the truth."

"It seems so," observed Dick with a thoughtful frown, "don't go after him, Alan. He will tell us all to-morrow, and you needn't be afraid of his running away, since his revelations mean that he gets a share of the gems."

"But we have to confront him with Jotty; and where is the boy?"

Dick shrugged his shoulders as they resumed their walk to Belstone. "Who knows? But even if he doesn't appear Bakche won't keep silent, for in that case he will lose his reward. Hum! I wonder if Jotty—as he infers—murdered Grison?"

"Well, Jotty is a greedy little beast, and admired the peacock. As he was a protégé of Grison and could run in and out of his room at will, it might be that he stole in when the man was sleeping and killed him. Bakche seems to hint at that. And then," added Fuller, warming to his theme, "remember how Miss Grison took charge of the lad. Perhaps he gave her the peacock and the stiletto, which she took down to The Monastery to implicate Sorley and revenge herself on him."

"She denied plainly enough that she took the bird to Belstone," replied Latimer, shaking his head, "and if Jotty had the peacock she would have guessed that he had murdered her brother. Seeing how she loved the man she would not have condoned Jotty's crime in any way. No, Alan, I don't agree with your theory. Better wait and hear what Bakche has to say and then we can be certain. But the stiletto? I thought that was missing?"

"From Mother Slaig's house," said Alan quickly, "but Marie and I found it in the secret cupboard where Sorley keeps his own private collection of jewels. Either he is guilty, and concealed it there, or Jotty—who came to warn him—did so; or Miss Grison did in some way manage to get the weapon and hide it. But then her possession of it would certainly entail her knowing the truth, and she would not—as you said before—spare the murderer of the brother whom she loved so dearly."

"Perhaps Bakche is guilty and is using Jotty as a screen," suggested Dick with a shrug; "however it is no use speculating, Alan. What we have to do is to watch to-night in The Monastery in the hope that Sorley has returned there, and to-morrow hear what the Indian has to say."

This was very good advice under the circumstances, and the young men took this very natural course. They arrived at the vicarage in time for dinner after calling at the big house to arrange with Granny Trent about sleeping there for the night. All the evening the vicar and his wife asked questions about the gems, and built castles in the air along with Marie as to the best use to be made of the money. Mention was made in the course of the evening by Mrs. Fuller that Miss Grison was staying with her dressmaker friend, and when Alan and Dick left to take up their quarters at The Monastery, they felt convinced that the woman had some idea of the whereabouts of her enemy.

"She's on the watch," said Fuller, as they walked to the big hole, "and if Sorley really has returned to hide, she will smell him out. I daresay he treated her and her brother badly, Dick, for Sorley is an utterly selfish creature, and perhaps deserves what he has endured. But what a vindictive person Miss Grison is."

"Hell hath no fury like a woman scorned," quoted Latimer sententiously, "and since Sorley scorned his true wife by making love to another woman, and used her love for her brother to free himself, you can scarcely wonder that she hates him as the devil hates holy water. She would be more than human if she did not. I am sorry for Miss Grison, or rather, as we should call her, Mrs. Sorley."

"She doesn't want to take that name," said Alan, shaking his head; "but if her husband gets off through Bakche's evidence, she may do so in order to show him up and spite him. As long as Sorley lives he will have to pay for his behavior."

"Serve him jolly well right," said Latimer grimly, and the conversation ended on the steps of the great house, where Henny Trent stood to receive them.

Granny was annoyed that her young mistress was sleeping at the vicarage, as she maintained that the noises were only due to ghosts, and that there was nothing to be feared. She scouted the idea that Sorley had returned, although she admitted that the old mansion was full of hiding-places where he could conceal himself. Her point was the same as Marie had mentioned, that the fugitive would require food, and knowing that all in the house would be loyal to him, he would not have hesitated to reveal himself had he actually sought refuge at The Monastery. The young men heard all these arguments passively, without seeking to contradict them, and then retired to bed wondering if granny was right and they were wrong, or if the reverse was the case.

It is not quite precise to say that they retired to bed, for they did not remove their clothes, and simply lay down, ready to spring up when the noises called their attention. They wore slippers, however, instead of boots so as to move softly about the place, and thus pounce unawares on anyone—Miss Grison or Sorley—who might be haunting the place. "But if it is a ghost, Alan, all our dodging and preparations won't be of much use."

"I don't believe in ghosts," said Alan curtly.

"I do," said Dick with equal terseness, but was too tired to argue the knotty point, and then they lay down, clothed as they were, to snatch a few moments of sleep.

Latimer certainly fell into a deep slumber, but his friend was too excited to follow his example. It occurred to him that if Sorley really were in the house and given to explorations by night, that he would assuredly haunt the library, if only to look at his beloved jewels. Hour after hour the young man dwelt on this point, and by the small hours of the morning had worked himself up to such a pitch of excitement that he could no longer endure inaction. Without disturbing Dick, who was sleeping in an adjoining chamber, he rose and stole down the stairs cautiously, making scarcely any sound, since he carried his slippers in his hand and walked in his socks. Also he had a revolver in his hip-pocket, lest the intruder should prove to be Bakche, admitted by Miss Grison through one of the numerous secret entrances. The Indian would be certain to show fight even if the woman did not. But of course, as yet Alan had heard no sounds, and was beginning to think that Marie's report was due to imagination.

He opened the library door cautiously, shading the candle he carried with his hand, after thrusting the slippers into the pocket of his tweed coat. The room was in complete darkness, as the shutters were closed, and there was no sign that anyone was about. However, as Alan assured himself once more, Sorley, if on the spot, would certainly come to the library, so the young man extinguished his candle, and concealed himself behind an Indian screen near the middle French window. Here he lay down on the carpet and waited patiently.

An hour passed and then another, and the night wore on to dawn. Still the room was quiet and Alan at length began to feel drowsy, for his long vigil was telling on his tired body. Through the shutters he saw a thread of cold light, which showed that day was breaking, and heard the early outburst of song with which the birds greeted the dawn. He shifted himself into a more comfortable position, and closed his eyes, when suddenly he opened them again widely, and every sense intensified its power. There was certainly a noise—that of shuffling footsteps, hesitating, dragging, doubtful, as though the individual was in deadly terror of discovery. Then after a pause came the cautious opening of the library door, and Alan peering round the corner of the screen, saw a gleam of light. It came from a candle held in a man's hand, and the glimmer shone faintly on the haggard face. The newcomer was Randolph Vernon Sorley, and he looked like a ghost of his former self, bowed-down, white-faced, and lean.

Closing the door he went to the cupboard where the golden bird had been found by him, and opened the same. In a moment or so Alan heard the sound of eating, and saw that Sorley was eagerly devouring food. Apparently in his prosperous days he had established a larder in the cupboard against the time when he might be hunted down. The sight gave Alan the idea that the man might be guilty after all, since otherwise he would not have prepared for such a contingency. However, there was small time to consider this reason and that, for Sorley having eaten, might slip away to his hiding-place, and then in the rambling old mansion it would be impossible to discover him. When the man left the cupboard and came to the table, he placed his candle thereon, took a long drink from a flask—it probably contained whisky and water—and then shuffled to the panel marked with a cross. Slipping this aside he held the candle so that he might admire his jewels. Alan thought it was now time to make his presence known in the least startling way possible.

"Mr. Sorley!" he said softly, and rising with caution.

"Oh God!" gasped the man, dropping the light, and suppressing a scream.

In the darkness Alan groped his way forward. "Don't be afraid. It is Alan Fuller. I am your friend.

"Alan," the young man heard the click of the door, and knew that the fugitive was making for his hiding-place. But he halted when hearing the voice and the name. "Alan," said Sorley in the darkness, and his quavering voice hinted at relief. "Oh thank heaven you have come! How did you guess—"

"Marie and granny heard certain noises," said Alan quickly.

"Yes," muttered Sorley, lighting another candle which he apparently took out of his pocket, since the fallen one was lying near the panel. "I was not so careful as I should have been. But it could not go on for ever, so I am glad you have come, Alan. I want help," his voice trembled piteously, "yes I want help to escape."

In this turn the young man lighted the candle he had kept beside him, and in the radiance of the two tapers surveyed the broken-down creature before him, who looked quite his age, if not more. His face and hands were black with dust and dirt, his clothes were stained and torn, while his beard had grown considerably, and despair lurked in his sunken eyes. In place of the alert, soldierly man of yore, Alan beheld a trembling, shivering, cringing thing, wincing at every sound, shrinking from every shadow. Guilty or not, Sorley was surely paying in full for his sins, since the agony and terror of his soul was made manifest in his body. "And I am innocent," he muttered again and again.

"If you are innocent why do you wish me to help you to escape?" asked Mr. Fuller gravely.

"Because I can't prove my innocence," said Sorley with sudden energy. "I am in a net woven by that infernal woman."

"Your wife?"

"Oh, so she told you that, did she? Yes, I admit she is my wife, and a bitter one she has been to me. But this is not the time or place to talk of these things. I could defend myself on that score if necessary, but there is no need. Place me in safety, Alan, and I can explain everything. You do not believe that I, am guilty; surely you don't?" and he looked piteously at the young man, shaking like a leaf.

"No, I can't say that I am absolutely convinced of your guilt," admitted Alan cautiously, "but when you gave yourself up why did you run away again?"

"I can explain that," replied Sorley with a cunning look, "only give me time, and all will be explained. I got away in the fog and came down here on my motor bicycle which I had kept ready in town. Now I am hiding here in a secret place below the earth—down in the cellars. There are ranges and ranges of cellars here, you know, Alan. I come up here at night to get food which long ago I placed in that cupboard"—he pointed to the recess with a trembling hand—"biscuits and potted meat, whisky and claret."

"That storage looks as though you expected to be accused," said Alan dryly.

Sorley nodded. "I was never sure of Louisa," he muttered shuffling with his feet. "I knew she would get me into trouble some day, and she has done so. She is here now. Yes, I know that, for I saw her from a peephole yesterday evening wandering round the house. I daresay she entered it, for she knows all its secrets as well as I do. And if she finds me"—he gripped Alan's coat —"she will give me up. I must get away; help me to fly beyond the seas until such time as I can prove my innocence. I won't take the peacock with me," he went on eagerly, "you can have that, and you can find the treasure. I shall only take my own jewels," and he glanced at the panel which was still open.

"The treasure has been found, Mr. Sorley."

"What—what—what!" the man would have fallen had not Fuller held him up.

"Marie and I solved the riddle!" and to quieten the babbling creature Alan hurriedly related everything in as few words as possible. "The peacock and the jewels are now at Yarbury's Bank, so things are all right in that respect, and Marie is now wealthy."

"She has the jewels," muttered the old man jealously. "Oh, the beautiful jewels. They are beautiful, are they not, Alan?"

"Don't trouble about what is not yours," said Fuller sharply, "what we have to do is to come to an understanding. Miss Grison is here, staying with Mrs. Millington, while Morad-Bakche is at The Red Fox, and I shrewdly suspect that Inspector Moon will come down this very day, since he guesses that you are here, because Marie let drop a word or so about the noises she heard."

Sorley staggered to the door. "I am surrounded by my enemies," he gasped, "but I sha'n't give in. I shall go back to the cellars and hide myself."

Alan ran forward and grasped his arm. "No," he said strongly, "you must act like a man, Mr. Sorley, and give yourself up. If you are innocent you need fear nothing, and I shall stand by you throughout the trial."

"The trial! the trial!" wailed Sorley; "no, no, I cannot, I dare not. Louisa is too strong for me, indeed she is. Unless he knows the truth."

"He. To whom do you refer?"

"He—I mean—I mean—ah, you asked me why I ran away again after giving myself up. Stop here and you shall see, you shall see with your own eyes, Alan, I swear you shall see," and wrenching himself free, Sorley flung open the door and passed hastily out of the room.

Alan had half a mind to follow, since once hidden again, it would be difficult to discover the old creature. But then Sorley believed that he would help him, so Fuller was satisfied that he would return, although he could not conjecture the reason why he had gone away. It seemed impossible for him to produce any proof to show why he had fled in the fog. Fuller determined to wait, and meanwhile opened the shutters. The cold searching light of the morning penetrated the large room in a chill manner, and Alan shivered in the keen air when he opened the middle French window. But he did not shiver when the sound of Sorley's returning footsteps was heard and when the door re-opened to show the old man dragging a miserable object forward by the arm.

"Jotty!" cried Alan with a bewildered stare.

"Yes, Jotty," echoed Sorley; "and now you know why I bolted."

CHAPTER XX

WHO IS GUILTY?

The urchin presented a more dilapidated appearance than he had ever done before even when in his native slums as a street-arab. The neat serge suit with which Miss Grison's kindness had supplied him was smeared with green slime and covered with cobwebs, besides being torn in many places. But Alan did not look so much at the lad's clothes as at his face and figure, for he was terribly emaciated, and so weak, apparently with hunger, that he could scarcely keep his legs. When he saw Fuller he burst into tears, and Sorley allowed him to drop on to the carpet.

"How does the lad come here?" demanded Fuller indignantly, "and what have you been doing to him that he should be in this terrible state?"

"He knows the truth," snarled Sorley, who looked quite wolfish at the moment, and cast a vindictive look at his victim, "and I have been trying to starve it out of him."

"But y' haven't," murmured Jotty feebly, game to the last, "gimme sumthin' t' eat an' drink, mister, or I'm a goner," and his head dropped as though he would die then and there. But Sorley only laughed at his sufferings.

"I was certain that the boy knew the truth," he declared savagely; "and when he came to warn me I lured him to the cellars and locked him up."

"Without food?" questioned Alan with horror, and knelt by the boy to put one of the biscuits Sorley had left on the table between his lips.

"No, I fed him occasionally," said the man sullenly, "but kept him short so that starvation might make him speak."

"But it didn't," murmured Jotty again, trying to eat the biscuit.

"Little devil!" cried Sorley in a transport of rage. "I'll make you admit that you are in league with that woman to ruin me before I've done. It was because you were locked in the cellar and no one but I knew where you were, that I bolted from Moon in London. If I had been locked up you would have died of starvation, and, bad as you are, I didn't want that. And now you know," he said defiantly to Alan, "why I changed my mind after giving myself up. It only occurred to me that Jotty might starve when I was in the cab driving to Bow Street with Moon. I therefore determined to get away in the fog, and I did."

"You should have told Moon where the boy was to be found," said Fuller in sharp tones. "Hand me that flask of whisky; the boy is nearly dead."

"Oh I hope not, I hope not," said Sorley in alarm, and anxiously watching the young man moistening Jotty's lips with the powerful spirit. "I didn't mean that he should die, for then he would take his secret with him, and I might be hanged through Louisa's lies. As to telling Moon about the cellars, I wasn't such a fool," he went on in an injured tone. "I wasn't going to reveal my hiding-place, which I knew would come in useful, if I were driven to extremities. But I'm poor old man, and everyone is against me," he ended sobbing bitterly.

Fuller was too disgusted with the man's behavior to say a word, but busied himself in feeding Jotty cautiously with biscuits soaked in whisky. The boy soon began to pick up, and eagerly demanded more food, which Alan refused to give him lest he should suffer from overeating, after being so long without nourishment. Besides he thought that the whisky might make him drunk, which was not to be thought of, since the boy had to give his evidence and tell his secret, whatever that might be. So while Sorley wept and maundered on about himself in an agony of self-pity, Alan lifted Jotty and placed him in a deep armchair. By this time the color had returned to the lad's face, and he was much stronger for the moment, at all events, so Fuller thought that it would be just as well to question him.

"Why did you warn Mr. Sorley after betraying him to me?" he asked.

"'Wanted quids,'" admitted Jotty frankly, and with a malevolent glance at Sorley; "'knew he'd pay t' git awaiy fro' th' coppers. 'Said es he would, an' tole me, es his cash was in his bloomin' cellars. I was fool enuff t' g' daown, I was, an' he shoved me int' one of 'em an' keeps me wiffout grub till I fair screeched wiff 'unger. But I'll 'ave th'lawr of him, I will," said Jotty vindictively and very humanly.

"Why didn't you escape?"

"'Couldn't, nohow. Thet cove lock'd th' beastly door, he did."

"Couldn't you cry out?"

"I cried and hollered till I was fair sick, but it warn't no' good, nohow, es I soon sawr, mister. He guv me grub et toimes t' keep me fro' becomin' a deader," acknowledged the lad grudgingly, "but he ses as he'd not feed me up till I tole. But I didn't, you bet I didn't."

"Tell what?"

"The truth about the murder," sobbed Sorley; "he knows it, the reptile."

"I dunno no nuffin;" murmured Jotty sulkily; "give me another bisket, mister, 'cept y' want t' play the saime game."

Fuller gave him what he wanted, and a little more whisky and water to bring back his strength. Then he turned his attention to Sorley, and wondered what was best to be done. "You will have to surrender yourself and stand your trial, you know," said Alan firmly, "things can't go on in this silly way, Mr. Sorley."

The old man pitched forward, sobbing at Alan's feet, while Jotty, who was now top-dog, grinned delightedly at his enemy's downfall. Fuller stooped to pick up the wretched creature, and to repeat his determination when he heard Dick rushing down the stairs shouting his name.

"Alan! Alan Where are you?"

"In the library. Come in. What's up?"

Latimer burst into the room with dishevelled hair and untidy clothes, just as he had leaped out of bed, and evidently was greatly excited. He was on the eve of imparting the cause of his hurried coming, when he stopped short on beholding Sorley and the missing lad. "Well I'm hanged!" said Dick, and gasped with amazement.

"I shall be, I shall be," groaned Sorley still grovelling on the floor, "if Louisa has her way. And you hate me, Latimer, you know you do. You will give me up after all my trouble in coming back to hide here."

"Oh so you did hide here," said Latimer slowly, "and Jotty?"

"He lock' me up, cuss him!" whimpered the boy, "'cos I wouldn't tell him things es I ain't agoin' to tell, nohow."

"What re—" began Dick wonderingly, when Alan cut him short.

"You'll hear later, old man. Meanwhile what's up, that you rush in like a whirlwind?"

"I missed you when I woke up, and wondered where you were. I looked out of the window of my bedroom and saw a woman coming up the avenue with a man. As they came nearer I saw that it was Miss Grison and Moon."

"I'm lost, I'm lost," shouted Sorley scrambling to his feet; "let me hide, oh let me hide," and he rushed to the door.

"Ain't no go, mister," yelled the malignant Jotty, nibbling at his biscuit, "fur I

210

knows yer hole an' I'll sell y' fur a sneak."

But in spite of this assertion, Sorley, in a fever of terror would have fled, but that Alan caught him by the arm. "Stay here and face things like a man," he said sternly. "Dick run out and ask Moon and Miss Grison to come here. Then dash down to The Red Fox and bring Bakche to prove the poor devil's innocence."

"What—what—what," gurgled Sorley, as Dick lost no time in obeying, and sprang out of the French window which Alan had opened. "Can he—"

"I think so; I am not sure," said Fuller sharply. "However you shall stay here and face the best or the worst."

"Louisa will hang me," murmured Sorley, sinking into a chair and covering his face with two grimy hands. Jotty grinned, and did not seem disturbed at the announcement that Bakche would prove his captor's innocence, which made Alan think that the brat could not be so guilty as the Indian had hinted.

Feeling weary with his long watching and the late exciting events, the young man went to the window to inhale deep breaths of the keen morning air. The sun was now rising, and the eastern sky was radiant with golden floods of light, while the chill atmosphere felt perceptibly warmer. Trees and lawns and beds of early flowers presented themselves with photographic distinctness in the crystalline clearness of the dawning, and there was a feeling of freshness, as if all old things were being made new by the magical workings of nature. But Fuller had small time to gratify his jaded senses with this cool beauty, for crossing the lawn were Inspector Moon and Miss Grison. Dick had just delivered his message and had left them to dash down the avenue to Belstone, while the woman and the officer advanced towards the open window, as they had been directed. Alan stepped down to meet them, quite satisfied that the vindictive Jotty would keep a close watch on the miserable old man. The tables were now turned with a vengeance.

"How are you, Miss Grison? and you, Mr. Inspector?" said Alan quietly. "I heard that the lady was here, but you sir?—"

"I brought him," said Miss Grison triumphantly, and looking wooden and washed out and as hard as ever. "I wired for him last night, for I was certain that Sorley would come back to The Monastery."

Moon nodded, and looked curiously at Alan's drawn face, and disordered clothes, and especially at his feet which were without slippers. "I came down late last night to Lewes," he explained, "and drove over early this morning. That is why I am here at so unexpected an hour. And even if Miss Grison had not wired me, I should have come, although perhaps later. Miss Inderwick's remark about noises in her house—"

"Yes! yes!" interrupted Fuller with a shiver, for the dewy grass chilled his feet. "I guessed that you would come after that unconscious hint."

"Well of course Miss Inderwick naturally; wants to save her uncle—"

Miss Grison interrupted the inspector in her turn. "She won't though, try as she will. I know all the hiding-places in The Monastery, and wherever Sorley may conceal himself I can hunt him out."

"He doesn't wish to conceal himself," said Fuller coldly, for the look of malicious triumph on her sallow face was terrible. "He is in the library and wishes to give himself up."

"He did so before," remarked Moon dryly, "and then ran away."

"Because he had Jotty locked up in a cellar here, and feared lest the boy should starve to death. Come in, Mr. Inspector. This is surely the beginning of the end."

"The end, the end," cried Miss Grison joyfully, and absolutely chanted the words as if they were the funeral hymn of a victim, "the end of the beast and all his wickedness. I hope they'll let me see him hanged. And he'll have no coffin, but be buried in lime and—"

"Hold your tongue," said Moon roughly, for even his tried nerves gave way with a quiver when the vindictive woman expressed her unholy joy. "Come on, Mr. Fuller. I'm glad you didn't help this man to escape."

"I never intended to," Alan assured the officer as they stepped into the room through the open window, followed by Miss Grison, who slunk behind like halting Nemesis, silent and sinister. "I forced him to stay and surrender."

"He sha'n't escape this time," growled Moon, looking at Sorley who stared rigidly from the chair he was seated in, not at the officer of the law, but at the cruel face of the wife who had hunted him down. He seemed like a rabbit fascinated by a serpent, and could utter no sound. Even when Moon again recited the formula of arrest he did not speak.

But Miss Grison did. "Ha!" she jeered, pointing a finger of scorn at the motionless man, "now do you receive the wages of iniquity, you beast!"

"Be silent," said Alan tartly, while the inspector turned to address a few words to Jotty, who looked at him impudently.

"I shall not be silent," raged the woman; "you know what I am, and who I am in every way, Louisa Sorley—that is my name." Moon overhearing, turned with a blank look of astonishment. "Yes, you may look and look and look!"

she taunted, snapping her fingers. "Louisa Sorley, and that fiend's lawful wife. Ah!"—she turned furiously on her husband—"you cast me off, you made me hold my tongue by threatening to imprison Baldwin so that you could marry the wealthy slut you set your mind on. I could do nothing, because I had to save my brother; all I could do I did, and that was to steal the peacock. And now the secret has been guessed and the jewels belong to your minx of a niece—"

"Stop that," cried Fuller in a fierce way; "not a word against my promised wife, Miss Grison."

"Mrs. Sorley, if you please," retorted the woman making an ironical curtsey, "and the girl is my niece by marriage as well as your promised wife. But she has the jewels, and much as I hate her I am glad, since this sneaking reptile will not get them into his clutches. I have waited for this hour; for years have I waited; lying in bed, walking during the day, working or playing I have plotted and planned and thought and striven to bring you down to the dust. You scorned me, who loved you, you tortured Baldwin who was your friend, and you drove us both in disgrace from this house. Now it is your turn—yours! yours! yours!" She pointed her finger again and laughed with savage delight. "You shall be driven from the house; you shall go to jail; you shall be hanged by the neck until you are dead, and may God *not* have mercy on your soul."

Moon caught her by the arm, and shook her sternly. "You mustn't talk like that, you know," he said in a peremptory manner.

Miss Grison—as it is more convenient to call her—wrenched herself free, and her little lean figure quivered with unrestrained rage. She wore the long black velvet cloak, the early Victorian bonnet, and the drab thread gloves in which Alan had seen her when she had been surprised by himself and Marie in the library. But she was no longer demure, no longer did she compress her thin lips and stare in an unwinking unmeaning way. Her terrible triumph had stirred up the depths of her nature, and she acted like a woman bereft of reason, as indeed she was for the moment.

"Damn you, let me be!" she screeched, getting free at the expense of a torn cloak. "I can speak to my husband, I suppose. Ha! ha! A nice thing it is for me to have a murderer for a husband."

"I am not a murderer," wailed Sorley tremulously. "I left Baldwin alive and well. She—she—she—"

"She—she—she," mocked his wife, "you, with your she—she—she. You are a murderer; you had the peacock; you have the knife which killed My darling brother. Deny it if you dare."

"I do deny it," stammered Sorley with an attempt to assert his dignity. "I had the peacock, because you brought it here secretly."

"You lie, as you have always done. I did not. Perhaps you will say that I brought the knife—the dagger—the thing with which Baldwin was stabbed also, you animal!"

"No—no—no. I have never seen the knife. But I believe you would have brought it if you could, so as to make me out to be guilty."

"You liar!" raged the woman, while both Moon and Alan stood aside silent, wondering what would be brought forth next. "I came here on that day when I warned you, and walked all over the place while you were snoring, like the hog you are. Here!" she brushed Moon aside with a force surprising in so small a woman, and marched to the open panel. "I looked in here, where I always knew you kept your bits of glass, and I intended to take some, so as to make you suffer, just as I did with the peacock; just as I did with the peacock, you wretch! But I found hidden there the dagger which was used to murder my dearest brother, so I left things alone knowing you were the beast who murdered him, and knowing that I at last had you in my power to hunt down." She thrust her arm into the recess and tore out tray after tray of jewels which scattered themselves about the floor, and finally pulled out the stiletto which Marie had found and Alan had seen. "There! oh there you are! Do you see this, policeman? blood on the handle? Yes, take it, and bring it up in the evidence against him."

Moon handled the stiletto with a frown. "This looks bad," he said to the terrified Sorley; "is it yours?"

"It was—it was," stammered the old man, shaking with nervous fear, "but if I were truly guilty I would not dare to say so. I bought it in Venice—in Italy—where I—I—" he broke off with a cry rising to face his wife with what courage he was able to summon to his heart. "And you stole it over twenty years ago, along with the peacock; you stole many things—you know you did, Louisa. I believe—yes—I believe—"

"That I put it there," interrupted Miss Grison with a shrill laugh. "Oh I daresay. To save your own bacon you can say no more and no less. Liar and murderer and wife beater that you are! You struck me once, you did, you did, and now I have come back to repay the blow with interest. Man!" she faced round fiercely to Moon, "why don't you put the handcuffs on him? Make him a shame and disgrace in the village where he has lorded it for so many guilty years. I could—" she dashed forward with a raised arm, her face working with furious passion.

Fuller caught her back. "Steady! steady!"

"Beast!" she turned and struck him full in the face, whereupon Moon came to the young man's assistance, and the two forced her back into a chair. For a few minutes she struggled, screaming, spitting, kicking and fighting with all the abnormal strength which her fury against her husband gave her. All at once she collapsed, and became as weak as an infant, to burst into tears, and huddle up, a nerveless heap, in the deep chair.

"She's finished now," said Moon, wiping his red face; "all the fight's gone out of her. Whew! I've seen women in the cells like her before. She's a crazy bit of goods."

"She's mad, quite mad," quavered Sorley, wringing his hands in a senile manner, "I always said that she was."

"Then you sent her mad," muttered Alan, who did not think Marie's uncle was wholly the injured person he presented himself to be.

All the time Jotty surreptitiously devoured all the biscuits within reach, and enjoyed what was to him quite a performance—and a well-known one at that, as often he had seen Mother Slaig and others of her kind raging in just such an animal manner. "She's a oner, ain't she?" he said grinning, "but not a bad ole gal, oh no, not at all."

Miss Grison, who was lying back apparently exhausted, unclosed one eye and then two, shooting such a malevolent glance at the boy that he held his tongue and looked away uneasily. Moon was about to take up again the stiletto which he had cast carelessly on the table in order to ask questions, when Latimer, hot with rapid walking, made his appearance through the window followed by Morad-Bakche, who looked uncomfortable. The inspector nodded to both, but did not speak for the moment, as his attention was taken up with Alan's attempt to pacify granny and the two servants who had been attracted to the library by Miss Grison's screams. The three wished to stay, and argued the point, but Fuller managed to finally turn them out and then came back to witness what would doubtless prove to be the final act of the drama. Meanwhile neither Bakche nor Latimer said a word, and Miss Grison still lay back in her chair broken up much in the same way as was her husband. They were both wrecks, the sole feelings predominating being terror in the man's heart and hatred in the woman's.

"Well, sir," said Inspector Moon, turning sharply on the dignified Indian, "and what do you know about this matter?"

"I have some idea of the truth," answered Bakche quietly, and now more at ease, "and I am willing to state what I know on the condition which I arranged with Mr. Fuller yesterday. Indeed, Mr. Fuller, so to speak, suggested the condition some time ago, and I came down here to see Miss Inderwick as to whether she would be willing to fulfil it."

"If you know the truth, you must tell the truth without any condition. That is the law of this country. If you impede the course of justice by keeping back necessary information you are liable to a penalty."

"I am willing to take the risk," responded the Indian dryly, "since I have so much at stake. I appeal to Mr. Fuller as to whether he is willing to agree to my condition?"

"On behalf of Miss Inderwick I am," said Alan quietly, "since she leaves me free to use her jewels in any way likely to free her uncle from this charge of murder brought against him by Miss Grison."

"Mrs. Sorley, if you please," murmured the woman without unclosing her eyes.

Bakche took no notice. "I want half the jewels," he stated coolly.

"You shall have a third," answered Alan.

"Then I don't speak."

"What's that?" cried Moon. "Let me tell you, that if you don't, I shall arrest you as being concerned in this crime."

"You have no warrant!" said the man uneasily.

"I shall arrest you without a warrant, and make good my reason afterwards."

The Indian looked uncomfortably from one to the other, and finally seeing that the Inspector was in earnest, he yielded to circumstances too strong for him. "You agree to give me a third of my family jewels?" he asked turning to Alan nervously.

"Yes; I shall put it in writing if you like."

"No; I am willing to take the word of an English gentleman. That lad," the man looked at Jotty, "also knows something of the truth; at least I think that he does."

"Don't know nuffin," muttered the boy truculently, for the drink was telling on his weak condition. "If I did, I wouldn't tell when that cove," he pointed to Sorley, "lock'd me up."

"Tell," said the inspector sharply, "or I'll box your ears."

"Sha'n't, sha'n't, sha'n't," babbled Jotty, "wot I knows is wuth quids, an' quids I'll 'ave or say nuffin."

Sorley scrambled on the floor and swept together some of the gems. "Take these; take these and save my life," he implored, thrusting them into the boy's hands. "You wouldn't tell by force but these are worth money, so—"

Jotty played with the gems and put them into his pocket. "If they're wuth quids," he said thickly, "I'll split."

"Do you know the truth?" asked Latimer quickly, "I always thought you did."

"Perhaps you saw the murder committed," Alan remarked, and they all stared hard at the boy.

"No I didn't," snapped Jotty, "but I sees sumthin', and I think es I kin spot who did it."

"Who did it then?" demanded Moon impatiently.

"Sha'n't speak till thet cove does," muttered Jotty, pointing his chin at Bakche with an obstinate look; "don't b'leve he knows tho'."

"Don't I?" cried Bakche drawing himself up to his stately height, "I was at Rotherhithe when the man was murdered by his sister."

"Miss Grison!" cried Alan confounded. "Good Lord! Miss Grison killed him?"

"Yes," said Bakche, "Miss Grison killed him."

CHAPTER XXI

THE TRUTH

The accusation of the Indian, which seemed to be emphasized by Jotty's silence, brought Miss Grison, still weak and broken, to her feet. "It's a lie! a lie! a lie!" she stammered, holding on to the chair for support.

"It's the truth," insisted Bakche deliberately.

"But it's impossible," murmured Fuller, who was quite bewildered, "she loved her brother dearly."

"I did, I did. Bless you for saying that, Mr. Fuller," cried Miss Grison in a tremulous tearful way. "Why should I murder my darling Baldwin?"

"To get me into trouble," quavered Sorley, who had got back into his chair and was nervously plucking at his chin.

"I wouldn't have sacrificed him to you," retorted Miss Grison, dropping back again into her seat and taking out her handkerchief.

"Perhaps if I tell my story," said Bakche appealing to the inspector, "you may be convinced of the truth."

"Go on," said Moon curtly, and took out his pocket-book.

"She killed him—"

"I never did, I never did," wept Miss Grison, "you did it yourself."

"I did it! How dare you say that!"

"Because it is true. You admit having been at Rotherhithe on the night and about the time poor Baldwin was murdered. You wanted the peacock, you know you did, and told me so. When I said Baldwin had it—"

"I went to try and get it from him," finished Bakche, "that is quite correct, madam. I did, and I tried hard to get him to part with it. But he refused and you urged him not to give it to me, even for money. When you visited your brother—"

"I never visited him," snapped Miss Grison, whose strength was coming back, and whose eyes were again beginning to flash ominously.

"You did," retorted the Indian, "you went frequently, I disguised myself as a lascar and followed you. I overheard your conversations with him many a time, madam."

"Ah!" she flashed out, "you were eavesdropping."

"Yes," admitted the man candidly. "I had too much at stake not to take all the means in my power to safeguard my interests. And a few days before the murder you urged your brother to write to Mr. Sorley and make an appointment for the thirteenth of November."

"Ah!" murmured Moon, making a note, "the night of the death."

"Yes! yes! yes!" cried Sorley, his voice growing stronger; "I got that letter, and wrote an answer saying that I would come."

"Jotty found the answer," put in Alan quickly, "and sold it to me for two pounds. Mr. Latimer passed it on to you, Mr. Inspector."

Moon nodded. "I have it at my office. Go on, sir."

"Miss Grison—as I overheard—urged her brother to make this appointment with Mr. Sorley, and then tell him that the peacock was to be given to me."

"Ah!" cried the woman sarcastically, "and yet you say that I urged my brother not to give it you. You contradict yourself."

"I am not responsible for your frequent changes of mind," said Bakche in chilly tones, "sometimes you told your brother to make terms with me so that Mr. Sorley—whom you seemed to hate—might be disappointed, and then you tried to prevent him even seeing me, let alone handing over the peacock. But you got him to make the appointment for the night of the murder with Mr. Sorley, that I'll swear to. There was another thing that I overheard. Your brother confessed with tears and terror that he had murdered that gentleman to rob him outside Chin Chow's opium den."

"What if he did?" said Miss Grison boldly.

"You blamed him for the shame he was bringing on your name."

"I did, but that does not say that I should have denounced him."

"There was no need for you to do so," said Moon coldly; "sooner or later the truth would have become known. Grison was already suspected."

"So he told his sister," said Bakche quickly, "and for that reason she reproached him."

"Why not say that I murdered him?" sneered the woman quivering.

"You did, but not on the night you advised him to make the appointment with this gentleman." He pointed to Sorley huddled up in his chair.

"When then, if you please, liar that you are?"

"I am no liar, and you know it, madam. It was on the night that the appointment was kept that you killed your brother. I determined to come on that night, so as to overhear the interview between Mr. Sorley and your brother, and I did. Mr. Sorley wanted the peacock and Grison refused to surrender it. Then Mr. Sorley left."

"And Grison was alive? Grison was alive?" cried the man in question.

"Yes," said Bakche, answering the question and a look of Moon's. "Grison was alive. Mr. Sorley is perfectly innocent."

"Thank God! oh thank God!" wept Sorley hysterically, and sliding from his chair he knelt down covering his face with his grimy hands. Alan nodded to Dick in a somewhat triumphant way, as he had never been sure of Sorley's guilt, and Dick nodded penitently in return, admitting silently his error.

"Was Miss Grison at Rotherhithe on that night?" asked Moon rather unnecessarily, seeing that Bakche accused her of committing the crime.

"Yes. I was on the watch, and I saw her coming."

"Did Mother Slaig see her?"

"Not on that night, I fancy. Miss Grison always slipped into the house and out of it like a shadow," said Bakche, after a moment's reflection. "Sometimes Mrs. Slaig saw her and sometimes she did not. The house was always filled with people coming and going, and in that shabby dress"—Bakche referred somewhat superciliously to Miss Grison's worn attire—"no one noticed her."

"Everyone knew that I came to comfort mm brother," said the woman sharply.

"I am not denying that. But on that night you hovered round the place and saw Sorley come and go. He came at seven and went away by eight. Grison afterwards came down and got a drink, after which he retired to bed at ten o'clock as was stated at the inquest. He did not see you when he was down stairs, as you did not speak to him. But you followed him up and were with him in his room. No one but I saw you, as no one paid any attention to your brother, save I who was on the watch. After ten—I can't state the exact time —you came out of the room and slipped away unnoticed. I followed you to the end of the slum, madam, and then returned to see if you had been urging Grison not to give me the peacock. I looked in and he was on his bed quite dead."

"Why didn't you give the alarm?" asked Alan impatiently.

"Ask yourself why I did not, Mr. Fuller," said Bakche pitying this denseness. "Here was I, who wanted a valuable object possessed by Grison, disguised as a lascar. Had I given the alarm I should have been arrested for the crime and would have had a great difficulty in clearing myself."

"Yes," said Moon, "that is perfectly true. Well?"

"Well," echoed Bakche, "what more do you wish me to say, sir. Grison was alive when this lady entered his room, and when she came out he was dead. I knew also that she carried away the peacock."

"How do you know?" asked Latimer, while Miss Grison sniffed disdainfully.

"Jotty told me."

"Yuss," said the boy, brisking up, for he had nodded in a sleepy way during the recital, "he guv me a quid fur tellin' him; he wantin' thet there blessed peacock, somehow."

"But how did you know Miss Grison had it Jotty?" questioned Alan.

"Sawr it afore him es was good t' me was buried. I wen up t' 'er house in

Bloomsbury es I'd orfen gone afore, fur him es was good t' me, and I ses as 'er brother was a deader. Sh' sawr me in 'er room an' I sawr 'er smuggle awaiy thet peacock and thet thing," and Jotty pointed to the stiletto, which was lying on the table where Moon had thrown it.

"You liar! oh, you little liar!" shrieked Miss Grison, shaking her fist.

"It's trewth, fur sure," insisted Jotty, "an' cos I knowed too much, y' tuck me int' yer bloomin' ouse an' guv me thet button suit. I didn't say nuffin, I didn't, es y' wasn't a bad ole gal, an I oped t' maike quids out of y'. An' when y' come daown 'ere, t' the fun'rel of him es was good t' me, y' tuck awaiy thet peacock an' thet stabbin' thing. Oh, I kep' m' eye peeled, y' bet, fur I wanted thet peacock m'self, wuth plenty of quids it is anyhow. Sawr's y' packin' them in a bag when y' thought es I wasn't lookin'. But I ain't no fool, nohow, tho' y' did git me t' help t' git thet Sorley cove int' trouble."

"How was that, Jotty," asked the inspector while Miss Grison ripped her handkerchief to shreds in silent anger.

"Why sh' fun' out es I'd got that letter fro' him," he pointed to Sorley "an' she ses, as I'd better taike it t' Mr. Fuller there, who'd give me quids fur it anyhow. An' I did, gettin' two quids fur it. An' then I was 'opin' t' git more quids fro the Sorley cove, and comes daown 'ere t' saiy es the gaim was up, an' show'd him th' noospaiper. She," he indicated Miss Grison with his chin, "made me tell 'er as Mr. Sorley 'ad the peacock, es I'd seen the doring of it on Mr. Fuller's taible and missus she ses as there wasn't no dorin' maid, an' thet Mr. Fuller mus' 'ave got it fro' the Sorley cove. 'An' ses she, 'he's cort naow, so I'll tell the noospaipers es my poor brother was killed for the bloomin' peacock's saik.' An—"

"Lies! lies! all lies!" cried Miss Grison, who had been gradually working herself up into a passion "you want to save that beast of a husband of mine, you know you do, you know you do."

"He is saved already," said Moon sharply; "the evidence of Mr. Bakche, supported as it is by Jotty, proves that Mr. Sorley is innocent, and that you are guilty."

"And what is more," put in Alan severely, "you evidently laid a trap for your husband. That is proved by your telling Jotty to bring me the letter and thus implicate him. And not until you knew that the peacock was in Mr. Sorley's possession—as you guessed from the drawing having been made, knowing that none had been made before—did you make public the fact that your brother had been murdered for the sake of the bird."

"Yes, yes," quavered Sorley, who was still kneeling and weeping, wholly broken down by his providential escape; "it was a trap, I always said so. I knew that she placed the peacock in that cupboard; I told you so, Alan. I never knew that she hid the stiletto with my jewels, as I never came across it. But now that I know, I am sure that she put it there to get me into still further trouble. And I admitted that the stiletto was mine, didn't I, Alan I didn't I, Mr. Inspector?"

"Yes, yes," said Moon nodding, "the case is clear enough. Miss Grison I arrest you on a charge of murdering your brother."

The woman was silent and glared at him fiercely, but made no effort to evade him as he advanced, clinking the handcuffs. "Wait a moment," she said suddenly, "you needn't put those on yet. What motive had I to kill the brother I loved so dearly?"

"That I can't tell," said Moon hesitating.

"She is mad," cried Sorley, "she was always mad."

"You drove me mad," shouted Miss Grison turning on him furiously. "I loved you and you scorned me because you wished to marry a rich woman. But that you could have put Baldwin in jail for that forgery I should have told the truth about my marriage; and much as I hated you I should have taken my true position here as your wife. But you were too strong for me and too strong for Baldwin. He was never wicked, but only weak, and you ruined him as you ruined me. I vowed to be revenged."

"And you have failed," said Sorley brokenly, yet with a note of triumph.

"Failed. Yes, I know I have failed, and what is more I have fallen into the trap I set for you. That makes me question the justice of the Eternal. He gave me misery all my life, and you happiness. Yet here you get the better of your evil, and I am condemned to the scaffold. Baldwin is better off. At least I saved him from being hanged."

"Oh," said Moon, while Alan and Latimer started, "so you admit having murdered your brother."

"Yes," said Miss Grison darkly, and throwing back her head. "I did evil that good might come of it. Listen and before you take me away policeman, I am willing to tell the truth."

"What you say will be used in evidence against you, remember."

"I don't care. I have fought and lost." She moved forward to the table and facing the men adopted quite an oratorical attitude. Beginning her story calmly enough she gradually worked herself up into a furious passion, as a sense of the wrongs she had endured came home to her. And the fact that the man who had inflicted those wrongs was now free, was not the least bitter drop in her cup of sorrow.

"Four men against one woman," said Miss Grison scornfully, and drawing up her small figure stiffly; "five, if that brat can be called a man, instead of an ungrateful beast. How brave you all are, how very brave."

Moon glanced at his watch. "Time presses," he said coldly, "say what you have to say, for I must take you up to London as soon as possible."

"Oh, I shall say my say quick enough," cried Miss Grison savagely, "is that the way to speak to a lady, you low policeman. For I am a lady." She flung back her head haughtily. "I always was a lady, as Baldwin always was a gentleman, bless him."

"Yet you murdered him," hinted Moon coldly.

"And for why?" she demanded clenching her hands, "because I wished to save him from himself and from the gallows, and from further disgracing the honored name left by our father. I tell you all that I loved Baldwin, but I knew his weakness I knew his faults, knew that unless he had some one stronger than himself to cling to, he was always dropping into the mud. Oh, the poor soul, who can blame him? Not I, though the world may, and the world did. If Sorley had treated Baldwin properly, he might have lived and died here in honor."

"I did my best," quavered her husband faintly, "but he drank and—"

"Oh, he had all the vices and you all the virtues," interrupted Miss Grison scornfully; "but you might have put up with his weaknesses for my sake. I was your wife, and deserved some consideration. But you drove me away and you drove Baldwin."

"I gave you money to set up that boarding-house."

"Yes; and I took it as my right, although I could have spat in your wicked face for insulting me by the offer. I only held my peace when you were courting that slut who died, because you could have put Baldwin into jail. He and I went away to try and live out our ruined lives as best we could. Baldwin was too much afraid to think of revenge, but I was not, and I swore that you should pay for your wickedness. He told you that he had the peacock, which I had given him, after I took it from here, as it was a toy to him. You came and came, but I prevented Baldwin giving it to you, although he wanted to, for money that he might go to the colonies."

"That would have been a wise move," murmured Alan nodding.

"It would not," contradicted Miss Grison, "what do you know about it, Mr. Fuller? although I have no quarrel with you, as you have always treated me like a gentleman. It would not have been a good move, because Baldwin was so weak that unless he was constantly looked after, he was always getting into dangerous trouble. He was a fool; yes, I who loved him, and who sacrificed my life to him, say that he was a weak fool. I did my best to keep him in the straight path, I allowed him a weekly income, and comforted him, I did all that a sister and a woman could do. But it was all of no use, as you may guess, you men who are bullying a poor weak woman. When Baldwin confessed to me that he had murdered that man outside Chin Chow's opium den I knew that the end had come."

"What end?" demanded Moon stolidly.

"The end of my patience, the end of the sinful years which Baldwin was permitted to live on this miserable earth," cried Miss Grison. "He told me that he was suspected, and implored me to save him. I promised to do so, and I did in the only way that I could. I killed him, I stabbed him to the heart, and that was an easy death compared to being hanged."

So fierce and wild did she look as she said these words, that all present shivered, and Sorley moaned, "A terrible woman, a terrible woman."

"A merciful woman! a good woman! a bold woman!" cried his wife, overhearing. "A weaker woman would not have acted as I did. But it was the only way, if I wished to save him from being hanged and the honored name of our father, Dr. Theophilus Grison, from being further smirched. I determined to kill Baldwin, and also to use his death as a means to hang you."

"You wicked woman!" cried Alan indignantly.

"Wicked? Why wicked, since this beast ruined both me and my brother? I was only dealing out justice to him, as I dealt out mercy to Baldwin. And I made my plans cleverly. I knew that Mr. Bakche was haunting Mother Slaig's, and counted on him recognizing my brute of a husband on that night, since he had already seen him here when he came to make inquiries about the peacock. I made Baldwin write to Sorley to appoint the thirteenth of November night as the time to come up. Baldwin showed me the reply, and I knew that he would be there. I took the stiletto which belonged to Sorley as I stole it along with the peacock when I left this house. Since it was his I thought it would make the evidence against him more certain. I went to Rotherhithe and watched. I saw Sorley go, and then I went up to Baldwin's room and stabbed him. It doesn't matter how I cajoled him to lie down and rest, and chose my time. I stabbed him to the heart and that is enough for you to know."

Again her listeners shivered, for there seemed to be something terrible about this small frail woman admitting such a dreadful deed so callously and boldly. She smiled as she saw their feeling. "What a lot of cowards you men are," she jeered, "you wouldn't have acted so bravely; no, not you."

"Go on, go on," said Moon impatiently, "there's no time to be lost."

"I have nearly finished," said Miss Grison tartly, "don't hurry me, as you must admit that my confession is interesting. I killed Baldwin with this," she added, taking up the stiletto which lay on the table, "and I took it away, along with the peacock, intending to hide both in this house. Jotty—ungrateful little reptile that he is—saw me with these when he came to Thimble Square to tell me of the murder. Ha! ha! of the murder which I had committed. I wept and wailed, as I was bound to do, since my dear brother had been murdered by Sorley. Then came the inquest, and I said nothing, for I waited my chance. The funeral took place here, and I stayed at Mrs. Millington's, she has been a good friend to me. I came to this house on the day you know of, Mr. Fuller," she went on, addressing herself to Alan who nodded in answer, "and while you and Marie were in the grounds, and this man—if he can be called a man —was asleep, I placed the peacock in that black-oak cupboard and the stiletto in the place behind that panel marked with a cross, where I knew Sorley kept those bits of glass—"

"They are jewels, valuable jewels," cried her husband irrelevantly.

"Oh, get on with the confession," said Latimer sharply, for the prolonged scene was getting on his nerves, "you hid the stiletto and peacock."

"Yes," said Miss Grison snappishly, "and then I waited, guessing that Sorley would probably seek Mr. Fuller's help to solve the riddle of the bird. That was why I introduced the subject of cryptograms on that day when we were at tea, Mr. Fuller. When I learned that Jotty had Sorley's reply to the request of Baldwin I sent him to you so that it might implicate this beast of a husband of mine. Then when Jotty told me about the drawing of the peacock, I knew that Sorley had consulted you, since no drawing had ever been made of the thing. My trap was set, and by making the matter of the peacock public, I closed it on the man I hate."

She shut her mouth with a snap, and idly dug the stiletto into the table as if she had finished. "What else?" questioned Moon imperiously.

"Nothing else," said Miss Grison raising her pale eyes; "you know all. The trap caught the bird, and my revenge would have been complete had not this fool learned more than he should have. You, I mean, you," said Miss Grison walking slowly towards the Indian, "why couldn't you let me have my way?"

"I wanted the jewels," said Bakche stolidly, and not moving even when she was face to face with him.

"You shall never have them," cried Miss Grison unexpectedly, and before anyone could move she raised her arm. In a moment the stiletto was in the Indian's heart, and he fell like a log on the floor.

"Great God!" roared the inspector and sprang forward.

Miss Grison put out her frail arms. "Go on, put the handcuffs here," she mocked coolly. "I have settled the beast who balked me of my revenge!"

"He is quite dead," said Alan lifting a pale face from an examination.

"And that beast Sorley lives," snarled Miss Grison viciously, and spat at her husband.

CHAPTER XXII

CALM AFTER STORM

In the month of July the park of The Monastery was in full leafage, and presented a glorious sea of shimmering tremulous green. The gardens glowed with many-colored blossoms, and especially there was a profusion of roses, red and white and yellow, for Marie Inderwick, loving flowers, had planted quantities immediately after her return home from the Brighton school. The whole place was radiant with color under a cloudless and deeply blue sky, and the hot sunshine bathed everything in hues of gold. It was like the Garden of Eden, and neither Adam nor Eve were wanting, since the lovers were walking therein, arm in arm, talking of the past, congratulating themselves on the present, and looking forward to a serene and glorious future. The storm was over, and now a halcyon calm prevailed.

"It's like heaven," sighed Miss Inderwick, whose face glowed like one of the roses she wore at her breast, from sheer happiness, "and to think that we shall be married to-morrow, Alan dearest."

"Then it will be more like heaven than ever," laughed the young man, who looked the picture of content. "Let us go to St. Peter's Dell, Marie darling; for it was there that we found the jewels."

"Rather the papers which led to the finding of the jewels," corrected Miss Inderwick gladly, "and it's a nice place to make love in, Alan, for I have planted it with roses."

"The Gardens of Shiraz, where Omar Khayyam sang," said the happy young lover, and quoted the well known lines softly:—

> "Here with a loaf of bread, beneath the bough,
> A flask of wine: a book of verse—and Thou,

227

Beside me singing in the wilderness,

And wilderness is Paradise enow."

"Oh, we don't want the bread and wine," laughed Marie indolently, as they took their way to the dell along a path riotous with blossom.

"Bread and cheese then."

"You have left out the best thing, dear."

"Kisses, eh? Well then." Alan stopped, took her into his strong arms and kissed her twice, thrice, and again on her rose-leaf lips.

"I wish you'd behave yourself," said Marie sedately, "as to bread and cheese we have something better than that now."

"*You* have," said Alan quickly, "the jewels have brought close on one hundred thousand pounds, which all belong to you."

"What is mine is yours, darling. You know that."

"Yet nasty people will say that I married you for your money, Marie."

She pouted. "What a compliment to me, as if I were an ugly girl."

"Quite so, instead of being the most perfect woman ever created."

"Oh," Marie sighed from sheer pleasure, "say that again."

Alan did so with a laugh. "Marie, will you ever have enough flattery."

"It's not flattery, it's the truth, and I like you always to tell me the truth," said Marie as they entered the dell. "Come and sit down on the edge of the pool, Alan, and have a talk."

"Why not call it the well?" he asked, while they balanced themselves on the circle of stones, and he placed his arm round her waist to support her.

"Simon Ferrier called it the pool, and I think it's a very good name."

"Darling, he only did so because he was unable to find the name of a gem which began with 'W'."

"I'm very glad he did," said Marie quickly, "and that he could not find one which began with 'K'. If he had we should never have solved the riddle."

"Oh, don't let us talk any more about the riddle or the sad events connected with it," cried Fuller, a shade passing over his happy face; "let us leave the past alone and live in the present."

"I am living in the future when we shall be husband and wife."

"That desirable state of things will come into being to-morrow."

"I know," Marie nestled in her lover's arms. "But I want to talk of all that has happened Alan. Then we will say no more about it."

"But, Marie, we have talked over everything again and again."

"I dare say; but I want to ask questions and to be quite satisfied in my own mind that everything disagreeable is at an end."

"Very good," said Alan, resigning himself to the inevitable with a good grace, for he knew Marie's obstinacy of yore. "What do you wish to say?"

"Well, in the first place, I am still sorry that poor Mr. Bakche did not live to get his share of the jewels. For you know, Alan, they really did belong to him as a descendant of the Rajah of Kam."

"My dearest, the jewels were legally assigned to George Inderwick for a very great service. I am sure that the Rajah of Kam in those days would rather have lost his jewels than his wife and only son. As to Bakche, I am sorry that he died in so terrible a way, and had he lived, undoubtedly I should have kept the promise made on your behalf and handed over one third of the treasure. But Bakche did not act well, or honorably."

"What do you mean?" asked Marie opening her azure eyes very widely, "If he had not spoken out, poor Uncle Ran might have been hanged."

"Quite so, dear. But he only spoke out when bribed to do so. He knew all along that Miss Grison was guilty, and yet held his tongue."

"He wouldn't have done so had Uncle Ran been brought to trial?"

Alan smiled grimly. "I shouldn't like to have given him the chance," he said in a skeptical tone. "Bakche, like most people, acted in an entirely selfish way, and was ready to sacrifice every one for the sake of gaining his own ends. Had Miss Grison given him the peacock, and had he solved the riddle and secured the jewels, he would not have confessed what he knew."

"But Jotty might have done so."

"It's not improbable," admitted Fuller musingly. "Jotty was wonderfully greedy, and was willing to sell anyone for quids, as he called them. He certainly sold Miss Grison for the sake of the few gems your uncle gave him. However, let us hope that the reformatory Inspector Moon has placed him in will improve him into a decent member of society. He's sharp enough and clever enough to do well in the world."

"But he hasn't had a fair chance, dear."

"Perhaps not; but he has one now. Miss Grison gave him one also, but only because he knew too much and the brat was aware that he had her under his thumb. However, Marie, I have told Moon that when Jotty improves you and I will give him enough money to go to America and make a new start. So that disposes of Jotty."

"I wonder Miss Grison didn't stick that horrid stiletto into him," said Miss Inderwick with a shudder "seeing how he betrayed her."

"He would not have done so had not Bakche told his story, and it was Bakche she hated most. It was truly wonderful how cunningly she managed to get close to the man to stab him. None of us thought when she walked up to him so quietly that she intended murder. And she drove it right into his heart, weak as she was. I expect," added Alan musingly, "that is what Bakche meant when he said that a weak arm could drive a stiletto into a sleeping man as easily as a strong one could. I thought at the time he meant Jotty, but he referred to Miss Grison, little thinking that the very next day she would prove the truth of his words on himself."

"But she was mad, Alan, quite mad."

"So it was proved at the trial," said Fuller with a shrug, "but I have my suspicion, Marie, that Miss Grison was acting a part. I don't think that her brain was quite properly balanced, but her cunning in planning and plotting to implicate your uncle in the crime very nearly succeeded. She certainly was not mad when she acted in that way."

"Mad people are always cunning and clever; Alan," insisted Miss Inderwick.

"Well, let us give Miss Grison the benefit of the doubt. She can do no more harm now that she is shut up in that asylum as a criminal lunatic, and your uncle must be relieved to think she is safely out of the way."

"All the same he has gone to live in Switzerland in a little mountain hotel, my dear," said Marie nodding wisely. "He told me that he never would be satisfied until he had placed the ocean between him and his unhappy wife, and chose Switzerland as the best place to stay in."

"Which means that he has only placed the Channel between him and his bugbear," said Fuller dryly. "Well, Marie, I can't say that I am sorry Mr. Sorley came to that determination, as it leaves us The Monastery to ourselves, and such is his dread lest his wife should escape that he will never come to England again, even for a visit."

"I don't think you are quite fair to Uncle Ran, dear."

"Marie, you have said that again and again, and there is no truth in it, I assure you. I have every desire to be fair to the miserable man, and so has Dick, let alone my father and mother. But now that his deeds have come to light they all mistrust him. He certainly did not murder Baldwin Grison, but he assuredly ruined his life by driving him away, even though the poor wretch gave certain provocation for his dismissal. And you can't say that he behaved well to his wife. He married her for her good looks, and then grew weary of her, as such a selfish man would. When he had her under his thumb through the love she bore her brother, which impelled her to save him from arrest for forgery by sacrificing herself, your Uncle Ran, whom you think so highly of–

–"

"No I don't. But I'm sorry for him, dear."

"I don't think he needs your sorrow, or deserves your pity," said Alan in a grave tone. "He was quite ready to commit bigamy for money because he knew that Mrs. Sorley would not speak of her marriage on account of the hold he had over Baldwin. Luckily the rich girl he wished to marry died, so another complication was avoided. He is selfishly happy in Switzerland with his jewels, and because he knows that the woman he wronged so deeply is shut up. I think we may as well do our best to forget Uncle Ran."

"Yes, but Alan, he was very good to me as my guardian."

"I don't agree with you, Marie, and if you think so, it shows what a truly sweet nature you have. He sold furniture which belonged to you and took your income, and kept you short in every way. He didn't bully you, I admit, but he didn't look after your welfare in any manner whatsoever. You know that what I say is true."

"Yes," sighed Marie. "Well then, we won't talk any more about him. I know that he is quite happy where he is, and I'm sure I don't want him to come and make an inconvenient third in our lives, Alan."

"He won't," her lover assured her seriously. "He is far too much afraid of Miss Grison, or rather Mrs. Sorley, escaping from her asylum. He is out of our lives, Marie, and as he is happy in his own selfish way, why there is no more to be said. There are plenty of pleasanter subjects to talk about, my dear. Indeed, I never liked your uncle, and I always mistrusted him, as I had every reason to."

"I shan't talk of him any more, as I know you are right. And now that the jewels have sold so well and we have plenty of money we can repair The Monastery and improve the grounds, and you can be country squire."

"My dear, I am a solicitor, and I shall always be one. I can't live on my wife, you know."

"But Alan, you will be away all the week."

"Not at all. I can come down every night. It isn't a long run to town."

"I want you all to myself here," pouted Marie, "what's the use of my having this horrid money unless I can have you. And half of it is yours, Alan, for unless you had solved the riddle it would not have come into my possession."

The young man was quiet for a few moments revolving what she had said. Much as he liked his profession, he secretly admitted that it would be very pleasant to play the part of a country gentleman. And certainly the discovery of the jewels was due to him. Also it was he who had saved the girl's uncle from a disagreeable death, and thus had prevented her from suffering a life-long shame and regret. Finally there was much to be done in connection with the house and the park and with certain lands which Marie wished to buy back, as having belonged to former spendthrift Inderwicks. Alan thought that he could do a great deal of good as the squire of Belstone, especially as his father was the vicar of the parish. Therefore he began to consider that it would not be a bad thing to give up the dingy office in Chancery Lane and come back to the land.

"And of course I could enter Parliament," he muttered, following his line of thought. "Yes I could do good there."

"Of course," cried Marie, clapping her hands, and guessing what he had been thinking about, "and perhaps you'll get into the Cabinet and the King may give you a title and—"

"And the moon is made of green cheese," laughed Alan, giving her a hug. "I dare say I shall give up the law, Marie, since you wish it, and we can do a lot of good down here on your money."

"Yours also, darling, yours also."

"Very well, mine also. But we can talk of this on our honeymoon when we are strolling over those glorious Cornish moors. Now, Marie, let us go back to the house. You know Dick is coming to be my best man, and he is bound to walk over here as soon as he arrives at the vicarage."

"I asked him to come with your father and mother, who are due here to afternoon tea," said Marie slipping off the circle of stones.

"Oh!" Alan looked at his watch. "Four o'clock. Then I expect they have arrived. Come along, my darling."

"Only one more question," said Marie as they, walked away from the dell.

"What is it?"

"You know that Simon Ferrier went back to India after burying the gems."

"He didn't bury them, he put them in Yarbury's Bank, dear. You forget."

"Well, you know what I mean," said Marie impatiently. "He hid the gems so that Julian Inderwick wouldn't get them."

"Yes; that's old history. Well?"

"Well," echoed Marie. "Simon Ferrier went back to tell George Inderwick where the jewels were to be found and never anticipated capture."

"True, oh queen! But what does all this lead to?"

"To this! Simon Ferrier had arranged the enigma of the peacock before he left England, and at a time when he never anticipated that he would have any difficulty in speaking personally to his master."

"I see what you mean. Well, my dear, all I can suppose is, that Ferrier was an over-cautious man, and made ready the enigma in case anything should prevent his reaching George Inderwick, as he certainly never did. When in captivity he worked out his scheme with the ring and the peacock exactly as he had planned it in England."

"But there was no need to when he was here," insisted Marie.

"No. But as I said before Simon Ferrier undoubtedly was an over-cautious man; witness the fact that he made so ingenious a cryptogram—if it can be called so—that even the man he designed to benefit could not solve it. And in its very ease lay its difficulty. I can't answer your question in any other way, dear. Not that it matters. We have the money, and everything is right, so let us enjoy our good fortune, and be thankful that none of those wasteful ancestors of yours solved the riddle. Had they done so I fear you would not be so rich."

"I think that is very true," said Marie with a laugh; "but here we are, darling, and there is Mr. Latimer."

It was indeed Dick arrayed in white flannels looking big and burly and genial, and more like a good-natured bear than ever. He held out a hand to each at the same time, and walked towards the house between them. "How are the happy pair?" he asked gaily.

"We won't be a truly happy pair until to-morrow," said Alan.

"Speak for yourself, dear," said Marie lightly. "I am happy enough now."

"You deserve to be," said Dick smiling, "for you have come through a lot of trouble, and that always makes hearts grow fonder. But do come and give me some tea, Mrs. Fuller—I beg your pardon, Miss Inderwick, but you and Alan do look just like a married couple."

"What's that about marriage?" asked the vicar appearing at the drawing-room door—the trio were in the house by this time, "have Marie and Alan been studying the prayer-book."

"Of course," said the girl, running forward to kiss Mrs. Fuller. "I know the ceremony by heart."

"It's more than I do," wailed Latimer with a shrug, "and as best man, I am sure to be a dismal failure."

"Oh you'll pull through somehow," the future bridegroom assured him.

"You must give me hints then. And when you are off for your honeymoon to Cornwall, I shall find it dismal in those Barkers Inn chambers all alone."

"Get married yourself then," advised the vicar.

"Upon my word I must think seriously about it," said Dick. "What do you say, Mrs. Fuller. Can't you find me a nice girl?"

"Not one so nice as Marie," said Mrs. Fuller, looking fondly at the graceful form of Miss Inderwick as her hands hovered over the tea-cups.

"No, I agree with you there, mother," said Alan, taking up a plate of bread and butter; "Marie is a rare bird."

"A rare bird indeed. Why not a peacock?"

Mrs. Fuller shuddered. "Oh don't talk of peacocks!"

"Why not?" asked the vicar, "all the happiness of the present is really due to the peacock. Marie, my dear," he observed as he took his tea, "I used to laugh at the idea of your fetish, but really things have come about so strangely that I think there is something in it."

"Behold our benefactor," cried Alan, pointing towards the bay-window at the end of the vast room, and there on a pedestal under a glass case was the famous bird, which had to do with so strange a history.

And even as the young man spoke, there came a burst of sunshine through the window which bathed the golden bird in radiant light. The gems flashed out into rare beauty, and in the dusky room, the fetish of the Inderwicks shone like a rare and magnificent jewel. So unexpected was the sudden glow and glory that everyone muttered a cry of admiration.

"It's an omen!" cried Marie, "the omen of the peacock."

"Let us drink its health in tea," said Dick raising his cup.

And with laughter they all did so, applauding the beneficence of the peacock, even though the vicar hinted that they were acting heathenishly. The fetish of the Inderwicks radiated glory from its gold and jewels in the burning sunshine until it glowed like a star of happy destiny. And all present accepted the omen as a hint of the future.

THE END

Lightning Source UK Ltd.
Milton Keynes UK
UKHW010701070820
367857UK00003B/757